A

Ray French
Irish parent
with people with disabilities, as a stagehand,
labourer, cartoonist, archivist and in libraries. He
now lives in Leeds, the Milan of the north, with his
partner and their daughter. Further information and
writing can be found at www.rayfrench.com.

Ray French

ALL THIS IS MINE

VINTAGE

Published by Vintage 2004

2 4 6 8 10 9 7 5 3 1

First published in Great Britain in 2003 by
Secker & Warburg

Vintage
Random House, 20 Vauxhall Bridge Road,
London SW1V 2SA

Random House Australia (Pty) Limited
20 Alfred Street, Milsons Point, Sydney
New South Wales 2061, Australia

Random House New Zealand Limited
18 Poland Road, Glenfield,
Auckland 10, New Zealand

Random House (Pty) Limited
Endulini, 5A Jubilee Road, Parktown 2193,
South Africa

The Random House Group Limited Reg. No. 954009
www.randomhouse.co.uk/vintage

A CIP catalogue record for this book
is available from the British Library

ISBN 0 099 45533 1

Papers used by Random House are natural, recyclable products made from wood grown in sustainable forests. The manufacturing processes conform to the environmental regulations of the country of origin

Printed and bound in Denmark by
Nørhaven Paperback, Viborg

'Of course I don't believe in the little people – but they're out there, all the same.'

Elderly woman interviewed on
RTE radio in the late 1940s.

'Life can only be understood backwards, but it must be lived forwards.'

Søren Kierkegaard

To my parents, Nancy and Paddy

'He fancies himself, doesn't he?'

Colin didn't like the way the new boy was ignoring everyone. He was leaning against the wall, eating an apple, gazing up at a jet plane streaking through the thin white clouds.

'He thinks he's better than us.'

'Maybe.'

I wasn't sure. Still, he'd only started school that morning, he had no right acting so relaxed in our playground. He should have been hovering anxiously on the edge of our game, charging off to fetch the ball every time it went out of play, a big sucking-up smile on his face when he rushed back to hand it over, slowly plucking up the courage to ask for a game.

The sides are even.

What if I go on the side that's losing?

No, it's too close, there's only one goal in it.

We were stood around, waiting. Preece had kicked the ball over the wall into the street, then made Joe 90 go and get it. He was taking ages. Preece was fed up waiting. He started walking over to the new boy. I nudged Colin.

'Look.'

He wasn't even going to wait till after school, he was going to get him right there, in front of everyone. No hair, staring eyes. Heading straight for him. I held my breath. One of the teachers, Thommo, came round the corner, hands behind his back, whistling *The Dam Busters*. Preece heard him, turned round and slipped into the bogs for a fag instead. The new boy carried on eating his apple, no idea what a narrow escape he'd had. I could have given him a run-down on who to keep in with and who to avoid, might even have offered him the chance to team up with Colin and me. But he didn't seem bothered whether anyone liked him or not, so now he'd just have to find out how things worked in our school the hard way.

'About time, you spaz!'

Joe 90 was back with the ball. The game restarted with a throw in. Now Preece had gone for a fag, our side was one man down; the new boy could have had a game if he'd wanted, but he just carried on gazing up at the sky, eating his apple.

Marek, that was his name.

★ ★ ★

Preece barged into Marek on the way out of school.

'Oi! Fucking watch where you're going, you spaz.'

'You bumped into me.'

Preece searched his face for signs of nerves, but Marek looked irritated, not scared. A crowd started gathering.

'Don't you know who I am?'

'No.'

Everyone was supposed to have heard of Preece. He shoved his face into Marek's.

'You soon will.'

There was some pushing as kids jostled for position, eager not to miss anything.

Marek turned to go, Preece stepped in front of him, pointed to the patch sewn on to his anorak. A white eagle on a red background.

'What's that?'

'The Polish flag.'

'It's shit.'

I watched the anger flare up in Marek's eyes, then him struggling to gain control of it.

'Excuse me.'

Preece let him past, a sneer on his face. He started making the chicken noise, but Marek didn't turn round. Preece walked over to his mates and grinned. He wasn't in any hurry.

★   ★   ★

Colin couldn't see it.

'He isn't chicken.'

'Oh yeah, then why didn't he fight him?'

That was a laugh. Colin would have run a mile.

'I don't know . . . but it wasn't because he was scared of him. It was something else.'

'Ha!'

'Ha!' I shouted back, louder. He was getting on my nerves. We walked the rest of the way to the railway crossing in silence. The sun glinted off the rails. My favourite smell, burning tar, drifted past on the breeze.

'Why are you taking his side?'

'Why are you taking Preece's?'

He hesitated, picked up a stone, threw it at a rusting tin.

'He's all right.'

'He's a bastard.'

He wouldn't look at me. I said it again, louder this time.

'Preece is a bastard. Isn't he?'

He finally turned and looked at me.

'Yeah, he is.'

'What was that? I didn't hear you.'

'He's a bastard.'

I jumped in front, stood in his way.

'*Who's* a bastard?'

'Preece is.'

'Then tell him, like this.'

I threw back my head, made a loudhailer with my hands.

'PREECE – YOU'RE A BASTARD. A BLOODY BAAAA-STAAARD!'

'Oi, you. Watch your language.'

An old man stood on his doorstep, pointing at us. He looked a right miserable old git. I ran across the road, shouting.

'BASTARD! BASTARD! BASTARD!'

He was shouting something back at me, but I kept on running. I didn't slow down till I was out of sight. When Colin caught up I put my arm around his shoulder.

'Silly old bugger.'

'Yeah, sod him.'

We turned down our street. I took my arm away, in case anyone saw us and thought we were a couple of nancies.

* * *

Monday was boiled bacon and cabbage. Clouds of steam rolled across the kitchen as Mam drained the saucepans. I laid the knives and forks on the table, then sat down next to Michael, the spaz. Dad came in the back door.

'I'm home. The working man is ready for his grub.'

He bent down to take off his bicycle clips, then went into the bathroom. Mam served the dinner. Slabs of thick, sweaty bacon, a pile of steaming spuds, dark green water oozing from the cabbage. Michael began to look queasy. Mam sat down, wiped the sweat from her forehead, blew out her cheeks.

'Oh God, I'm killed. I wish your father would eat a salad in the week.'

Salads were for Sundays – corned beef, lettuce, tomatoes, pickled onions and salad cream or brown sauce. Dad came back from the bathroom, covered his chair with yesterday's paper so he wouldn't stain it with his working clothes, then beat it flat with his hand.

'Now then . . .'

Mam handed him his cup of cabbage water. He slurped it down. Michael pulled a face.

I put my head down, started shovelling it all in as quickly as I could.

'For God's sake Liam, it's not a race.'

The only way to get through a plate of boiled bacon and cabbage was to pretend you were a robot imitating a human, and that you couldn't really taste anything. There was only one thing worse – crubeens; pigs' trotters. Dad ate them cold, with a glass of buttermilk and some soda bread.

'I've finished.'

'You'll give yourself indigestion.'

'Leave him be,' said Dad. 'At least he likes his grub, not like the other fella.'

Michael was still nervously cutting his first slice of bacon.

'Can I leave the table, please?'

I rushed to the toilet, locked the door behind me, lifted the seat. Stuck my fingers down my throat. My dinner came out like a flood. I flushed the toilet twice, washed my hands and face, drank some water from the tap. When I went back into the kitchen Michael was trying to force a tiny piece of soggy cabbage into his mouth. He'd be there all night.

'Can I go and see Colin now?'

'All right.'

His house was only a few doors away. I ran down the back lane, knocked on their door.

'Hi-ya.'

'Hi-ya, Liam. Come in.'

They were having pie and chips from the chippie. Colin's mam smiled, said, 'There's some chips left, they always give you too much at Alonzis.'

'Thank you.'

'Help yourself to bread and butter.'

5

I took a couple of slices from the plate in the middle of the table, some chips from the bag on top of the cooker, made myself a butty.

'Don't they feed you at home?' said Colin's dad.

He always said that. I ate the butty leaning against the cooker. They got their dinner from the chippie three or four times a week. At the weekend they ate their dinner sitting in front of the telly. I'd have loved that.

* * *

Everyone knew what was coming. When Marek walked through the gate at the end of the day and saw the crowd waiting, he knew too, he must have, even though he looked as though his mind was somewhere else. Preece walked right up to him, blocking his way.

'My dad says Poland is a commie country.'

He pushed Marek in the chest.

'Commie.'

Marek went rigid.

'Take it back.'

'What?'

Preece was acting dumb, taking his time, getting his own back on Marek for not knowing who he was, for not being frightened of him.

'Take it back, I said.'

He started to shout.

'I'm no communist.'

'Are you calling my dad a liar?'

'Yes.'

Preece's head snapped forward. Marek's legs buckled, he staggered backwards, eyes wide with pain and bewilderment. It wasn't fair, Preece hadn't given any warning.

'Cheating!'

One of Preece's mates pointed at me, shouted, 'Shut your face, Bennett.'

Marek slumped against the wall, put his hands out to steady himself. Preece stayed where he was, gloating, waiting to see if he'd recover. The crowd tightened around them.

'Go on, Preecey, get him.'

Marek shook his head, straightened up, brought his fists up in front of his face. Preece sneered, closed in. He had to get away from the wall or he was finished.

Preece swung for his head, but Marek was ready this time, ducked, then caught Preece a beauty right on the nose. He swerved to the left, then moved to the right, wrong-footing Preece, moving out from the wall. When Preece turned to follow him, there was blood streaming from his nose.

Yes.

There was a crazed look on Preece's face. He hated Marek for not being scared, for fighting back, for drawing blood in front of everyone. His punches were wild, the ones Marek didn't dodge caught him on the arms or shoulders. Marek timed his perfectly, drove his fist into Preece's face two, three, four times.

Come on, Marek.

I had to bite down hard on my lip, force the words back down my throat, keep them from escaping. It frightened me to realise how much I wanted to see Preece beaten. He'd been lording it over us for years. Had us all where he wanted us, under his thumb. We bored him. He'd needed someone new to bully, thought he'd found him. But he'd finally met his match. Now I was ashamed of pretending to like him, laughing at his jokes, letting him dribble past me when we were playing football even though he was useless. He'd made my life hell when I first went to school. Waited for me outside every night with a couple of his mates, pushed me against the wall.

'Count to three.'

'What?'

'Count to three.'

'Why?'

He pushed his knuckles into the side of my head.

'Do it.'

I could see it was a trick, knew it would just be the beginning. But what was the catch?

He shoved me in the chest with the flat of his hand, my head bounced off the wall.

'Go on.'

'Wun, too, tree.'

They howled with laughter.

'Shut up!'

Wun, too, tree. See dat over dare. A cup of tay. I sounded like Dad back then. Mary Dwyer and Caroline Duffy weren't picked on by the other girls; Pat Roche, Sean McGuinness and Tom Daley didn't come till later. I was the one who got it all.

'Hey, Bennett, how many goals did United score at the weekend?'

I'd turn away.

'I tink it was tree.'

Ha ha ha. Ha ha ha. Ha ha ha.

Let them laugh, I told myself. *They're just being stupid, it doesn't bother me.*

It did. I hated it.

I looked around, at Colin, Joe 90, some of the others, could see they felt the same as me, wished they'd fought back, were struggling to force cries of *Come on Marek* back down their throats too.

Then suddenly Preece was bellowing like a bull, charging at Marek, ramming him back into the crowd, scattering boys. The two of them rolled across the pavement, kicking, gouging, tearing at each other's clothes. Preece elbowed him in the nose. Before Marek could recover he had him in a headlock. Preece dragged him to his feet. His eyes were crazy. He rammed

Marek's head into the wall. The sound sickened me. He grabbed a handful of hair and scraped his face down the bricks.

'Cheating!'

It was Joe 90 this time. One of Preece's mates shoved him and his glasses went flying into the gutter.

Preece got him back in a headlock.

'Give in?'

Marek wouldn't say yes. I willed him to get up, throw Preece off, but it was over. Preece had won. A sour taste fetched up in my throat. Preece tightened his grip.

'Give in?'

Marek was trying to prise Preece's arm away from his neck, but he barely had the strength to stand.

'Do you want some more?'

Preece's face was burning red, his teeth bared.

He was going to ram his head into the wall again. He was going to kill him.

'There's someone coming.'

'Where?'

I pointed to the school.

'Someone was watching from the window. Just now. I think it was Thommo.'

'Are you sure?'

'Yes, yes!'

'Let him go Preecey, Thommo's coming.'

'Give in or I'll smash your head. Give in, give in.'

'Leave it, Preecey. Come on, let's go.'

A couple of his mates dragged Preece away. Colin and I helped Marek up. He was a state.

'Bad luck. You put up a good fight.'

He spat on to the pavement.

'His father's a liar.'

His face was battered and scratched, his jumper torn. His hands were shaking.

'Are you OK?'

He wiped blood and dirt from his mouth, felt his jaw. He was white as a ghost.

'I'm fine. Thank you.'

He didn't have an accent like ours. He wasn't posh, but he spoke very precisely.

'No one's ever beaten Preece.'

Joe 90 handed him his anorak. He snatched it from him, ran his hand carefully over the Polish flag, searching for any damage.

'He did over a boy two years older than him in the summer holidays,' said Colin, 'because he thought he was looking at him funny.'

'No one would have blamed you if you'd given in. You could have . . .'

The contempt in his eyes stopped me in my tracks.

'He insulted me. I would have died rather than give in.'

Before I could reply he turned and started walking away.

*   *   *

Tuesday was boiled bacon and cabbage again. The left-over bacon from Monday reheated in a bowl on top of the saucepan, bright pink, curling up at the edges. Dad beating the newspaper into submission on his chair.

'Now then . . .'

Mam handed him his cup of cabbage water. He took a sip, licked his lips.

'Grand.'

He noticed Michael staring at him.

'Would you like some?'

Michael shook his head. Dad pushed the cup in his direction, Michael pulled away so sharply he nearly toppled the chair over.

'Brendan, would you eat your dinner and leave the boy alone?'

'It's cat altogether trying to eat with that fella squirming around on his chair and pulling faces and picking at his food like a bleddy auld scalded tinker. He'd put years on you.'

He pointed his knife at Michael's plate.

'Are you going to eat that or what?'

'I don't like it.'

Dad's eyes lit up, he started roaring.

'Who asked you to like it, ya whelp ya? Get it down you.'

'Don't take any notice of him, love.'

He turned on her.

'No wonder he's like he is, you have him soft.'

He was right. Michael shouldn't be allowed to leave the table till he'd eaten every last bit. Then drunk a cup of cabbage water. That'd teach him. I looked away, started clearing my plate.

'Look at Liam, he loves his grub, he can't get it down quickly enough.'

'Liam, slow down.'

Dad leant back, looked at Michael as if he was seeing him for the first time. Nodded to himself, working something out. He emptied the cup, banged it down on the table, pushed it away.

'Never again. That's the last time. No more cabbage water for me. I wouldn't want to upset yer man's delicate stomach. Oh no, that'd be terrible, I wouldn't be able to live with myself if I did that.'

Mam shot him a look, but he'd already bent over his plate to spear his first spud. He chewed it thoughtfully. Suddenly he looked up again, excited, as if he'd just had a brilliant idea.

'Do you know what I'll do? Take the advice of that fella I was reading about in the *News of the World*.'

He waited. Mam knew it was a mistake, but she couldn't stop herself from asking.

'What advice?'

'There's nothing better for the health than drinking a glass of your own piss every day.'

'Brendan!'

Michael's eyes filled with tears.

'For God's sake, man, we're trying to eat, don't be so disgusting.'

'There's nothing disgusting about it at all. They reckon it's full of goodness and it helps you live longer. You'd be surprised how many are at it. They interviewed a 108 year old Scotsman, he's up at the crack of dawn every day, drinks a glass of piss, makes himself a bowl of porridge, then hops on his bike and off he goes, down to his allotment, rain, hail or shine.'

He pointed his knife at Mam.

'And women improve their complexion by washing their face in it – one day piss, the next milk, aye. But sure I knew that already, Des Furlong's grandmother used to be at that. She was a fine-looking woman.'

'That's enough.'

Mam's knife and fork clattered on to the table. Michael was staring at the floor. The room began to ice over. Dad shook his head.

'What's the matter with you all?'

'I've finished.'

'Good man.'

He turned to Michael.

'Look at that now, your brother has cleared his plate before you've even started.'

I rushed to the toilet.

★　★　★

The ball flew off Preece's foot over the wall into the street. Joe 90 lowered his head and set off. Preece took out his packet of fags, stuck one in his mouth, started searching for his matches. His mates started laughing.

'You're mad, you are. What if one of the teachers sees you?'

'I'll ask them for a light.'

They laughed again.

Marek had been leaning against the wall watching Preece, now he started to walk into the centre of the playground. He was trying not to limp, but his face tightened every time he moved his right leg. The scratches down his face looked raw and sore, his top lip was swollen. Preece watched him, something new sinking into his face: doubt.

Maybe I went too far this time.

He didn't like the new feeling, threw his head to one side, hawked, tried to gob it out on to the ground. But he couldn't get rid of it that easily. He opened his packet of fags, held them out to Marek.

'Want a smoke?'

He made it sound like a challenge but I'd never seen him offer anyone else one. Marek looked down at the packet, then back up at Preece.

'I don't smoke. And I don't slander people.'

'What?'

'You called me a communist. Take it back.'

Preece frowned, his mouth slackened. It took him a moment to realise he was being challenged.

'I said take it back.'

Preece's eyes turned cold.

'Make me.'

'I'll see you after school tonight.'

No one moved. The only noise was the girls' skipping song drifting over from the other playground.

My name is Juliana, Juliana, Juliana,
My name is Juliana from over the sea.

Preece clenched his fists.

'You're dead.'

Marek limped back to his spot by the wall. Joe 90 rushed back with the ball, red-faced, breathless. He followed everyone's gaze to Preece's stunned, furious face.

'What's happening? Aren't we playing any more?'

* * *

Davies squeezed up next to me in the corridor.

'What are you up to, Bennett?'

I ignored him. He dug his elbow into my ribs. I pushed him away.

'Get lost, Davies.'

'Yesterday, when Preecey was winning, you said someone was coming.'

'So?'

'There wasn't anyone, was there?'

'There was.'

He narrowed his eyes.

'You'd better not try anything like that again tonight, all right? I'll be watching you.'

He tried to close in on me again, I used my arm to hold him off.

'Come on, come on, get a move on, you two.'

Thommo rushed up behind, waving his hands at us. We went back to our classroom. I shared a desk with Colin in the middle of the left-hand row. Davies sat next to Preece at the back. They were behind me, watching, whispering. Deciding I was the enemy. Colin leaned closer.

'Marek must be mad. Have you seen the state he's in? Preece will murder him.'

Marek sat just across the aisle, next to Pinnell. No sign of nerves, sitting perfectly still and calm, straight-backed, as stony-faced as Eliot Ness in *The Untouchables*. I thought of the way he'd looked at me yesterday when I said no one would have blamed him if he'd given in.

You're frightened like all the rest.

He hadn't spoken a word to me today, not looked at me once. I wanted him to like me. I couldn't bear to see him lose again.

He insulted me. I would have died rather than give in.

Someone had to stop it.

How?

I'll be watching you.

There was only one way. I had to tell one of the teachers.

Sneak.

Sneak.

Sneak.

No, not that.

When Robert Kennedy was shot we all had to close our eyes, bow our heads and say a silent prayer. We were in Thommo's class then, I shared a desk with Joe 90. I could feel there was something wrong with him straight away. I opened my eyes, saw the panic, his chest and shoulders tighten as he struggled to keep it inside. But it was too late. It forced his mouth open, exploded into the room. A huge belch.

'Who made that revolting noise?'

Joe 90 stared at the desk, rigid with fear. Everyone around us knew it was him.

'If the person responsible doesn't own up, you'll all be punished.'

Joe 90 kept his head down, mouth closed.

'Just think of that. You'll all have to suffer because one person sitting amongst you hasn't the decency, or the guts, to own up.'

There were tears in Joe 90's eyes. His arms were folded tightly across his chest, a nerve in his cheek was out of control, jumping like a cricket.

'This is your last chance, is anybody here going to tell me who did it?'

We got fifty lines.

I must not make revolting sounds in class.

Preece made his life a misery for months afterwards, but he didn't tell.

But sometimes you had to take risks, fight dirty. Like double agents in the war. They went through hell. Terrified they'd be discovered by the enemy, hated by their own. Forced to hold their tongues, knowing that the truth could only come out when the war was over. I'd walk home alone every day, my back covered in spit. But eventually, when the full story came out and they understood why I did it, they'd all rush to shake my hand and slap my back, name their children after me. A film of my life. Starring Steve McQueen. Huge queues around the block to see it.

The Unsung Hero – Retained For Tenth Great Week!

'I said are you all right, Liam?'

It was Miss Mellon, staring at me. I felt myself blushing.

'Yes, Miss.'

'Are you sure?'

She looked worried. Miss Mellon was lovely, the nicest teacher in the school.

'Yes, Miss, I'm fine, thank you.'

'Good, then we'll . . .'

Do it now. I tore some paper from my exercise book, folded it up, shoved it into my pocket along with a pencil. My hand was up in the air before I realised what I was doing.

'Yes, Liam?'

'Please, Miss, can I go to the toilet?'

She nodded.

'Yes.'

Down the corridor, my footsteps pounding out a drumbeat, back into the playground, empty now. The toilets were in the corner. I locked the door of the cubicle, sat down. It was calm in there, dark and cool. Murmuring pipes, a dripping tap, the sharp smell of disinfectant. It was easy to disguise my hand-writing, I'd spent hours practising my autograph.

Preece is going to beat up the new boy Marek outside school tonight.

I folded the note up carefully, put it in my pocket, pulled the flush in case anyone had come in. Walk, don't run, you've got nothing to hide. Back down the corridor, past our class, to Miss Partridge's office right at the end.

Headmistress. Please knock before entering.

The cold silence seeped out from under the door. She was in there, hearing everything. I leant down, pushed the note under her door, ran.

Miss Mellon gave me an odd look when I came back. I put my head down, made my way back to my desk. Colin nudged his knee against mine.

'Number two?'

'Yeah.'

I'd done it. I couldn't meet his eyes, I was sure he'd be able to tell.

Sneak.

Sneak.

Sneak.

I waited. The afternoon went by in a flash. A spelling test, reciting the times tables, something else, I couldn't remember what. It was all happening to the others, not me. They were still living in their innocent kid's world. I'd just betrayed someone. I'd stepped over a line, there was no way back. I was on my own now. Like Marek.

The bell rang.

Walk, don't run.

Past Miss Partridge's door, still silent inside, through the hall where we had assembly, out into the street. Marek was already there, folding up his anorak, then placing it carefully against the wall behind him, some other kids standing to one side, watching. Preece came through the door, a grinning gang behind him, face taut, doubt banished, feeling *he* was the one who'd been insulted.

'Ready?'

Marek rolled up the sleeves of his shirt, making him wait. Preece's eyes said, *Go on, push me a little more.* Finally, anorak folded, sleeves rolled, he nodded.

'Yes, I'm ready.'

Where was she? Maybe she couldn't read my autograph-style writing, perhaps I should have done it in capital letters? There were about twenty of us gathered outside, how couldn't they notice? Preece and Marek moved towards each other. The crowd squeezed in. Suddenly my back froze, I turned around.

'You and you – in my office.'

Miss Partridge was standing in the doorway, shouting. Thommo was next to her.

'The rest of you – home. Now!'

I turned away, trying to look as shocked as the others.

★ ★ ★

Wednesday was corned beef, spuds and peas. It was OK, if you mixed it with plenty of brown sauce. The brown was too hot and spicy for Michael, he could only take the tomato. I found tomato sauce a bit dull for my taste nowadays. When I'd finished I went into the front room and started reading *Shoot*. It was full of pictures of Man Utd's European Cup win at Wembley at the end of last season. Nearly everyone in school was a Man Utd fan. I supported Liverpool. There was a photo of Eusebio crying after the final whistle. I couldn't stop looking at it.

The great Eusebio, of Portugal and Benfica, sheds a tear after finding himself on the losing side once more at Wembley.

The other time he'd lost at Wembley was when England beat Portugal in the semi-final of the World Cup. I liked Eusebio. He scored great goals, had a brilliant name, and a nice face. You could tell he wouldn't be stuck up if you ever met him in the street.

Eusebio! How's it going?

Not too bad, like, how about you?

That was the thing I remembered most about the final, Eusebio being led off the pitch in tears, feeling my own chest tightening as I watched. Colin and his dad didn't even notice, they were too excited about Man Utd winning.

Mam rushed into the room, turned on the telly, started shouting.

'Brendan – the news is starting.'

A chair scraped across the floor, then Dad came rushing through, stuffing one last bit of corned beef into his mouth, muttering, 'The news, the news, the news!'

Mam flopped into her chair, lit a fag. Dad stood in the middle of the floor, wiping his hands.

I decided to watch the news too, I couldn't bear to look at any more photos of Man Utd.

It was bad. Very bad. The man reading the news didn't need to say anything, you could tell from his expression. He looked as though he'd been trying all day to find a way of breaking it to us gently, but it was no good, he was stumped, he was just going to have to give it to us straight.

'Early this morning, hundreds of Russian tanks and thousands of troops crossed the border into Czechoslovakia, occupying the capital and deposing the Czech president.'

There were pictures of huge tanks squeezing through narrow, cobbled streets, rolling slowly through a square crowded with people shouting and pointing angrily at them. Some of the people climbed up on to the tanks, pleading with the drivers.

Please leave us alone.

'Oh Christ, it's started.'

'What's started?' asked Mam irritably, puffing on her fag.

'That's exactly how the last war began. It was the Germans

then – they marched into the same place in 1938 and no one lifted a finger. They just let them get on with it, and hoped to Jayzus they'd be satisfied with grabbing Czecho and leave everyone else alone.'

He arched his back, narrowed his eyes.

'By Jayzus, they soon found out not to trust the Hun. The next year the Germans invaded Poland, and everyone was dragged into a world war.'

'Everyone went to war over Poland?'

'They did so.'

No one had rushed to help Marek when Preece attacked him. We should have. It was wrong to leave him on his own like that. Dad nodded at the telly.

'It's history repeating itself. God help us all this time next year. You may start saying your prayers, boy.'

'Brendan – for God's sake, man.'

'What's wrong now?'

'Do you have to be so gloomy?'

His eyes blazed like the floodlights coming on at the start of *Sportsnight*.

'Are you blind or what?' he asked, pointing at the telly. 'Will you just look at what's happening right in front of your eyes, for Christ's sake? If only Kennedy were alive. He was the fella that knew how to deal with the Russians. Jayzus, he soon put the wind up them when they tried to move those missiles into Cuba a few years back. "Just you fecking try it," says he, "I have my finger on the nuclear button and I'll fecking well press it if you don't back off." Christ, they soon did what he wanted.'

'Oh God,' said Mam, 'don't remind me.'

'Oh no, Kennedy wouldn't have stood for this, there'd have been missiles raining down on the bleddy Ruskies as soon as they stepped over that border – "Get back, you cunts!" But that fecking Johnson is a dead loss, he'll let them do what they want.'

He was clenching and unclenching his fists, his voice growing louder, edgier.

'The Russian is a dangerous bastard – I'm telling you, I've seen them up close. I was in Berlin with the army after the war and a Russian officer came up to me and slapped me on the shoulder. Jayzus, the *size* of him, he was built like one of them lads that lifts the weights at the Olympics. "Hey, English!" he said – bleddy *English* if you please, the ignorant fecker – "Hey, English! We will meet again some day in your country, yes?" I tried to walk away, the bastard was reeking of drink and I didn't want to get stuck with him. But he grabbed me by the arm and pulled me back. "One day we will liberate *you* too. One day every country in the world will be communist. You like?" And he laughed in my face.'

Mam pursed her lips, angrily flicked some ash into her cupped hand.

'Do you really think Liam wants to hear about that kind of stuff at his age?'

She thought I couldn't understand, but I did. It all made perfect sense now, explained the terrible atmosphere in the house. Most days it felt like somebody had knocked a glass off the table and I was holding my breath, waiting for it to shatter on the floor. So *this* was what had been hanging over us, the thing that no one dared mention. It was almost a relief to finally discover the truth.

'He might as well know what kind of future he's got to look forward to. It's not going to go away just because *you* don't want to think about it – Jayzus, you're no better than bleddy Chamberlain.'

I *did* understand.

It was time for us all to be saying our prayers.

There was going to be another world war by next year.

That's the kind of future I had to look forward to.

★ ★ ★

The next morning there was a special assembly. Thommo was trying to make out he was really the one in charge, but he couldn't stop fidgeting. He'd put his hands in his pockets, take them out, hold them behind his back, change his mind, shove them back in his pockets again. Miss Mellon looked sad, stood with her hands clasped in front of her, head slightly bowed. Miss Bute sat behind the piano, looking like she'd just remembered something she'd been trying to forget. Miss Partridge was in the centre of the stage, completely still except for her eyes, moving expertly over the rows of children. *That one's a troublemaker, that one's easily led, she's a liar, he'll never amount to anything.* She stepped forward, the silence deepened.

'This morning I'm going to talk about responsibility.'

She paused to let us know what a serious matter it was.

'Each and every one of you is responsible for maintaining the good reputation of this school. A reputation that has taken many years to build up, but which can be destroyed . . .'

She clicked her thumb and finger together, *crack* – it rang out across the hall like a rifle shot.

'. . . like that. We must not let our standards slip. This school's very survival depends on it. And don't think there aren't plenty of people who wouldn't rejoice at our failure.'

Her voice became lower, graver.

'We are a tiny island of Roman Catholics in a sea of Methodists.'

'What's a Methodist?' whispered Joe 90.

'Shut up, you spaz,' hissed Colin.

I didn't know either, but I tried to look as though I did.

'Most people in Crindau have probably never even met a Roman Catholic. Now, what kind of impression do you think they'll get if they walk past this school and see a couple of boys brawling in the gutter, cheered on by an unruly mob?'

She stopped too suddenly. No one realised she wanted us to answer. Her face tightened, she took a deep breath, tried again.

'WHAT KIND OF IMPRESSION DO YOU THINK THEY'LL GET?'

The answer rumbled slowly through the hall.

'A bad impression, Miss Partridge.'

'Exactly. And what kind of impression do we want to create?'

She paused again. We were ready for her this time.

'A good one, Miss Partridge.'

Thommo was nodding his head, as if we were answering *him*. Miss Mellon was still looking down at the floor.

'I shudder to think what might have happened if I hadn't come out when I did yesterday. And do you know *how* I managed to come out just in time?'

I felt a chill run through me.

I found this note pushed under my door.

Eyes smouldering behind her glasses, she slowly scanned the faces in the front row. She looked like a THRUSH agent, trained in ruthless interrogation techniques.

So, Mr Solo, we meet at last. I trust those handcuffs aren't too tight?

She leant forward, lowered her voice a fraction.

'Because I know *everything* that goes on in this school.'

She was lying. She'd never have known if it wasn't for my note.

'I know what you're planning before you've even thought of it yourself.'

She *looked* as though she knew. Maybe she *had* read my mind, directed me to her office by hypnosis. Used me. It was possible. It happened. I'd make myself believe it. That way I had nothing to feel bad about any more. I'd been putty in her hands. Released after years of solitary confinement thanks to new evidence, a free man wrongly convicted. The guards lining up to shake my hand.

We're sorry, Mr Bennett.

I forgive you.

Walking through the prison gates in my best suit, a brown

23

paper package tied up with string under my arm. Miss Partridge was raising her voice again.

'Before you go to your classrooms, I want you all to join me in singing "Faith of our Fathers".'

Miss Bute started playing the piano. You could see she was happier now she had something to do.

'FAITH OF OUR FATHERS, HOLY FAITH,

'WE WILL BE TRUE TO THEE TILL DEATH.'

It was my favourite. We belted out the words at the top of our voices. It was more like a football song than a hymn, 'You'll Never Walk Alone' for Catholics. You wanted to march down the street singing it in a huge gang, swaying from side to side, your scarves held above your head.

'Stop that!'

Thommo got down from the stage, started rushing along the rows, trying to spot who was stamping their feet. You couldn't help doing it once you'd started singing 'Faith of our Fathers', you wanted to swing your arms too, and march on the spot.

'WE WILL BE TRUE TO THEE TILL DEATH.'

I looked round, and spotted Marek, head thrown back, singing at the top of his voice.

★   ★   ★

I'd tried to like him.

I had.

But he was sly. He was always finding ways of coming between me and Mam.

'Mammy, Liam hit me, then made me promise not to tell you or he'd hit me even harder.'

She never believed me. She always took his side.

'Show me where he hurt you.'

He'd roll up his sleeve, or hold up his leg, or bend down to show her the top of his head, but there was never a mark on him. I never hit him *that* hard, just enough to keep him in his place, no more, or less, than other people hit their kid brothers. Sometimes she was bored with it, you could tell, and he'd have to start bawling before she made a fuss of him.

She was always telling me off for shouting at him, or snatching something out of his hand, or pushing him, but she never wanted to know *why* I'd done it. He provoked me. He'd try the patience of a saint.

I could never get her to myself any more, he was always there first. Forever under her feet, following her around when she was trying to do the housework, climbing up on her lap when she was trying to watch the telly, snuggling up closer to her when he knew I was watching. Why didn't she tell him to go away?

I didn't understand it. He never blew his nose. He was stupid. Was always crying. He was ugly. What did she see in him?

He caused all the arguments. Dad got annoyed when he saw Mam slobbering over him.

'You're spoiling him, he'll be good for nothing.'

She'd snap back, then he'd lose his temper, and the room would freeze over. Everything had been fine till he came along. We were happy then, me and Mam. And her and Dad, they'd been happy too, I think.

Yes, I think they were.

★ ★ ★

We were in Colin's front room. Kneeling on the floor with his dad, looking through his record collection. The LPs in a long row under the music centre, the singles and EPs in a brown plastic box with a handle and little lock on the front like a suitcase. More packed into shoeboxes. Every now and then Colin would pick one out and hand it to him.

'This one?'

'Penny Lane'. I liked that.

'No.'

He didn't even look to see what it was. He was funny like that, he didn't mind you looking through his records, never even told you to be careful, but he'd never let you choose one to play. Singles were scattered across the floor in front of him.

DECCA. LONDON. PARLOPHONE.

The Decca singles were my favourite. *DECCA* in silver letters on blue and red backgrounds. Thin white lines running down the orange covers just like a football shirt, along the bottom: *full frequency range recording*.

'This one?'

'Sunny Afternoon.' *PYE*, black letters on pink background, *Words and music by Raymond Douglas Davies*. I liked that one too, even though it was sad. Most of the Kinks' records were sad. The singer had a sad voice and a sad face.

Mr Williams glanced at it.

'No, I'm not in the mood.'

I loved looking through his records, kneeling on their carpet. You wanted to put your head on it, curl up and go to sleep it was so soft and deep. Blue with red and orange flowers. The one in our front room was orange with red and blue flowers. Mr Williams stacked the singles on the spindle, brought the plastic arm across, locked them in place. The music centre would play six singles in a row, without you having to get up and change them. It was wooden, looked a bit like a sideboard till you noticed *High Fidelity* in swirly gold writing across the top. Speakers at either end, a long row of knobs, a radio with the stations' names in gold – *Luxembourg, Radio One, Brussels, Riga, Stavanger, Rome*. Our record player was a pale green plastic box, two knobs, volume and tone, no speakers, a handle on the lid. It looked like a girl's suitcase.

'Hey!'

Mr Williams flashed Colin a dangerous look. He'd bumped into one of his dad's guitars, the electric one. You weren't allowed to touch them.

'You knock that over and there'll be trouble.'

'Sorry.'

The electric guitar was a Fender. A Fender Telecaster – a fab name. Black around the edges, red and orange in the centre. A sunburst finish, that was what Mr Williams called it. He'd bought it from Joe's in mint condition, handed over his old one in part exchange. His acoustic guitar was next to it, black, in one corner a sticker. Two fingers giving a V for Victory sign, in the colours of the American flag. *Cliff* painted in white underneath.

Mr Williams closed the lid, went and lay down on the sofa, opened the *New Musical Express*. Inside the music centre things were happening. A high-pitched whine, a sharp click, then the quiet plop of the single dropping on to the turntable. Behind the rumbling, a hum that you got when the volume was turned right up. It was exciting not knowing what he'd chosen, like waiting to see if you'd won something.

At first the guitar sounded all wrong. Like it was out of tune, or there was a big ball of fluff stuck to the needle. Then you realised the wonky beginning was deliberate. It was a warning something bad was about to happen. Something that no one had told you about, that it was too late to run. I felt the bass hit me in the stomach. Then the singer came in.

One, two.

'Like this,' said Colin.

He puckered his lips, put his hands on his hips, started strutting about like a chicken.

I did the same, setting off in the opposite direction. The Rolling Stones. 'Jumpin' Jack Flash'. I'd seen them doing it on *Top of the Pops*. The guitar players hid in the shadows, daring you to look them in the eyes. Mick Jagger with white stripes painted on his cheeks like an Indian brave, rushing at the camera mouth open, like he was going to take a bite out of it. I pumped my legs up and down, stretched my mouth wider, wider, till it was big enough to swallow the room. When I reached the door I turned around, saw Colin jump on to one of the chairs. He pretended to hold a microphone in one hand, wagged the index finger of his other at me, shouting, 'One, two – get down.'

I looked at Mr Williams, he was still reading his paper, waggling his feet on the arm of the sofa, his big toes bursting out of the holes in his socks. He was supposed to be keeping an eye on us while Colin's mam popped down the road to see a friend.

He wasn't going to do anything.

I climbed up on the other chair, pretended to hold a microphone, pointed at Colin.

'One, two – get down.'

He pointed at the painting above the fireplace of the sad gypsy lady with the rose in her hair.

'One, two – get down.'

I pointed at the Welsh doll on the mantelpiece with the tall black hat and white frilly apron.

'One, two – get down.'

We pointed at the plate with the picture of the Pope giving the blessing from his balcony in Rome.

'One, two – get down.'

Colin swung around to point at the lady walking past outside in the street, toppled over the side of the chair, fell on his head. I burst out laughing. He staggered to his feet, wide-eyed with the pain and shock, strutted to the middle of the room, fishy-lipped, punching the air in front of him with both fists. I jumped off the chair, put one hand on my hip, the other behind my head, pushed out my lips, wiggled my bum.

'One, two – get down.'

Mr Williams licked his finger, turned a page. The guitar faded out. We staggered towards each other, laughing. My heart was hammering. My ears were destroyed.

'That was brilliant.'

'I fell off the chair deliberately, it was a joke.'

I nodded. A quiet plop as the next single hit the turntable. I was having too much fun to tease him. Five more to go.

★ ★ ★

Joe 90 carried on down Ruperra Street, Colin and I turned into Tredegar Avenue.

'See you tomorrow.'

I returned his wave. Colin started shouting over his shoulder.

'See you tomorrow, Joe. Bye, mate.'

He turned to me.

'I wouldn't like to be him.'

'Why not?'

'It's Wednesday.'

'So?'

He leant into me, gave me a look that meant *I haven't told anyone else this before.*

'I was round there once on a Wednesday. Guess what they were having for their tea?'

'What?'

'Cat food.'

'Get lost.'

'Really, every Wednesday and Thursday, and sometimes Friday too – it's all they can afford. His dad's on the social, see, he's not fit to work.'

'What's wrong with him?'

He started swinging his satchel back and forth as he walked.

'He's nearly blind, has to wear special glasses, the lenses are as thick as the bottom of a pop bottle. Joe's mam has to tell him where everything is – "Chair three steps to your right. Salt and pepper to your left, tomato sauce to your right, Kit-e-Kat straight in front of you." '

'I don't believe you.'

'Have you been in their house?'

'Only in the hallway.'

Joe 90 had told me to stay there while he ran inside to get a jumper. It was dark and smelt of cabbage and something else horrible that I didn't recognise, something to do with toilets or sickness. I didn't want to put my hand on anything. I wanted to get out as quickly as possible. Before I found something that I'd never be able to forget about. After he'd been at our house the first time Mam shook her head and said, 'Ah, God love him anyhow.'

'Well then, how do you know what it's like? I've been in every room downstairs, I know what I'm talking about. In the kitchen, right, there was a dirty nappy in one of the chairs, covered in flies.'

'Ugh.'

'They all wear glasss – his dad, his mam, the three brothers and his sister.'

'He's got a sister?'

'Yeah, she's fourteen. Looks like Olive from *On the Buses*.'

Something was nagging at me.

'Joe 90's kid brother, Gary, he's in Michael's class, he doesn't wear glasses.'

Colin looked at me like I was thick.

'Of course he doesn't wear them to *school*, he doesn't want people to know he's Joe 90's brother. He'd get picked on, he'd be given a nickname.'

'Come on, Colin, what about . . .'

Something heavy fell right behind us. We nearly jumped out of our skins.

'Bloody hell!'

'Good afternoon, gentlemen.'

It was Marek, a mysterious smile on his face, arms folded across his chest.

'Where did you come from?'

He looked up at the branches of the tree spreading out above us. His expression didn't change. It took a moment for it to sink in.

'What were you doing up there?'

'Waiting for you.'

Colin and I looked at each other.

'What do you want?' asked Colin suspiciously.

'To thank you. You two were on my side the other day when I had the fight with Preece. You two and the one with glasses . . .'

'Joe 90.'

Marek looked puzzled.

'If you say so. You two and him were the only ones who stayed behind afterwards to see if I was all right.'

This was pretty strange. I'd never had a conversation with someone who'd just dropped out of a tree before. I couldn't decide if he was barmy, or it was *us* who'd got the wrong end of the stick. Maybe we were behaving oddly and Marek was the normal one.

'What happened in Miss Partridge's office?' Colin asked.

Marek made a little movement of his head, shrugged.

It's hardly worth talking about. It's no big deal, being hauled before the head teacher.

'She tried to get us to say why we were fighting, who started it, that kind of business, you know how teachers are. Then, when she got nothing out of us, she got even angrier, made us empty out our pockets. That's when she found Preece's cigarettes.'

'Did Preece look scared?' I wanted him to have suffered.

Marek nodded.

'He was trying not to show it, but he was. I could tell. She's going to write to his parents about it.'

31

He frowned.

'Tell me, why does he have no hair?'

'He fell out of a tree when he was young. His hair dropped out with the fright.'

'Don't ever ask him about it though,' I said. 'He hates being reminded of it.'

'Is she going to write to your parents?'

'Yes.'

'Are you worried?'

'It won't be the first time. I often have trouble when I start a new school.'

'Preece's dad will kill him,' said Colin, 'he . . .'

'He's the barman at The Engineer's Arms, where all the gyppos, prozzies and criminals go. He drinks most of the beer himself, gets down on all fours, crawls around licking up the slops off the table at the end of the night, picks up the butts from the floor and smokes them. Once, when they'd run out of *Brains*, he climbed onto the roof and howled like a wolf. The police came with nets and took him away.'

Colin's dad told us. Well, the bit about him drinking most of the beer himself, Colin and me guessed the rest.

Marek nodded to himself. 'So,' he said quietly. We waited for more, but that was it.

'How did you know which way we go home?' I asked.

I could see he was pleased I'd asked that.

'I know lots of things.'

'We live in Price Street,' I said. 'In Pill, near the gasworks. Are you coming that way?'

'No, I live in Cat's Ash. I have to go the other way. I just wanted to thank you.'

He held out his hand. I stepped forward and shook it first, then Colin. When we'd finished, Marek nodded.

'Now we are friends.'

I was delighted. Now I could study him, learn how not to be

afraid of anything.

'Can you meet me here on Saturday morning at ten?'

'Yeah.'

'Good. I will bring you to my house and show you a secret. You will be the only people outside my family who have ever seen it.'

We were stunned, we didn't know what to say.

'I'll see you then.'

He nodded, then walked away. We watched him go.

'What do you think?'

I gave his shoulder a push.

'Last one to the end of the avenue has the pox.'

We started running.

★ ★ ★

I didn't use one of the best glasses from the cabinet in the front room, I took one of the plastic ones that Mam had got with Green Shield stamps. I went into the bathroom, locked the door behind me. When I'd finished it was about half full. It was clear, it could have been water or lemonade. I took a deep breath, raised the glass to my lips.

Full of goodness, and they reckon it helps you live longer.

Imagine pouring piss down your throat. Feeling it slosh around inside your stomach when you walked. *Jesus!* I wanted to heave. It was no good, I couldn't do it. I unlocked the door. Clouds of steam rolled through the kitchen, Mam wiping her forehead with the back of her hand, sunlight pouring through the open door.

'Jesus, I'm killed.'

Michael was out the back, playing with his toy soldiers. I acted casual.

'Are they commandos?'

'No.'

'Infantry?'

'No – yeah, infantry.'

He was making little machine gun noises, there was a bubble in the corner of his mouth struggling to get out. I pretended to drink from the tumbler.

'Hot, isn't it? Would you like a drink?'

'Yeah!'

'Here you are.'

I handed him the tumbler, he took it without even looking up. He was too easy. I waited. He carried on playing, holding it in his hand.

'Go on, what are you wating for?'

He stiffened, pulled back. I'd given the game away, sounded too eager.

'Don't want it.'

He tried to hand it back.

'It's nice.'

I grabbed his wrist, not too tight, just to reassure him.

'It's special lemonade, it's good for you.'

'Take it away.'

'Don't be such a spaz.'

I pushed it towards his mouth, he clamped it shut. The gate flew open, Dad barged in, pushing his bike before him.

'What's the matter with youse two?'

Red-faced, sweating, the stench of oil from his overalls. I let Michael go.

'I was only offering him a drink – first he said he wanted it, then he tells me to take it away.'

The little spaz started whining, 'Don't want it.'

Dad scowled.

'Ah shut up, willya. What is it?'

There was sweat pouring off him, big drops hanging off the end of his nose.

'Lemonade.'

'I'll have it – I've a terrible thirst on me.'

34

He grabbed the glass, emptied it in one huge gulp, handed it back to me.

'Jayzus, that's queer tasting lemonade.'

He pulled a face, wiped his lips with the back of his hand, then pushed open the shed door.

'Now then, let's put this bike away, wash my hands and get some grub.'

★ ★ ★

Colin and I were on the rec, sitting on the swings. The sun was starting to go down, the younger kids had already been called in by their mams. There was something I wanted to ask Colin.

'Do your mam and dad argue?'

'Yeah.'

The way he said it – like it was no big deal. I wished I'd asked earlier now. It had been gnawing away at me for months. For no reason. We were like everyone else after all.

'They start shouting and yelling at each other over the slightest thing.'

Yes!

'Mine too.'

'The worst thing about it is . . .'

Normal, we were normal.

'. . . a couple of hours later they're slobbering all over each other again.'

He made a face.

'How about yours?'

He was still picking at the scab, but looking straight at me now. Something in his eyes told me I'd given the game away, got too excited when he'd told me they argued.

'Yeah – they get like that too.'

I started swinging again, leaning back, pushing with my feet to get higher. Dad had given Mam a hug when we were on holiday in Ireland last summer. It was Gransha's birthday, the house was full. All the adults had been drinking. Uncle Matt had brought his accordion. Aunt Kate had sung.

Won't you step outside, my sweet col-leen,
Come take me by the hand.
With your nut-brown eyes and your golden hair
You're the fairest in all the land.

Then she and Mam had got up and danced. Everyone cheered when they'd finished and when Mam sat down again Dad laughed and grabbed her round the shoulders.

'She's a fine-looking woman, ain't she?'

His eyes were nervous, you could tell he'd only done it because everyone was watching. It wasn't like when the others had hugged. He'd almost pulled her off the chair. It was more like wrestling. *This is Ken Walton at the Civic Hall, Crindau. The first bout is between Mr and Mrs Bennett, the winner is the first to score three falls or a submission.*

'So . . .'

He wasn't going to let it go.

'You've seen them kissing.'

'Yeah, loads of times.'

I didn't look at him. I swung higher, faster, till the air roared in my ears like the sea.

* * *

I'd never been to Cat's Ash before. The houses were bigger than the ones in Pill. They weren't joined up, they stood apart from each other. Marek's house was on the corner. It had a hedge around it, its own gate with a loud, clanking, heavy latch and steep steps up to a neat lawn. Marek let us in. On the inside of the front door was a little wire basket for catching letters. I'd have loved one of those. There was a grandfather clock in the hallway, a slight pause before each tick, as if it was catching breath.

36

'In here,' said Marek, turning the handle. Colin and I followed him in on tiptoe, hardly breathing, even though there was no one else in. We'd never been in such a posh house before, it was making us nervous. The room was packed with dark, heavy wooden furniture, thin grey light sneaked in through the curtains. A piano stood against one wall, above it hung a large wooden plate, with a painting of the Virgin Mary in the middle. Marek walked over to a chest of drawers, grabbed the little brass handles on either side of the top drawer, then turned to Colin and hissed, 'Close the door. I don't want them to know I've brought strangers in here. If someone comes in, we'll sneak out through the window. Right?'

'Right.'

When Colin had closed the door, Marek said, 'This is just between the three of us. You're not to tell anyone else.'

'OK.'

'Swear on your mothers' graves.'

I didn't dare look at Colin, in case I started giggling. We swore on our mothers' graves, our hands on our hearts. It was stupid, but exciting at the same time.

He opened the drawer, took out an old photograph album, opened it. He turned a few pages, then pointed.

'That's our house in Poland.'

It was a huge white house, with a porch. The porch had a roof and pillars of its own. It stood in a meadow, there was a road leading up to it, and a row of trees behind.

'How come you've got two houses?'

Colin was getting ready not to like him. I could see it.

'That's where Tata was born.'

That's what he called his dad.

'But after the war the communists gave it to someone else.'

'Who?'

'A bunch of peasants. Now there are holes in the roof, half the windows are broken and they keep chickens in the rooms

37

downstairs. Now you see why I don't like being called a communist.'

'Why did they let it get like that?'

Marek shrugged.

'It's not theirs, so they don't care what happens to it.'

He turned another page.

'That's Tata.'

It was a pilot standing in front of a Hurricane. He was looking up at the sky as if he'd just noticed something.

Jerry, eight o'clock high, coming straight out of the sun. Scramble! Scramble!

'What's he doing in the RAF? I thought you said your father was Polish,' asked Colin.

'The Poles were the best pilots in the Battle of Britain. They had their own squadrons. Look.'

He pointed to the top of his dad's sleeve in the photograph; it had *Poland* written across it.

'Tata shot down eighteen German planes.'

Colin went quiet. The next pages were full of photos of his parents' wedding, and his brothers and sisters as babies.

'Let's see the one with the Hurricane again.'

While Marek was putting the photograph album away, I noticed framed photos of Marek's brother and three sisters on the mantelpiece. There was another one at the end, face down. I picked it up. It was a photo of another girl, the eldest, in a mortar board and gown, clutching a scroll with a ribbon tied around it.

'Who's this?'

Marek frowned.

'That's Hanka – we don't mention her any more.'

Behind Marek, Colin raised his eyebrows. I put the photo lying face down again. Next Marek took out a wooden box with a swirly gold design on the outside. He put it down very slowly and carefully on top of the chest of drawers. He was like a priest handling the host or communion wine. He took a key from another part of the drawer, unlocked it.

'This is Tata's most precious possession.'

He opened the lid.

Colin and I looked inside, then looked at each other. We burst out laughing.

'It's dirt!'

'No it's not!'

'Yes it is – look.'

I tried to grab a handful, but Marek snapped the box shut.

'Hey! Careful.'

'It's not dirt. Dirt is what you find in the street, dirt is what you scrape off your shoes.'

'OK, keep your hair on.'

He was going red in the face.

'This is Polish soil.'

He clutched the box to his chest.

'When the Germans took over Poland, Tata decided to make his way to Britain and continue the fight from here. He filled his pockets with this Polish soil before he crossed the border in 1939, just like everyone else around him, so that they would always have something to remind them of their homeland.'

Colin nodded at the box.

'Can we see it again? I promise we won't laugh.'

'Please, Marek,' I said. I'd never seen Polish soil before. I wouldn't have called it dirt if I'd known.

'OK.'

He'd calmed down a bit. He opened the box again. Colin and I leaned forward. He snapped it shut.

'Not too close.'

We leant back. He opened it a tiny bit. We stayed where we were. He nodded, slowly raised the lid, tilted the box slightly towards us.

'You have to be careful. Once, when my sister, Eva, was young, she dropped it on the floor. It took ages to sweep it all up, then pick out all the bits of hair and fluff from the carpet.'

'It looks different to Welsh soil.'

'That's probably because it's been blessed, at the Polish church in London.'

We stared at it for a bit longer.

'I'm going to put it away now.'

'Thanks, Marek, that was tidy.'

'Excuse me?'

'It's what we say in Crindau when we think something's really great – *tidy!*'

He frowned. 'Ah yes, they say this in the Valleys too.'

He made it sound like a black mark against us. I looked around again. There was a huge map on the wall opposite. It said *Polska* in red letters in the corner. Marek saw me looking at it.

'When I grow up, I'm going to become a resistance fighter and free Poland from the communists.'

He put his hands on our shoulders.

'I know how to use a gun. I've fired Tata's.'

'Show us it.'

'I don't know where it is any more.'

'You're making it up.'

'I'm not. When we lived in the Valleys he kept it inside a box in his shed, wrapped in a cloth. But I don't know where it is now.'

'What sort of gun was it?'

'A revolver, the one that he had in the RAF.'

'Where did you fire it?'

'I took it out to my den in the woods – it was surrounded by sharpened stakes and booby traps – and I shot a pigeon and cooked it over a fire. I was always making fires out there.'

'Liar.'

'I'm not lying.'

He didn't avoid my eyes or raise his voice. His hands weren't trembling.

'How many shots did you fire?'

'Two. I missed the first time. The gun was heavier than I'd expected, I had to use both hands to keep it steady, and the kickback from the shot nearly made me lose my balance.'

I'd read that that was what happened when you fired a gun. It all fitted perfectly. I looked at Colin, he was nodding to himself.

'What did the pigeon taste like?'

'Gorgeous, the breast was the best bit, really juicy. When I'd finished eating it I destroyed all traces of the fire, and wiped my fingerprints off the gun before putting it back. It was good practice. You have to know how to survive in the woods if you want to be a resistance fighter.'

'Your brother Jan, the one who's just left school, is he going to become a resistance fighter?'

'No, he's training to be an accountant.'

There was a long pause, then Colin asked, 'Why did you move from the Valleys?'

'One day Tata saw the red flag flying from the town hall, came straight home and told us to start packing.'

'Why?' asked Colin.

'It's the Russian flag.'

I knew that.

'Would you die for Wales?' he asked Colin.

'Depends.'

He squeezed my shoulder.

'How about you, Liam? Would you die for Wales?'

I shrugged.

'Might do.'

He looked disappointed.

'I would die for Poland.'

41

He was mad. I liked him though.

'You have to be mad to be a goalkeeper,' Colin said on the way home. Since he'd started playing football with the rest of us we'd discovered Marek was the best keeper in school, he threw himself around like a maniac, scratching and scraping his knees and elbows on the tarmac. He was always bleeding at the end of a game.

'Die for Poland, I would die for Poland. Die for Poland, I would die for Poland!'

That's what we started chanting at Somerton Park that afternoon, when Colin's dad took us to see Crindau. He was mad about football, had changed the Saturdays he worked so that he'd be off when Crindau played at home. I started it, then Colin joined in. We always stood on the same spot on the Shelf, the side opposite the clock, just to the right of the tea hut, so Mr Williams's mate could find us. He always turned up just as the match was starting, with a bag of chips stuffed into his jacket pocket.

'Back for more punishment?'

'It was either this or going shopping with the wife.'

He unwrapped the chips and started eating them. He never offered us any. Crindau were playing Doncaster Rovers. Nothing happened for a long time, then our centre forward had a shot, it hit one of their players in the head and flew into the goal with their keeper diving the other way.

'Yes!'

Everyone went wild.

'They've actually taken the lead, it's a bloody miracle.'

At half-time Mr Williams bought us orange juice and crisps; cheese and onion for me, salt and vinegar for Colin. A very tall man walked around the edge of the pitch carrying a giant packet of Wrigley's Spearmint Gum under his arm, while they played the music from the advert over the Tannoy, and everyone laughed and cheered.

Shortly after half-time, Doncaster equalised.

'Here we go, normal service is resumed.'

Mr Williams started smoking one fag after another. When Doncaster scored again he started swearing. Then the Crindau keeper let a soft shot straight through his hands.

'Jesus wept.'

One of our players was sent off, then Doncaster scored a fourth. That's when we started chanting.

'Die for Poland, I would die for Poland. Die for Poland, I would die for Poland!'

People started looking at us, they didn't have a clue what we were talking about. When the fifth goal went in, Mr Williams said, 'Come on, I've had enough. See you next time, Dave.'

'Not likely, I'll be going shopping with the wife.'

'Die for Poland, I would die for Poland!'

We chanted it all the way to the bus stop, till Mr Williams told us to shut up or we could walk home.

* * *

I leant into the heavy front door with *Public Library* in curly, oldy-style writing in the glass, my head down, slowly pushing it open with my shoulder.

Yo heave ho.

I slapped my feet down hard on the tiles in the corridor, ran my hand over the trees, flowers and birds carved into the green and yellow tiles on the wall. The adults' library was on the right, the children's on the left. I held my breath as the librarian checked the books I was returning: *The Wild West*, *The Plains Indians*, *The Bumper Book of Ghost Stories* and *Coral Island*.

She didn't wear glasses like the librarians in films, and her hair wasn't tied back in a bun. She could have done with losing a bit of weight.

'That was in there when I borrowed it.'

A greenie, squashed flat in *The Wild West*, right in General Custer's face. She glanced up at me, annoyed, slipped a piece of paper in to mark the page. She was always annoyed about something, I'd never seen her in a good mood. It was all right though, she knew me, knew how well I took care of books. Joe 90 was suspended from the library because he'd messed up so many. She checked each book just as carefully as the last. I liked that, even though it made me uncomfortable, she was doing her job thoroughly.

'All right.'

Don't smile, you'd crack your face.

I was going to say that to her on my last day, just before I joined the adults' library.

She put *The Wild West* to one side, the others back on the trolley. I went to the History section. I wanted a book on the Battle of Britain. I took out four books on the Second World War, but when I looked through them at home there was nothing about Polish pilots. I didn't understand, they were the best, why weren't they mentioned?

I wondered what it would be like having a war hero for a dad. My dad had been in the war, but wasn't a hero. He hadn't mentioned shooting any Germans, he didn't have any medals. Colin's dad was only a kid in the war. Uncle Ronnie had worked on the docks. I wondered if Mr Sikorski had nightmares. Sometimes Dad woke up in the middle of the night, shouting.

'They're coming! They're coming!'

Mam would start roaring at him.

'Wake up, Brendan. For God's sake, man, you'll have the whole street hammering on our door.'

Michael would be blubbering.

'Mammy!'

'Ssssh, it's all right, go back to sleep.'

I was frightened, but I wasn't going to let him know.

In the morning, I'd ask her, 'What was he dreaming about?'

'Things he saw in the war. You have to try and understand that's why he's like he is. He can't help it, it's his nerves, God love him.'

'What did he see?'

'Never you mind.'

I asked her about communists. She was making soda bread, her hands were sticky with dough. It clung to her like little fat globs of wet cement.

'God almighty, Liam, what's brought this on?'

'They're in charge of Poland, aren't they?'

I could see her wondering whether to tell me to go away.

'They are so. It's a shame, the Poles are great Catholics.'

'If they're all Catholics, how come the communists are in charge?'

'They're very sly.'

'But . . .'

'What?'

'Why are they so bad?'

'They don't believe in God. If they got the chance they'd burn down every church and lock up all the poor priests and nuns. They're a terrible crowd.'

'Are there any in this country?'

She had to think about that.

'There are a few, I think. But the police have their eye on them. I wouldn't worry about it.'

I told her about Marek.

'He said they had to move down here from the Valleys because the communists were taking over there. They were even flying the Russian flag.'

'Is that so?'

She looked shocked. She turned away and started mixing the dough faster, so I knew she wasn't going to answer any more questions.

'Dad, are the communists taking over?'

He was out the back, putting things in the wheelbarrow, getting ready to go to the allotment. He stopped in his tracks, looked round to see if anyone was listening, then leant down so that his face was next to mine.

'Fecking right they are. But try telling your mother, it's like talking to a brick wall.'

He was making me nervous. I wanted a proper answer.

'They won't rest till they've taken over the world. No one will be able to stop them. Napoleon, Hitler, all those fellas came a cropper when they took on the Russians.'

'So the Russians are the communists . . .'

'That's right, yeah.'

'Why do they want to take over the world?'

'They want to turn us all into communists. Well, just let them try it with me.'

He grabbed the axe from the wheelbarrow, waved it in the air.

'The first one that comes over that wall will get this in their gob.'

'You all right there, Brendan?'

It was Mr Williams, shouting over the garden wall. He'd just come in from the back lane. Dad laughed.

'I'm getting ready to defend my property against the communist menace.'

'Oh aye.'

Mr Williams gave him a funny look, took the fag from behind his ear, lit it, flipped his lighter closed, slid it into his shirt pocket.

'Expecting them to arrive any minute, are you?'

He winked at me like we were in on the joke together, blew some smoke from the side of his mouth.

'You never know, boy. They could strike without warning, look at the Japs at Pearl Harbor.'

'Well, Brendan, I have to go, my tea is ready. You give me a shout if you see anything, and I'll come out and give you a hand.'

When he'd gone in, Dad said, 'Dozy long-haired divil.'

I didn't like it when he said that, Mr Williams was a great laugh.

He rubbed his hands together.

'Well now, Liam, I'd love to talk more but I'm far too busy. I've work to do down the allotment.'

He grabbed the handles of the wheelbarrow.

'If there's anything else you want to ask me about . . .'

'Yeah, thanks.'

'Right so.'

He stepped into the back lane, and was gone.

★ ★ ★

Colin and I were uptown. I made Michael walk five paces behind. He wasn't allowed to speak unless one of us spoke to him first.

Every now and then I'd turn round and shout, 'Five paces!' Then one time I turned to shout at him and he wasn't there.

'I'll bet he's still in the market.'

We checked upstairs, where they sold the kittens. No.

'Michael! Michael?'

People turned and stared at us. I hated him. I was scared.

We checked downstairs. The comic stall. No.

'The fish stall?'

'No – he hates the smell. Wait, I know.'

Near the other entrance was a stall that sold broken chocolate for half-price.

'There, there, love. There, there.'

The lady who worked behind the counter was holding his hand. He was snivelling, but he was enjoying it too. As soon as he saw us, he started bawling.

'Are you his brother?'

I nodded.

'You should be more careful. Don't let him out of your sight again, d'you hear me? What if he'd been run over? What if someone had run off with him?'

She gave him a bar of chocolate. A Galaxy, my favourite. I took his hand and led him out of the shop. As soon as we were round the corner, I twisted it up his back and gave him a dead leg. I snatched the bar of Galaxy off him, gave half to Colin.

'Come on, you. And keep up this time.'

We walked down the narrow street that ran along the side of the market, where the rough pubs were. Michael wouldn't stop crying.

'If you don't shut up I'm going to push you into The Prince of Wales and let the mob from the Valleys get you.'

They came down on the trains from the Valleys every weekend to Crindau to drink and fight. You only had to look at them the wrong way and they'd bottle you.

'They're communists,' said Colin.

'They'll take you back to the Valleys in a sack and put you to work in the mines. You'll never see daylight again. You'll have to dig coal all day long, and there's no toilets down there. You'll have to do number one *and* number twos in the dark, listening to the rats scrabbling about.'

I loved making things up to frighten him. I don't know where they came from, I didn't even have to try most of the time, the lies just flew out of my mouth on their own. It was exciting, lying without stopping to think about it, like trying to keep a ball up in the air.

'They have special communist tortures. After an hour you'll be begging them to kill you. But they won't, they'll carry on.'

'And on.'

'And on, till you go mad. No one will hear you crying down there. If you shout for help, they'll just laugh in your face.'

It was brilliant, I was scaring myself.

Michael was blubbering like a baby. I grabbed him by the arm, tugged him towards The Prince of Wales.

'Come on.'

He started screaming.

'No! No!'

I nodded at Colin, he grabbed his other arm. He started shaking his head and dragging his feet along the ground.

'No! No! I don't want to go to the Valleys.'

We were right in front of the door. I could make out rippling shapes behind the frosted glass, like reflections in water. I tugged the door open. The sour smell of beer rushed out at us. There was a poster on the wall.

It's Brains You Want!

'Are there any blokes from the Valleys in there? Here's someone wanting a job down the mines. Can you take him back with you?'

He was screaming, turning red in the face. It was getting difficult to hold him.

A lady stopped in the street behind us.

'What exactly are you boys doing?'

The way she asked it, I knew she was a teacher.

'Mind your own business.'

Her face went tight.

'You cheeky . . . what's your name?'

'Napoleon Solo.'

'And I'm Illya Kuryakin,' said Colin.

We ran off, laughing.

★ ★ ★

I was on a mission. Walking down the street, not too fast, not too slow, careful not to catch anyone's eye. False papers in my pocket in case I was stopped. A gun I'd use rather than let myself

49

be taken alive. At the top of the street I turned left into Courtybella Terrace. My ankle started to itch, but I didn't stop to scratch it, I didn't want to attract any attention. This was no time to take chances. Others were depending on me. Back in the camp, the men were digging secret tunnels with knives and forks. Hiding the earth in their turn-ups, then spilling it on to the ground when the guards weren't looking. It would take them months just to reach the fence. Time was the one thing we didn't have. Someone needed to get a message out.

I reached the address I'd been given.

Stay calm. Try to act normal.

I pushed the door open. The room was crowded, smoky. I ignored their stares, walked up to the counter, whistling. The man behind the glass looked up from writing something in a book.

'Yes?'

'Half a crown on Laughing Boy, please.'

'Is that for Ronnie?'

'Yeah.'

I often went to the betting shop for Uncle Ronnie when his leg was playing up. He and Auntie Val lived at number 100. They were as old as my Nana and Gransha in Ireland. I stopped at Sullivans on the way back.

'Ten Woodbines.'

'Is that for Ronnie?'

'Yeah.'

You always had to say who they were for when you bought cigarettes, otherwise he wouldn't sell them to you.

'And a bar of Galaxy, please.'

Uncle Ronnie always told me to get myself something.

It was his birthday. We had tea in their front room. I'd never been in there before. There were white pieces of cloth on the arms and backs of the chairs that looked like the things they used to line the plates on cake stands.

'Sorry.'

I kept knocking the white things on to the floor. I couldn't help it. You only had to touch them with your hands or the back of your head and they flew off.

'Sorry.'

They were driving me mad.

'Why don't you relax, Liam?'

'I am relaxed.'

'You don't look it.'

I was sitting right on the edge of the seat, my hands on my knees, so I wouldn't knock them off any more.

'What are these?'

'They're called antimacassars,' said Auntie Val.

'What are they for?'

'They look nice.'

'Oh.'

I looked at Uncle Ronnie. He was laughing at me. I didn't mind though. One of the antimacassars from his chair was lying at his feet, but he hadn't noticed, he'd opened his birthday card from Liverpool again.

'"To Ronnie, best wishes from Bill Shankly."'

He smiled to himself.

'Tidy!'

Uncle Ronnie's brother Owen worked as a steward at Anfield. It was him who'd got Shankly to sign the card as a favour.

'Hey, Owen told me the latest Shanks story, do you want to hear it?'

'Yeah!'

I was smiling already. Shankly was my hero too. He cracked me up.

We beat them 4–0 – and they were lucky to get nil.

'He bumps into this player who's just signed for Everton in the town centre and says, "Never mind, son, at least you'll be able to play next to a great team." '

He slapped his thigh, threw back his head and wheezed. I roared. Auntie Val said, 'Oh, that's cruel, that is.'

It was Uncle Ronnie who'd got me supporting Liverpool. If it hadn't been for him I might have ended up supporting Man Utd like all the others.

'That's a nice little job Owen has got for himself there. The money comes in handy now he's retired from the docks, and he gets to see the games free.'

I'd give anything to stand on the Kop, singing 'You'll Never Walk Alone' with all the others, applauding Shankly as he marched, chewing gum, back ramrod straight, to his seat in the dugout. Shankly chewed gum brilliantly, I'd never seen anyone look so tough while they were chewing gum. His walk was tough too. Even his hair looked tough.

Shankly! Shankly! Shankly!

The away teams felt like they were walking into the Lions' Den. The fear beginning to gnaw at them as they clattered down the steps in their football boots to the low tunnel that brought them on to the pitch. Their hearts missing a beat at the sign above their heads at the entrance to the hallowed turf.

This Is Anfield.

The Liverpool players all reached up and touched it for luck. Short-arses like Callaghan and St John had to jump, Big Ron Yeats just stretched out a giant paw. The visiting team looked away, their legs turning to jelly. If I ever had to move from Crindau, Liverpool was where I'd like to live. As well as being able to watch all Liverpool's home games, you could get the ferry across the Mersey every day, *and* the Beatles lived there. Next door to each other in a terraced street just like ours. Except even though each of them entered through a separate front door, inside it was one big house with loads of space. It was true, I'd seen it in a film.

'Of course, according to Owen there was never anywhere

like the docks in Liverpool, thinks he's a big city slicker now, that we've nothing like it in Wales. But Crindau Docks were a great place in the twenties and thirties, people would come from all over to visit. It had a reputation, you see.'

'For what?'

Auntie Val gave him a look I wasn't supposed to see. He hesitated for a moment and took another swig of his pale ale before he continued.

'Somewhere you could let your hair down and have a good time without it getting back to some busybody. Coomassie Street was lined with honky-tonks in those days.'

'What's a honky-tonk?'

'A place where you can have a drink, listen to music and have a dance with one of the working girls.'

'Ronnie!'

'And the Fez Club at the end, many a night I had to be carried home from there.'

'Another biscuit, Liam?'

'Yes, please, Auntie Val.'

They were chocolate digestives, delicious. I bit off a piece and slowly sucked all the chocolate off, letting it slowly melt in my mouth.

'You never heard such a noisy place as Coomassie Street. There was a cage outside every door with a bird inside screaming its head off. Cockatoos, canaries, and parrots . . . the parrots were the worst. They knew some choice language, they'd turn the air blue. The coppers would come round and tell people to bring them inside the house, they were creating a public nuisance.'

He started to laugh, it turned into a coughing fit. He slapped his hand down on the arm of the chair and the other antimacassar flew across the room. Auntie Val started tut-tutting, went over and picked it up, placed it back carefully on the chair.

'For God's sake, try and keep *one* room in the house a bit respectable.'

Uncle Ronnie took another swig from his glass.

'Don't worry, I'll be in my box soon enough, then the place will be spotless.'

'A box now, is it? I thought you were going to be cremated, and have your ashes scattered on the pitch at Anfield.'

Uncle Ronnie gave her an offended look, took out a huge white handkerchief, blew his nose. It sounded like someone trying to play a tuba.

'There'd usually be some bloke wheeling a barrel organ round the streets with a little monkey perched on his shoulder, dressed in a little red hat and gloves, the monkey would be screeching away, the parrots cursing, the coppers hollering at everyone . . .'

'If you were up the town you could spot someone from the docks a mile away,' said Auntie Val. 'You'd always hear them first, it was so noisy down there, everyone had to shout at each other to make themselves heard, see. So even if they were standing right next to each other, they'd be bellowing at the top of their voices, and of course everyone around them would be cringing.'

Auntie Val shook her head and started laughing. Then Uncle Ronnie joined in. I was glad Colin wasn't there, that I didn't have to share Uncle Ronnie and Auntie Val, their stories, their chocolate digestives, with anyone else.

'I remember as if it was yesterday coming down on the train to Crindau as a young bloke. It was the first time I saw a Chinaman laugh,' said Uncle Ronnie, lighting a Woodbine. 'There was a group of them sitting opposite, gambling with shells – fan-tan, they called it.' He cocked his head at Auntie Val. 'What was the other game they played called now?'

She sipped her Babycham.

'Paka . . . puku . . . paka pu, I think it was.'

'Aye, that's right, paka pu. They all worked in the laundries up the Valleys, and they'd come down to the Docks to gamble, see, when they had a day off.'

'You weren't born in Crindau?'

'Born and raised in Merthyr, I was. Christ, what a dump. Rough as boots. A couple of my brothers joined the army just to get away from the place. I came down to Crindau for a night out, had the time of my life, I did. Never went back to the Valleys.'

'Why? Because of the communists?'

He looked at Auntie Val and grinned.

'You haven't been talking to your dad about the Russian menace, have you?'

I didn't like that. He was making fun of me. I didn't say anything.

'He's probably building an underground bunker for you all down in that allotment of his right now.'

Auntie Val laughed, then Uncle Ronnie joined in. It was all going wrong.

'Was that you?'

Auntie Val winced, screwed up her eyes at Uncle Ronnie.

'What?'

'Oh, it's disgusting.'

He frowned, then shook his head.

'It wasn't me, you cheeky mare.'

'It wasn't me!' I said.

It smelt as if someone had heated up rotten eggs in the oven for an hour, then flung open the door. Auntie Val pulled out the handkerchief she always kept tucked into the end of her sleeve, clutched it over her nose.

'Oh, it's that filthy dog.'

Uncle Ronnie prodded him with his shoe.

'Butch! Wake up!'

He twitched, spluttered, bared his teeth.

'Have you been putting pale ale in his bowl again?'

'No, I haven't.'

He had, I'd seen him do it. Auntie Val left the room, came back in with a broom, poked Butch with it.

'Out! Get out of here, go on.'

Butch woke, struggled upright, then nearly bent double with a sneezing fit. Auntie Val poked him again.

'Out, you smelly bugger, go on, go out and get some exercise – oh, the dirty rotten bugger's done it again.'

'You startled him.'

I pinched my nose with my finger and thumb. Using the broom, Val prodded Butch towards the door with one hand, kept the handkerchief to her nose with the other. She shoved him out into the hall, then through to the kitchen – 'Go on! Keep going, you stinker!' I heard the kitchen door open, Auntie Val shouting 'Out!' The door slammed behind him. She came back in, waving her hand through the air in front of her.

'His insides must be rotten.'

'Ah – there's nothing wrong with him.' He leaned towards me. 'Butch may be getting on, but he's a great guard dog. If anyone ever went for me, he'd soon have them.'

Auntie Val sat back down, blowing out her cheeks. Uncle Ronnie leaned over, touched my arm with his hand.

'Your dad should get a dog like him.'

'Why?'

'He'd be a great deterrent.'

'What's a deterrent?'

'A weapon so horrible that your enemies are scared to attack you in case you use it against them. Oh yes, if your dad had Butch he wouldn't be so worried about the Russians coming for him.'

He started cackling. A prickly heat spread its tentacles across the top of my head.

'I've trained him to blow off if someone attacks me – worse

than mustard gas, it is. He could repel a whole regiment of the Red Army with one of those.'

Auntie Val was sniggering.

'That's it, that's what we'll do – ask Brendan to take the dirty so-and-so off our hands.'

'He's not for sale.'

Uncle Ronnie lowered his voice, winked.

'You never know when you might need a dog like Butch. On constant red alert, he is.' His voice dropped to a whisper. 'Primed with pale ale!'

Auntie Val reached for her drink.

'Liam's dad has given us some laughs down the years, hasn't he?'

I didn't want to hear any of it, I didn't want to find something new to worry about.

'Aye, he has all right, but never mind about that now – Liam, instead of sitting there with that long face, why don't you go and make yourself useful and get me another bottle of pale ale from the kitchen?'

★ ★ ★

Colin, Joe 90 and I stood under an oak tree in Cwm Wood. We raised our hands, ready to take the oath.

'Repeat after me, "I am not afraid to die for the cause." '

'Die?'

Joe 90 lowered his hand. Marek stared at him.

'You have a question?'

'You never mentioned anything about dying before.'

'Go home, forget you ever came here, forget that you ever saw us.'

He wouldn't be able to forget he saw us, he was in our class, we'd see him in school on Monday.

He started fiddling with his glasses.

'I was only asking . . .'

'Go on, this is no place for you, you're not ready.'

'But . . .'

'Go! You don't have what it takes to be a member of the resistance. You're still a boy.'

Joe 90 looked at me and Colin, we looked away. He put his hands in his pockets, started trudging off, kicking leaves as he went.

'Any more questions?'

Colin and I shook our heads.

'Good.'

I felt sorry for Joe 90, but him having to leave also made what we were doing seem more exciting and dangerous now. Marek repeated the oath.

'I am not afraid to die for the cause.'

He paused, fixing us with his eyes, letting us know he'd be able to tell if we didn't mean it. The light was just beginning to fade, there was a chill in the air. We said it.

'I am not afraid to die for the cause.'

'I will never reveal the names of my comrades to the enemy, no matter how badly I'm tortured.'

Somewhere in the distance, bells rang out.

'I will never reveal the names of my comrades to the enemy, no matter how badly I'm tortured.'

'I will obey my commanding officer at all times.'

Colin and I looked at each other.

'Hang on, who's that?'

Marek looked annoyed.

'Me!'

We dropped our hands.

'Who said *you* could be commanding officer?'

'You didn't even know there was an Anti-Communist Resistance till I told you about it this morning.'

'Yeah, but that doesn't mean . . .'

'So you've known about the resistance for less than a day, while the Poles have been fighting communism since before you were born, but you still think you should be commanding officer?'

'But there's only three of us, why do we need a commanding officer?'

Marek stamped his foot.

'You have to have a leader. And I'm the tallest.'

Colin said, 'We could be like the Three Musketeers – one for all and all for one!'

Marek narrowed his eyes.

'That's communism.'

'Oh.'

'If you want to join, you have to obey the rules.' Marek folded his arms. 'If you don't want to join, it's no skin off my nose. Make your mind up.'

'We could form our own resistance group,' said Colin.

I knew what would happen if we formed our own resistance group, we'd never be able to decide on anything. We'd spend all day mucking around and telling jokes. We *did* need a leader.

'No,' I said, 'I think we should join Marek's, and he should be commanding officer.'

'What?'

Colin was staring at me.

'You're joking.'

'Give us a minute,' I said to Marek.

He shrugged and turned away. Colin and I walked to where Marek couldn't hear us.

'What's the matter with you?' hissed Colin.

'Come on, let's give it a go. We can always leave if we don't like it.'

He tapped his forehead with his finger.

'He's mad.'

I nudged him.

'You have to be mad to be a goalkeeper.'

He nearly smiled, but caught himself just in time.

'It could be great fun. We'll get him to bring his dad's gun.'

Colin snorted, stamped on a piece of wood lying amongst the leaves; there was a loud crack as it snapped.

'There *is* no gun.'

'This is our chance to find out if there really is. Come on, it won't be the same without you.'

'He's too bossy.'

'Just try it for a bit. If you don't like it, we'll both leave. You're my best mate, I don't want to join without you.'

He stared into the trees, biting his lip.

'Come on, Colin.'

'OK.'

We walked back. Marek was scratching something into the tree with his penknife.

'We both want to join, and we both agree to you being commanding officer.'

Marek nodded, folded his penknife up, put it in his pocket. He didn't look surprised, or pleased, just eager to carry on. I liked that.

'Good men.'

We finished swearing oaths.

'I will not rest till Poland is free again.'

And:

'I will not rest till the last communist is driven out of the Valleys.'

We held a minute's silence for all those who died in the Warsaw uprising, then Marek handed over his penknife and we carved our names into the tree next to his.

Marek Liam Colin Crindau Resistance October 5th 1968

We did ten press-ups, then went home for our tea.

★ ★ ★

Michael was sitting on the coal bunker, swinging his legs, humming to himself. He pretended not to see me walking up to him.

'Mam made me promise never to tell you.'

I waited. He looked up.

'Tell me what?'

'That you were adopted.'

His face fell.

'The gyppos left you on our doorstep. There was dog's mess in your hair and you were covered in sores. Dad wanted to hand you in to the council, but Mam stopped him. She felt sorry for you.'

'It's not true.'

I shrugged.

'Suit yourself.'

'It's not!'

His voice was cracking, there were tears in his eyes. I walked away.

'See you.'

It started to rain, but he didn't come in. I watched him through the window for a while, sitting there, staring into space, then it was time for *Thunderbirds*.

★ ★ ★

'What's *he* doing here?'

It was Sunday, the resistance were meeting in Cwm Wood again, but this time I had to bring Michael with me. Mam was in bed with flu, Dad had gone down the docks road, foraging for more wood.

You can never have enough wood, you'd never know when you might need it.

'It's all right, I'll make him stand over there, with his face to that tree.'

Marek shook his head.

'No, it's not that easy.'

'Why?'

'It's a breach of security, bringing him here. Now he knows where we meet, who we are. If he stays here he has to join or die.'

'OK, then he dies.'

Michael flinched.

'We could strangle him, then bury him in the wood, no one would ever know.'

'No, I'll tell Mam.'

'What? That we killed you?'

Colin burst out laughing. I pinched the back of Michael's arm and he squealed.

'Don't be such a worm.'

I turned to Marek.

'I don't want him to be a member. I'm sick of him hanging around me all the time.'

Marek thought about it.

'We could make him a Friend of the resistance.'

'A Friend?'

'A Friend is different to a member. He has to obey the rules but he's not really one of us, he's not allowed to hear our secret passwords or sit in when we make plans.'

Colin said, 'We don't have any passwords and we haven't made any plans.'

'That's because we wasted a lot of time last week arguing over who should be leader when we could have been doing something more useful.'

There was an awkward silence, then Michael shouted, 'I want to be a member.'

I cuffed him round the back of the head.

'You'll be a Friend and like it.'

'Friends of the resistance still have to swear an oath. Raise your right hand.'

Michael was still rubbing the back of his head. I grabbed his hand and yanked it up for him.

'Are you deaf?'

'Repeat after me, "I will obey my commanding officer at all times."'

'And me, otherwise I'll thump you.'

'And me,' shouted Colin.

Michael was cowering, his hands over his head. I pushed him in the back.

'Stand up straight when your commanding officer is speaking to you.'

Marek swore him in as a Friend. There was no minute's silence, no carving his name into the tree with Marek's pen-knife, but Michael still looked delighted, he thought he was one of us now. He started hopping from one foot to the other with excitement.

'What shall we do first?' he said.

I grabbed his arm, turned him round.

'Go and stand over there and face that tree.'

'What?'

'You heard me. No talking, no peeping, no moving at all. Stand to attention, your nose one inch from the tree exactly. I'll come and get you when it's time to go.'

His bottom lip started to tremble. I pushed him.

'Go on!'

He lowered his head and walked away.

★ ★ ★

'Tina! Got a minute?'

Mrs Williams looked flustered.

'I'm up to my neck here.'

We were in Glamourpuss, me, Colin and his dad, the hair-dressers' where she worked. It was Saturday, nearly lunch-time, the place was packed. A line of ladies sat with their heads under space helmets, flicking through magazines, not worrying about their hair overheating and catching fire.

Mr Williams took all the notes except one from his wallet, held them out to Mrs Williams.

'Here – I want you to keep hold of my money till this evening.'

'What?'

She laughed nervously, stepped backwards. He followed, pushing the money at her. Colin and I looked at each other. Something funny was going on.

'I swore I wouldn't waste any more money on that shower, but I don't trust myself. It's not easy to break the habit of a lifetime. You've got to help me – take it!'

'What are you . . . I'll be with you in a minute, love.' She waved her hand at a lady with wet hair, and a towel around her neck, who was frowning in her direction. Mr Williams stared at the floor.

'I hate them.'

He clenched his fists and the notes crumpled and twisted between his fingers. His head shot up again.

'I realised this morning. I've actually hated them for years, I just haven't been able to admit it to myself.'

'Hated *who*?'

'The Steelmen.'

That was our nickname. West Ham were the Hammers, Sheffield United were the Blades, Crindau FC were the Steelmen.

'I thought they couldn't get any worse. I thought I knew what to expect, and I'd learnt to live with it. But that last game . . .' He shook his head. 'Never again. NEVER AGAIN, DO YOU HEAR ME?'

'Sssssh!'

The ladies were looking up from their helmets.

'Dad!'

Colin was tugging at his sleeve.

'We *are* going to the match, aren't we?'

Mrs Williams snatched the notes from his hand, stuffed them into the pocket of her pink nylon overall.

'Satisfied?'

'Thanks, Tina.'

He kissed her.

'Go on, you daft bugger.'

Another lady in a pink overall gave a wolf-whistle. I felt myself blushing.

'See you later. Come on, boys.'

We headed up town.

'Dad . . .'

'No.'

'You haven't heard what I'm going to say yet.'

Mr Williams took the fag from behind his ear.

'No, I'm not taking you to the game. I'd sooner go for a guided tour of the sewage works . . . I'd sooner go and watch bloody Cardiff City.'

He stopped, looked around nervously to see if anyone had heard him. You could tell he was ashamed at saying such a terrible thing. *Cardiff City!* He reached into his jacket pocket, flipped open his lighter, lit his fag.

'Now let's hear no more about it.'

He jerked his wrist and the top of the lighter flipped itself shut.

'Let's go.'

'Where to?'

'The market.'

That was OK, I liked the market.

Colin looked sick. He was mad about the Steelmen, he had hundreds of their programmes stacked under his bed, and he was always asking me to test him on their history.

'Biggest victory?'

'Six–one versus Tonypandy Town – "the Townies", Welsh Cup, 1903.'

'Biggest defeat?'

I asked him that one every time.

'Seventeen–nil versus Tranmere, 1947, Fourth Division.'

He'd give me a dirty look.

'Our keeper had a stomach bug.'

He always said that.

But I wasn't that bothered. What I enjoyed most about match days was walking up town with Colin and his dad, marching through the narrow streets to the ground, an army of us taking over the pavements, spilling on to the road, bringing traffic to a halt. The shouts of the programme sellers, the smell of sausages and onions frying in the snack vans outside the ground.

'Sauce with that, mate?'

'Yes, please.'

'There it is, on your right. That's a tanner. Next.'

Sausage, roll, sweet slithering onions and tomato sauce all mashed up together in your mouth. Lovely. The roar on the terraces when Crindau got a corner. The jokes and insults. The swearing. The songs:

Come on, you Steelmen

and

I'd walk a million miles for one of your goals, O Crindau.

But Mr Williams was right, they were rubbish.

As we walked up the High Street a man yelled, 'Hi-ya, Cliff, off to the match?'

He shook his head, rushed straight past.

'Everyone's going except us,' said Colin. 'It's not fair.'

Mr Williams speeded up, so that we had to nearly run to keep up with him. Past Slape's Hardware, Browns For Bargains!, Woolworths, the monument to the South Wales Borderers, The Parrot Hotel.

There was a man outside the entrance to the market holding up a newspaper and shouting.

'General strike now!'

I'd never seen him there before. He was wearing a duffel coat, had long hair and little round glasses like John Lennon.

'Force Wilson to arm the Vietcong!'

I gave Colin a nudge, but he didn't look up, he was still sulking. The man wasn't any good at selling papers, everyone was ignoring him. It was all wrong, he was too young, didn't have the right kind of voice, he pronounced the words too carefully. He was too eager, kept turning to people and shoving the paper towards them. The man who sold the *Argus* outside the post office was ancient, wore a brown coat and a cap, sounded like someone mental losing their temper.

HAAAAAAAAAAAAAAAARRRG!!!! LATEHAAAAAAA-ARRG!!!

He never tried to catch anyone's eye, he looked as though he just enjoyed shouting at people, as if he didn't care whether anyone bought a paper or not, but he sold loads.

I wondered where the new paper seller had come from. I didn't like the look of him.

The market was packed. We pushed through the crowds and raced up the stairs, where the best stalls were. Past the foreign coins, The Tea Hut, The Bible Store. We stopped at Criminal Records. Mr Williams nodded at the man behind the counter, started flicking through the LPs. I loved watching him. He held the records steady with his left hand, flicked them forward with one finger of his right hand. His face was creased with concentration, his body taut, like a hunter poised to strike. When he saw an LP he liked, he plucked it out in a flash, checked the price, turned it over and looked at the back using one hand. Before he bought it, he'd take the record out of the sleeve and check its surface for scratches.

Colin was still moping.

'I bet they win this week, and we won't be there to see it.'

He was dreaming.

'Why don't you look through the singles, see if there's anything you like?' said Mr Williams.

Colin didn't move, so I had a look. I tried to flick through them the way Mr Williams did the LPs, but I couldn't get the knack of flicking just one at a time. When I tried, about five or six fell forward at once and I had to go back and start again, slowly. After a while Colin came and stood beside me. I found a Roy Orbison single, 'Oh, Pretty Woman'. I took it out of its sleeve and checked it for scratches.

'Do you want that?'

Mr Williams was nodding at me.

'Yeah!'

'Here, I'll get it for you.'

'Thank you very much.'

I handed it to him. The man behind the counter put it in a brown paper bag along with the two LPs Mr Williams had chosen. Mr Williams paid for the records, then we had tea and beans on toast at The Tea Hut. When we'd finished, Mr Williams lit another fag and took the records out of the bag.

The first LP was called *Cream*. There were three men with long hair in funny clothes on the front, staring out. The second was called *Introducing John Lee Hooker*, a black man, smiling, like he knew a secret about you, his hands draped over a guitar.

'I'll be able to treat myself every week now that I've stopped wasting money on football.'

'Cliff!'

It was Mr Richards.

'Tony! Hi-ya, mate.'

He sat down beside us, signalled to the lady behind the counter.

'Mug of tea and a pork pie, please, love.'

He turned to Mr Williams, took out his wallet.

'Here's that fiver I owe you.'

'There's no rush.'

'That's not what you said the other day.'

'Next week will do.'

'No, I wouldn't hear of it. Go on, I've just had a win on the gee-gees.'

'No.'

'Go on!'

He shoved the fiver into Mr Williams's pocket. The lady brought his tea and pie. Mr Williams looked anxious.

'Right, I'll have this, then we'll head off to the game.'

Colin's eyes lit up.

'Not me, I'm never going again.'

'What?'

Bits of pork pie flew across the table like shrapnel.

'You're joking.'

Mr Williams shook his head. He told Mr Richards how he hated the Steelmen.

'What's wrong with you, man? You'll be telling me you're switching to rugby next.'

'Piss off.'

Mr Richards started laughing.

'I can just see you standing with all the bloody bumpkins from the Valleys, passing round the raw turnips and cheering on a crowd of stupid Welshies knocking each other senseless. Aye, just up your street.'

'Leave it, will you?'

'Come on, man, don't be so soft.' He checked his watch. 'If we don't get a move on we'll miss the kick-off.'

Colin saw his chance.

'Dad! Please!'

'How can you let the poor kiddies down like this? I'll bet they've been looking forward to it all week, haven't you, boys?'

'Yes,' said Colin. He nudged me.

'Yes,' I said. 'We have.'

Mr Williams winced. I bit my lip so I wouldn't burst out laughing.

'See! Just look at their faces. How could you do this to them? What kind of a bloke are you anyhow?'

Mr Williams pushed a baked bean round his plate with his fork, squirming with embarrassment.

★ ★ ★

The Walsall players were just coming on to the pitch when we arrived. We joined in the booing. Then they played the theme from *2001*, Crindau ran out and we all cheered.

There was an announcement over the Tannoy.

'There is a late team change for Crindau. John Alwyn will now be replaced at number eleven by Stevie Venus.'

'Which one is Venus?'

'There he is. Christ, he looks a right stick insect. They'll have him for dinner.'

In the first minute one of our defenders tried to pass back to the keeper, but he booted it too hard and it hit the post and started rolling along the goal line. Our keeper dived on it just before a Walsall player got there. Mr Williams shook his head, lit a fag.

Then, the first time Venus got the ball he skinned their full back, raced down the line and put over a brilliant cross, right on our centre forward's head. He was unmarked, the keeper was nowhere. He headed it wide. Everyone groaned.

'Christ, he couldn't hit a cow's arse with a shovel.'

A few minutes later, Venus nicked the ball off a defender, went past their centre half, rounded their keeper, slotted it into the net. Everyone went mad.

'Bet you're glad you came now.'

The next time Venus got the ball a Walsall player kicked him to the ground.

'You dirty bastard! Go back to . . . where the bloody hell *is* Walsall anyhow?'

'Up north.'

'Go back to north Wales, you dirty bastard.'

Everyone laughed. I didn't get it.

Venus was all right again a few minutes later. He had two men on him every time he got the ball now; they were terrified of him.

Mr Williams's other mate arrived. He was late today. He nodded at Mr Williams, took his bag of chips out of his pocket.

'I know I said I wasn't going to come back, but the wife's gone to visit her sister, and I got fed up sitting on my own watching *Grandstand*.'

He looked around, frowned.

'What's up?'

'What do you mean?'

'Why is everyone smiling?'

'We're one–nil up, we've got a brilliant new winger.'

He snorted.

'Oh aye, and I've got a date with Raquel Welch tonight.'

'GO ON, STEVIE BOY!'

He beat two of them, crossed, the keeper flapped at it, their centre half fell over and the ball dropped in front of our centre-forward, two yards out. He couldn't miss.

'YES!'

Two–nil. In the celebrations, Mr Williams's mate dropped his bag of chips and I grabbed my chance, kicked it down the steps before he could find it again. Served him right for never offering us any.

In the second half, Stevie boy got brought down in the area and we scored from the penalty, but he limped off ten minutes from the end with us 3–0 up. It finished 3–2. We all poured into the streets, singing and clapping our hands.

'Champions! Champions!'

On the bus back, Mr Williams was in a brilliant mood, laughing and joking and checking up on which teams Crindau were playing next in the programme.

'Scunthorpe United. They've got that bald bloke at full back, bandy legs, looks about fifty. Stevie Boy'll destroy him. That's another two points in the bag. Then home to Crewe, they're rubbish . . .'

We were going to be promoted. Mr Williams had bought me a Roy Orbison single, and I'd kicked his mate's dinner down the steps. What a fab day.

★   ★   ★

'Grand and peaceful, isn't it? This is the best part of the day, when the air is still fresh and clear and you have the place to yourself, when the rest of the lazy feckers are still snoring their heads off.'

It was half past eight on Sunday morning. Straight after breakfast Dad asked me to come down the allotment with him. He'd never done that before, but he said he had something to show me.

He went inside the shed at the end of his allotment, came out with a bottle of Guinness. I wondered what else he had in there, I'd never seen inside it. He slammed the bottle down on the side of the wheelbarrow, the cap flew off and he bent over and sucked at the foam surging out of the neck.

'Do you want some?'

'No, thanks.'

'I've no minerals, mind.'

That's what they called pop in Ireland. He held up the bottle.

'This is all there is.'

72

'I'm OK, thanks.'

He frowned.

'Suit yourself.'

He wiped his lips with the back of his hand.

'I often come down here for a bit of peace and quiet, to escape from your mother's yakking and nagging. She seems to think I'm interested in what the neighbours are doing, or what's happening in bleddy *Coronation Street*. Her head is filled with rubbish, she hasn't a clue what's happening in the world. I can talk to you all right though.'

He was making me feel nervous.

'Michael takes after his mother, but you're like me.'

'I am?'

'You're not easily fooled, am I right?'

'Yeah,' I said. 'That's true.'

'There now,' he took another swig of stout, 'I thought as much. Wait till I show you something.'

He opened the door of the shed again, beckoned me inside. There were hundreds of tins stacked up against the walls – none of them had any labels, and most of them were dented and buckled. He looked pleased with himself.

'What do you think?'

'Er . . . what's in them?'

He looked put out.

'Well, you'd have to open them to find out *exactly* what's in them . . . Christ almighty, what do you *think* is in them, only the usual kind of stuff you find in cans – beans, peas, peaches, fruit salad – all that kind of carry on. Look . . .'

He bent down, picked up the top one from a small pile of thin, rectangular tins with a little metal key in the corner that you used to pull back the lid.

'I'd say these lads are sardines.'

He turned it round in his hands, nodding to himself.

'Oh yes, those are sardines all right.'

'Why haven't they got any labels?'

His expression brightened, pleased at the question.

'I bought them off this fella down the cattle market a few years ago. Everything on the stall was shop-soiled, or fire-damaged, or *something* . . . I could see some people turning their noses up at it, but more fool them. There's nothing wrong with them apart from having no labels and a few dents in them, but that doesn't bother me – the important thing is what's inside them, not whether they've got labels or no. They were right bargains, it cost me hardly anything to get myself stocked up.'

He put the tin back on the pile, took a step back. He gave me a look I couldn't figure out.

'There's only one other person I ever invited in here, that was Ronnie from down the street.'

'What did he say?'

His face tightened.

'He stood right there, where you're standing now, for a long while, taking it all in. Then he gave me this quare look and said, "Brendan, you need a holiday." What do you make of *that*?'

He hawked and spat out of the door. There was an awkward silence. Through the gap I glimpsed a lorry coming along the road from the docks, throwing up a dust cloud behind it like the stagecoach in a western.

'Ah, sure he's getting on, the auld brain is probably starting to go on him. Anyway!' He waved the bottle at the rows of cans. 'I'm well prepared, aren't I?'

'For what?'

He looked at me as if I was an idiot.

'The war. I'd give it a couple of years at most before it breaks out. Europe's in a bad way, the Russians must be laughing. Everywhere you look long-haired wasters are pelting the police with petrol bombs and stones. France, Germany, Italy, they're completely rotten, the Russians'll cut through them like a knife.'

Everything Marek had said was right.

The Russians will never be content with what they've got, they'll always want more. Always!

'We're in the front line here in Wales. The Russians would love to get their hands on what we've got – the docks, the factories, the coal – Jayzus, Russia's a quare cold place. You'd never keep a house warm in Siberia. The temperature there drops so low that if you went outside without a pair of gloves you'd get frostbite after half an hour, and the fingers would drop off you.'

He picked up another can.

'Christ, I hate this tinned muck, but we'd be glad of it right enough if they landed tomorrow and it was all you could get. Better a tin of cold beans than nothing at all. And when things get really bad, you could barter with them.'

He held the tin in front of my face.

'You never know, the time might come when this tin could save your life.'

'How could a tin of beans save your life?'

'Your average Russian soldier is a thick peasant. He's the bogman of the East. Spends all his life dreaming of Western goods. His eyes would be out on stalks if you waved this in front of him. He'd swap his rifle for it in a second. That's the class of a fella you're dealing with now.'

'They wouldn't *really* bother with Crindau, would they?'

He raised his eyebrows.

'Oh, indeed they would, they'd strip it bare. I saw the Russians in action during the war; fecking hell, they're like mad dogs. Be Christ, I'm telling you, boy, they made the Germans pay. Some of the things I saw . . .'

He broke off, took a long swig. I felt a chill run down my back. I told him about Marek and his dad the Hurricane pilot, and their house back home that the communists had handed over to peasants.

'Jayzus, you've a grand friend there, boy. The Pole is very loyal, he'll never let you down. He's suffered so much, you see, the poor Pole, been stabbed in the back so many times, that he really values a good mate.'

He patted my shoulder.

'You won't let him down now, will you?'

I shook my head. I told him about Marek's dad seeing the red flag flying from the town hall up in the Valleys and them coming down here to live to escape the communists. He paused, squeezing his top lip between his thumb and forefinger, then took another swig from the bottle. He shook his head.

'Christ almighty,' he muttered, 'it's worse than I thought.'

★ ★ ★

'Mam, do *you* think there'll be another world war soon?'

'Not now,' she snapped. 'Can't you see I'm busy?'

She was only hanging washing on the line. She could talk and do that at the same time, I'd seen her.

'But what about what Dad said, you know, when we were watching the Russians invading on the news?'

She frowned.

'Go and play.'

She never wanted to talk. I stayed where I was.

'He said I should start saying my prayers because . . .'

'Will you give over?'

'But I don't know who to believe. Why do Mr Williams and Uncle Ronnie laugh at Dad, is there something wrong with him?'

She grabbed my shoulders, started shaking me.

'This is a normal family like any other, there's nothing wrong with any of us, do you hear me?'

'All right, all right!'

'Now what's done is done. I've made my bed and I've got to lie in it, and you're going to have to get used to it too, understand?'

No, I didn't, she was talking in riddles.

'Let go, you're hurting me.'

I thought she was going to scream, but, instead, she released me and rushed into the back kitchen. I waited a bit before following her. She was stood next to the sink, smoking a cigarette. Her hand was trembling.

'Mam, what's the matter?'

She turned away from me, sent a cloud of angry smoke rushing to the ceiling.

'Nothing's the matter.'

There were tears in her eyes.

'Please don't get upset.'

'I'm all right.'

'Is it Dad?'

She squeezed her eyes shut, bit her lip.

'Will I put the kettle on?'

'No, just leave me alone.'

I started kicking the cupboard under the sink.

'What's the matter? What is it?'

'Stop that.'

'Tell me.'

She jerked upright, her eyes blazing.

'I'll tell you what's the matter with me – it's you. You're the problem.'

I took a step back.

'You and your damn questions. You never stop. Why in God's name do you want to be worrying about things like war breaking out at your age? I never worried about that kind of thing when I was young. I was always out enjoying myself, running about in the fields, or collecting shells down the strand, not a care in the world.'

There weren't any fields around here. The nearest beaches were at Barry Island or Porthcawl, you had to catch the train.

'What kind of a child are you anyhow? You'd never run up to me and give me a hug and tell me you love me like Michael. You're no comfort to me at all.'

She took a long drag from her cigarette. Tilted her head back, sucked the smoke deep inside her.

'You used to be so affectionate when you were a little fella, but now! You've never been the same since Michael was born. You've always been jealous of him.'

'I'm not jealous!'

Not of him – he was a complete spaz, a waste of space.

'When he was a baby you'd give out to me – "You're always looking at him, you never look at me any more." Oh Jesus, you gave me a terrible time, you wouldn't do anything I told you to – you told me you hated me, you chucked things at me, you kicked me, you hit me . . .'

'I didn't.'

'Indeed you did. You've a very spiteful streak in you, Liam. I don't know where you get it from, not from my family anyhow . . .'

'You're making it up.'

She gave me a look then that I'd never seen on her face before. As if she was seeing me, *really* seeing me, for the first time, and didn't know who I was. It frightened me.

'What in God's name do you want from me? I try and do my best, Christ knows it isn't easy sometimes. Haven't you food in your belly, shoes on your feet, and a roof over your head? Just think of all the poor children in Africa who'd love to have what you have.'

'I don't care about them.'

I saw it coming just in time, swerved sideways, her finger-tips brushed my hair. It would have really stung if she'd caught me. By the time she'd recovered her balance I'd stepped back, giving myself enough distance to make a run for it if she tried again.

'May God forgive you, you rotten little divil.'

She cursed under her breath as she stooped to pick up her cigarette from the floor.

'I never thought I'd hear you say something like that.'

'I didn't mean it.'

I cringed at the sound of my voice – it was just like Michael's when he was on the verge of blubbering.

'Go away from me. Go on, get out of my sight.'

I ran down the back. Lifted the latch, pushed open the gate. It was Tuesday, the men were coming to empty the bins. Ours was just outside, Dad had put it out before he went to work. I kicked it once, twice. The third time it went crashing to the ground, spewing everything into the dirt. I started running.

★ ★ ★

We crept through the trees, hunched over, our faces blackened with dirt. The resistance was about to strike its first blow. Marek held back the wire while we crept through the hole in the fence, me first, followed by Michael, then Colin. We made our way along the edge of the embankment, the railway line below us. Colin checked the timetable again. He loved timetables, he'd got it from his uncle who worked on the railways.

'There's one that goes to the Valleys in a couple of minutes.'

Marek nodded. We took cover in the ferns. A fat raindrop landed on the back of my neck, slithered icily down my back, but I didn't flinch. There was a rumbling in the distance.

'Hold your fire till I give the order,' hissed Marek.

Colin rolled his eyes. My heart was pounding. The front of the train appeared through a gap in the trees, Colin pushed forward to get a better look.

'Wait!'

It was almost on us, so close I could see the driver yawning, his flask and sandwich box, the badge on his lapel. The first carriage went past.

'Now!'

We jumped up, Marek shouting at the top of his voice.

'DEATH TO COMMUNISM!'

Startled faces at the window, realising too late they were under attack. No time to duck or throw themselves to the floor before our stones rained down on them. I aimed my first shot at a man reading the paper. He was gone before I could see his reaction, replaced by a lady staring out at us, a cigarette in her hand, her mouth dropping open. I aimed at her head.

Crack!

The stone hit the glass right in front of her face, it must have nearly shattered the window. I saw one of Michael's stones fly harmlessly up into the air, then plummet into the ferns a few feet in front of us. But Colin and Marek were hitting the target. I fired again and again at the faces below. Suddenly the train was gone, the last stones falling on to the empty track.

It had gone brilliantly. We started jumping up and down and singing.

'HELLO, HELLO, WE ARE THE CRINDAU BOYS!'

'When's the next train to the Valleys?'

Colin brought out his timetable again.

'An hour.'

'Damn.'

'OK,' said Marek, 'back to base.'

It was over too soon. Michael was the only one who moved. We wanted more action. I heard something.

'What's that?'

Colin checked the timetable again, frantically turning the pages.

'Come on, come on.'

'That'll be the 11.30 to Cardiff.'

Cardiff.

Colin and I looked at each other.

'Yes!'

'No,' said Marek. 'The plan was to attack trains carrying communists to the Valleys. We must keep our discipline.'

'Cardiff's crawling with communists too,' I said.

'Yeah,' said Colin. 'The place stinks of them.'

It was getting closer.

'Come on, we haven't got much time.'

I could see it in his eyes – Marek didn't want to stop now either.

'OK, take cover.'

We squatted down in the ferns again.

'Hold your fire till I . . .'

'OK, OK.'

It was nearly here. A bigger train this time. A bigger target. Marek raised his arm, brought it down like a guillotine.

'Now!'

Colin and I jumped up, screaming at the top of our voices.

'OH CARDIFF CITY, WE HATE YOU.'

A blizzard of stones flew through the air. They didn't know what had hit them. They must have thought there were at least twenty or thirty of us. It was over in a flash, we stood there, exhausted, watching the train head down the line towards Cardiff.

We jumped up, punched the air.

'Yes!'

'Ha, that showed them. Go on – fuck off back to Cardiff, you bastards!'

We flashed V signs at the last carriage. We put our hands to the sides of our mouths, did Indian whoops.

'It's slowing down. Run!'

We scrambled through the hole in the fence, back into the wood.

'Liam! Liam!'

I looked behind, Michael had caught his anorak on the wire.

Marek climbed up on to a branch, was looking down on to the railway line.

'It's gone.'

Colin looked away. Marek dropped down from the branch.

'Who said it was stopping?'

Colin said, 'It wasn't me.'

It was. I pointed at Michael.

'It was him.'

'Liam!'

'He's such a spaz, I knew he'd muck things up.'

'Help me.'

I cupped my hand round my mouth, started shouting.

'They're coming. Hurry up.'

'Liam!'

We heard the fence shaking. Then a whimpering noise.

'He's stuck.'

'I can hear you,' shouted Michael, his voice breaking. 'I know you're there.'

'Come on,' I said. 'Let's leave him, it'll teach him a lesson.'

I heard the anorak tear.

I'd get the blame.

'Stop that! Stay still, don't move, I'll come and get you.'

He looked like the Hunchback of Notre Dame, he was hoisted up by his wrist and back, hanging out of the anorak. His eyes were red and tubes of snot oozed from his nostrils.

'I'm telling.'

I grabbed his hair and the front of his jumper, yanked him out of the anorak. He yelped, then collapsed on the ground, blubbering. Now with him out of the way it was easy to see where the anorak was caught, and ease it free. I chucked it down on to him.

'Be more careful, that used to be mine. I always took good care of it.'

Marek said, 'If someone had been coming, we would have had to leave him.'

'Do you hear that? You'll have to do better if you want to stay a Friend of the resistance.'

He wouldn't last five minutes when the war broke out.

★ ★ ★

'Here we are.'

I felt a sinking feeling in my stomach. It was all wrong. The sign said Coomassie Street, but it didn't look like the place Uncle Ronnie had described. Two long rows of grey houses, each one as stubby and drab as the last, stretched down to a buckled and torn fence with rusting junk piled up against it. No screaming birds in cages outside the houses, no men with little monkeys on their shoulders wheeling barrel organs up and down the street.

'Is this it?'

'Aye, it is. They've torn all the old places down, they said it was a slum, an eyesore.'

Behind us a dog barked like a machine gun. At the bottom of the street a gate slammed over and over in the wind.

'Lovely, isn't it?'

'No, it's a dump.'

He nodded. The drizzle grew heavier.

'Disappointed?'

'Yes, I am.'

'I tried telling you. I warned you it had all changed but you had to drag me down here so you could see for yourself.'

He grimaced. Butch was shivering next to him.

'This wet weather isn't helping my leg. I'll have to have a sit down.'

He was making me feel bad, but I was too embarrassed now to apologise. We walked on till we came to a big pub called The

83

Steam Packet which stood alone in the middle of some waste ground. When Uncle Ronnie pushed the door open, the smell of sour beer and stale smoke nearly knocked me to my knees. He pointed to a small room on our left.

'We'll go in the snug, no one'll bother us there.'

I sat on a bench while he went to the counter and rapped out a secret code with a two-bob bit that made the barman appear. His eyes flicked over me, then back to Uncle Ronnie, and he took the order without changing expression. Behind the counter, wooden shelves stretched up to the ceiling, crammed with a wonderful collection of things. Packets of cigarettes stacked in different colours – red and white, gold, white with a thick navy-blue band. Tins of cigars. Boxes of matches – Swans and England's Glory – one stack of each. Trophies for football, running and darts. Postcards of skyscrapers and tropical beaches and crumbling pillars in the sand. Foreign banknotes with strange heads and colourful flags.

Uncle Ronnie brought me a glass of lemonade and a packet of crisps, a bottle of pale ale for himself. I thanked him, tore open the packet, fished out the little blue twist of paper with the salt in, scattered it over the crisps, then shook them up and down. I offered Uncle Ronnie one first. He took some, lit a Woodbine, poured his ale. He took the empty ashtray off the table, poured in some ale, and put it on the floor for Butch.

The barman came back, reached up and took down a packet of cigarettes, disappeared again.

'That's Holy Jim's son,' said Uncle Ronnie, blowing a stream of smoke through his nose.

The rain rapped and slapped against the window behind us.

'Jim Jenkins was his real name. He ran this place till he retired, oh, ten years ago now at least. During the war, first the house on one side, then the other, was blown to hell by a bomb. And twice, *twice*, mind you, a bomb came through the roof and didn't explode. The *Argus* ran a story – *Pub's miraculous luck* – that's when everyone started calling him Holy Jim.'

In the public bar, someone put 'Hey Jude' on the jukebox. I ate another crisp, took a swig of lemonade. Butch had finished his ale, was licking his lips and looking up at Uncle Ronnie.

'Could you tell there was a war coming?'

'We had a pretty good idea, once we realised what sort of a bloke Hitler was, the signs were there all right.'

'What about now? Are the signs there now? Will there be another world war soon?'

He looked at me in a way he'd never done before, as if he'd just realised something about me he'd never noticed. I began to feel uncomfortable.

'What's this about? Are you worrying about something your dad has told you?'

The prickly heat crawled across my head again, I shifted uneasily on the bench.

'No.'

He kept staring at me.

'Yes.'

'Well? Spit it out.'

I told him about how desperate the Russians were to get their hands on our coal, how you could never keep a house warm in Siberia. Uncle Ronnie snorted, some beer went up his nose and he had a coughing fit. When he stopped he sighed, took a long drag from his Woodbine, brushed some ash from his trousers. Butch started whining and pawing his shoe. He poured some more ale into his dish.

'Do you ever have nightmares?'

I nodded. When I was Michael's age I used to have the same nightmare over and over, that I was being chased down the road by a giant Weetabix.

'Sometimes when you wake up after having a nightmare,

you're still shaken up for quite a while afterwards, the things that you dreamt about seemed so real, isn't that right?'

'Yeah, sometimes.'

'Well, your dad's worst nightmare is the Russians invading. He keeps having that nightmare over and over, he can't get it out of his head. But that doesn't mean *you've* got to worry about it too.'

'Why does he keep having it over and over?'

He blew out his cheeks, shifted his weight on the bench.

'Now that's a question for a doctor, a specialist, not an ordinary bloke like me. I can't really explain why your dad's mind works the way it does, but I do know enough about the world to know that the Russians aren't going to risk starting another world war over our coalfields. Now, anything else bothering you? Good, then I'm off to the Gents, my bladder is bursting.'

He shuffled out of the door and into the corridor, leaving me on my own. Butch had curled up on the floor and gone asleep. 'Hey Jude' had reached the bit where they go *Na na na, na na na na, naa naa naa naa, Hey Jude* over and over. A couple of blokes started laughing in the bar, then one said, 'That'll teach the bastard.' I didn't like the man's voice.

I hoped Uncle Ronnie wouldn't be too long, I didn't like sitting there on my own, I kept expecting someone to come in and shout at me.

Who are you?

I stuffed some more crisps into my mouth. The bad thoughts started coming.

Dad was imagining it all.

People who imagined things that weren't true were mad.

Michael takes after his mother, but you're like me.

I'd catch it off him, they'd come and take me away, lock me up in a big nuthouse surrounded by a high wall, topped with glass and barbed wire. Watchtowers on every corner, searchlights and guards with Alsatians patrolling through the night.

Holy Jim's son came back, took a box of matches, turned and looked at me accusingly, left again.

He could tell.

No. I wasn't mad, and neither was Dad.

This is a normal family like any other, there's nothing wrong with any of us.

It was Uncle Ronnie who'd got things muddled up. Old people were forgetful.

'Val, have you seen my slippers?'

'You're wearing them, you daft bugger.'

Ah sure he's getting on, the auld brain is probably starting to go on him.

It was him who'd imagined things. Coomassie Street didn't look anything like how he'd described it. It wasn't the first time he'd lied to me either. When I was younger, he told me the building at the end of Glanwern Road was a prison. One day when I was walking past with Dad, I told him that's where the Great Train Robbers were locked up and he roared.

' Jayzus, that's a great sentence.'

He pointed to a sign above the metal gates.

'What's that say?'

Brains Brewery.

I'd never noticed it before. I was furious with Uncle Ronnie for making me look dense, but when I told him what happened, he thought it was hilarious.

'I was only pulling your leg.'

I didn't see what was so funny about it. It was Dad who told me the truth then. He'd never pulled my leg.

Uncle Ronnie came back, grimacing slightly as he walked. He looked as though he was in pain, but he still managed to give me a wink and a smile. OK, so he didn't always tell the truth, he was forgetful and maybe he did imagine things, but he was a really fantastic bloke, one in a million. A heart of gold, that's what Mam said. I didn't like it when Dad talked about him as if he was just a silly old fool. It wasn't right. He should have more respect.

But then Uncle Ronnie laughed about Dad, and he'd told him he needed a holiday when he showed him his collection of tins, and that wasn't very nice either.

Waaa! Waaa! JudeJudyJudy!

It was noisy, the smoke was stinging my eyes, the man with the horrible voice was shouting again – 'I bloody warned him, I did, he had it coming.' I wanted to go, I couldn't think straight in there, everything was spinning round in my head. I didn't know who to trust any more. Then, out of the blue, I saw Marek's dad standing in front of his Hurricane, looking up at the sky. Thick black hair, the beginning of a smile on his face, squinting slightly in the sun. A war hero. Someone you could trust.

I had to meet Mr Sikorski.

★ ★ ★

Miss Mellon was telling us how lucky we were.

'A hundred years ago children younger than you worked all day for a penny. Imagine that.'

She usually read us a story in the last hour, from a big book with a bright yellow cover called *The Golden Treasury*.

'Just a couple of years ago you'd all have had to take the eleven–plus, and if you didn't pass you'd be labelled a failure for the rest of your life just because you did badly at one exam. Wouldn't that be terrible?'

'Yes, Miss,' nodded Sharon and Theresa.

Sent to a special school for thickos like Joe 90's brother, where you have to do PE and woodwork all day and join the army or deliver coal when you finish.

'Now you don't have to worry about that, now everyone will get an equal chance to make something of themselves. If you work hard there's nothing to stand in your way, there's no limit to what you can achieve. Some of you will go on to be teachers, or doctors.'

'Or footballers,' whispered Colin.

'Resistance fighters,' said Marek, but Miss Mellon didn't hear him.

'Lawyers, or scientists.'

Those were boring jobs. I'd play on the wing for Liverpool. Or be a pop star, or maybe a racing driver, I wasn't sure. But whatever I decided to be in the end, I had a great future, but Michael would end up a nobody, he was no good at anything. Miss Mellon smiled.

'Even, who knows, Prime Minister. Yes, why not? Just look at Nye Bevan, he was born just up the road, the son of a miner, and he went on to become one of the most important men in the government. He helped create the Welfare State. It's thanks to him you get free milk every day.'

There'd been yellow bits floating on the top of mine that morning. I'd got there too late, it was one of the last left in the crate.

'You'll have opportunities your parents never dreamt of.'

I didn't care about that, I wanted a story. I looked out of the window, at the silver drops of rain flickering in the light under the lamp-post.

'You may wonder why I'm telling you all this.'

Colin nudged me, put his hand over his mouth, pretended to yawn.

'I've noticed that one or two of you are not trying as hard as you were at the beginning of term. I won't mention any names.'

She paused. *Don't let her look at me.*

'But I think you know who you are. I just want to say that it won't be *me* you're letting down if you don't do as well as you expected at the end of the year, it'll be yourselves. There'll be no one else to blame. So some of you have some difficult decisions ahead of you, and need to think very carefully about what's most important to you – enjoying yourselves mucking about, or thinking about your future.'

She gripped the little gold crucifix she wore round her neck.

'Let me tell you there's nothing worse than looking back all the time when it's too late and wishing you'd done something you didn't.'

She looked very sad. I felt guilty even though I hadn't done anything. I liked Miss Mellon, we all did. She looked at her watch.

'Well now, I think it's time for a story.'

That was more like it. She brought out *The Golden Treasury*, licked her finger, began turning the pages. She stopped, and held a page flat with her hand.

'Fold your arms on your desk, and lay your head down on them.'

I closed my eyes, felt the soft wool of my blue jumper against my cheek, smelt the thick, gluey smell from the inkwell, heard the soft patter of rain against the windows. Miss Mellon read us the story of Theseus. How his father, the King of Athens, had to keep sending seven boys and seven girls as sacrifices to the King of Crete every few years. They were pushed into the labyrinth where a monster called the Minotaur lived. He tracked them down one by one and ate them alive. Theseus volunteered to go one year, strangled the Minotaur and found his way out of the labyrinth again using a special ball of unbreakable thread. It was a brilliant story, really scary. I was worried how it would turn out right up to the very end.

Afterwards we ran down the street, jumping in every puddle, shouting at the top of our voices.

'LABYRINTH! LABYRINTH! LA-BY-RINTH!'

It was a fab word, the best one I'd heard for ages. Joe 90 was with us.

'I still don't understand why the King of Athens kept sending sacrifices to the Cretins.'

'Cretans.'

I gave him a shove, he was always getting things wrong.

'LABYRINTH! LABYRINTH! LABY-LABY-LABY, RINTH-RINTH-RINTH.'

I wished we had a labyrinth in Crindau, I'd push Michael into it, and he'd never be able to get out again.

When I got home, Mam was in the kitchen, getting the dinner ready. I told her about Miss Mellon going on about how lucky we were. I wish I hadn't, she went berserk.

'She's right and all, you don't know how lucky you are. When I was going to school in Ireland, if you were poor you were treated like dirt. I had to sit at the back of the class because my father was a farm labourer and all the farmers' sons and daughters sat up front, next to the fire. If you got an answer wrong you had to go to the front and get the cane and be told how thick you were in front of everybody, how you'd never amount to anything, you were nothing but a stupid peasant who was wasting the poor teacher's time. But if the farmer's son or daughter got an answer wrong the teacher would just smile at them and say, "Never mind, you must try harder next time." '

The saucepan with the cabbage in it started boiling over. She rushed across and turned down the gas. I hated the sour, soggy, salty cabbage we had with nearly every meal. I'd often slip some of mine on to Michael's plate when he wasn't looking, then he'd get told off for not finishing it.

She lit a fag.

'What I went through now, it'd break your heart.'

I didn't want to know.

'Some schooling I got. No wonder I'm stupid, you'd be too

terrified to think straight. You were *always* hungry, always cold, waiting for the next belt round the head, the next insult . . .'

I wanted her to stop.

'The Irish lessons were the worst. I hated Irish, I could never get the hang of it no matter how hard I tried and you got a slap of the cane for every word you got wrong. There was nothing like Irish to get those bleddy teachers going, if you didn't know your Irish they'd fly into a rage straight away and start thrashing you and lecturing you about how the mother tongue had survived all these centuries despite everything the English had tried and now, just when poor old Ireland was finally free, our beloved language was going to die out because thick devils like us couldn't be bothered to learn to speak it. Don't talk to me about Irish.'

I wasn't. The saucepan was boiling over again but she hadn't noticed. She took another drag of her fag, flicked some of the ash into her cupped hand.

'Course the farmers' sons and daughters didn't get a lecture like that, let alone the cane. All they got when they couldn't remember the Irish word was "Never mind, you must try harder next time." Even now if I'm back home and I hear Irish being spoken on the radio a chill goes through me. I have to turn it off straight away, I can't bear the sound of it. You've no idea how lucky you are, when I was your age . . .'

She didn't notice me leaving. I went into the living room, turned on the telly, started watching *Top Cat*.

★   ★   ★

I helped Dad drag the sofa away from the wall, swivel it around on its castors and push it in front of the fire. He nodded towards the corner of the room.

'Now, turn off the light.'

When I did the only light in the room came from the warm

red glow of the fire and the flickering bluish light from the telly. I joined Dad on the sofa.

'Now we're snug! This is how it was in the old days back in Ireland, before we had electricity. Much better, isn't it? You'd get sick of that bleddy auld electric light scalding your eyeballs. You get a very harsh, unnatural light from a light bulb, it can't be good for you. I have to watch your mother, she's a terrible one for electric light, she's absolutely addicted to it. I'd be sitting here of an evening, peaceful and contented, me feet up, reading the paper after a long day at work and she'd rush in and say, "God, it's terrible gloomy in here, you'll ruin your eyes." Then she'd turn on the light, and fecking go out again!'

He stared at me, disbelieving.

Do you see what I have to put up with? Do you?

'And there'd be plenty of light, plenty! She thinks just because there's a switch on the wall, she has to turn it on. She must think I'm made of money. You should see the electricity bills – Jayzus!'

He leant forward, spat on to the fire. The bubbly white flob wriggled and jumped on the coals like an egg sizzling on a frying pan.

'And have you ever noticed how you can't ask your mother the simplest question without her flying off the handle?'

'Yes, I have.'

Can't you see I'm busy?

Go and play.

Will you give over?

Leave me alone.

'You know why, don't you?'

I shook my head, no. He looked pleased, he wanted to explain, for it to be a surprise.

'You see, Liam, when we were growing up back in Ireland in the twenties and thirties there was no such thing as electric light out in the country. Everyone had oil lamps. Your mother didn't come into contact with electric light on a regular basis till she came to this country. So you see, she's not used to it, she thinks she's able for it but she's not, she's no idea what harm she's doing to herself. Her eyes aren't made for coping with that bright, harsh glare all day. When we were courting back home she was always in a good mood, never stopped laughing. Now look at her. Do you see? The years of constant exposure to electric light have made her irritable and crabby. Christ, it's a shame.'

He chewed his lip, gazing into the flames. I tried to picture Mam with a smile forever lingering on her lips. Her and Dad sitting in front of an oil lamp, getting on great. I couldn't. Suddenly Dad slapped the arm of the sofa.

'Anyway! She's not here now, so we can turn off the light if we want to without having to listen to her squawking.'

She'd gone to visit her friend Bridie in Maes-glas. He laughed, opened a bottle of stout, poured some into his glass, sipped the foamy top.

'It's grand and peaceful without her, isn't it? She'll be all night at Bridie's, when those two get together they never stop gassing. God knows what they find to talk about for so long. Their poor auld husbands, probably.'

He clicked his tongue. 'Bleddy women.'

Laughing, he nudged my knee with his. 'Oh Jayzus, the mug on that Bridie, it's enough now to put a donkey off his oats.'

He made his face go thin, scowled, puckered up his lips. I burst out laughing. 'She looks like one of them gargoyles, the council should build a fence around her house to keep her from wandering the streets and frightening the locals.'

I roared. I didn't like her either. She was always slobbering over Michael.

Ah Michael a stór, you're a grand little fella, I'd say it won't be long now before you have all the girls chasing you.

Mam would beam with pleasure.

Ah now, Bridie, you're terrible.

Indeed I am not. I'm only telling you the truth, woman.

And Michael wriggling with pleasure, kicking his heel against the wall, ready to listen to her old guff all day. Then she'd turn to me.

Of course Liam's much too grown up to come and give auld Bridie a hug these days, aren't ya?

She was out of her mind. I'd never given her a hug in my life. Mam rolled her eyes. Bridie gave a wheezy cackle. She sucked on the Players clamped between her nicotine-stained fingers.

I bet you give your poor auld mammy a terrible time, don't you?

Dad was right, she did look like a gargoyle. Mam just stood there, a pained smile on her lips, not even trying to stand up for me.

Dad bent down, took a slice of bread from the loaf on the tray, then stuck it on the end of the toasting fork. He'd made it himself by tying an ordinary fork to the end of the spare poker with some wire, so that you could get enough distance to toast the bread properly without burning your hand. I loved toast done over a coal fire. It tasted completely different to toast done under a grill, smoky and succulent and soft.

I'd have been in bed by now if Mam was at home. As soon as Michael was in bed, she had put on her coat, grabbed her bag and said to me, 'Another half an hour, then up those wooden stairs for you, Liam.'

I nodded, but that wasn't enough for her.

'You'll make sure he goes to bed on time, won't you, Brendan?'

'Go on if you're going, willya?'

He was in the kitchen, putting some batteries in the oven. He hated buying new batteries for his bike lights so he'd heat up the old ones in the oven over and over to make them last longer. As soon as she was out the front door he came out of the kitchen, peered through the curtains. When he was satisfied she'd gone, he said, 'Would you like to stay up and watch the telly with me?'

'Yeah!'

'Good man, there's a very interesting documentary on later.'

Documentaries didn't come on till nine, so I knew then I'd get to stay up till at least ten.

He started humming as he toasted the bread, lifting it up and checking it every now and then to make sure it wasn't burning. When it was ready, he whipped it off the fork and chucked it on to a plate.

'There – that's yours.'

'Thanks.'

I spread loads of butter on, watched it ooze into the golden brown, closed my eyes and took my first bite before the butter had completely melted. Gorgeous.

'Good stuff, eh?'

He was smiling.

'Delicious.'

This was tidy. Outside the wind was howling, the rain lashed the windows. But we were inside, warm and cosy in front of the fire, eating toast, admiring the glowing coals. It was so much more relaxed without Mam there. Dad buttered his slice, checked the clock on the mantelpiece.

'Nearly nine o'clock.'

He got up, turned the sound up. The adverts finished.

And next on ITV, a chilling documentary about the threat to world peace posed by the Soviet Union – 'The Red Empire'.

'Now then.' He rubbed his hands together, settled back with his toast and stout. 'Tell us all about the dirty bastards, come on, we're waiting.'

The most powerful army in the world, seen here flexing its muscles on the annual May Day Parade in Moscow.

The people cheered and waved flags as the soldiers goose-stepped past, followed by hundreds of tanks. Next came huge missiles as long as our street hauled along by giant lorries.

On one side of the Iron Curtain lies the West, and democracy.

Laughing children on a roundabout. A man and a lady kissing on a street corner, the passers-by smiling at them. A policeman helping an old lady across a road.

On the other side lies the East, where communism rules.

Watchtowers, barbed wire, searchlights, armed guards with stone faces staring at the camera.

The Soviet Union has hundreds of missiles with nuclear warheads aimed at Western Europe.

Mushroom clouds, flattened buildings, people on their knees, crying in the rubble. It was terrifying. I looked at Dad. He was staring at the screen, mesmerised. His jaw was clenched, his body rigid, and at first I thought the fierce glare in his eyes was anger. *Just let them try it. The first one that comes over that wall will get this in their gob.* But when I looked more carefully, I noticed how one hand kept clutching nervously at his trousers just above the knee. Realised that his eyes were wide not with anger, but fear.

He can't help me, he's too terrified to do anything.

I thought of Preece's face when he was fighting Marek, when he turned round and everyone could see the blood pouring from his face. He was furious, but hiding behind the fury was fear. Wanting to hurt someone and wanting to cry, they were the same thing. No one thought Preece was afraid of anything, but he was. It was fear that caused his hair to fall out. That was why he hated anyone mentioning it. Fear that made him pummel Marek. And now I realised it was fear curled up inside Dad's temper, like a worm inside an apple. I turned away from the telly, squeezed my eyes shut, imagined Mr Sikorski in his fighter plane, racing to intercept the missiles.

Hot chocolate drinking chocolate.

The adverts had started. Dad nudged me with his elbow.

'Do you see? Do you see now what I'm telling you is true?'

97

It had to be, it was on the telly. He shovelled more coal on to the fire.

'That's a bastard of a night. You'd need a good fire on a night like this. Would you like some more toast?'

'Yes, please.'

'Righto. Hey, there's some of that cake left. Go and bring it in from the kitchen.'

It was in the cupboard on a plate, Mam had made it today, there was still half left. I brought it in, Dad cut it into four portions after he'd finished the latest slice of toast. He opened another bottle of stout, speared another slice of bread with the toasting fork. He winked at me.

'Jayzus, what a feast.'

He was laughing now, and I tried to forget how frightened he'd looked earlier on, tried to concentrate on the cake, the coal fire, the excitement of being up so late. The second half of the documentary began. Russian tanks entering a city. I'd seen this bit.

'Czechoslovakia,' said Dad.

That was it.

He laughed scornfully. 'Jayzus, would you look at that fella driving the tank. He's the real culchie.'

Culchies were big thickos from the bogs who didn't know anything.

'Oh Christ, I wouldn't want to be in any tank that fella was driving.'

For a moment relief flooded through me, I imagined the Russian army careering all over the place, crashing into each other like the Keystone Kops as they tried to invade. Then suddenly the pictures were of a man collapsing on the ground covered in flames. The commentator's voice said, *For this Czech student who set himself on fire as a protest against the invasion, death was preferable to living under the Soviet yoke.*

I gorged myself with cake. Light and crumbly, a soft creamy

vanilla filling that stuck to my teeth. I licked it off, rolled it up into a gooey paste, as thick as putty, rolled it to the back of my mouth, kept it there, biting down on it till the documentary was over. Dad got up, turned the telly off. He sat back down, poured the last of his stout. The silence lengthened, the only sounds the sharp crack of sparks in the fire, a gust of wind outside. When Dad spoke again his voice was hushed, there was a faraway look in his eyes.

'I'll tell you what the Russians are like. I was in Berlin with the army for a while, just after the war. One night I went out for a few drinks with the other fellas. On the way back I lost them. I didn't know where I was. It was freezing cold, sleeting, pitch black. I cut across some waste ground. Suddenly I heard someone screaming. I ran over to where it was coming from. There was a crowd of Russian soldiers, mad with drink, dragging a German woman off by the hair. Blood streaming from her mouth, half her clothes hanging off her, the fecking dirty bastards. And then . . .'

He broke off, took another swig of stout.

'This little fella in his nightshirt, no older than Michael, came running after her, bawling his eyes out, yelling "MOO-DER, MOO-DER, MOO-DER." "Max! Max!" she screamed back.'

He put his glass down on the arm of the sofa.

'This big fecker of a Russian walked over to the little boy and smashed his rifle into his face.'

He reached down, took the glass of stout from the arm of the sofa, emptied it in one long gulp.

'The *roars* from the mother . . .' Some coal shifted and fell, a spark flew out and glowed for a moment on the carpet, then dimmed and disappeared.

'Then he walked back, leaving the little fella in a heap on the ground, and they dragged the mother off. God only knows what she went through. I know the Germans were cruel bastards but Jayzus Christ almighty . . . That's the Russian for you. They don't know the meaning of the word mercy. The war opened my eyes for me, boy. I thought I'd seen cruelty and suffering enough in Ireland to last me a lifetime, but I'd seen nothing. Nothing. Man is a beast, he's sick inside. There's no limit to his cruelty, no end to his fecking greed. The bastard'll end up destroying every bleddy living thing on the earth. The stupid fecking eejit will turn the planet into a cinder.'

He got up, shovelled some more coal on to the fire. He put his empty glass on top of the mantelpiece, shoved his hands into his pockets. Rested his back against the wall, facing me.

'We've been warned – nobody can say we haven't been told what's coming. Didn't Our Lady of Fatima try her best to get it into their thick skulls?'

Our Lady of Fatima was the Virgin Mary. She'd appeared to three children at a place called Fatima in Portugal during the First World War.

'She predicted three things. Now the first two have already come true – the end of the First World War, and the start of the Second. But the third one, now they wrote *that* down on a piece of paper, sealed it in an envelope and handed it to the Pope. Now what do you think it says?'

'I don't know.'

Just the thought of it made me feel scared.

'How the world will end. The Pope was due to read it out a couple of years back but he didn't. They reckon it was so terrifying he changed his mind at the last moment, worried he'd cause mass panic.'

He fixed me with a piercing stare.

'The victory of communism, that's the third secret. The church destroyed. The Russians in control.'

He paused to let it sink in.

'We've got to get the women and children away. You and me know what's coming, we're well able to take care of ourselves. But Michael now, he wouldn't stand a chance. He'd only get in the way, bawling and screaming. And your mother would be the biggest liability of all. Jayzus, she's a nervous wreck already . . . many times in the past few months I'd be on my way home, my stomach howling with the hunger after being at work since seven in the morning, crossing my fingers that she's managed to make a bit of bleddy dinner.'

I didn't know that. Had no idea she was a nervous wreck. It explained a lot though.

'She used to keep the house grand and tidy when we were first married, you could eat your dinner off the floor. But now!'

He ran his finger along the top of the mantelpiece, looked at it, wrinkled his nose in disgust, then wiped it on his trousers.

'There's a solid inch of dust here – and there's bleddy cigarette ash everywhere you look, your mother's like a bleddy chimney. I hate smoking, it's a filthy habit, so it is. It nauseates me to see it going on in my own house. I tried reasoning with her, I didn't lose my temper, I only gave her the same information any doctor would – "Cut that out or you'll die roaring with cancer, you thick biddy." She couldn't look me in the face, she knew I was right, she just turned around and walked away, muttering to herself and . . . ah feck it anyhow, what the hell was I saying before I got sidetracked into talking about her bleddy filthy habit?'

'You were saying how she was a nervous wreck.'

'Oh, she is, definitely. I wouldn't like to bet on how much longer she'll be able to last, she'll end up in St Woolos if she's not careful.'

That was the mental home, out on the edge of town.

He shook his head sadly.

'Sure, didn't her own father try and warn me off her? He came around to the house the evening before we got married. "Brendan," says he, "are you absolutely sure you want to go through with this? Do you think you two will *really* make a good match?" Jayzus, I thought, that's a quare thing for the father of the bride to say the day before his daughter's wedding. But then, after a while, I started to see the cracks appearing – her moods, the complaining, the smoking and drinking, and eventually I understood what he'd been up to. He'd been trying to warn me that she was a nervous wreck, she'd never make a decent wife for anyone.'

He stretched one arm along the top of the mantelpiece, lowered his voice.

'I'm afraid, Liam, the stuffing's beginning to come out of your mother. Can you imagine what she'd be like in a war? I realise a young fella wouldn't enjoy hearing bad things about his mother, but I'm only trying to put you in the picture.'

He gave me a look that drew me in. Him and me, the men of the family, had to take control before it was too late.

'Christ almighty, the Russians will be mad for the women by the time they get here. I know she'd drive you round the bend with her nagging, and not a day goes by without me regretting marrying her but, Jayzus Christ, you wouldn't wish that kind of a thing on anyone. Can you imagine seeing your mother dragged away into the night by a gang of fecking drunken Russians? Can you?'

★ ★ ★

When I grow up I'll get married. I'd hate coming home to an empty house.

'Hi-ya, Liam.'

'Hi-ya, darling.'

It would be brilliant having someone to talk to when you were lying in bed at night in the dark. I love talking in the dark. I only ever got to do it once, when I stayed the night at Colin's. Michael is always asleep by the time I come to bed, and he's the last person I'd want a conversation with anyway.

My wife will be pretty, a bit shorter than me, with a nice

personality. We'll have two children, a boy and a girl. Twins would be nice, that way they'd never be alone. A house in Llanthewy, out on the edge of Crindau, where the countryside begins. One of those big old ones with turrets, and a porch. Its own road leading up to it, and a row of trees behind. A long garden, with enough room to play football in, and to have picnics in the summer. On the inside of the front door a little wire basket for catching letters. A grandfather clock in the hall, a piano in the front room. That's the kind of house I wanted. Colin wanted one like George Best's. A glass box, open and on display to every Tom, Dick and Harry. You could stand outside and watch Georgie make a cup of coffee in his kitchen, then walk through to his living room and sit down and drink it on his white leather sofa, hang around to see if he'd pick his nose while he watched the telly. I wouldn't want that. I liked my privacy. Colin just wanted it because Georgie had one, because it was the latest thing.

We'd need our own garage, so we wouldn't have to leave our red E-type Jag on the street, in case someone broke the aerial or tried to steal it. It wouldn't bother me if my wife wasn't a very good cook, we could have our meals from the chip shop on our laps in front of the telly. I'd nip down to Alonzis in the E-type while she and the twins were warming the plates and getting the knives and forks, salt and vinegar ready. In the summer I'd put the top down, my sunglasses on, and drive back down to Uncle Ronnie's and Auntie Val's, check if they were all right, go to the shops and bookies for them.

Yes, I'd still take care of all my old friends when I was rich and famous.

★ ★ ★

'Hi-ya.'

She didn't reply. Didn't even look my way. She was standing by the sink, her hands in a basin full of spuds.

'Mam?'

I'd just got in from school.

'Are you OK?'

She shook her head. I stepped closer, tugged at the corner of her apron.

'Mam?'

She lifted her hands out of the water, dried them on her apron, gently wiped her eyes.

'I am, yes.'

'What?'

'OK.'

She turned and faced me. Her eyes were puffy and red.

'I'm fine. There was something in my eye. Go and see what Michael's up to, will you?'

'All right.'

I didn't argue, I wanted to come back later when everything was all right. Michael was in the living room, watching *Jackanory*, his face a blank. Some eejit with a big bow in her hair was reading *Rumpelstiltskin*.

'Do you want to know how it ends?'

He ignored me. He was getting very good at doing that.

'The princess guesses his name. That's it, that's the end, then she lives happily ever after, nothing bad happens to her at all. It's a useless story.'

Not a flicker. I dug my finger right up into my nose, poked around, brought out some snot. I rolled it carefully between my finger and thumb till it formed a perfect ball, then flicked it at him. Direct hit.

'You've got snot in your hair.'

He carried on staring at the telly.

And then, just when the princess had forgotten all about the funny little man who'd helped her to spin gold . . .

I thought about going over and pushing Michael on to the floor, but I couldn't be bothered.

I took the stairs quickly, back ramrod-straight, chewing, the chants ringing in my ears.

Shankly! Shankly! Shankly!

On my way up to collect the FA Cup after beating Man Utd 8–0 in the final.

And they were lucky to get nil.

There were thirty-nine steps up to where the Queen was waiting to present the cup. I'd read that in *Shoot*. I stopped at the top to wave to all the Liverpool fans. Reached over to shake one of the hands stretching out from the crowd. Uncle Ronnie's.

'Did you get that birthday card?'

He was so overcome with joy he couldn't speak, just gripped my hand with both of his, tears rolling down his cheeks.

I'd sellotaped a sign to our bedroom door.

This Is Anfield.

I touched it for luck, went inside, got changed into my long trousers, a pair of red corduroys I'd got for Christmas, and my red pullover. All in red, like Liverpool. Came back downstairs again holding the cup between my hands now, a big grin on my face, receiving the fans' tributes.

Shankly! Shankly! Shankly!

I sat back down on the arm of the sofa. Michael was still watching *Jackanory*, the same blank expression on his face. The snot had gone from his hair. I dug out some more, rolled it, flicked. It flew straight into his ear.

'Gotcha!'

He shook his head. Reached inside his ear and picked it out, shook it off his fingers on to the floor without taking his eyes off the telly. I went back into the kitchen to lay the table. Mam was standing on the back step, turned away from me, smoking. The spuds were still in the basin, not even peeled.

The dinner wasn't going to be ready.

'Mam!'

She slumped sideways into the doorway, let her head sag.

'I can't do this any more. I can't . . .'

'Mam – the dinner!'

Dad would be home any minute. I couldn't bear it.

'I just can't . . .'

I couldn't let it happen.

I filled the big saucepan with water. It was no good, I couldn't lift it up out of the sink, had to pour half the water out again before I could carry it over to the cooker. I lit the gas and filled the rest of the saucepan using the kettle.

Spuds next. I'd peeled spuds before, it was easy, I just wasn't as quick as Mam.

'Damn.'

When I tried to put the one I'd peeled on the top part of the sink it slipped straight back into the water. It shot out of my hand when I tried to pick it up again, as slippery as a bar of soap.

'Damn damn damn.'

Why was I doing this on my own?

Rushed back into the living room. *Jackanory* had finished, Michael was watching *Top Cat*.

'Mam's not well, Dad will be home any minute – you've got to help me make the dinner.'

He didn't bat an eye.

'Come on!'

He had another thing coming if he thought he could ignore me.

'Oi, shitface!'

He made a sound like a kitten whimpering when I twisted his arm behind his back and dragged him from the chair. I marched him into the kitchen.

'YOU'RE – GOING – TO – HELP – ME – MAKE – THE – DINNER.'

Mam hadn't moved, she was still stood in the doorway. I shoved Michael in front of the sink.

'Right – when I've peeled a spud I'll hand it to you, and you put it in the saucepan, OK?'

He wasn't listening, he was looking beyond me, at Mam. His eyes were big and round. He looked as if a trapdoor had just opened under him. I grabbed his mouth, pulled him closer.

'Listen – you've got to help me. I can't do this on my own, understand?'

He looked like a jellyfish. I let go.

'Here.'

I handed him the spud I'd already peeled.

'PUT – THIS – IN – THE – SAUCEPAN.'

I couldn't carry on talking like that, it was making me feel like a Dalek. He stared at the spud in his hand, frowning. I hadn't time for this. I gave him a slap.

'IN THE FRIGGING SAUCEPAN, YOU FRIGGING SPAZ!'

He did it. I started peeling another spud. I heard a sniffing sound, looked round at Mam. Her shoulders were trembling. What had gone wrong with her?

Was it my fault?

You've a very spiteful streak in you.

'Aaaagh!'

'What is it?'

I dropped the knife. The blood was running into the water.

'Oh Jesus, Mary and Joseph . . .'

Mam grabbed my hand.

'Let me see that.'

It stung like hell.

'For God's sake, Liam, what are you playing at? Michael – get away from that saucepan before you tip it over. Come on.'

She led me to the bathroom with one hand, wiped her eyes with the other. I held my finger under the running tap while she poured some TCP into a cup, then added water.

'Jesus Christ, I can't turn my back for a minute.'

She was trying to pretend nothing was wrong. Trying to act like she normally did, but it wasn't quite right. It was like a mirror with a crack running through it.

'Here.'

She dried my finger.

'Careful.'

'Now – let's have a look . . . Ah, you'll live.'

'Do you think I'll need stitches?'

She laughed, then sniffed and swallowed.

'I'd say a plaster would be enough.'

That was better. More like her real self. She bathed my finger in the TCP. I took a sharp breath.

'Is it stinging?'

'Yeah.'

'Then it's doing its job. You'll be all right in a bit.'

Then a plaster.

'There – that's grand now.'

She ran her hand through my hair.

'You're a Holy Terror – Oh Jesus – the dinner!'

We rushed back into the kitchen.

'Michael – help Liam lay the table.'

She had the spuds peeled and in the saucepan in a jiffy, then opened the tin of corned beef, cut it into slices, chucked them on to the plates. One piece missed and fell on the floor. She ran it under the tap and slapped it down again, wiped her forehead.

'He's late, thank God.'

Suddenly she went rigid.

'The cabbage. I forgot the cabbage.'

'We could have beans,' I said.

'You're right, one night without cabbage won't kill him.'

By the time Dad got home everything was ready.

'Oh Christ, I've had a terrible time getting home. I had a puncture. I had to wheel the bleddy bike all the way from Maes-glas.'

We all held our breath as Mam put the plate down in front of him.

'Beans?'

She didn't say anything, just nodded.

'Christ, I couldn't care less *what* I eat tonight as long as there's plenty of it. My stomach's howling with the hunger.'

We'd made it.

★ ★ ★

Yes!

I wanted to punch the air.

Yes! Yes! Yes!

It had been so easy. We'd been walking home from school, Colin had been telling Marek about his dad being in a pop group.

'Has he been on *Top of the Pops*?'

'No.'

'What was their last record called?'

Colin looked annoyed now, as if Marek had tricked him.

'They haven't made one yet.'

Marek frowned.

'They play in pubs.'

'And he earns enough to support you and your mother?'

Colin wouldn't look at Marek any more when he spoke.

'He works in a factory in the day.'

I jumped in and said, 'What does your dad do, Marek?'

'He fixes cars. He owns a garage.'

I hadn't expected that. A war hero working in a garage? It didn't seem right. But when I tried to picture *what* I imagined him doing I drew a blank. I could only see him as an RAF pilot.

'It's *his* garage?' asked Colin. 'He doesn't have a boss?'

'No, *he's* the boss. He's in charge of two men.'

'He's lucky, the foreman at my dad's factory is a right bastard. He's always on my dad's back. Dad's just waiting for someone

109

to discover him so he can pack in his day job. I'm going to be my own boss.'

Marek nodded enthusiastically.

'Good for you, Colin.' He clasped him on the shoulder, nodded again, 'Good man.'

I took a deep breath.

'I'd like to meet your dad.'

'OK.'

'Eh?'

'I'll meet you on Saturday and take you to the garage.'

'Yeah? Straight up?'

'Pardon?'

'Really?'

He looked at me strangely.

'Yes, really.'

'We haven't got time for all that,' whined Colin. 'We're going to the football on Saturday.'

'If we went in the morning we'd still have time.' I turned to Marek. 'Is it all right to come in the morning?'

'Of course.'

'There you are,' I said to Colin. He was pulling a face.

'Maybe.'

We were at the corner of Tredegar Avenue. This was where we parted ways.

'Well,' said Marek, 'it's up to you. Let me know if you can make it.'

He said goodbye. Colin started muttering about missing the game if we weren't careful.

'Look! If you don't want to come with me – fine. Just stop going on about it, will you?'

His face fell. I hadn't meant to sound that angry, but it was too late to take it back now. We walked on, our heads down.

★ ★ ★

Colin and I ran down the back lane, shouting at the top of our voices.

'Scramble! Scramble!'

The rec was nearly empty. We stood on the swings, pushing, jerking the chains, working ourselves higher, higher, till it felt like we were taking off.

'Jerry eight o'clock high, coming out of the clouds.'

Soaring through the air, making machine-gun noises till spit flew from my mouth and my head throbbed.

'Take that, you blighter.'

'Bye bye, Fritz. Good shooting, Ginge.'

We'd just been watching *Reach for the Sky*.

What ho, chaps. Ginge Ginge Ginge! Wilko Wilko Wilko! Chocks away!

When we'd finished on the swings, we did the Douglas Bader walk. Legs dead straight, gritting our teeth, swaying from side to side with every step.

'Oi, that's cheating.'

I caught Colin bending his knees. The other kids were staring, they didn't know what we were up to. We kept it up all the way across the rec. When we reached the roundabout, we slumped down on to it, puffing and blowing like a couple of pensioners.

'It's knackering, isn't it?'

'Imagine if you had to walk like that all the time. Imagine waking up and finding you didn't have legs any more.'

I didn't want to think about that.

Doctor, I can't feel my legs.

Sorry, I'm afraid we had to cut off your arms.

Uncle Ronnie knew a man who worked down the docks who had a wooden leg.

'After a few drinks the bloody so-and-so would start swaying around and he'd stamp on your foot with this great lump of wood. Couldn't help it of course, never understood why you were screaming blue murder at him.'

The most frightening part of the film was when Douglas Bader was shot down and the cockpit caught fire but his metal legs got jammed between the pedals and he couldn't move. He had to pull himself out of them so he could bail out. It must have been agony, I was curled up in a ball on the sofa watching it. He threw himself out, pulled the ripcord, floated down on to enemy territory, empty trousers flapping in the breeze.

Did you see the state of Bader coming home from the pub last night? He was completely legless.

He must have been one of the bravest men in the whole war.

Colin struggled to his feet, started doing the walk.

'Come on, Bennett, I'll race you to the airfield.'

'You're on, Williams. Last one there's a filthy Hun.'

I lurched after him, swaying from side to side.

★　★　★

Colin, Marek, Joe 90 and me were walking down Ruperra Street. Number 29's front door was wide open. I'd often wondered who lived in there. There was a model of the *Cutty Sark* in the window. Beautifully painted, no splodges of glue showing, perfect cotton rigging, like something out of a museum. The man, the dad, must have taken ages over it, been very patient, his son sitting alongside him, helping. They had tropical fish too, you could see through the window, and a selection of board games piled on top of each other in the corner – Monopoly, Cluedo, Spy Ring, Snakes and Ladders, Ludo. It looked a fabulous place to live. I stepped inside, started walking down the corridor. I could feel the others watching me from the street. A kettle started whistling in the kitchen.

'Hello, Mam, I'm home.'

I made myself believe it – this *was* my home. It was easy. My name was Paul, I had a big brother called John, we had our own rooms. My dad worked in an office, my mam stayed at home, kept the house nice and tidy, cooked lovely meals. They never argued. Sometimes when we all sat down on the sofa to watch the telly together, Dad put his arm around Mam and she rested her head on his shoulder. We had a caravan in Porthcawl where we went every summer. A dog called Spot who fetched sticks. John and I had won *Blue Peter* badges, our trophies for football and running had pride of place on the mantelpiece. It was Tuesday, cottage pie with Bisto gravy and Birds Eye crinkle-cut chips, lovely.

I walked on, a bit slower now, in case someone was just behind the kitchen door. I couldn't stop. Couldn't bear the thought of leaving. This was where I really belonged, a house like this. I called out.

'Is Dad back from the office yet?'

No answer.

'I've brought some friends home for tea, could you lay another three places at the table?'

A door opened upstairs.

'Who's that?'

A woman's voice. Shocked, getting ready to be angry.

'Liam! What are you doing?' Colin hissed at me. 'Get out of there.' I turned around, he was waving me towards the street with his hand. Joe 90 was nearly in tears, ready to bolt at any minute. Marek was shaking his head, grinning. *You crazy son of a bitch.* I'd finally done something that impressed him. When I wasn't even trying, when I'd forgotten they were there. Then, footsteps on the landing.

'I SAID WHO'S THAT?'

I ran for it. The others were ahead, laughing. By the time I caught them up they were at the end of the street. I hadn't looked back once. We slowed down. They surrounded me, breathless.

'You're mad.'

I forced myself to laugh. They were staring at me, waiting for me to say something. I shrugged like Marek.

It's no big deal.

'What if you'd been caught?'

'What made you do it?'

There was a burning sensation in my chest. I didn't want to talk about it. I wanted them to leave me alone.

'What's the matter?'

'Nothing.'

'Are you sure?'

It felt like I'd lost something.

'Yeah. Yeah, I'm fine, let's go.'

And I'd never get it back.

★   ★   ★

'Down here.'

The road veered to the left, under a railway bridge. Icy water dripped from above. Our footsteps echoed along the damp, dark walls. In the middle, half on the pavement, half on the road, an abandoned car, a thick crust of pigeon shit on the bonnet and roof. We came out the other end, carried on past a patch of waste ground. A rusting cooker and a scorched mattress lay in a pool of dirty water in the middle. I'd never been to this part of town before. I didn't like it. It was drizzling and cold. I stepped on a loose paving stone, a wave of water surged up from below it, soaking my shoes. I felt my heart sinking.

'Are we nearly there?' asked Colin, putting up the hood of his anorak.

'Yes, nearly,' said Marek.

We came to a warehouse. A man in overalls stood in the doorway, smoking a fag.

'Lost?'

'No, we're going to the garage at the end of the road.'

'It's closed down, son.'

Colin and I looked at each other.

'It opened up again,' replied Marek angrily.

The man smirked, took another drag.

'What's the matter, sonny? Wheel come off your Noddy car?'

Marek ignored him, began to walk faster. Colin had shrunk inside his anorak like a snail inside its shell. He stuck his hands in his pockets, bowed his head.

'Are we nearly . . .'

'There it is.'

Marek pointed to a building at the end of the road. There were three cars parked outside. Above the entrance a sign that read *Honest Ted's Garage*.

'Is that your dad's name?' I asked.

'My father's real name is Tadeusz, but when he came to this country, he found that no one could pronounce it, so instead they called him Teddy. Now that's become the name he always uses outside the home. In fact his real name is very easy to pronounce. Listen.'

He stopped, turned to face us.

'Ta-DAY-oosh.'

We repeated it.

'Ta-DAY-oosh.'

He beamed with pleasure.

'Very good. You speak Polish very well.'

It was easy.

'Usually his garage is in a very nice part of town,' said Marek suddenly, sounding less confident than usual. 'But we wanted to move as quickly as possible, there was no time to search for a place up to his usual standard so . . . but once he's been here for a while, and people get to know about him, he'll get lots of customers and buy a bigger place.'

There was a forecourt next to the garage. Under an awning a

bloke in overalls was poking about in a car. His hair was long and greasy, his face was covered in pimples. He looked up when we walked in.

'Hi-ya, kidder.'

Marek scowled at him.

'Good morning, Nicky.'

We walked into the garage. It was gloomy and cold inside.

'Tata! Tata?'

In the corner was a car with its bonnet up. Mr Sikorski slowly eased his head from under it.

War hero.

Straight back, shoulders held high, ready for action. His overalls looked perfect, as if they'd just come back from the dry-cleaners two minutes ago. He looked better in them than Dad did in his suit. Black hair swept back, greying at the sides. Eyes that took in everything in an instant. His face relaxed.

'Aha, here are the chaps. One minute, please.'

He bent down again, picked up a rag, carefully wiped his hands. I looked at Colin, who'd been making out he wasn't that bothered about coming, especially when it started raining, but now I could see he was as excited as me. Then I looked back, saw the slow, stiff way he was walking towards us. It hit me like a blow to the stomach.

I gripped Colin's arm, whispered, 'Look.'

'What?' he hissed.

'His legs.'

'What about them?'

'Look how stiff they are.'

'So?'

I dug him gently in the ribs.

'They're like Douglas Bader's.'

He frowned.

'Eh?'

'They're not real – they're metal.'

Colin's eyes nearly popped out of his head. There was no time to take it in. He was nearly on us.

'Well, Marek, aren't you going to introduce me to your friends?'

'This is Colin.'

He bent down, shook Colin's hand.

'Pleased to meet you, Colin.'

Colin was still goggling at his legs. He'd gone pale. Slowly, he raised his head. He tried to say something but his mouth dropped open, no words came out. He swallowed hard, tried again.

'Hi-ya,' he replied, in a thin, weedy voice as if his lungs had turned to straw.

Mr Sikorski smiled, gently patted Colin's shoulder.

'Please, no need to be shy. You are very welcome.'

Colin blushed, made a funny little movement with his shoulders.

Now me. *Don't think about his legs, concentrate on his face.*

'And this is Liam.'

I was ready. I'd waited for this. I met his eyes. They were bright green. The eyes of a hunter. They saw right inside me. I shook his hand. A dry, cool palm, strong fingers, covered with calluses. Hands that had guided a Hurricane through a blizzard of bullets, and came out the other side unmarked, doing a victory roll. Hands that had sent enemy planes screaming to the ground in a trail of black smoke and flames. Hands with blood on them. The hands of a hero. I squeezed tight.

'Hello, Mr Sikorski, pleased to meet you.'

He smiled, held my hand for longer than he'd held Colin's.

'And I'm pleased to meet *you*, Liam.'

He liked me. A weight lifted from my shoulders. Deep inside, where it mattered, I was good. He'd seen that. Made me able to see it. There was nothing to be afraid of. Things would get better. He liked me.

'So, would you like some refreshment?'

'Yes, please, Mr Sikorski.'

He turned awkwardly and started walking towards the tiny office in the corner. The slow, very deliberate walk of someone whose every step caused him great pain. No! I ran after him. He was handicapped. *You* were supposed to do things for handicapped people, not the other way around.

'Please, let me. Sit down.'

He laughed.

'No, *you* must sit down, you are the guest.'

'But . . .'

'*I'll* do it,' said Colin, suddenly springing back to life. I jumped in front of him, blocking his way.

'No, let me. I asked first.'

'Stop,' shouted Marek. 'Sit down, both of you. Don't insult us.'

Insult them?

'Marek, don't shout at our guests.'

He bent down, put one hand on Colin's shoulder, another on mine.

'Look, chaps, I appreciate your offer, but in Poland we have a saying – "A guest is God in the house." He is not allowed to lift a finger. In fact, if he does it reflects very badly on the host. It's a matter of honour. And when I come to visit you, I would certainly expect the same treatment. Now do you understand?'

He had us. We nodded: yes, Mr Sikorski.

'All right, now please come with me into the office and sit down.'

The office was tiny. There was a desk against the wall, above it three shelves lined with folders and telephone directories. Opened on the desk was a ledger filled with small writing and figures, a pen resting in the middle. Hanging from a nail below the shelves, rosary beads, the cross at the end hanging over the phone. Mr Sikorski brought a stool in and Marek dragged the chair away from the desk.

'Please . . .'

We sat down. I let Colin have the chair, he still looked pale. I sat on the stool, Marek leaned against the wall.

There was a sink in one corner. Mr Sikorski took four mugs from the draining board, made Marek, Colin and me orange squash, tea for himself.

He was *trying* to move normally but I could tell he was suffering. Probably he needed new legs, had had the same ones since the war, and now they were turning rusty. I'd write to *Blue Peter*, ask them to start a campaign – *Send in your milk bottle tops and help raise money for a new pair of metal legs for handicapped war hero*.

Hundreds of vans filled with sacks of bottle tops arriving at the BBC; me being interviewed for John Craven's *Newsround* – 'It all started one rainy Saturday morning when I visited him in his garage . . .'

John Noakes coming to Crindau to make a film about him, me meeting him at the station.

'Hi-ya, Noakesy.'

'Hello, Liam – flipping heck, get down, Patch!'

Being asked to go to the *Blue Peter* studio.

'It's been the most amazing response to any campaign we've ever had – and it's all thanks to you. It's only right that you should be the one to present Mr Sikorski with his new legs.'

'Are you all right, Liam?'

I cleared my throat, wiped my eye.

'Yes, thanks, I just got something in my eye.'

I'd write the letter tonight. He'd have the new legs for Christmas.

Mr Sikorski took a packet of fig rolls from the top drawer of the desk, opened them, handed them to me.

'Please, help yourself.'

I took one, passed them on to Colin. It was cosy in there, even though it was so small. Mr Sikorski pushed some things aside and, moving slowly and carefully, sat on the desk. He sipped his tea. Colin and I sat watching him, eating and drinking.

'How's your back, Tata?'

His *back*?

'It's OK.'

He turned to me and Colin.

'I slipped this morning when I was getting out of the bath and fell right here.'

Moving cautiously, he touched the bottom of his spine very gently with his hand. He brought his hand back up, kissed his index finger and the one next to it, then touched the crucifix very gently with them.

'Nothing broken, thank God. But I've been as stiff as an old man all morning.'

I could feel Colin glaring at me. The burning sensation climbed from my neck right up to my forehead.

'Your legs are OK?' Colin asked. Mr Sikorski looked puzzled.

'My legs? Yes, my legs are perfectly OK, thank you, Colin.'

An awkward silence spread like a stain. I stared at the floor. It wasn't my fault, it was an easy mistake to make. *For God's sake, somebody say something.*

'Fig roll, Tata?'

Mr Sikorski reached out, took one.

'There's hardly room to swing a cat in here. It's not the kind of place I had in mind, but it will have to do for now. And it was cheap – very cheap in fact. But now I realise why.'

He stretched out a hand, opened a drawer, took out a pile of letters.

'Every week there are more – unpaid bills, final demands, letters from solicitors . . . Every week I write back to these people explaining that the last owner left without leaving any forwarding address, that I have nothing to do with him. Then there are the angry customers who come back with their cars in a worse state than when they brought them in. This man was obviously a complete scoundrel. But . . .'

He pointed at me and Colin, held our eyes.

'In this life you must make the most of what you have. If they stop swearing and shouting after I've explained that he's left, I offer to fix their cars for them for a very small charge. Of course they are suspicious at first, for now they hate all mechanics. But they go away delighted once they find I've sorted the problem out.'

'Last week a man came back to thank Tata – he gave him that.'

Marek pointed to a bottle of whisky standing in the corner of the desk.

'Ah yes, Mr Sefton – "It's like having a new car, I can't believe it," he said.'

Someone you could trust.

Nicky poked his head around the door.

'Kettle just boiled?'

Mr Sikorski tensed.

'Have you finished with Mr Prosser's car yet, Nicky?'

'Yeah, are those fig rolls?'

'Have you cleaned it?'

'Uh . . .'

Mr Sikorski gave him a stern look, he spread his hands in front of him.

'Then the job isn't finished.'

Nicky groaned.

'It was like a pigsty when he brought it in – sweet wrappers and crushed biscuits and old carrier bags . . .'

'I don't care. How many times must I tell you? The job isn't finished till the car is spotless inside.'

Nicky pulled a face, went back out again. Mr Sikorski and Marek exchanged a secret look.

'I have to watch this boy all the time. Maybe it's not his fault, maybe he has picked up these slovenly habits from his family, I don't know. But now he must pull his socks up.'

He took another swig of tea. Marek took another fig roll, passed the packet to me and Colin.

'Maybe you think I'm being too hard on him?'

We shook our heads.

'Listen,' said Mr Sikorski, picking up the pen from the middle of the ledger, tapping it against the edge of the desk. 'I'll tell you a story.'

He paused to collect himself, started rolling the pen between his hands.

'After Poland fell in 1939, thousands of us crossed the border into France, determined to continue the fight. I joined a French squadron. When I got into the cockpit of a plane after a Polish mechanic had serviced it – mmm!'

He blew a kiss to the ceiling.

'It was beautiful – you'd swear it was brand new, straight from the factory that morning. But if it had been serviced by a Frenchman – pah!'

He pulled a face.

'The first time I climbed into my plane after a French mechanic had been working on it I climbed to two thousand feet.' He guided the pen upwards. 'And, at full throttle, with the cockpit open I . . .'

The pen soared downwards.

'Dived down to one thousand feet in a few seconds.'

He widened his eyes.

'Suddenly I was under attack.'

He drew his shoulders in as if to duck, covered his head with his hands.

'Bombarded with screws, washers, cigarette butts. Then . . . BANG!'

He struck the side of his head a glancing blow with the flat of his palm.

'A hammer hit me on the side of the head so hard I nearly passed out.'

He stood up, threw up his hands.

'That was the last time I ever got into a plane serviced by a French mechanic without cleaning it out first.'

He shook his head. The muscles around his mouth tightened.

'I hate that "this will do" attitude. You must do your job to the best of your ability, you must believe that what you are doing is important otherwise . . .'

He raised his shoulders, arched his eyebrows.

'It's time to find something else to do. How can you expect other people to respect you if you have no pride in what you do?'

'You can't,' said Marek.

'This young man Nicky, he probably dreams of having his own garage one day. Of being the boss, and telling other people what to do. Well, if that's the case, he needs to buck up his ideas. Last week I checked a car he'd been working on and found cigarette ash all over the seat. Now how do you think the owner would have felt if he'd driven home, got up and discovered that his trousers were covered in ash? He would have said, "Filthy Pole! I'm never going back to that garage again," that's what he would have said. How am I supposed to build up a business if things like that happen?'

'I can't stand the way he calls me kidder,' said Marek.

'Well,' said Mr Sikorski, waving his hand back and forth in front of his face, 'enough complaining.'

He broke into a smile, gestured towards me and Colin.

'So, Marek, these are your friends. Liam and Colin.'

Not Colin and Liam.

'I think we're going to like it here, Marek, don't you?'

'Yes, Tata.'

'This is a good town. The people are good people. They are friendly, respectful. We have nice neighbours, they have made us feel very welcome.'

He looked at us, smiled.

'And now, now you have made friends at school.'

He raised his mug.

'To the future.'

We raised our mugs. I quickly swallowed my last chunk of fig roll so I could join in. I loved toasts.

'The future.'

Mr Sikorski beamed.

'Down the hatch.'

We all took a swig of our drinks. Mr Sikorski rubbed his hands together.

'Well, now I think I'd better be getting back to work.'

He walked out of the office, gazed up at the grey clouds through the open door.

'I would hate to still be living in the Valleys on a day like this. The clouds seem to hover just above the rooftops, pressing down on you like bad luck. The rows of houses climbing up the mountainside looked like they were trying to escape. What a place.'

He shook his head.

'Never mind, now we are living in Crindau. Things are different here.'

He smiled at me and Colin.

'And what do you boys usually get up to on Saturday?'

'We go to watch Crindau Town – with my dad.'

Mr Sikorski turned to Marek.

'You like football, Marek, you should go.'

Marek looked uncertain for once.

'I will some time.'

'Why don't you come with us now?'

'Yeah!'

'I . . .' He frowned, avoiding our eyes.

'Yes, go with your friends. Here . . .' said Mr Sikorski, taking his wallet from his back pocket, handing Marek a ten bob note. 'No need to spend the day kicking your heels on your own when you have friends. What are friends for?'

★ ★ ★

There was a buzz in the air at Somerton Park. We were having our best run for years, we were fifth from bottom, the highest position anyone could remember. We were playing Reading today and everybody hated them. Mr Richards met us there, holding up the programme, pointing at the line up.

'Dougie Blute is back.'

'Aye, about time and all,' said Mr Williams. 'He'll put some backbone in the midfield.'

He'd missed the beginning of the season because he was in hospital after crashing his car into a lamp-post.

'He's up in court in a few months' time,' said Mr Richards. 'They reckon he'd had fifteen pints. Wasn't in any state to walk home, let alone drive.'

Crindau ran out in the pouring rain, started the kickabout. We all booed Reading when they came out a minute later. They beat us 1–0 at home every year. Last year they'd beaten us 1–0 at home *three* times – once in the league, once in the League Cup, once in the FA Cup. Each time they stole a goal, then spent the rest of the game with every player behind the ball, defending like mad.

Just before the game started a gang of giggling teenage girls arrived and stood just in front of us. They wore plastic macs, miniskirts and long boots. Mr Williams and Mr Richards looked at each other and smirked.

'Aye aye.'

Mr Williams's other mate rolled up with his bag of chips. Mr Williams nudged him, nodded at the dolly birds.

'Seen that?'

His face froze.

'What are they doing here?'

Mr Williams and Mr Richards laughed. We laughed too. He opened his bag of chips, started stuffing them into his gob and muttering.

'Is there nowhere left where you can escape from bloody women for a couple of hours?'

The game started. The first time Stevie Boy got the ball the dolly birds huddled together and started shouting at the top of their voices.

'STEVIE! STEVIE! WE LOVE YOU, STEVIE! WOO-HOO!'

They stood on their toes and waved – *waved!* At him. We all turned away in disgust, we'd never seen anything like it at a football game before. Stevie Boy beat one player, but another slid in and nicked the ball off his toe before he could get away. That's how it went for most of the half, Crindau kept trying to get the ball to Stevie, but there were always two players right on him, sometimes a third hovering just behind. Reading had everyone behind the ball as usual. Then, after about half an hour their number 10, the blond one who'd scored against us in every game last season, turned so sharply our centre half slipped trying to keep up with him. He set off for our goal, with only the keeper to beat.

'For Christ's sake.'

Dougie Blute came from nowhere. He was like a runaway train. He collided with the blondie forward, sent him crashing to the ground face first. He lay in a heap, not moving. Everyone cheered. Mr Richards handed Mr Williams a fag, said, '*That's* what we've been missing. We've been letting teams walk all over us.'

The referee ran over, but Dougie already had his hands up in the air, as if to say *he just ran into me, what could I do?* He took a couple of steps backwards, hands still up, trampled on blondie's hand. When he started roaring, Dougie turned round in surprise, a horrified expression on his face – *Sorry, mate, didn't see you there.* Mr Richards couldn't light his fag for laughing.

'Now that is an artist at work.'

Reading's trainer ran on, sat blondie up, pushed a sponge into his face. He flinched, rubbed his jaw tenderly, then held out his hand for the trainer to look at. He was nearly bawling.

'Get up, you great poof, he hardly touched you.'

We started chanting, 'Bring on the dustbin.'

When the referee finished telling Dougie off, he turned to the crowd and winked. We cheered again.

'Attaboy, Dougie.'

Marek was watching it all wide-eyed.

'Great, isn't it?'

'Yes, it is. I've never been to a football match before.'

I felt sorry for him.

'You can come with us any time you want.'

'Thank you.'

Reading's free kick went out for a goal kick.

'What did you do in the Valleys on Saturdays?'

'I would help Tata at the garage, or maybe go for a walk. It wasn't so bad.'

We paused while Stevie Boy put in a cross. Their centre half cleared it. Marek was leaning on me to get a better view. He rested his arm on my shoulder.

'This is much better.'

I was glad he didn't have to go for a walk on Saturday after-noons any more, glad that we were his friends, and that we could take him places.

It was 0–0 at half time. The rain was coming down harder

now, puddles were beginning to form on the pitch. Marek, Colin and I had crisps, a Mars bar and orange juice. Mr Richards took out a little bottle of whisky from inside his coat, poured some into his and Mr Williams's tea.

'That'll keep the cold out.'

'Tidy.'

The second half was just as bad. Stevie Boy looked fed up, his long hair was hanging in rat's tails, his sleeves hung down over the end of his fingers. The dolly birds huddled together, shivering under their two spotty umbrellas. For a long time nothing much happened. The ball skidding about on the wet surface, bouncing crazily from one side to the other like a pinball.

'Top up?' Mr Richards handed the whisky bottle to Mr Williams. The raindrops ran off the end of my nose down the neck of my anorak.

Suddenly blondie got the ball in space, started running towards our goal with no one near him.

'Come on, who's picking him up?'

Dougie charged after him, but blondie was fast, and he had a ten-foot start. We had to do something, quickly, otherwise we were going to lose 1–0 again. Everyone felt it. All at once the whole ground started chanting.

'SIX FOOT TWO, EYES OF BLUE, DOUGIE BLUTE IS AFTER YOU!' Blondie looked nervously over his shoulder, saw the runaway train hurtling down the line towards him in a cloud of steam, whistle screaming. Our voices roaring in his ears like a hurricane.

'SIX FOOT TWO, EYES OF BLUE, DOUGIE BLUTE IS AFTER YOU!'

Blondie's legs turned to water, he lost control of the ball, ran it out of touch. The cheers shook the ground, as loud as for any goal. Blondie's head dropped, his shoulders sagged. We started making chicken noises.

'Baaaaaawk-bawk-bawk-bawk-baaaaaaawk!'

That's what he'd get every time he touched the ball now. There was nowhere to run, nowhere to hide. He was destroyed. They might as well have taken him off there and then.

'Ha!' Marek clenched his fist. 'I like this Blute.'

That was the moment the match turned. From the throw-in Stevie Boy got a lucky bounce and was away from both of the players marking him in a flash. He dribbled past another defender, was into the area.

'Go on, go on.'

The keeper saved his shot. The ball spun up into the air. Stevie Boy kept going, jumped like a salmon and headed it into the net before any defender could reach him.

'YEEEEEEEEEEE-EEEEEEEEES!'

Colin, Marek and I hugged each other, jumped up and down on the terrace. Squish squash slop went the water in our shoes. We didn't care. Stevie Boy ran behind the goal, one hand in the air, one finger raised, just like Georgie Best.

Reading were on the run. When Crindau attacked again Stevie Boy poked the ball through the legs of one defender, sent the other sliding on to his backside with a wiggle of his hips.

'OLÉ!' shouted the dolly birds.

Mr Richards frowned, the whisky bottle halfway to his mouth.

'Olé?'

'Olé now, is it?' said Mr Williams, pulling a face.

Mr Richards put on an ooh-la-di-da voice. 'Olé – I speak Italian, you know.'

'It's Spanish,' said someone behind.

'Ah, shut up, Bamber.'

But he was nearly smiling, there wasn't going to be any arguing, everyone was in too good a mood.

★　★　★

We sat in a thick fog on the bus home – cigarette smoke and the steam rising from everyone's clothes. Marek said to Colin, 'I enjoyed coming to watch the football. Your dad is good fun.' Then he turned to me. 'What about you, Liam? When am I going to meet your family?'

A sudden chill ran through me.

'Ummm . . . soon.'

'How soon?'

A panic gripped me, then guilt, then the panic returned.

'Soon . . . you must come round to our house . . . soon.'

★ ★ ★

They rounded up the survivors, marched us at gunpoint through the town centre, nothing but blackened ruins now. Everywhere you looked there were Russian bogmen, staggering about mad with the drink, searching through the rubble for fancy Western goods. They made us line up in front of the remains of the market. Big wet flakes of snow whirled in the chilly wind.

'Mammy!'

I squeezed Michael's hand.

'Stop crying, don't attract attention.'

He hung his head, blubbered more quietly. The sobs caught in his throat, his shoulders shook with the effort of holding them in. They dragged out the priests and nuns, lined them up, formed a firing squad. I was careful not to let my face betray anything. You daren't let anyone know you were a Roman Catholic. The Russians wouldn't think twice about putting a bullet into you if they found out. Best to keep yourself to yourself, avoid talking to strangers, especially friendly ones who asked too many questions.

'Excuse me, mate, do you know where I can find a mass round here?'

'Sorry, mate, no idea, try asking one of those Roman Catholics.'

You never knew who you were talking to.

We are a tiny island of Roman Catholics in a sea of Methodists.

They were working hand in hand with the Russians, hunting us down like dogs. The soldiers in the firing squad raised their rifles, took aim.

'Fire!'

'Liam! For God's sake.'

'Fire!'

A light was blinding me, someone had hold of my wrists.

'Fire!'

'Calm down, there's no fire.'

It was Mam. I looked around. I was in my bedroom. The blue flowery wallpaper, my Liverpool FC poster, the Airfix model of a Spitfire on top of the chest of drawers, my clothes draped over the chair. Michael was in the bed opposite, propped up on his elbow, looking like a startled hamster.

'The priests, the priests and nuns, they were going to shoot them.'

'Sssh now.'

She let go of my wrists, put her finger to her lips.

'I was left on my own with Michael. I was trying to stop him from crying, where were you?'

She ran her hand through my hair.

'You had a bad dream, but it's all right now.'

'Is it?'

My voice sounded like glass splintering. Mam pressed gently down on my head with her fingers.

'Yes, it is. Michael, go back to sleep now, love.'

He closed his bleary hamster eyes, lay back down, turned away from the light.

'Come on now, Liam, you too. Lie down.'

'I want to look out of the window.'

She frowned. 'What?'

I was already sliding out of the bed. I had to see.

'Please – just a quick look, then I'll go back to sleep, I promise.'

I walked over to the window, pulled back the curtain. The row of houses opposite with their curtains drawn, empty bottles on the doorsteps, ready for tomorrow. Another normal day.

'Liam.'

'Mam.'

'What is it?'

'I'm scared.'

Her knees cracked as she bent down behind me. She squeezed my shoulders. I smelt Palmolive soap, a faint tang of cigarettes. I wanted her to myself. I wanted to push her away.

'Oh, Liam a stór, what are we going to do with you at all?'

I wanted her to promise that nothing bad would happen. But my throat was cracked and sore and the words dried up inside.

'Come on now, get back into that bed.'

I let her guide me back, tuck me in. It was usually Michael who woke up in the night, he was the one who always needed calming down. It was always her who came, never Dad. He was too busy having his own nightmares.

'Mam, I don't want anyone to come and take you away.'

She laughed. Too loud. Too long.

'Fat chance of that. Who'd want me?'

No, that wasn't the right thing to say. She hadn't understood at all. That look on her face – *The life I've had, it'd make you weep*. I lay down, waited for the soft click as she closed the door behind her.

★ ★ ★

I was in Cwm Wood, crouching in the ferns at the side of the railway track. Preparing myself. I had to be ready for the worst. Only the toughest would survive. You had to learn to conquer fear. You couldn't let fear conquer you. The train was getting closer. I shifted on to my haunches, like a runner waiting for the starting gun. Here it comes. I blessed myself.

Thirty yards away. Twenty yards. Ten.

Now.

I sprang out, ran across the track in front of it, yelling at the top of my voice.

'GERONIMO!'

Everything was a blur. My heart was thumping like a jackhammer, trying to burst through my chest. Someone was screaming inside my head.

I was alive. I was on the other side of the track, still running. There was a donkey braying somewhere. No, it was me. The sound of my breathing as I pushed myself up the bank. I couldn't stop running. It was mad. I was desperate to get as far away from the railway track as possible. As if the train could veer off the track and chase me up the bank. I stumbled, cut my knee on something, tried to get up, stumbled again. Clambered on all fours to the top. Collapsed on to the wet grass.

'Oh God. Oh God.'

I started crying. I don't know how long I lay there. It seemed like hours. When I looked up again I expected it to be getting dark, but the sky looked the same. Something was falling on me. It was raining. It took a huge effort to get up. My body felt like lead, like I was pulling myself out of the swimming baths after being in the water for an hour.

'Come on, don't be soft. Be a man.'

I was on my feet. I'd done it. Done something I thought I was too frightened to do. On my own. I felt better for it. I did. This was nothing compared to how terrifying a nuclear war would be. But it was a start. I'd begun preparing myself. I'd passed the first test. No one had seen me cry. I'd be ready.

★ ★ ★

Sunday morning. We were on our way to the allotment. Dad stopped just before we reached the railway bridge, pulled a couple of old copies of the *Argus* from the wheelbarrow, held one over his head.

'What are you doing?'

'This is a pigeon shit blackspot.'

He passed the other one to me.

'Here, protect yourself.'

I covered my head with it. We steeled ourselves, went in. Over us a restless fluttering, in front a series of loud, sickening splats.

'Dirty bastards – they're worse than the fecking Luftwaffe. I'd love to take a flame-thrower to the lot of them.'

We got to the other end unscathed, chucked the papers back in the wheelbarrow. Uncle Ronnie and Mr Alonzi were already there when we reached the allotments.

'Allo, Mr Bennett, nice day.'

'It is, yeah, a grand day.'

He bent down, whispered, 'As long as the fecking Russians don't launch an attack. Jayzus, then these two would have a heart attack.'

He shook his head.

'Jayzus, they wouldn't know *what* had hit them.'

Uncle Ronnie was sitting on a stool outside his shed, reading the *Sunday Mirror*, a flask by his feet, Butch stretched out just beyond, gnawing at a bone.

'Hello there, Ronnie.'

'Hi-ya, Brendan, Liam.'

He winked at me, stuck his head back in the paper. Butch got a tighter grip on the bone with his front paws, tilted his head, gnawed, grunted.

There was no warning. The explosion came from behind us. Something screamed past our heads, thumped into Uncle Ronnie's shed.

'AAAAGH!'

Dad clutched his leg. Collapsed on to the ground. Butch sprang up, barking furiously.

'What the . . . ?'

Dad was squirming at my feet. He grabbed my leg, tugged.

'Get down! They're coming, the fecking Russians are coming.'

I threw myself to the ground next to him.

'Take cover, youse two, for feck's sake.'

Uncle Ronnie's mouth hung open, pages from the *Sunday Mirror* spilled on to the ground. Mr Alonzi had one hand over his heart, was pointing behind us with the other.

'Look.'

'A fecking sneak attack, just like Pearl Harbor.'

I waited breathlessly for the drone of aircraft, the scream of missiles, the desperate shouts and cries of the terrified and wounded, the bitter, choking smoke. But all I could hear was Butch barking.

'Shut up, you stupid mutt,' said Uncle Ronnie.

Then:

'Looks like it's *you* they're after, Brendan.'

'What?'

Mr Alonzi said, 'Your shed – he exploded.'

We looked round, saw the shattered window, burst cans littering the ground.

'What the . . . ?'

Dad's face froze. His mouth dropped open.

'Fecking hell.'

He grimaced, picked up a burst can of beans and sausages lying next to him, stared at it in disbelief.

'It damn near broke my leg.'

Uncle Ronnie clicked his tongue.

'The Russians must be running short of ammo – firing tins of beans now, they are.'

Dad pushed himself up, his hands balled into fists.

'Years of work down the bleddy drain.'

He limped over, unlocked the shed door, went inside.

'FECKING HELL!'

Rushed back out, covering his mouth and nose with his hand.

'What is it?'

He waved his hands frantically at us.

'Stay back, don't go in there. The bleddy tins have exploded.'

He took out his handkerchief, held it over his face, pushed the door open again, went back inside. I got up, ran over. Uncle Ronnie called after me.

'Liam – stay where you are!'

I made a mask with my handkerchief, went inside. Pineapple chunks, meatballs in gravy, spaghetti in tomato sauce, tapioca, diced carrots, splattered all over the floor, walls, ceiling.

The smell.

My stomach heaved. I ran outside and threw up.

Uncle Ronnie shuffled over, gripped my shoulder as I retched again, bringing up the last of my breakfast.

'Attaboy – get it all out. You'll be all right in a minute. GET AWAY FROM THERE!'

Butch was licking at the sick. Uncle Ronnie gave him a kick up the backside. He yelped, ran off. Mr Alonzi came over with a cup of water.

'Here – drinka this.'

I gulped it down. Dad ran back out, coughing. He snatched the handkerchief away from his mouth.

'I'll kill the cunt!'

Uncle Ronnie tightened his grip on my shoulder.

'Christ, I'm the luckiest man alive, if I'd arrived a couple of minutes earlier I'd have been in there when they blew up, they'd have taken my head clean off.'

Uncle Ronnie gave him a withering look.

'And Liam's.'

It was true, I could have been killed. Suddenly my legs were shaking.

'"The only reason they're so cheap is that they've got no labels, that's top quality stuff inside, you're getting yourself a fantastic bargain there, mate." The lying hoor – they were fecking rotten. I'd have poisoned myself if I'd tried to eat any of that stuff.'

'What were you doing with all those tins anyhow?' asked Mr Alonzi.

'I chucked a few of them out only last weekend – they were swelling up like fecking footballs, you'd never seen the like. Christ knows how old they were already when I bought them. Jayzus, if I ever find him . . .'

'He saw you coming all right,' said Uncle Ronnie.

Dad cursed under his breath, turned and gave the shed door a mighty kick with his hobnailed boot. The top hinge snapped and came away. There was a groaning sound, the second hinge broke, the door crashed to the ground.

'I'll track him down if it's the last thing I do, the fecking . . .'

'Come on,' said Uncle Ronnie, guiding me towards his allotment. 'You can give me a hand till your dad calms down.'

★ ★ ★

It was Wednesday, Mam's night for visiting Bridie again. Dad ignored all her comments about making sure I was in bed in half an hour, but as soon as he heard the front door shut he rushed to the curtains and peered out to make sure she'd really gone. Then it was time to bring out the tray of bread and butter, drag the sofa in front of the fire and turn out the light. Next he opened a bottle of stout, poured it, stuck a slice of bread on the end of the toasting fork. He'd calmed down about the tins exploding now, seemed to be in a good mood again.

'Is there another documentary?'

He looked a little offended. I felt a sharp pain in my chest.

'No, there isn't. I thought you might like to stay up for a while and keep me company.'

'I would. Yes.'

'You're sure you're not tired now?'

'No, I'm not.'

He smiled.

'Good man. You're not a baby any more, like Michael. You're well able for a late night or two, aren't I right?'

'I am. I hate going to bed early, sometimes I lay awake for ages, not able to get to sleep.'

'And there'd be all sorts of things going through your mind.'

'Yeah.'

Worrying. About the third world war starting. Someone finding out I'd told on Preece. No one *really* liking me.

'I'm the same meself. I don't like to go to bed till I'm completely worn out, otherwise I'd be likely to lay there for hours, worrying about this thing and that thing . . . had I locked the back door, was the bathroom window shut, oh Jayzus . . .'

He turned the bread over.

'There'd be no comfort, no comfort at all.'

I picked at a loose thread snaking out from the arm of the sofa.

'The fellas at work are a decent enough bunch but they'd be forever gassing about bleddy football and as for your mother . . . well, you know yourself what she's like . . . you'd go mad trying to find someone to have a serious conversation with.'

He paused, took a swig of his stout, checked the toast.

'Nearly ready. But now you're a bit more grown up I'm able to talk to you man to man – it's a great relief, so it is.'

He reached forward, plucked the toast off the end of the fork, handed it to me.

'A great relief.'

I buttered it, watching the gold melt into the brown, feeling the heat from the fire burn my knees.

'Do you remember the other week, when I was telling you how we'd have to get your mother and Michael away from here before the Russians invaded?'

I nodded.

'Well . . .'

He looked around as if half expecting someone to be listening.

'Do you know the best place for them – for us all in fact?'

'No.'

'It came to me this summer, when we were on holiday.'

We always stayed with Mam's family when we went on holiday to Ireland – Aunt Kate, Uncle Sean, my cousins, Mary, Margaret, Nuala, Tom, Kevin and Ned, Gransha and Nana. Dad had fallen out with his relatives, it was years since he'd spoken to any of them.

'I was up, had my breakfast and out the door by six. Jayzus, it was a grand morning, I got on the bike and headed off for Spanish Point with the fishing rod. There was no one about, not a soul. The only sound was the wind whistling in the telegraph wires overhead, and the wheels turning on the road. You know how if you're up early in the morning here you'd always come across *someone* – a milk van, a few cars, some other fellas off to work, you know.'

He shook his head.

'Not there. Eventually I came across this auld fella bent over the engine of a car outside his house. One look was enough to tell you he'd been hunched over that engine, cursing and swearing at the side of the road, every morning for the last ten years. Jayzus, it was nothing but a heap of scrap, it looked as though it was held together with Sellotape and string. He'd never dare take it out on the road in Wales, the police would arrest him before he'd got to the end of the road and tow it straight to the scrapyard.'

He took another sip of stout, laughed.

' "Grand day!" says I. "It is that," he says. I stopped the bike. "Do you know what? You're the first person I've come across since I got up this morning. They're a right bunch of fecking lazy bastards here. A grand day like this, and they're all still in bed snoring like pigs. Jayzus, no wonder the country's in the state it is. If the Russians wanted to invade, all they'd have to do was land early in the morning and the whole country would be overrun in a day." The auld fella screws up his eyes, takes a long look at the car, the pile of junk in his yard – a door with a great hole in it, broken old chairs, blackened saucepans, a bike frame, a rusty old potty. Then at the cow dung splattered across the rotten bleddy road full of potholes, then back at me. "They're fecking welcome to it," says he.'

Dad slapped his knee, roared with laughter. I finished the toast, wiped the crumbs from my fingers.

'Jayzus, afterwards I got to thinking about what your man had said – and started looking around at the fecking awful state of the road, and the dirty auld buildings and the way everything you laid your eyes on looked broken, or patched back together and well on the way to being broken again. And how I only had one brother and one sister still left at home, how all the others, all fecking ten of them, myself included, had fecked off out of the place to Wales and England, Australia, New Zealand, the States. And your mother's three brothers and one of her sisters too . . . Christ, there's hardly a family I know of over there that's not scattered all round the world. "They're welcome to it" is right – the people can't get out of the place fecking fast enough. Then it came to me!'

He clicked his fingers.

'Who *would* want it – fecking no one! Christ almighty, what would the Russians do with it anyhow? Dublin is a dirty fecking shit hole, there's nothing but bleddy bogs in the middle, and take away Galway and there's feck all worth having on the west side.'

Eyes shining brightly, a big smile on his face, he pressed his elbow into my arm.

'That's the genius of it.'

His face was glowing. He looked like he'd just won First Prize. I didn't get it.

'For centuries the Irish have been invaded. The Vikings, the Normans, that cunt Cromwell . . . and what happens when they all finally piss off and the Paddies have got it back to themselves? They sit on their arses and let the place go to the dogs. And then laugh about it.'

It was true – every time something didn't work, or was late starting, or was cancelled, Uncle Sean and Auntie Kate would roll their eyes and say, 'Ah Jayzus – only in Ireland!'

'I used to think the country was in such a terrible state because they were no good for anything, but now I realise what they've been up to all along.'

He sat back, smiling to himself, staring into the coals.

'Think about it – a tiny country like that with no army or navy, no money to spend on fancy radar systems and missiles and underground bunkers and all the rest of it. What chance would they stand in a war? Instead they've come up with a very cunning form of defence – make sure the country's in such a shambles that no fecker would want it. Ha! The genius of it!'

He was laughing again.

'The Yanks spending millions trying to protect themselves from the Russians and *still* it won't do them any good. But Ireland, oho, Ireland'll be OK. Ireland will just keep its head down and carry on quietly, minding its own business – just the same way it avoided getting involved in the Second World War.'

He paused, shifted his weight on the sofa, spat into the fire. He grinned.

'Now then – what do you think of that?'

I didn't know what to say, I was finding it all difficult to follow, the way he jumped around. But before I could say anything he was off again.

'Just think of it – all these years Irish fellas have travelled all over the world, building roads and railways and towns in *other* people's countries while their own has gone to rack and ruin. And now you see why. Oh yes, Brendan won't be bothering to buy any more bleddy rotten tins, we're not staying here to be slaughtered like cattle – Ireland's the place for us.'

★ ★ ★

The next day I ran my finger along the window sill, held it up to the light. Absolutely filthy. Worms of cigarette ash across the carpet. Dirty clothes piling up in the bathroom. Unwashed breakfast things still lying in the sink.

The place was going to pot.

How could I not have noticed?

There'd been a gravy stain on my school shirt since Monday, and Mam still hadn't gone on at me to change it. Dad was right. She was a nervous wreck. Was letting everything fall apart around her. You couldn't blame him for getting angry. A bloke had a right to expect his dinner to be ready when he came back home from work, the house to be clean and tidy. It was only fair, after all, he was holding up his end of the deal. He never missed a day's work. He was bringing home the bacon. What did she have to do all day but a bit of dusting and cleaning, washing and getting the dinner ready? The place was a pigsty. She was hanging by a thread. Dad was the only one I could rely on.

★ ★ ★

We were in Colin's bedroom, sitting on his bed, setting out the chess pieces on the board. We played nearly every night now. Ever since an episode of *The Man from U.N.C.L.E.* a few weeks before. Illya had been captured by a mad scientist who was going to launch nuclear missiles against America if they didn't pay him a hundred million dollars. He challenged Illya to a game of chess. They played next to a pool of piranhas, their next meal, Illya.

Good luck, Mr Kuryakin, you'll need it. Ha ha ha.

Evil scientists always laughed at their own jokes. The game was fantastic, as exciting as any shoot out or car chase. Jazzy music. Illya sneaking anxious glances at the pool. The board slowly emptying. The scientist frowning, realising too late what a good player Illya was. Taking longer and longer to make his moves. Down to the last few pieces. The *tsk tsk tsk* of cymbals. A voice, Illya's, saying 'Check . . .' *tsk tsk tsk* '. . . mate!' The scientist's eyes brimming with rage and humiliation.

'Guards!'

Too late. Illya was already out of his seat. One swift punch sent the scientist flying into the pool. Illya ducked as the guards opened fire, sprinted across the room, threw himself through the window.

Colin kept the score in a notebook. I was leading 158 to 156.

'Can I play?'

I'd forgotten Michael was there. Sitting in the corner, looking through Colin's old Crindau programmes.

'*You?*'

He nodded. We burst out laughing.

'I'm not going to spend all night trying to teach you the rules.'

'I know how to play.'

'No, you don't.'

'Yes, I do, I've been watching you.'

'Go on, let him have a game,' said Colin.

That annoyed me. It was all a big laugh to Colin. He had no idea what hard work it was keeping a kid brother in line. Today it was chess, tomorrow it would be coming to the football, or to Mr Sikorski's garage with us. Colin got up from the bed, grinning like an idiot.

'Go on, sit down and play Liam. I'll watch.'

Michael walked over to the bed, his eyes down.

'You start,' I said.

I took three of his pawns, then a rook, in lightning quick strikes. Six moves, four–nil. None of *his* moves made any sense. He didn't know the first thing about defence, I was slicing through him like a knife through hot butter. Next to fall was a knight, clacking into the wooden box before he'd finished drawing back his arm from making his last move. I winked at Colin. He nodded at the board. Michael had moved his queen into an attacking position. He looked up at me for the first time.

'Checkmate.'

Something vital slipped out of me, dribbled on to the floor. I looked again. I couldn't move to my right, one of his bishops was covering there.

'He's got you,' said Colin.

I looked back at Michael, his head was down again.

'He's got you.'

'You just said that.'

I looked at the board again, there was no way out. Wanted to scream and knock the board across the room. No. I couldn't lose my temper in front of Colin, he'd never stop going on about it.

You should have seen him when his kid brother beat him at chess, he went mad.

The thing to do was forget about what had just happened and concentrate on winning the next game, bounce back straight away.

'Best of three.'

Michael shrugged. That was the worst thing of all, the way he acted like it didn't matter. A gloating smile would have been easier to take. He wouldn't dare do that though, he knew I'd murder him.

This time I was more careful. Took my time. Took more notice of *his* moves. Saw his bishop getting too close, took it with a rook. Blocked his Queen from moving out with a knight. Now I was back in control. I brought out my second rook, then my Queen, the beginning of a pincer movement that would bring us level. His rook took my knight. How could I have missed that coming? I brought up another pawn to gain time. He moved his bishop.

'Checkmate.'

I couldn't bear to look up at him this time. Could hardly bear to bring myself to look at the board. Didn't need to. I could feel I'd lost. Could tell, already, that he was amazing. The George Best of chess.

Colin was laughing.

'He beat you easy. Twice!'

I got up from the bed. I couldn't speak, couldn't look at either of them. I had to keep my cool or I'd go under. After all, it was only a game.

'You play him.'

'All right.'

I stood to one side, my hands in my pockets, watching. Michael beat him just as easily. Colin spent longer staring at the board, trying to figure a way out of the trap Michael had sprung, than one of our games usually lasted.

'He's got you, Colin.'

'Best of three.'

I knew he'd say that. Even after Michael had beaten him just as easily the second time he couldn't accept it, insisted on playing the last game, lost that too. He couldn't look me in the face afterwards. Thought it was worse for him because it was *his* bedroom, *his* chess set. But it wasn't. It was worse for me. Far, far worse. I'd just discovered my kid brother was a genius.

★ ★ ★

'This way – it's quicker.'

Marek led us down an alleyway. It was pelting down. We'd abandoned our training in Cwm Wood for the day, it was practically a swamp. The alleyway came out near the top of his road, we turned right, reached Marek's house in a minute. Just as we ran through the gate one of his sisters opened the front door, shouting, 'I'll be back by six.'

'You be sure you are,' shouted a voice behind her.

She put up an umbrella, squeezed past us with barely a glance. We stumbled into the hallway.

'Marek! Just look at you.'

His mother stood perfectly still in the middle of the hall. I knew at once that she thought people who rushed were fools. Black dress, black hair, long silver earrings. Piercing eyes, fierce mouth turned down at the corners. I'd have loved to have seen her and Miss Partridge trying to outstare each other. It would have been as exciting as any boxing match. She turned her attention to us.

'And you must be Liam and Colin.'

She knew the right order.

We nodded and she smiled. I hadn't expected that. Not after the way she looked when we came in the door. It was a wonderful smile. But it made me nervous too. It was a smile that expected a lot from you. Made you realise that friendship was a very serious thing. You had a duty to your friends, and they to you. You didn't let them down. That smile could disappear without warning, never return.

'You are all soaked. Give me your coats and I will hang them up to dry.'

We handed them over.

'Now go into the living room and warm yourselves up.'

As we entered Jan charged out, brushing angrily past Marek. From the hallway, he turned and shouted back into the living room.

'There's more to life than adding up columns of figures in a stuffy office.'

Marek stared at him. Jan glanced back, sneered, rushed up the stairs. Mr Sikorski was sitting on the sofa, a pile of paperwork on his lap. He took his glasses off – I never realised he needed glasses – and shouted, 'What do *you* know about life?' But it was too late, Jan was gone.

'What's the matter, Tata?'

'Your brother – hardly out of short trousers, and already he knows better than me.' He gestured towards the stairs, raised his voice. 'He won't be told. That young man is heading for a fall.' He looked at us for the first time.

'Gentlemen, you are soaked. Come in – get next to the fire and dry yourselves.'

We huddled around the grate. Steam began to rise from our clothes, tickly prickly heat climbed our legs. The table between us and Mr Sikorski had bowls of chocolates and fruit on it. Mr Sikorski noticed me looking.

'Please help yourselves.'

I took a chocolate with a drawing of a plum on the wrapper, chucked the wrapper on to the fire. Colin copied me.

'What's the name of this film, Tata?'

'I don't know, Jan put it on, then sat in that chair with his feet up on the arm, sniggering. Suddenly everything's funny to him. When I told him to sit in the chair properly, and reminded him that he should be studying for his exams, he jumped up and stormed out of the room. He turned it on – so it's his responsibility to turn it off, not mine.'

I couldn't understand why Jan would behave like that. How could you argue with your dad if he was a war hero?

The film was all *Tally Ho! Crikey, Ginger!* and stuff.

'Mr Sikorski, why are there never any Polish pilots in these films?'

He shrugged that way he did with his shoulders and hands, which seemed to say so much. I'd never known anyone else who did it.

'These types of films are made *by* English people *for* English people. In English films it's the English who win the war. This is normal. In American films Americans win the war. They don't want a bunch of Poles grabbing the glory. People have short memories. After the war was over they held a Victory Parade in London. All the Allied forces took part. Except the Poles.'

'Why?'

'Because Stalin had declared the Poles to be fascists. And the British government didn't want to offend their Russian friends.'

That was a terrible thing to do, I couldn't understand why we used to be friends with the Russians and so spiteful to the Poles, after they'd helped us so much. It didn't make sense. Mr Sikorski nodded at the telly where a toff sat in an armchair, smoking a pipe and patting a labrador's head.

'Everybody thinks this is what all RAF pilots were like.'

The toff squinted up at the sunny sky.

'Jerry's quiet today.'

A second later the alarm went.

'Scramble!'

They all shot out of their chairs, raced to the Spitfires, the labrador lolloping behind them, barking. I took another sweet.

'It's a beautiful sight, isn't it?' said Mr Sikorski, nodding at three Spitfires flying in a perfect V formation.

'Yes, it is.'

I'd love to have a Spitfire more than anything, even a red E-type Jag. Me, Marek and Colin, flying them in a V formation above Crindau, everyone straining to look. The chocolate coating was dark and thick, the plum filling sweet and sticky. I took another one while no one was looking.

'Of course, it was a quite ridiculous way to fly in a war. The RAF insisted on formation flying like this, we spent hours practising it when we were training. But we spent so much time trying to fly in pretty patterns that there was no time left for target practice!'

I'd always loved the way they flew in those formations, it reminded me of knights riding side by side into battle. But I kept my mouth shut.

In the film, one of the pilots cocked his head as he listened to a voice buzzing in his ear.

'Wilko – there they are! Jerry at seven o'clock.'

'OK, let's go introduce ourselves.'

They turned like three graceful birds and swooped down on the Germans, guns blazing. Mr Sikorski smiled.

'We Poles completely ignored their orders, and flew in pairs. They thought we were hotheads, that we had no discipline, or that we were too stupid to follow their orders. But we understood only too well that war was not about flying in perfect formation. While the English pilots had been finishing their education we had seen our homes destroyed, our mothers and sisters killed, our country enslaved by the Germans. We had no illusions about what the enemy was like. We were not gentlemen. We did not want to go to war against the Germans flying in a formation.'

He leant over, took a chocolate, unwrapped it, popped it into his mouth.

'But they soon stopped complaining when they saw how many German planes we shot down. The Poles had the highest kill rate in Fighter Command. We knew what we were doing all right. We employed panic. A couple of us would fly straight at the Germans, holding our fire until we could see the colour of their eyes. They thought we were madmen, that we were going to ram them. They scattered in all directions. And that's when the rest of us would dive down on them from above, and pick them off one by one. Those were *our* tactics. It was not gentlemanly, but it was very effective.'

On the telly a German fighter went down in flames.

'Good shooting, Ginge.'

Two more Messerschmitts were shot down, then a Spitfire was hit.

'Cripes, Ginge, I've bought it.'

'I've seen this,' whispered Colin. 'He can't get his parachute to open – told you.' On the telly, the RAF pilot was twisting through the air, falling to his certain death.

'There were always stories about our exploits in the newspapers – wait, let me show you something.'

As soon as he left the room, Colin and I ran to the sweet bowl. Marek stayed where he was, giving us his most scornful look.

'Like pigs at a trough.'

I didn't care, those sweets were delicious. Mr Sikorski came back in, holding a yellowing card. We gathered around him.

'This is my old RAF identity card.'

There was a photo of Mr Sikorski underneath the RAF wings.

'Do you notice anything strange about the name?'

It said *Captain Teddy Singleton*.

'But that's not . . . but it's you in the photo.'

'All Poles were issued with false IDs – if an English pilot was shot down and captured, he was treated like an officer and a gentleman. Poles were shot.'

'Why?'

'Hitler liked and respected the English. He wanted them on his side. He hated the Poles. Thought we were fit only to be used as slaves. He thought we had been crushed. He was furious when he discovered that Poles were inflicting such terrible damage on his beloved Luftwaffe. But we were determined to show him that we were not beaten. We defended this country as if it were our own.'

He took another sweet from the bowl.

'But I'm afraid people soon forget such things.'

Mrs Sikorski came in carrying a tray with three steaming bowls of soup.

'Sit down, boys, this will warm you up.'

It smelt gorgeous. We sat down and she handed us each a bowl. Mr Sikorski beamed at his wife.

'You will like this – Polish soup is delicious.'

From upstairs came the sound of a saxophone. Someone playing along to a jazz record. Mr Sikorski's face hardened. He turned to his wife in exasperation.

'Does that sound like someone revising for their accountancy exams to you?'

She shrugged. 'He must have a break, he can't study all the time.'

'How many times have I told him about the importance of a career?' Mr Sikorski put his hands to the side of his mouth, shouted at the ceiling.

'JAN!'

A teenaged girl with long blond hair, a miniature version of Mrs Sikorski, dressed in a brown duffel coat and blue corduroys, came into the room. She looked really tidy, the kind of girl you'd see dancing on *Top of the Pops* in a jazzy outfit. Tossing her hair and smiling, paying no attention to the camera zooming in on her.

'Tata, can I have some money for bus fare? I'm going over to Sian's for the afternoon.'

Mr Sikorski shot her a suspicious glance.

'We're going to revise together for our mocks.'

'She's going to meet a boy,' said Marek.

'Shut up, you.'

'Barbara!' shouted Mrs Sikorski, then, to Marek, 'Don't tell tales.'

The saxophone got louder, faster. It sounded horrible, like someone drilling into a wall and hitting a brick. Mr Sikorski put his hands to the sides of his head, screwed up his eyes.

'Why is he like this? Why does he always have to provoke me? Does he really think I'm going to stand for this in my own house? I'm going up there now and . . .'

'Tadeusz, let him be, please.'

'Tata! Can I?' asked Barbara.

'I've *seen* her with boys.'

'Marek—'

A little girl Michael's age ran in, flung herself at Mr Sikorski's lap.

'Where's Susan? She should have been here an hour ago.'

Mr Sikorski looked imploringly at Mrs Sikorski.

'Who's Susan?'

'Her imaginary friend.'

He threw up his arms in frustration.

'My God – dealing with the Luftwaffe was a piece of cake compared to this.'

I think he was just joking.

★ ★ ★

It was dark, sleeting, my shoes and trouser legs were sodden from crouching in the ferns. We were the only ones standing between freedom and the forces of evil. The Few. Like Mr Sikorski and the other Poles in the Battle of Britain. *We had no illusions about what the enemy was like. We were not gentlemen.* We stiffened as we heard first a noise, then a minute later saw lights cutting through the gloom. In an instant we were on our haunches, ready for action.

'Now.'

We jumped up, letting out a blood-curdling cry of 'DEATH TO COMMUNISM'.

My hands were frozen, the first carriage was past before I could get them to work properly. By the end of the second I'd found my range. Halfway down the third a ginger-haired man leant out of the window, smoking. He looked like a ringleader. I could just see him at the head of a gang of drunken Valley yobbos searching for Roman Catholics to drag in front of a firing squad.

He was mine.

I let fly. He roared like a bull. A shower of sparks burst from the window as his fag flew through the air. He covered his face with his hands, disappeared.

'Jesus!'

Suddenly no one was firing any more. The rest of the train rattled past. Nothing to break the dreadful silence except the ghostly kerchunk, kerchunk fading into the darkness.

'Bloody hell,' said Colin.

The ginger-haired man was lying on the floor of the corridor, blood pumping from his head. Women and children screaming.

Is there a doctor on board? For God's sake, somebody pull the emergency cord.

A direct hit, right between the eyes – he would have been dead before he hit the ground.

I was going to jail for the rest of my life.

'You've really done it now,' said Colin.

'Let's go,' said Marek.

I was frozen to the spot. Michael was whimpering, pushing at me to get past. My life was over, I was ruined. A murderer. I threw back my head, started bawling.

Marek grabbed hold of my shoulders, shook me so hard he nearly pulled me off my feet.

'Pull yourself together. We have to get out of here – now!'

'Yes . . .'

'MOVE!'

He pushed me. We scrambled through the hole in the fence, stumbled through the sodden leaves and clinging mud till our legs buckled and snot slid down the backs of our throats. We collapsed against a tree, gasping, our lungs scalding. It was Marek who spoke first.

'We go home separately. Me that way, Colin in that direction, you and Michael through there. We haven't seen each other today, understand?'

We nodded. No arguments over who was leader now. No one else knew what to say, or do. I was glad he was there. He pushed me again.

'GO!'

★   ★   ★

I sat in school the next day, desperately trying to think of the ways a murderer gave himself away. Fidgeting. I kept my hands in my lap. Stammering. I kept my mouth shut. Afraid to look other people in the eye. I looked Miss Mellon in the eye. She smiled, exactly as if it were an ordinary day. But she was a teacher. Detectives could spot a murderer a mile away. One look was enough. You could never hide your guilt from *them*. They had ways.

A door slammed, I stiffened.

Here come the police.

Outside, someone shouting; I nearly jumped out of my seat.

Here come the police.

Footsteps in the corridor; I broke into a cold sweat.

Here come the police.

Ever since I woke up, a terrible pain in my stomach; it felt like rats trapped inside me, trying to claw their way out.

Colin was terrified, it was written all over his face, but Marek looked the same as usual, stony-faced as Eliot Ness.

'Marek, I'm worried, I . . .'

'Not here!' he hissed. 'Someone might hear us.'

We were in a corner of the playground.

'We'll meet after school, talk then. Come on, let's go and play football, just like we would any other day.'

★ ★ ★

We met in a little square off Caradoc Road. A couple of benches surrounded by a low hedge, a ruined flowerbed, littered with empty cider bottles and crushed cigarette packets. Colin stared at the ground, chewing the remains of his fingernails. Marek kept his hands in his pockets, looking one way, then another, every few seconds.

'I didn't mean to kill him.'

Marek snapped at me.

'Pull yourself together. We've no idea how seriously he's injured. All communists are cowards, a tiny little scratch is enough to set them off bawling. Now listen, we have taken an oath of loyalty. All of us are engaged in the war against communism, fighting side by side, taking the same risks.'

'But I'm the only one to have actually *hit* somebody.'

'I am the commanding officer, *I'm* the one who told you to fire, you and Colin were only obeying orders. So if anyone should be really worried, it's *me*.'

I wanted to believe it.

'We must maintain discipline. None of us will ever say a word about what happened to anyone outside the unit – *on pain of death*. The three of us were nowhere near Cwm Wood on that day – we played football on the rec, then went up to Belle Vue Park afterwards. Refuse to say anything else without a lawyer being present.'

'I haven't got a lawyer,' whined Colin.

'Just do what I tell you.'

'But . . .'

'Pull yourself together!'

Colin muttered something.

'What was that?'

He shook his head. A light went on in an upstairs window to our right.

'Remember they have no evidence. As long as we keep our mouths shut they can't do a thing. We just need to keep our nerve, OK?'

We nodded. I repeated it to myself. I chucked the stone. But I was only following orders. We were all in this together. That's how it was.

'Right, this meeting is over.'

We said goodbye to Marek at the top of Tredegar Avenue. Then Colin was off, surging down the street like an Olympic walker, going so fast I had to nearly run to keep up with him.

'What's the hurry?'

'I'm hungry, I want my tea.'

That wasn't it.

'Slow down – the last thing we want to do now is attract attention.'

'It's a bit late to think of that, isn't it?'

It felt like he'd slapped me.

'What do you mean?'

He stared straight ahead.

'What do you mean?'

Suddenly he was running. I chased after him.

'Colin!'

I caught up with him at the end of the avenue, pulled at his shoulder. He shrugged me off, stumbled. I grabbed the collar of his anorak and pulled. Nearly wrenched him off his feet.

'Fuck off.'

'Make me.'

We stood eyeball to eyeball, waiting to see who would throw the first punch. Neither of us moved a muscle.

'What did you mean by that?'

I watched the panic and rage fighting it out in his eyes.

'Nothing.'

The poisoned silence hung in the air between us.

'You heard what Marek said – we're all in this together. Any one of us could have hit that man with a stone.'

I waited for him to say it.

But you were the one who did.

'Colin, don't do this to me.'

His eyes filled with tears.

'We'll all go to hell. We'll burn for ever.'

He buried his face in his hands.

'No, we won't. We may have broken the law, but the Church would be proud of us. This is a war between communism and the Holy Roman Catholic Church – and we're in the front line. We're heroes! If the priests and nuns knew what we're doing, they'd be queuing up to shake our hands, give us their blessing, sprinkle us with holy water. They'd put up statues of us in Lourdes, and grateful Catholics would come from all over the world to lay flowers.'

I paused for breath, I was making it up as I was going along, desperately hoping he'd swallow it. Anyway it was true. I think it was.

'*And* it was an accident. I didn't *mean* to kill him. Just put the wind up him.'

He wiped the corners of his eyes with his knuckles, ran his finger under his nose.

'Heroes.'

He said it like someone who'd been put in a trance, told what to say by a hypnotist.

'That's right.'

He started gnawing his lower lip. It began to bleed from where he'd been at it before.

'I'm right, aren't I?'

He looked at me vacantly. He'd never be able to take the pressure. I loved him like a brother – not *my* brother, someone less spasticated – but he was spineless, I saw that now. I had to handle this very carefully, like a doctor treating a hysterical patient.

'Aren't I?'

He nodded. I didn't know whether he'd understood, or was just agreeing with me so I'd stop asking him questions and let him go home.

'Good man.'

I patted his shoulder.

'We're heroes, remember. OK, let's go.'

We walked the rest of the way in silence.

★ ★ ★

I grabbed the *Argus* from the floor, brought it into the living room, sat down on the sofa. I hadn't made the front page, the headline was *Llis-werry Man Up In Court For Neglect Of Dog*. I checked the other pages, every one – nothing. I didn't understand. Maybe it was a trap. A deadly game of cat and mouse, the police hoping I'd relax, and give myself away. In a few days, maybe next week, there'd be a knock on the door late at night, a detective and a couple of coppers standing outside.

The game's up, Bennett – the house is surrounded. Are you going to come quietly?

Or maybe he wasn't actually dead. They'd *always* report a murder, surely? Maybe I'd blinded him.

There he is, see him struggling up the steep streets of the Valleys with his new guide dog and a white stick.

'Oh God!'

Mam popped her head around the door.

'Is that the *Argus* you're reading?'

'Yeah.'

She looked at me oddly.

'Since when have you been so interested in the news?'

'Mam – do they have stories about the Valleys in the *Argus*?'

She pursed her lips.

'Now and then . . . not very often. They have their own papers up there. Why?'

'No reason.'

Whatever she'd been wondering about she put to the back of her mind, left the room.

★ ★ ★

I waited till Mam was doing the washing up, Dad was in the bath, then pulled Michael into the hall.

'Do you know what'll happen if you don't keep your mouth shut about the other day?'

He wouldn't look at me. He did that now. Tried to ignore me. He knew though. Knew something was coming. But he didn't know what. I grabbed a handful of his hair, twisted his head around so that it faced the cellar door.

'I'll push you down there again, and I'll lock you in this time.'

I waited.

'The . . .'

'What?'

'Key's missing.'

'That's what you think.'

I reached inside my pocket, held up a key in front of his face.

'See that?'

I'd found it in the street a couple of weeks ago, knew it would come in useful.

'See – I'm always one step ahead. I'm much smarter than you. And much stronger. And better looking.'

I pushed the key into his cheek. He tried to turn away. I pushed harder, till tears filled his eyes.

'I'll tie you up, stuff a dirty rag from under the sink in your mouth. Lock the door behind me, leave you to rot. No one will ever think of looking down there. They don't know I've got a key. It'll take you weeks to die. Choking on a rag stinking of cherry blossom polish, pissing yourself in the dark and cold.'

It was his own fault I was this nasty to him. He drove me to it. If he wasn't so pathetic I'd be able to stop. Why couldn't he stand up for himself just once?

I rammed his face into the cellar door. He made a pathetic bleating noise.

'Are you going to keep your mouth shut?'

'Yes.'

I let him go. Normally I would have spun it out, but I didn't have the heart for it right now. I had too much else on my plate. There was something else I needed to do urgently.

★   ★   ★

I felt better as soon as I walked inside the church – the soothing silence, the welcoming soft glow of the candles in the corner, the gentle clacking of shoes on tiles as someone walked up the aisle. I had to make a confession. Had to. If I was run over by a bus when I had a mortal sin on my soul I'd go straight to hell. Ask God to forgive me, even though it was an accident, and I was only defending the Church against communism.

I entered the confessional, closed the door behind me, knelt and kissed the punctured feet of Jesus writhing on the cross. Behind the screen I could make out a shadowy figure bent over, murmuring a prayer. He finished, my cue to begin. Suddenly my throat, my tongue, were paralysed. What was wrong with me? *Come on, don't be soft. Be a man.* It was only Father Gillespie, poor old Gillo.

Ah, God love him, the poor auld craytur.

That's what Mam and Bridie said whenever anyone mentioned him. He was practically an invalid. Sometimes, during mass, his eyelids would start to flutter, his mouth begin working away on its own.

P . . . P . . .

Come on, Gillo, you can do it.

P . . . P . . . P . . .

Good man, you're nearly there.

Pea . . . Pea . . .

We're all rooting for you.

Peas . . . Peas . . .

Attaboy, Gillo!

Peace be with you.

Yes! He did it! Gillo! Gillo!

It was only Gillo, the poor auld craytur, what was I waiting for? I took a deep breath, opened my mouth.

'Are you ready to start?'

I nearly hit the roof. Jesus, it was Father Walsh. What was *he* doing here? It was *always* Father Gillespie on a Wednesday. Mad Dog Walsh, that was what Preece called him. I could just picture Father Walsh stealing through enemy lines in the dead of night, his face blackened, a dagger in one hand, swift and deadly, slitting the guard's throat in one expert movement. That kind of thing would be right up his street. But he hadn't joined the commandos. He'd become a priest. And now, instead of wreaking havoc behind enemy lines he was separated from me by only a thin wooden wall and a square of black wire mesh, and beginning to lose his temper.

'I'm waiting.'

He was always losing his temper when he was training altar boys. He'd hit one so hard he'd sent him tumbling down the steps. Pulled another into the air by his ear when he didn't swing the incense the right way.

You're not a Red Indian sending smoke signals, ya whelp ya.

'Hello, is there anyone there?'

But he was still a priest. Bound by a holy oath. Like that priest in the film. He'd been the only witness to a murder. The murderer knew the priest had seen him do it, went and confessed to him before he had a chance to go and tell the police. That way he was safe – a priest could never reveal the secrets of the confessional box. He had to take them with him to the grave.

'I haven't got all night.'

The chair behind the screen creaked as he shifted position irritably. The priest in that film was gentle and sad. But this was Father Walsh. He'd start screaming blue murder as soon as I began to tell him what had happened, no chance of being able to explain how I was only defending the faith, that if the communists got into power they'd round up every last priest and nun. He'd rip out the wire mesh and grab me by the throat before I got on to all that.

Ya evil little whelp ya! What the divil were you thinking of, chucking stones at people like that? I'll teach you a lesson you'll never forget.

'Right, I'll count to five, and if you haven't started by then . . .'

I got up from my knees. Slipped out the door, put my head down, headed straight out of the church. Didn't even stop to dip my finger in the holy water and bless myself on the way. As soon as I hit the street I started running.

* * *

The lunch hour was over, we were on our way back to class. Marek bent down to tie up a shoelace. I dropped back.

'I'm worried about Colin.'

'You're right to be worried.'

'He's—'

'I know.'

He finished tying his lace, stood up.

'Leave him to me. I know how to deal with Colin.'

I didn't like the strange glint in his eye. After school we met in the square off Caradoc Road again. It was freezing, beginning to snow, big wet flakes settling on Colin and Marek's hair, the tips of their eyelashes. Marek said, 'Are you ready?'

'For what?'

He took out the knife. My heart started racing.

I know how to deal with Colin.

He pointed it at Colin. Gave him a long look, allowed him plenty of time to see how sharp the blade was. How snugly it fitted into his hand.

See – carrying a knife is no big deal to me.

My guts churned. I got ready to jump between them. Then, without taking his eyes off Colin, Marek raised his other hand, sliced into the fleshiest part of his thumb.

'What are you doing? You're mad!'

I didn't get it. Then I did. Fantastic, what better way to make Colin keep his trap shut?

'Now you.'

Marek grabbed Colin's hand. Colin gasped as the blade cut him, stared in horror at the blood seeping out of his thumb.

'Aaaagh!'

Me next. I held out my thumb, looked into Marek's eyes. *Go ahead, cut me open.* Felt the blade slashing into me, the sharp, shocking pain, the hot, urgent flow of blood. I bit down on my lip, never moving my eyes from his.

'There.'

Marek held out his bleeding thumb. I raised mine.

'Colin.'

I watched him finally get it, move across and join us.

We pressed our thumbs together. It stung like hell. I had to

163

hold my breath so I wouldn't flinch. The blood pooled, slid down our hands, inside our sleeves, trickled down our arms. I began to feel light-headed, the way I did after Holy Communion. We looked at each other in a new way, each weighing the other up, wondering how far we might have to go now we'd done this. Colin looked scared, Marek looked like he was ready for anything. I was scared and excited at the same time.

'Now we are blood brothers.'

I could stop worrying about Colin. Now he'd *have* to keep his trap shut. I'd seen it in a film. Two braves, Running Bear and Cunning Fox, became blood brothers. Running Bear was captured by the cavalry, made to work as a scout, hunting down his own kind. Many years later, in the heat of battle, his blood brother, Cunning Fox, jumped him from behind. He wrestled Running Bear to the ground, had a knife at his throat before he realised. *You!* He recoiled in horror.

'How *could* you?'

He spat in Running Bear's face, he burst into tears, let him go. Cunning Fox threw away the knife, walked straight in front of a cavalry officer pointing his gun.

Go ahead, shoot, I don't want to live any more.

Bang, right in the head. Running Bear burst into tears, picked up the knife, cut his own throat. That's how it was. You stuck by your blood brother, no matter *what* he did. We had a special bond that would last forever now, Marek, Colin and I. Our loyalty to each other was stronger than anything else in the world. Even if Poland and Wales were at war, it wouldn't make any difference, we'd still lay down our lives for each other. Marek was a genius.

★ ★ ★

Nothing in the *Argus* the following night either. Were they toying with me? The terror was creeping back; even having two

164

blood brothers who'd have to cut their own throats rather than give evidence against me didn't make me feel better. I looked out the window, saw Dad pulling the wheelbarrow out of the shed. I'd go out with him, it would be much better than sitting inside on my own, waiting for the knock on the door. I ran outside.

'Can I come?'

'Hurry up.'

I rushed inside, pulled some more clothes on, ran back out and caught up with him at the end of the back lane. We headed down the Docks Road.

'Christ, it's raw today – that wind's straight from Siberia.'

It cut right through me, even wearing my bobble hat, scarf, gloves, anorak and two jumpers. Dad wore his donkey jacket and cords, the only extra clothing he'd put on was a scarf. He'd lost his gloves and wasn't wearing his hat.

'Where's your hat?'

'I chucked it away. You must allow the head to breathe – ventilation is the key to all knowledge – if your head can't breathe, you won't be able to think straight. A fella from Ballymurphy I met on the boat last summer told me that.'

We went past the allotments, beyond the turning for the docks, where the town dribbled out into scrubby countryside. If they came for me now, out here, I'd make a run for it across the fields; they'd never find me.

'You can never have enough wood. People are soft nowadays, they think everything they need is always going to be laid on for them and they'll never have to lift a finger to help themselves. But you only need a power cut, or a big fall of snow, or for some of these lazy feckers to go on strike and suddenly everyone's in the shit.'

The road here was more like an Irish one – uneven, breaking up, full of potholes. A low sky the colour of wet cement hung over us. There were no buildings to break up the fierce Siberian wind, just a rusting corrugated fence stretching down one side of the road for a few hundred yards.

The hailstones came without warning, stinging my face, spraying the fence like buckshot, bouncing across the road. Dad started laughing. He had to shout to make himself heard above the din.

'Only mad dogs and Paddies go out in weather like this.'

I was cowering under the barrage of icy pellets, but Dad hardly batted an eyelid as the hailstones pinged off him. *Do your worst, fecking communist weather*, he seemed to be saying. *You'll not get the better of Brendan.* He's invincible, I thought, a man of iron, nothing bothers him. Why don't you just tell him what you've done, he'll help you. He'll be proud of you!

You fired stones at the communists? Good man, that's the only language those fellas understand.

Then he turned to one side, pinched his nostrils with his thumb and finger, fired a double barrel of snot on to the ground, became just Dad again, and the moment passed.

The hailstones began to ease off as we approached the railway line. Suddenly Dad's eyes lit up, he veered off the road, the axe clattering about in the wheelbarrow as he juddered across the frost-hardened bumpy ground. Stopped next to a pile of uprooted, neatly stacked sleepers by the side of the railway line.

'Oho, we'll have these lads.'

'Is it all right to just take them?'

'Who's going to stop me?'

He was already reaching for the axe.

'We'll never get them home, they're massive.'

He looked at me sharply.

'Oh, I'll get them home all right, don't you worry about that, boy.'

He adjusted his stance, began swinging.

'Uggghhn!'

Thunk!

'Uggghn!'
Thunk!
I stood and watched him.
'Uggghhn!'
Thunk!
'Uggghn!'
Thunk!

He was like a machine, didn't pause, slow down, or weaken for a second. It was a contest between him and the wood, and there was only going to be one winner. He was strong as a bull, he'd knock the police aside like skittles if they came for me.

The first one of you that lays a hand on my son will get this axe in their gob.

I had to stick close to him. He was my best chance of staying out of jail.

'Uggghhn!'
Thunk!
'Uggghn!'
Thunk!
'Uggghn – yafecker!'
Thunk!

It was in half. He stepped back, panting, mouth hanging open. He stared at his handiwork.

'Am I strong?'

'Yeah.'

He smiled, wiped a thread of spittle from his lip, winked at me.

'Fecking right I am. It'd take a hell of a blow to put me down.'

He chucked the axe into the wheelbarrow, spat on his hands.

'We've got to get the bastard home now. Are you a chip off the old block?'

I nodded.

'Good man, then you can give me a hand.'

Dad laughed to himself.

'Jayzus, "a chip off the old block", they have some quare expressions. Come on . . .'

I kept the wood steady while he pushed the wheelbarrow. Every few feet I thought I heard something.

Here come the police.

'You're quare jumpy today, what's the matter with you?'

'Nothing.'

He laughed scornfully.

'Do you think some fellas from British Rail are going to come after us?'

'No – yeah.'

'Well, you can stop worrying, we're not going to meet anyone else on a night like this.'

I hoped not. Who knows what might happen once they got you down the police station? Begin by accusing you of stealing wood, end up dragging a murder confession out of you. He started laughing again.

'You could push a barrow-load of sleepers down the main street in Ireland on Saturday afternoon with a big sign on it saying *Property of the Irish Railway Board*, wearing a bleddy mask and no one would take a blind bit of notice of you. Least of all the bleddy gardai – they're nothing but a bunch of thick culchies.'

That's when it hit me. It was so obvious, why hadn't I thought of it sooner? We had to move to Ireland. As soon as possible. The perfect place if you were on the run from the law. Everyone knew how useless the gardai were, they never caught anyone. Just look at Uncle Sean's car. The tax disc years out of date, no insurance, a hole in the floor, no wing mirrors, cardboard filling one window. Drove it past the gardai station at Ballyhack every morning and every evening.

If I took this out for a drive in Wales I'd be arrested on the spot and me poor auld car towed off to the scrapheap. But I've been driving it for years over here and never had any trouble from those eejits – Jayzus, officer O'Laurel and officer O'Hardy I call them.

'Dad – how long before we move to Ireland?'

'Well now . . .'

'A couple of weeks?'

'Jayzus, what's come over you?'

'I've just been thinking about what you said – how we need to get Mam and Michael away from the front line.'

'Good man, I'm glad at least *one* other member of the family has some common sense. We have to sell the house first, of course.'

'Why?'

He laughed.

'Because we need the money, ya eejit.'

'How long will that take?'

'Jesus, I don't know, boy. Two or three months, maybe.'

Two or three months! I couldn't stand another two or three months of this! I'd go mad.

'Let's just go!'

He burst out laughing.

'Christ – will you hold your horses. The first thing we have to do is persuade your mother.'

'How long will *that* take?'

'It won't be easy. I'll need your help.'

'OK.'

He laughed, clapped me on the shoulder with his huge paw.

'That's the spirit. Jayzus, we'll make a great team.'

★ ★ ★

'You seem very nervous these last few days, Liam. Is everything all right?'

Miss Mellon had taken me to one side. This was bad. Terrible in fact. She wasn't even a detective. If *she* could see how scared I was, what chance did I have of fooling the police?

'Nothing, Miss, really. Thanks for asking.'

She stepped closer. Her perfume was as sweet and mysterious as incense. Her hair fell forward, and I watched as she slowly pushed it back behind her ear.

'Are you *sure*, Liam? Whatever you say in this room will just be between you and me.'

The classroom door was shut, everyone else was out in the playground. *Tell her!*

'Well?'

Tell her. You couldn't tell Father Walsh, you couldn't tell Dad. You'll go mad if you don't tell someone.

'I . . .'

'Yes?'

She smiled, a beautiful smile, a smile that said *you know I'd never tell anyone else.*

'I . . .'

'Mmm?'

'I've got a stomach ache – I've had it for days now.'

The disappointment on her face. She didn't buy it for a minute. I hated lying to her, she'd always been lovely to me. She was the only one who'd asked if I was OK, Mam and Dad hadn't noticed anything different about me. I *wanted* to tell her. I couldn't. She'd hate me if I told her the truth.

'Have you told your mother?'

I shook my head.

'I will though – tonight.'

'Yes, I think you should, Liam.'

She paused, gave me a last chance to tell her what it *really* was. I hung my head. She sighed.

'OK, run along now. We'll talk again some other time.'

'Yes, Miss.'

The moment I was back out in the corridor, I felt a sinking sensation in the pit of my stomach. *You should have told her.*

★ ★ ★

I was walking down Pugsley Street with Marek and Colin after school. Saw a copy of the *Argus* on a bench. Ran over, grabbed it. *There'll be something in there today, I can feel it.*

Nothing on the front page.

'Shit!'

Tore it turning it over too quickly. Colin couldn't understand why I was so frantic.

'It's only the *Argus*. Don't you get it delivered?'

Second page – no.

Third page – no.

Marek said, 'What are you looking for?'

'This!'

There – on the fourth page. A photo. I felt an iron band tighten round my chest.

'Look!'

'What?'

'It's him.'

'Who?'

'*Him!*'

'Who?'

'The ginger-haired man – look.'

I pointed at the photo. A bloke about Mr Williams's age, staring into the camera, looking sorry for himself, a plaster covering the bridge of his nose.

'He's alive!'

An enormous weight lifted from me. The feeling you got after you'd been to confession; no, a hundred times better. Weightless, dizzy, giddy, giggly. I jumped on to the bench and punched the air.

'I'M INNOCENT!'

An old lady walking her dog looked round, startled. Her dog started barking at me. I was laughing.

'I'M A FREE MAN!'

Marek grabbed the *Argus*, stared at the photo, scowling.

'A scratch, nothing but a scratch on him. Didn't I tell you all communists were cowards and cry babies?'

I jumped down off the bench. I did a mad Red Indian dance around Marek and Colin, my hand over my mouth, whooping and singing.

Hey na na na, hey na na na!

Then I remembered to get angry, pointed my finger at the photo of the man.

'Bastard – putting me through all that for nothing.'

Colin peered over Marek's shoulder at the photo.

'Putting *us* through it.'

'Stinking coward, I *speet* on you!'

I sucked, hawked.

'No!' shouted Marek, snatching the page away. 'I want to read it.'

What was there to read? He was alive, what else did we need to know? Colin punched me playfully on the shoulder.

'I was behind you all the way, mate. They could have pulled my teeth out one by one with rusty pliers and I *still* wouldn't have . . .'

'Yeah, thanks.'

The worst thing was, I think he actually believed it. Marek slapped the paper with his hand.

'Look, look at what they're saying about us.'

He held up the page for us to see, pointing to the writing beneath the photo.

Mark Evans – victim of mindless thugs.

'Hey – we're not thugs.'

That was libel. We could sue them.

172

'Listen to this,' said Marek. ' "For months passengers have been demanding action about the growing problem of hooliganism on the Valleys line. Trains have been pelted with stones every day at dozens of places along the route." '

'Dozens of places?'

'How dare they lump us together with a bunch of mindless thugs.'

'But . . .'

'What?'

'Maybe there are other branches of the anti-communist resistance,' said Colin.

'No, I would have heard about them. We are the only genuine resistance movement. There are nothing but yobbos further up the line, believe me.'

'Damn.'

It started to rain, big fat drops soaking the page, Marek folded it up quickly, stuffed it under his arm. I didn't care, I'd heard all I needed to know. I was innocent.

'It's pouring, let's go.'

I raced Colin down the street, laughing, punching the air, jumping in puddles.

'I'M A FREE MAN!'

* * *

Dad stuck his head round the back door, looked at Mam struggling with the steaming saucepans, puffing and blowing like a stoker.

'Oh God, I'm killed.'

Caught my eye, beckoned me outside. He stooped down and winked at me.

'Tonight's the night.'

'For what?'

'To begin stage one of Operation Move Back To Ireland – Brainwash The Wife.'

I'd forgotten about *that*, now that I was a free man again. It wasn't fair, I'd hardly had time to draw breath since discovering I was innocent, why did we have to do it *now*? But I'd promised to help, *begged* him to move to Ireland as soon as possible, couldn't turn around and say I'd changed my mind a day later.

'Now of course I'd be within my rights to just *demand* she does whatever I say.'

He pulled a fierce face, jabbed his finger in the air.

'"Go upstairs and pack your bags, we're moving back to Ireland. *Go on, willya, get a bleddy move on!*"'

A smile crept across his face as he imagined the scene.

'After all, when we were married she took an oath to love, honour and *obey* me. Oh yes, I'd be well within my rights. But here's some advice for you, Liam – be careful, women are a different kettle of fish entirely to a man.'

He peered into the middle distance.

'If you've got a dispute with another fella, you can take him to one side and sort it out man to man – lay your cards on the table, call a spade a spade, and he won't take offence.'

He paused, reflecting on something.

'Unless he's had too much to drink of course, then he's likely to call you a cunt and punch you in the gob.'

He chewed his lip.

'Oh aye, you want to watch what you say in a pub near closing time. But!' He hurried on, determined not to get bogged down. '*Usually*, a couple of fellas will be able to sort out any problems after a bit of straight talking. But women aren't like that. They take offence more easily than a man. They store up grudges. They'd turn against you and you wouldn't know why, and then you'd never get a civil word out of them for the rest of your life.'

He shook his head sadly, a head brimming with a store of bad memories.

'It'd take yer man fecking Sherlock Holmes to work out what was going on in their heads, there's no rhyme or reason to it. That's why you have to use *cunning!*'

He paused, smiling, delighted with his explanation so far.

'Your mother can be a very stubborn woman. It's no use trying to reason with that one, she hates reason like a cat hates water. No, we're going to try a different approach.'

He tapped his forehead.

'We're going to use *psychology*, do you see?'

'No, I don't.'

'Ha! You will. I'll soon have her eating out of my hand. What are the Irish famous for?'

'Eating spuds.'

'No!'

They were.

'For *blarney!* A magical way with words – all the Paddies have it, it's in their blood. Do you understand now?'

'Yeah.'

I didn't, not really.

'Good man. I'll go in first, and when I give the signal you come in and back me up. You got that?'

'What do you want me to do?'

'Agree with me.'

★ ★ ★

'Mmmm,' said Dad, after the first mouthful of his dinner. 'Your mother's a grand cook, isn't she, Liam?'

He gave me a meaningful look. I swung into action.

'Yes, she is.'

Mam paused, the fork halfway to her mouth, a startled expression on her face. Dad shoved another piece of stringy beef into his gob.

'Ah yeah, grand grub, grand grub . . . considering.'

175

Mam stiffened.

'Considering what?'

'What you've got to work with – your basic ingredients, like. These spuds for example, they're terrible waxy auld things, nothing like the lovely spuds you'd get back home in Ireland – Jayzus, balls of flour, they are. And this beef, Christ, if I'd seen the poor auld craytur when it was still alive I'd have called the RSPCA, and had them put it down. Ah no, you can't beat a good bit of *Irish* beef.'

Mam dropped her knife and fork.

'*You* go and buy the food for a change if you think you can do any better.'

Usually Dad would have started roaring, but his face softened, he held up his hand.

'Ah now, you're missing my point.'

'What *is* your point?'

'You'd never get the grand natural ingredients here you would back in Ireland. So, no matter *how* good a cook you are, the food would never be as delicious as it would be back home.'

He began eating again. Mam looked like she was going to say something, changed her mind, slowly picked up her knife and fork.

'Ah Jayzus, you'd miss the auld country all the same, wouldn't you?'

He *smiled* at her. My mouth fell open. Mam's mouth fell open. Even Michael looked startled. I couldn't remember the last time one of them had smiled at the other. Dad ploughed on, not noticing how stunned we all were.

'Ah no, if you grew up in the countryside like you and me, you'd never really be happy in a town. Always breathing in petrol fumes, tiring your feet out walking on concrete all day, treading in dogshit, bleddy pigeons shitting on your head, factories pumping muck into the air – a town is a terrible place for a housewife, she'd put out clean washing in the morning and it'd be dirty again by the evening before she'd even taken it off the line.'

He clicked his tongue, shook his head.

'A woman's work is never done in a town.'

'And what about the boys, do you ever stop to think how *they'd* feel about living in Ireland?'

'Jayzus, let's ask them.'

He gave me another of his meaningful looks.

'Liam, do you miss Ireland?'

It was my cue to spring into action again.

'Yeah.'

Mam stared at me, furious and dismissive at the same time. I felt myself withering. She turned back to Dad.

'What are you up to?'

Dad looked offended.

'I'm just making conversation.'

'You don't usually make conversation.'

'Well, I am now, so don't bleddy well keep interrupting me.'

Irritation flickered briefly across his face, then he got it back under control.

'Now, where was I? Ah yeah, there you are, you see, Liam misses Ireland. His *true* home.'

He gave me a triumphant look. *Are you watching? This is called psychology.*

★ ★ ★

It was lunchtime, pouring down outside, we were all stuck in the classroom.

'I'm bored.' said Colin.

'Me too' said Joe 90.

Marek nodded, then rested his chin in his hand, stared at the floor.

'Yeah, me too,' I said, 'I'm *so* bored. My God, I'm bored. Bored, bored, bored.'

I was absolutely delighted. Happy as Larry. I'd never complain about being bored again, was looking forward to being bored rigid for the rest of the day. I'd had enough excitement these last few days to last me a lifetime. I didn't want to do anything. I yawned. I stretched. Tried to look miserable. A quiet life, that's what I wanted from now on. Wasn't going to get upset about anything ever again. Then Thommo peered in the door.

'Ye gods, look at them, it's like something from *Planet of the Apes*. Why don't you go out and get some fresh air?'

'It's raining, sir.'

'You big girl's blouse. When I was a lad . . .'

I couldn't bear to hear about Thommo's childhood again. How he walked ten miles across dale and hill to school, wading through flooded fields, his shoes tied around his neck.

Then I noticed the chess set he was carrying under one arm.

'Sir – do you like chess?'

'I do, as it happens, Bennett. How unusually observant of you.'

He thought he was hilarious. He didn't know about my secret weapon.

'Would you like a game?'

He laughed.

'What, with you?'

'No, sir, with my brother Michael.'

The smile vanished.

'Are you trying to be funny, lad?'

'No sir, he's brilliant. He beat me and Colin easy.'

Thommo snorted.

'Is that supposed to impress me?'

'Are you a good player, sir?' asked Colin, copping on.

'Well, I'm not one to blow my own trumpet . . .'

I didn't know where to look, he never stopped boasting.

178

'I was telling Michael what a good chess player you were, sir, how much he could learn from playing you. He'd love a game, but he's too shy to ask.'

Thommo frowned. 'Well, if he . . .'

'Shall I get him?'

'Eh?'

I was halfway to the door.

'He'll be so excited.'

I raced down the corridor to the nippers' room. It was bedlam in there. They were climbing on the seats, shouting at the top of their voices, chucking paper aeroplanes, chasing each other round the desks.

Michael sat on his own, staring out of the window, expressionless.

'Come on, Thommo wants to play you at chess.'

I put my arm around his shoulder in the corridor, made my voice nice and soft.

'You can beat him.'

He looked away.

'Just play the way you did against me and Colin and you'll have nothing to worry about.'

He should be glad I was encouraging him. I didn't have to be this nice. It was big of me. I stepped in front of him, put my hands on his shoulders, stared into his eyes.

'You're my brother. I'll be behind you all the way. I'm here to take care of you. There's nothing to worry about.'

He looked straight through me. I didn't mean to pull the buttons off his shirt. The top two were loose already, flew off when I grabbed him. He asked for it. Here I was, sticking my neck out, telling people the little runt was brilliant and *this* is how he repays me. He could have put *his* arm around *my* shoulder, said, 'Thanks, Liam, I'll make you proud of me.' We could have walked into that classroom a team. But no, he had to provoke me.

'If you lose I'll bloody kill you. Now get in there, you ugly little spaz.'

I pushed him towards the door.

Thommo was setting up the chess set on the teacher's desk at the front of the classroom. Everyone had gathered round to watch, even Preece and his mates.

'Now then, lad, I hear you're a bit of a chess player.'

'He's a natural.'

'I'm sure he can speak for himself, can't you, Michael?'

He nodded. Thommo beckoned him over to the desk, leant down, laid his hand on his shoulder.

'You *do* know how to play, don't you?'

'Yes, sir.'

Thommo picked up a piece.

'What's this called?'

'A horse, sir.'

Thommo took a deep breath.

'It's a knight!'

He clenched his teeth.

'And do you know how the knight moves?'

Michael showed him.

'See, sir, he knows how to play.'

Thommo ignored me.

'Right, let's get started.'

They sat down on opposite sides of the desk, began to play. Thommo made the same mistake as me and Colin. Tried to get it over with quickly, crush him like a bug. He hardly glanced at Michael's moves, didn't think there was any point, carried on picking his teeth, gazing at the big fat raindrops streaming down the windows.

'What was that, lad?'

Michael's voice was barely a whisper.

'Checkmate, sir.'

Thommo frowned.

'Eh?'

I nudged Colin, did the David Coleman voice.

'One–nil!'

I loved the way he said that – it sounded like a guillotine coming down. There was no way back after Coleman said 'One–nil!' You'd had it. Thommo's eyes scanned the board, wondering how the trap had been sprung. A smile slowly formed on Preece's lips. Thommo's shoulders lifted, stiffened.

'Well played.'

His voice was low, hoarse.

'Told you he was good, sir.'

I knew what was coming next.

'Well, that was fun, wasn't it? Fancy a rematch?'

Michael looked up at me. I nodded. *Go on!*

'Yes, sir.'

Thommo hunched over the board now, taking longer over his moves, watching Michael's like a hawk. The action was slower this time. By the time the first pawn was taken, they'd already been playing for longer than the whole first game had lasted. I couldn't work out who was winning. Thommo was blocking Michael's attacking moves, but he hadn't managed to threaten Michael's king with any of his own. Colin started to fidget.

'Why's he taking so long?'

'Relax,' I hissed.

More kids from Michael's class streamed in to watch. Miss Mellon standing behind them, arms folded. Michael struck like lightning, Thommo was completely different, stepping up the pressure bit by bit, slowly building up a head of steam, cranking and grinding away like a big, heavy machine. The minutes ticked by. Michael was defending well, but how long could he keep it up? He needed to break out.

'Check.'

Michael reluctantly moved his queen across to protect his

king, knowing it was only delaying things. Thommo picked her off with one of his bishops.

'That's checkmate, lad, if I'm not mistaken.'

A groan went up from the crowd.

'What went wrong?' whispered Colin.

'Don't know.'

Michael wouldn't look at me, the little spaz.

'Hard luck, Michael,' said Miss Mellon. 'That was a wonderful game, wasn't it, children?'

'Yes, Miss.'

'Are you going to play another game, Mr Thompson?'

The way she said it gave the game away, very slowly and deliberately, like she was talking to someone who didn't understand English. She was asking Thommo to let Michael win the next one. No chance. Not Thommo. I didn't want that either.

'Best of three it is, then,' said Thommo, not meeting Miss Mellon's eyes.

It was a replay of the second game. Thommo like a machine cranking and grinding, Michael blocking and dodging. My heart sank. Michael winning the first game had put Thommo on his guard, but now he was charging at Michael all guns blazing. It was stupid to think Michael could have beaten an adult. He thought the knights were called horses, for Christ's sake. Beating me and Colin had been a fluke. If I played him again tonight I'd beat him easy.

'What's wrong with him?' hissed Colin.

'I . . . wait, look.'

Suddenly Michael was attacking again, taking a pawn, a knight, another pawn. He brought up a bishop. Thommo took one of Michael's knights. Michael's queen took the knight. Thommo blocked the queen, left a gap in his defences for Michael's bishop to make his move.

'Checkmate, sir.'

Everyone held their breath. It had happened too fast for anyone to take in properly. We waited for Thommo to say, 'Not quite, lad,' block the danger, put the pressure back on Michael.

Miss Mellon said, 'Are you all right, Mr Thompson?'

He didn't reply. Just carried on staring at the board. No one dared move or speak. Miss Mellon stepped forward, put her hand on Michael's shoulder.

'Well done, Michael, you've won.'

A huge cheer went up. Michael looked at me, a bewildered mouse caught in a headlight. I clenched my fist, grinned at him.

Yes!

It had worked, I'd terrified him into beating Thommo. I was like Shankly, he made hard men like Big Ron Yeats and Tommy Smith shake in their boots. That was the only way to get results – to make your players more frightened of you than the opposition.

Thommo sat in a pool of silence. He turned his head like a robot, reached out an arm, began stiffly gathering up the pieces, dropping them back into their box. Miss Mellon leant down, so that her face was level with Michael's.

'You have a real gift.'

'Thank you, Miss.'

I elbowed some of the younger kids out of the way.

'Where did you learn to play?'

'I taught him, Miss.'

She looked my way, smiled, turned back to Michael.

'I'll bet you were a quick learner.'

'He was very slow at first, Miss, but I kept on pushing him, because I could see he had talent.'

She nodded.

'He thought I was bullying him, but I'll bet he's grateful now that I pushed him so hard.'

'I'll bet he is.'

Her smile looked forced, I thought she was going to ignore me. Then her face softened.

'That was very thoughtful of you, Liam.'

She was impressed. No wonder. Not many people would have done that for their kid brother. A chair scraped along the floor, Thommo got to his feet. Miss Mellon said, 'Thank you, Mr Thompson, that was very entertaining.'

He glared at her.

'Was I?'

She reddened, opened her mouth to reply.

'So glad you enjoyed it.'

He blamed her. He hated her. Was going to find some way of making her pay. He picked up his chess box, stomped out. I didn't mean for that to happen.

Kids were scrambling all over each other to get close to Michael.

'Well done, mate.'

'You showed him.'

Slapping his back, shaking his hand, ruffling his hair. I was pushed to one side, my part in the victory forgotten. He'd be nothing without me to push him, the spineless slug. Even Colin was joining in, patting his shoulder, grinning like an idiot.

'He's my mate's brother. I was there the night we discovered he was a genius.'

A couple of the nippers were reaching out to touch the sleeve of Michael's jumper, as if some of his genius would rub off on them. He was a superstar. It would be all over the school by the end of the day – *Michael Bennett is the George Best of chess, pass it on*. I could feel it already, I'd made a huge mistake, had done something I'd never stop regretting. I'd opened Michael's cage, pushed him out, let him taste freedom, now I'd never get him back inside again.

★ ★ ★

Dad speared a spud, started bringing it up to his mouth, then hesitated.

'Did you hear about the Irish fella who died of a broken heart?'

Mam gave him a look, carried on with her dinner.

'I read it in the paper from home. He'd lived in this country for over thirty years. Strong as a horse, never missed a day's work in his life. No one ever saw him with a cold or flu. He was as fit as a fiddle when he retired, anyone passing him in the street would have thought he was a man of fifty. And do you know what?'

Mam kept her head down over her plate. Dad rapped on the table with his knife.

'Hey – did you hear me?'

'I heard you,' she muttered, not looking up. He scowled, carried on.

'He died a few months after retiring. The doctor couldn't find a thing wrong with him. Completely baffled, he was. Then he noticed how the fella's room was filled with mementoes of the auld country, and piles of tear-stained letters from his family back in County Cork wondering when he was coming home. And the doctor – a medical man now, not some thick bleddy peasant – the doctor said the only conclusion he could come to was that he'd died of a broken heart. Isn't that a terrible story?'

He stared at Mam, waiting. She turned to Michael, prodded his arm gently with her hand.

'Come on now, Michael, eat up your cabbage.'

Dad took a deep breath.

'Wouldn't that be an awful thing to happen?'

Mam ignored him. He faltered for a moment, then gave me the look.

'Liam – do you miss Ireland?'

'Yeah.'

'You hear that? Wouldn't that be a terrible thing for a mother to have on her conscience?'

'What?' she snapped irritably.

'For her son to have died of a broken heart because he was missing Ireland so much.'

She screwed up her face.

'Jesus, I can't stand much more of this.'

She got up, left the room. Dad nudged me, smiling.

'She's cracking. What did I tell you?'

★ ★ ★

Preece walked over to where Michael was signing autographs in the corner of the playground. Waited, hatchet-faced, till he'd finished writing his name on Gina Esposito's plaster cast. Then gripped his shoulder, tugged him away from the jostling crowd, marched him away.

Jesus Christ!

My stomach knotted. Where was he taking him? I had to do something, couldn't let Preece pick on my brother without putting up a fight, I'd never be able to hold my head up in the street. I'd just have to hope Marek and Colin would back me up. I looked round but they weren't there. Shit. Preece was steering Michael round the corner, out of the playground. Our kid. The baby of the family, dragged off by the meanest kid in school.

Come on, don't be soft. Be a man.

I had to rescue him. Now. I raced after them. They disappeared behind the bike shed. I slowed down, tried to control my breathing, got my hard-man scowl in place, rehearsed my opening line.

Come on, Preecey, pick on someone your own size.

Or:

Just leave him, all right?

Or even:

Back off, baldy.

I turned the corner. Preece was leaning against the wall,

talking, Michael standing next to him, not daring to meet his eyes, staring down at his shoes.

'I used to think you were a complete spaz, like Liam, but you're all right.'

A freezing hand grabbed my guts and squeezed. A truce, that's what I thought me and Preece had. Old enemies no longer at war. Not friends, no, never. There were certain things I'd never forget. *Wun, too, tree.* But a slowly growing respect.

A complete spaz like Liam.

Cold sweat prickled my forehead. I'd been fooling myself all this time. I needed to go to the toilet. I wanted the ground to open up beneath me.

'I can still see the look on Thommo's face.'

It had taken me years to carve out a niche for myself in school. Years of fights, bitter arguments, anxious stand offs. Till eventually I gained a foothold, a place where I had respect, a reputation, a name. Years. Now Michael had the whole place grovelling at his feet in ten minutes flat.

Thanks to me.

A complete spaz like Liam.

I didn't want to hear any more. I had to get out of there, quick. I dragged a piece of glass across the ground under my sole as I turned. Preece's head shot round.

'What are you doing here?'

'I thought . . .'

Michael's eyes glided over me, no sign of recognition or interest. No idea of the risk I'd taken to make sure he was all right.

'Fuck off.'

He didn't even wait to see if I'd gone before he turned back to Michael, reached inside his pocket.

'Want a fag?'

★　★　★

We were sitting on the sofa in the Sikorskis' front room. Mr Sikorski was going through the same photo album Marek had shown us a few months before, Colin and me pretending it was all new to us.

'That's Ludwik, he was in my squadron. That's how I always remember him – sitting in his plane, waiting.'

The faintest tremor crept into Mr Sikorski's voice, a tiny hair-thin crack in the corner of a pane of glass.

'In his first week of action he was shot down. His plane caught fire. He managed to escape from the blazing cockpit and get his parachute open, but his legs were badly burned. He was so frightened of fire afterwards that he couldn't bring himself to light a cigarette. He would put one in his mouth and close his eyes while I lit it for him. He couldn't run any more – he'd never have reached his plane in time during a scramble – and naturally the commanding officer would have declared him unfit for duty if he'd found out. So he sat in his Hurricane for hours on end, waiting. I would often go and keep him company.'

He gently tapped Ludwik's head with his finger.

'*That* is courage.'

It was the bravest thing I'd ever heard. That and Douglas Bader. I looked at Ludwik again. He was smiling but his eyes were haunted. Mr Sikorski turned to me.

'It's OK to be frightened.'

He *knew*. He could tell how scared I got, was letting me know it was OK.

'Without fear there can be no courage.'

I tried to understand, *nearly* did, but it was like trying to grab a piece of paper blowing in the wind. Just as you thought you had it, it flew away again. I gave up trying, decided to store his words away till later, when I was on my own, when I could bring them out and examine them without anyone looking over my shoulder.

'Poor Ludwik.'

'What happened to him?'

'After the war, he tried to settle in this country, but he got homesick and eventually he returned to Poland. The communists made his life hell because he had fought in the RAF, and in their warped minds, that made him an enemy. He was framed – they accused him of spying for the British. They found him guilty, of course, then they shot him.'

The air flew out of my lungs. I looked again at Ludwik, sitting in the cockpit of his Hurricane. *They murdered a war hero. An invalid war hero.*

'See the things they do? If I ever got into an argument with a communist I'd tear him limb from limb.'

They rounded up priests and nuns, burned down churches, stopped the Poles from marching in the victory parade, had hundreds of nuclear missiles aimed at us.

They had to be stopped. We were the men to do it.

'Ah!' said Mr Sikorski, checking his watch. 'It's nearly time. I want you to hear something.'

He got up, turned on the radio on the writing desk, pulled the aerial up. I closed my eyes, listened to the whine from the radio as Mr Sikorski moved the dial. It reminded me of Dad, trying to find Radio Eirann in bed at night, his ear pressed up to the transistor, one of Mam's old stockings pulled down on his head, listening out for the diddley diddley music hidden in the snowstorm.

'The reception isn't very good today, it's probably – ah! Now I've got it.'

An angry man speaking very quickly in a strange language, every word sounding like an insult. Then the pips started.

'Now.'

A bugle playing a slow, haunting tune. It was like the Last Post, forcing you to be silent, still, to avoid catching anyone's eye while it lasted. Sadness filled the room. Then, without warning, right in

189

the middle of a note, it stopped. Mr Sikorski got up again, switched the radio off, noticed how puzzled Colin and I looked.

'That's how it's supposed to end.'

'Why?'

'Every day a man climbs to the top of the clock tower of Mariacki church in the marketplace in Cracow and plays that tune on the hour. Every hour of the day, every hour of the night, 365 days a year, to remind us.'

'Of what?'

'Hundreds of years ago, in that same tower, the watchman saw invaders coming – the Tartars. He grabbed his bugle and started playing the alarm, but before he could finish he was hit in the throat by an arrow, and the Tartars burnt Cracow to the ground. The most beautiful city in Europe, reduced to ashes and rubble. Ever since, a bugler plays that same tune, stopping at exactly the same place the watchman was killed. It's always been on the radio – even the communists wouldn't dare to try and change it. It is the sound of the Polish soul.'

We fell silent for a moment. What a way to go – an arrow in the throat. Colin clutched his throat, turned pale.

I loved this. This was men's talk. We'd waved goodbye to our childhood. None of the others in school had any idea of how dangerous the communist menace was, how near the third world war. Sometimes I envied their ignorance; it wasn't easy, facing up to how cruel and unfair and terrifying life was, but there was no turning back now.

* * *

Marek was excited.

'I've got something to show you.'

We were back in Cwm Wood for the first time since the day we'd attacked the train. He led Colin and me past the usual places, up on to a winding, overgrown track. We trudged over frozen, rutted mud. We fought through brambles and broken branches.

'Flipping heck, Marek, where are you taking us?'

The track got steeper, the trees thinned out a little as we neared the top. Marek came to a halt, breathing hard, pointed to the left.

'There.'

Partly hidden in the long grass, a concrete bunker.

'That, gentlemen, is our new HQ.'

'You're joking.'

'No.'

'I discovered it weeks ago. It's the perfect top secret location for the resistance. Come and have a look.'

We followed him. It was fantastic, looked just like something from a war film. Even had a slot in the front to fire a gun through.

'Look how high we are,' said Colin, making his hands into binocular shapes, 'you can see right out to sea.'

'That's the Bristol Channel,' said Marek. 'It's just England on the other side.'

Colin was annoyed.

'From here we can easily spot anyone who tries to attack from the front, and we can build defences to prevent a sneak attack from behind.'

We'd be invincible.

'Let's go inside.'

We followed him through the door, down steps into the murky, damp darkness.

'Phwooar!'

It stank of piss.

'Christ, it's colder in here than it is outside.'

'We'll be dry, and out of the wind. As for the cold, we can light a fire.'

That would be brilliant. I loved lighting fires. We'd soon have it spick and span and shipshape. No one else had a bunker.

Preece and his mates had to hang around on street corners till they were moved on. That was the difference between a gang and a resistance movement. Between a rabble and a disciplined unit. Between blood brothers and a crowd of yobbos. We were much more grown up than them, already knew things they never would; we deserved something special that no one else had. Like a concrete bunker. It was ours. We'd defend it to the death. Marek clapped his hands together.

'OK – let's get to work.'

* * *

First we built an early warning system, stringing up empty tins between trees. Then we started digging the mantraps. The work went slowly and we had to take turns; we only had one shovel, which Marek had nicked from his dad. By the third day, we'd dug six mantraps, covered them with long branches.

'Good work, men.'

We were sore, stiff, blackened, parched. Marek said, 'Let's celebrate.'

We followed him into the bunker, watched him take two bottles and three plastic cups from his bag. First he poured orange squash into each cup, then a slug of clear liquid from the other bottle.

'What's that?'

'Vodka.'

He savoured our shock, then handed us each a cup.

'Vodka is the perfect drink. It's guaranteed to blow your head off. It mixes well with just about anything, and it smells of nothing, so no one will know you've been drinking.'

My throat tightened

It's guaranteed to blow your head off.

Would I be man enough?

Marek raised his cup.

'Gentlemen, a toast – to the resistance.'

We held our cups in the air.

'The resistance.'

Slowly, carefully, like a man handling nitroglycerine, I brought the cup nearer to my mouth. I took a sip. A searing heat blasted through the sweet taste of the orange squash, charged down the back of my throat. It took my breath away, burnt my lungs, flooded my eyes. I turned away for a moment, took a long, deep breath.

Fuck!

My lungs were charred. My teeth were chattering. Marek looked at me, grinning.

'It's Polish vodka – the best. It has quite a kick, doesn't it?'

A strangled cry came from Colin. He dropped the cup, jumped to his feet. Stuck his hands round his throat like he was going to strangle himself. He looked like a man who'd just swallowed a bottle of rat poison.

'Uuuuggggggggghhhhhhhnn.'

'Try drinking it a little slower next time,' said Marek.

'Where did you get it?' I gasped.

'I siphon some off from Tata's bottles, a little at a time, so he won't notice.'

He drained his cup. It didn't seem to have any effect on him.

'Another?'

After his third cup, Colin was staggering around, chest out, singing.

'I'LL WALK A MILLION MILES FOR ONE OF YOUR GOALS, OH CRIIII-NDAU!'

'Let's get him home,' said Marek, packing his bag. 'I can't stand any more of this.'

I tried to get up, fell. Tried again, stumbled, started giggling.

'Here.'

I took Marek's hand, let him pull me up.

'Thanks, mate.'

'TWO-FOUR-SIX-EIGHT, WHO DO WE APPRECI-ATE?'

I leant on Marek to steady myself. We watched Colin wave an imaginary football scarf in the air.

'Ha ha – *lookarhim* – he's drink, I mean he's . . .'

'Help me grab him.'

We tried a pincer movement but Colin giggled and swerved at the last moment, ran up the steps. Marek rolled his eyes.

'Come on.'

There was a chilling scream. We rushed outside, saw a pair of legs flailing in the air.

'He's fallen into one of the mantraps.'

We dragged him out, brushed him off, calmed him down. It was getting dark by the time we got back to the bench where we'd left Michael. He jumped up as soon as he saw us. He'd been crying.

'You've been ages. People were staring at me.'

'Which people?'

'The same man went past twice. He asked me if I was on my own.'

Our kid. The baby of the family. I'd been too hard on him. Suddenly I was filled with a deep, fierce love for the little spaz.

'It's all right now, your big brother's here.'

I held out my arms to give him a hug, stumbled, threw up down his front.

★ ★ ★

Face down on the sofa, dying. My head splitting. The slightest movement in either direction and a scarlet, screaming pain shot through my skull. I was never going to drink vodka again in my life. My tongue lay thick and swollen in my parched throat, a dead slug. I made a superhuman effort, forced out a whisper.

'Michael.'

He was sitting on the chair opposite, reading a comic.

'Michael.'

He wouldn't look up. He'd heard me all right.

'Michael – can you get me a glass of water?'

He turned a page, folded it over. I'd kill him. When I recovered. The effort of saying so much had drained me. I closed my eyes, tried not to move, prayed for sleep to come and put me out of my misery.

★ ★ ★

Colin and me were cycling down the Docks Road to the Transporter Bridge. The first sight of it, when you turned the corner into Brunel Street, always twisted my stomach. It was the best bridge in the world, and it was ours. Towering over everything, huge pylons on both sides of the river, rows of steel cables stretching from the top across the road, over the rooftops and beyond.

Once I heard a bloke with a camera say they had one in Middlesbrough. He was lying. We had the only one.

This morning there were three cars and about a dozen people waiting. Colin said, 'It's still on the other side.'

He meant the platform that took you across. It hung from chains, suspended over the river. We cycled to the barrier, stood on our pedals, leant on the top.

'The gate's still open.'

There was a gate at both ends of the platform. When it wasn't very busy they'd wait a few minutes in case someone else turned up – the man who opened and closed the gates leaning on it, finishing his fag.

'Look.'

'Here it comes.'

Gliding silently, slowly across, like a slow-motion sequence in a film. It took four minutes to get from one side to the other, I'd timed it. As it got closer to our side, the drivers got back inside their cars, started the engines. Colin and I moved away from the gates. A bump and shudder, the man opening the gates on the platform, then the ones on the road. We were first on, parked our bikes, got a place on the benches at the front, wire stretching to the wooden roof to stop you falling into the river. The man waved one set of cars off, the next on. When it was busy I loved watching the careful way he directed the cars and lorries on to the platform, packing them on so close there was hardly an inch between them.

The driver sat in a cabin on top of the roof on the other side. It looked like a little pavilion, with a red peaked roof, a flagpole on top, the Welsh dragon fluttering in the wind. He was having a cup of tea from a flask. We stared at the sandwich box. Colin's dad had forgotten to take it into work and his mam had given us sixpence to bring it to him. It was making us hungry.

'Shall we open it?'

'No.'

'Just to see what he's having for lunch, just out of interest.'

'No.'

The gates closed, bell rang, platform shuddered gently, moved away from the barrier. I had one more go.

'Shall we open it?'

He hesitated.

'Shall we?'

'OK.'

He pulled off the lid. Two sandwiches, Ritz crackers, a piece of fruit cake, four biscuits and an apple. Colin pulled open the sandwich.

'Ham and mustard.'

Mustard, disgusting, it set your mouth on fire. He took out one of the crackers, broke it in half.

'We deserve something for coming all this way.'

I bit into it, rolled the salt crystals on my tongue. Tried to make it last, couldn't. I wanted another one. Colin finished his, reached inside again.

'What's this?'

A note slipped between the sandwich and the fruit cake. Colin took it out, unfolded it.

'What does it say?'

He was frowning. I looked over his shoulder.

Fancy an early night tonight? (nudge nudge!)

He looked embarrassed, tried to fold it back up, but a gust of wind blew it out of his hands.

'Shit!'

It wrapped itself around the netting, fluttering madly, like a trapped moth, then the wind sucked it out.

'Uh-oh!'

We knelt on the bench, our faces pressed against the wire, watching it soar and swoop in the wind, then drop down, disappear into the grey water.

★ ★ ★

We found Mr Williams's factory, the old man at the gate told us to go to Shed 6. Another man there told us he hadn't seen him for about half an hour.

'Try looking over there.'

Pointing to the hundreds of wooden crates stacked up outside.

'We'll *never* find him.'

'Hear that?'

'What?'

'Music.'

Coming from behind some boxes. We peeped through a crack, saw Colin's dad leaning back on his fork-lift truck,

197

smoking a fag, reading the *Daily Mirror*. He had a little tranny next to him, turned down low.

'Dad!'

'Fuck!'

He jerked upright, the *Daily Mirror* flew out of his hands.

'Jesus Christ, don't *do* that!'

We wheeled our bikes inside. He'd made a den in there just big enough for the fork-lift truck to fit.

'Just in time. I'm starving, I am.'

He poured some tea, opened the sandwich box, took a bite out of a sandwich.

'Like it? This is one of my hide-outs. Somewhere to escape from that bastard foreman.'

He took a sip from the tea.

'Herr Evans.'

A short, stout man with an angry face squeezed through a gap in the boxes.

'Speak of the Devil.'

'There you are – I've been looking for you for the last twenty minutes. What do you think you're playing at?'

'It's my lunch break.'

Evans checked his watch.

'It's one minute past midday. It's taken you more than a minute to pour that tea, start drinking it, and nearly polish off that sandwich.'

'Eh?'

'You've obviously knocked off early, and started having your lunch in the company's time.'

'Are you serious?'

Evans puffed himself up.

'I'll tell you how serious I am . . .'

'You're a right little Hitler, aren't you?'

It was as if Mr Williams had flipped a switch and sent an electric current through him.

'How dare you. I fought against Hitler. I went to war to preserve freedom for long-haired layabouts like you.'

'You were conscripted like everyone else.'

'You degenerate. You'll be sorry you said that.'

Mr Williams yawned and lay back, reaching for the tranny.

'Now if you've finished interrupting my lunch hour . . .'

He turned the tranny right up. A blood-curdling scream – 'Fire' by The Crazy World of Arthur Brown. Evans winced, stepped back. Then puffed out his chest.

'We've got your card marked, Williams.'

'Eh?'

'There are some big changes coming, and there'll be no room for shirkers and layabouts.'

Mr Williams tensed.

'What you talking about?'

Evans smirked triumphantly, knew he had him on the ropes now.

'You'll find out soon, don't you worry.'

★　★　★

I helped Dad carry the record player and records into the living room. Mam looked up from the *Argus*, rolled her eyes, looked down again. It was ages since Dad had played music. They only had three LPs – *The Kilfenora Ceilidh Band*, *Paddy's Green Shamrock Shore*, and *The World of Val Doonican*.

Hello there!

That one was Mam's. All the ladies were mad about Val Doonican, loved his smile and his colourful jumpers.

Dad put *Paddy's Green Shamrock Shore* on, the cover a thatched, whitewashed cottage in a field surrounded by a dry-stone wall. He turned his back to Mam, took a peeled onion from his pocket, held it under his eyes. An orchestra started up, a tinkling piano, warbling voice.

In a little white cottage in Ire-land, that's where I was born
Oh, how I rue the day I left, one frosty winter's morn.

The tears ran down Dad's face.

'Ah God!'

Mam's head shot up in surprise.

'What's the matter with you?'

He wiped his eyes with the back of his hand, sniffed.

'Wouldn't it break your heart?'

'What?'

'This song. Wouldn't it make you want to pack your bags and get the next boat back home and live among your own folk?'

She gave him a withering look.

'No, it bleddy wouldn't.'

There was a knock on the door, she got up to answer it. Dad clicked his tongue.

'Did you see that now? You see how she is?'

He tapped his head.

'But don't worry, I'll bring her round with the old psychology.'

His jaw tightened. He turned up the volume, bent over, stuck the onion into his face again.

'Christ! That's a quare powerful onion.'

He stood up, blinking frantically, a big fat tear rolling down his face. Bridie stood in the doorway, mouth open, staring at him.

'What's the matter with Brendan?'

Mam popped her head around the door.

'He's breaking his heart over poor auld Ireland, and it's not even St Patrick's Day yet. Have you ever seen the like?'

Dad angrily wiped away tears.

'What the feck are *you* doing here?'

'Nice to see *you* again too, Brendan a stór.'

Mam put on her coat.

'We're going out.'

'*Out?*'

'I have to get out of here, you're driving me mad going on and on about Ireland every bleddy night.'

'But . . .'

'We're going to play bingo. I'll be back about ten. Half an hour now, Liam.'

Now here I am in A-mer-i-kay, many miles from home

I'd give anything to see once more the land where I was born.

'Jesus,' said Bridie, frowning at the record player, 'that miserable auld song would put years on you. I'd prefer Val Doonican myself.'

'Who asked you your opinion, you interfering bleddy . . .'

She winked at me, took Mam's arm, left the room. A brief burst of laughter from the hall, the door slamming. Dad stared at the onion resentfully, couldn't understand why it had let him down.

'Do you see what I'm up against now, do you?'

He shook his head.

'What did I say? It'd take Sherlock fecking Holmes to figure them out.'

★　★　★

We were on a scouting mission. Going deeper into Cwm Wood than ever before. Eyes peeled, ears straining for any sign of the mindless thugs who'd been stoning trains.

'Look!'

Marek pointed to something halfway up the hill to our right.

'What?'

I couldn't see anything.

Marek waved us over to where he stood.

'See now?'

A van. In the trees.

'Let's go have a look. Spread out. Keep your heads down.'

We edged forward, scuttling through the undergrowth. It was wedged tightly between two trees. White, patches of rust around the headlights, the bumper hanging off.

Marek put his hands to his mouth, shouted.

'Hello. Is anyone there?'

No answer. He picked up a stone, flung it at the side of the van.

CLUNK!

Silence. He threw another.

CLUNK!

'Come on.'

He waved us forward. He tried the door. It opened about an inch before hitting the tree.

'That's what I call a tight fit.'

It was the same on the driver's side. The window was wound right down. Marek hoisted himself up with his hands, looked inside.

'See anything?'

'No.'

He dropped down again. I pointed to the hill behind.

'See the tyre tracks coming down there? I'll bet it made those – come on, let's go have a look.'

We followed the marks to the top of the hill, where they met a road.

'He must have been driving too fast, didn't see the bend till it was too late, ploughed straight down the hill.'

We looked at the tyre tracks weaving crazily through the trees. Colin whistled.

'If he'd hit one of those trees . . .'

'He'd have gone head first through the windscreen. Or the van might have burst into flames.'

'That was one lucky hombre.'

'Sí señor.'

'The odds against it must be incredible.'

'A foot either side and he would have smashed into a tree and been killed, or very seriously injured. There are no houses near here, no one would have heard his cries for help. He would have died a slow, horrible death.'

We froze. Imagined the horror of being trapped in a blazing van, your legs ripped off, the blood pouring out of you, feeling your flesh beginning to melt.

'I'll bet he still can't believe his luck.'

'Unless . . .'

Colin and I looked at Marek.

'What?'

'Unless he wound the window down, tried to get out but couldn't. But he managed to crawl into the back and . . . he's still there.'

Horribly wounded. Or dead, rotting on the floor, a mass of bloated, wriggling worms and insects.

'We have to go and check.'

Colin and I looked at each other. He was right. We *had* to. It was our duty as Roman Catholics. There might be another Roman Catholic in there, hanging by a thread, unable to move their arms to make the sign of the cross over themselves as their soul departed their dying body. Desperate for someone else to do it for them. A Methodist wouldn't know what to do. Or might spit in their face.

We set off back down the hill. Marek forging ahead, Colin and me behind.

'It's a good job Michael isn't with us,' I said to Colin. 'He'd be wetting himself by now.'

He'd sat on a bench at the edge of the wood, refusing to go any further. *I don't like it in there any more.*

'Yeah! Or Joe 90 – he'd run a mile.'

'Ha! Yeah.'

We fell silent till we reached the van again. Marek lowered his voice to a whisper.

'Whatever we find in there, we must remember to maintain discipline. No one does anything till I say, understood?'

We nodded. Marek took a deep breath, knocked on the door.

'Hello, is anybody there?'

No answer. He tried again.

'This is the anti-communist resistance. We mean you no harm.'

He paused.

'Unless, of course, you're a communist, in which case, you must surrender at once or face the consequences – we are armed and dangerous, we have killed before.'

'Marek!'

He gave me a sharp look, started pounding on the door.

'Hello, hello . . .'

Silence. He turned to us.

'OK, are you ready?'

We nodded. We weren't. Marek turned the handle, poked his head inside.

'What's there?'

He didn't answer. Opened the door wider, stepped in. We heard something heavy being dragged across the floor, a pause, then a ripping noise.

'Marek, what is it?'

'Come and see for yourselves.'

We clambered inside. It was packed with boxes, Marek already rummaging inside one.

'What's there?'

'Cigarettes.'

He held up a packet.

'Jesus Christ!'

'Just think what we can do with these.'

'I don't smoke.'

'Nor me,' said Colin.

'Neither do I,' said Marek, tossing the packet back into the box. 'So?'

'This van is hot.'

'*Hot?*' said Colin, frowning.

'Yes, full of stolen goods. There must be fifty or sixty boxes in here, and about one hundred packets in each box.'

'*But none of us smoke.*'

Marek slowly turned to face Colin, irritation etched on his face.

'But plenty of other people do.'

'So what?'

'So we sell them. Then we'll have the means to raise funds for the resistance. We'll be a much more professional outfit. No one will ever mistake us for mindless thugs again.'

* * *

The next day we bunked off school, met in the HQ at nine sharp. Marek paced up and down in front of us, hands clasped behind his back.

'OK, men, this is how it is. The smugglers could come back for their van at any time. Or someone else could stumble on it and help themselves to those cigarettes. So we have to act quickly. Can we do it?'

'Yes!'

He smiled.

'That's the spirit.'

The boxes weren't that heavy, but they were an awkward size. You had to really stretch to get a good grip, so that after a few minutes your arms and fingers felt as if they were being wrenched off.

I emptied myself of everything I didn't need to finish the job. I was a man. A member of the resistance. I didn't know the meaning of the word failure.

By two in the afternoon we were lying in a heap on the floor of the bunker.

Marek said, 'You know what this means?'

'We'll go home and sleep for a week.'

'It means once we sell these we'll have enough funds to equip ourselves with all the things that a top resistance movement needs – torches, binoculars, hunting knives, camouflage outfits . . .'

'Sub-machine guns.'

Arms rigid, spit flying from his mouth, Colin sprayed the bunker.

'Hand grenades.'

Marek pulled out a pin, bowled overarm.

'Flame-throwers.'

I dragged the noise up from deep inside my chest, aimed a jet of flame up the steps, sent the commies running.

Marek clapped his hands together.

'We'll start selling the hot goods next week.'

★　★　★

I was watching *The Avengers*, Dad cursing quietly beside me, slowly turning the black snake of his inner tube in the bowl of water.

'Feckit anyhow. Bastard fucking thing.'

Every night this week he'd thought he'd found the hole, patched it, wheeled his bike into the back with a flat the next day. The front door opened, Mam back from the parents' evening at the school. Her face pinched and anxious.

'Brendan!'

It was her bad news on the phone voice. Dad clenched his jaw.

'Jayzus.'

She came in, coat off, a glass of whisky in her hand.

'Do you know what that Miss Mellon said about Michael?'

It was *him* who was in trouble. Yes! He'd finally been caught.

Mrs Bennett, we're worried about Michael, he doesn't appear to be human.

Dad ignored her, kept on running the inner tube carefully through his hands.

'For God's sake, man, have you no interest at all in your own son?'

He looked up.

'Can't you see I'm busy?'

'Are you *still* trying to fix that? For crying out loud, would you ever buy a new inner tube like any other man?'

He glowered at her. She took a drink of the whisky. I don't know how she could stand the smell, like sour sick.

'She called him a child prodigy.'

He jerked his head back as if someone had put something raw and disgusting in front of him.

'What the feck?'

'She says he's a very talented chess player. He beat one of the masters at it.'

'Go on!'

He perked up.

'Is there money in it?'

Mam pulled a face: *that* wasn't it.

'She said someone like him needed special attention. We had to encourage him.'

Dad looked uneasy.

'How much will it cost?'

'Nothing. She's given me the address of a chess club. He needs to go somewhere where he can be with other prodigies.'

'Be Christ!'

He looked at the ceiling, frowning.

'A chess . . .'

'Prodigy.'

She'd never taken *me* to any clubs.

207

'Where in Christ did he get it from?'

'Not from me anyway, I'm as dull as a bat, God help me.'

I hated it when she said that.

'Did Miss Mellon say anything about me?'

She turned round, surprised, as if she'd only just realised I was in the room.

'She said you were doing very well – grand altogether.'

She wasn't even *trying* to pretend she was interested in me.

'*He* doesn't need taking to a chess club?'

'No.'

'Thank feck for that. Christ, one bleddy prodigy is enough for any family. We haven't time to be running all over town to bleddy fancy clubs.'

Mam laughed scornfully.

'*We!* Me, you mean, when have *you* ever done anything with them?'

She took a sip of whisky, went misty-eyed.

'Such a tiny little fella. It broke my heart the first day I left him behind at school. He didn't say a word, just stared at me with his eyes full of tears, his little lip trembling. I burst into tears myself as soon as I was out of the door.'

She shivered, slurped down some more whisky.

'But look at him now. Jesus, he may be small but he's got a quare powerful brain inside him.'

There was no escape. I had the little spaz shoved down my throat at school all day. Now at home too. I couldn't stand any more. I jumped out of my seat.

'Michael! Michael! Michael! I'm sick of hearing about bloody Michael. What about me?'

They froze, they gaped. Their shock disgusted me. They'd forgotten I was even there. I snatched the photo of Michael from the mantelpiece, flung it into the fire.

208

'Jesus Christ almighty!'

I ran out of the room. They had no idea what it was like being me. I hated them.

★ ★ ★

Marek did the talking. Colin and I stood slightly behind, looking nonchalant and tough. Colin examining his nails, me pretending to chew gum.

'Preece?'

He was crouching behind the bike shed on his own, sucking on a fag. He looked up, blew smoke through his nose, smirked.

'Christ, it's the Three Stooges. What do you want?'

Marek reached inside his anorak, took out a packet of twenty.

'Half price to you.'

Preece looked down at the fags, then up at Marek, eyes guarded now.

'Where did you get them?'

'Are you interested?'

Preece narrowed his eyes.

'Why come to me?'

'Because you are the biggest smoker in the school. It's an expensive habit. I can halve your costs.'

Preece glanced at us, then back at Marek. He took another drag, clicked his fingers.

'Let's see.'

Marek handed over the packet.

'Rothmans? They're OK,' he said dismissively, turning his mouth down at the corners. 'Capstan Full Strength are my favourites.'

'I can supply you with those, and also Players, Senior Service, Woodbines, Gold Flake.'

'Straight up?'

Marek nodded.

'All right then, I'll have four packets of Capstan Full Strength tomorrow. I'll meet you here at the same time.'

'OK, it's a deal.'

Preece handed back the Rothmans, glanced at me and Colin. 'They your gang then?'

'My business partners.'

Preece snorted. Let him laugh. He'd soon be funding the resistance.

★ ★ ★

Dad and Mam were roaring at each other in the kitchen.

'Grand floury spuds—'

'No.'

'Fresh fish from the sea every day—'

'No.'

'Your parents and sister just down the road.'

'No.'

'Grand countryside on your doorstep—'

'No.'

I *hated* it when they argued. It felt like I was being torn apart. That I'd never manage to join myself back together again. They never stopped, not really. When they weren't shouting at each other they were only resting, getting their strength back, before they started again.

Michael was reading his comic, oblivious. I wished I could cut it all out, like him. No, I didn't. There was something creepy about him. He wasn't like the rest of us. I was beginning to think he really was an alien. It would explain so much, like why he didn't even notice when people got upset or angry.

Why is that water pouring out of your eyes, earthling?

His true nature only came out when he was playing chess, that's when you saw what a ruthless, unfeeling killer he actually was.

He made me nervous.

Mam and Dad were still at it.

'Your washing clean on the line at the end of the day.'

'No.'

'Jayzus Christ almighty, is there nothing—'

'No.'

Smash! A plate shattered on the floor. I jumped. Michael didn't even blink.

'I'm your husband and I'm bleddy well telling you now we're moving back to Ireland. You took a vow to love, honour and obey, so start bleddy well obeying me.'

Her laughter was like a broken piece of glass scraping across concrete.

'Is that so?'

'But . . .'

'If you want to go back to Ireland, off you go. But I'm staying here with the boys.'

'You can't, you'll be in terrible danger if you stay here.'

'I'm in danger of going mad if you don't shut up.'

Holy Mother of God, would it never end?

★   ★   ★

Mam dragged me along to the chess club with her and Michael.

'It'll do you good to come along and watch your brother playing. Fancy throwing his photo in the fire like that. You've got a very spiteful streak in you. I don't know where you get it, not my side of the family anyway.'

Her side of the family weren't so great; nice to each other's faces, stuck the knife in afterwards.

Jesus, what a bore, I thought he'd never go.

At least Dad's family didn't beat around the bush.

Feck off, you.

No, you feck off, yacuntya.

211

She brushed something off her sleeve.

'I couldn't stick sitting on my own in a place like this all evening, surrounded by prodigies looking down their noses at me.'

It was just a big room with a row of tables in the middle. On each table two chessboards, two stop clocks. Nothing for spectators – no programmes, no stall with club scarves or pennants, no tea hut. Some club. Mam and I were the only spectators, sat on the row of chairs running the length of one wall like a couple of lemons.

She nudged me.

'Is Michael beating that auld fella?'

'I think so.'

The old bloke made his move, pressed a button on top of his clock. Michael made his, sat back. The old bloke wagged his finger irritably at Michael's clock till he reached out and pressed it. It was about the tenth time he'd had to remind him. How could such a spaz be so good?

'She's awful nice, that Miss Mellon.'

'She is.'

'I'd never have known Michael was a prodigy if she hadn't told me.'

She fidgeted with the straps of her handbag.

'Oh God, where does he get it from? Not from me anyhow, I'm as dull as a bat.'

If she said that once more I'd scream. *And Liam, he's as dull as a bat too*, that's what she meant. No, I wasn't, I just had too much on my mind at the moment to become a prodigy.

We'd be here all night. I'd get hold of Michael afterwards, warn him that next time he had to start losing or else.

'Jesus, I'm gasping,' said Mam. 'You don't think anyone would mind if I had a fag, do you?'

The resistance could have made a fortune out of her. *A packet every day, half price to you*. A few of the people smoked fags as they played, one bloke fiddled with a pipe that he couldn't get to stay lit. When Mam took her fags from her handbag, a small cardboard box fell out. She lit up, then bent down and picked it up, tossed it angrily on to the empty chair next to her.

'Isn't that your shamrock?'

'Indeed it is.'

It had arrived in the post from Ireland this morning, St Patrick's Day. It was Dad who was *really* keen on us all wearing it. I used to hate wearing it, you might as well have a great big bullseye painted on your chest.

Wun too tree.

But now I didn't mind so much. I was determined not to let Preece see how frightened of him I still was. And Thommo; I could tell from the irritable way he looked at the clumps of shamrock pinned to me, Mary Dwyer, Caroline Duffy, Pat Roche, Sean McGuinness and Tom Daley that it got up his nose. So I always made sure I kept walking past him on St Patrick's Day with my chest stuck out.

'I've no time for all that baloney about Ireland,' said Mam, cheeks caving in as she sucked on her fag.

'I always stay well away from the pubs on St Patrick's Night. I can't bear to see all those bleddy drunken Paddies crying into their beer over Ireland. How there's no place to beat it, the grand auld times they used to have there, how the Irish have suffered down the centuries, their poor auld mammies, and all the rest of it. Jesus, I've heard enough of that to last me a lifetime. Your father's no better. The way he'd go on you'd wonder why anyone had ever left such a fantastic place . . .'

She lowered her voice in imitation of Dad.

'You wouldn't need to spend a penny, no need to go work in a filthy auld factory, you'd live off fresh fish and spuds, burn some auld turf to keep warm. A grand, healthy life, you'd live to a hundred and twenty. Jayzus, look at Frank and Mary, they're an example to us all.'

It was a brilliant imitation. Something inside me caved in. It was scary, the way she could suddenly turn and cut people down to size. She snorted with laughter.

'Frank and Mary an example to us all – oh Jesus!'

Frank and Mary. Their names made my heart sink, but I couldn't remember why. Mam flicked the ash into her open palm.

'I remember when your father was a snotty-nosed whelp with no arse in his trousers, begging me and Kate for a piece of bread. Ha! He may have forgotten what it was really like, but I haven't. Grand life me arse.'

The old man playing Michael gave her a warning look. She lowered her voice.

'I couldn't wait to get out of it. He can go on all he wants about moving back to Ireland, but he'll never get me on that boat. Oh God, I'll never forget the day I left Ireland.'

She tapped her forehead with her finger.

'It's all in here, every last detail, burned into my memory, just as if it happened yesterday.'

She was starting to boil, soon her lid would be rattling. I saw now that Dad didn't have any chance of persuading her to move to Ireland, no matter how much auld blarney he used.

'Those bleddy customs officers at Rosslare—'

She hunched her shoulders, pulled a horrible face. The face of a bully.

'Big fat farmers' sons squeezed into fancy uniforms, great rolls of fat falling over their collars. They thought they were God almighty just because they'd passed their Leaving Cert and got into the civil service. Pulled every last thing out of my case, ran their great paws over everything, my underwear, *everything!* Holding it up piece by piece, letting everyone see what I'd got. Jesus, I was the last person who'd try and smuggle something out of the country, sure I had nothing, *nothing!* Oh no, they knew that well enough, it wasn't about *that* at all. They were trying to humiliate me. They bleddy *hated* me leaving. Someone like me – a farm labourer's daughter, she should have known her place. And stayed in it, which meant staying in Ireland, and not getting the hell out of it and trying to make a better life somewhere else. Another country, where they were no better than me. Where no one knew that their father was a big man, and that the family always sat in the same place on the front bench in mass on Sunday mornings and all that bleddy malarkey. No, in any other country they'd just be another big red-faced Mick straight off the boat, struggling up the road with a couple of heavy auld suitcases in the rain.'

She lit another fag with the butt of her old one, didn't notice the old bloke playing Michael was giving her an angry look over the top of his glasses.

'Oh no, they couldn't look down on me any more once I'd got across the water, so they were taking the chance to bleddy well rub my nose in it one last time.'

She paused, blew out a stream of smoke, crossed her legs.

'We came across in a force eight gale, there were people heaving everywhere you looked, what with that and the smell of the cattle's sick coming up from the hold . . . oh God, what a journey. We must have looked a right sight when we got off – nobody had been able to get a wink of sleep, nearly everyone had been sick. But the customs officers were lovely, didn't even open my case, just chalked a big cross on it and waved me on – "Go on, love, you're all right!" And then, when we arrived in Crindau, everyone was so friendly – the people I worked with, our neighbours, everyone! Fantastic friendly, the Welsh, didn't care where you came from or who your mother or father was, as long as you were willing to muck in you were soon one of the gang.'

Her eyes started filling with tears.

'The first time I ever felt like I'd been treated like a human being by anyone outside my family was here in Wales.'

She sniffed, pulled a hanky from her pocket, wiped the corners of her eyes. I felt the sadness welling up in my chest. For her, for all the other people on the boat, for me, forced to listen to more of her stories. *The life I've had, it'd make you weep.* She wanted Michael to stay her little pet, me to be the grown up one who'd listen, take her hand and say, *Oh Mammy, poor you. All that AND you're married to Dad.* Well, I wouldn't. I had enough of my own problems, she didn't want to hear about those.

Can't you see I'm busy?

Go and play.

Will you give over?

Leave me alone.

So why should I have to listen to hers?

There was no stopping her now. She was getting louder and louder, didn't notice people looking up, getting annoyed.

'If you ever got a bit low there was always someone asking you if you were all right, or pulling your leg, saying, "Cheer up, love, it might never happen." Or you could always go uptown and just mingle with the crowd – sometimes I'd join a queue and I wouldn't even know what it was for, I'd do it just for a bit of company, you know. I'd have a few words with the person in front of me, then pretend I'd forgotten something, and carry on.'

She laughed.

'God, sometimes I wonder if I'm right in the head at all.'

It *did* sound mad. I wished she wouldn't tell me about things like that either, they worried me. I wanted normal parents. A mam and dad who knew how to behave, not embarrass you in public. She dropped the ash from her hand on to the floor.

'Po-faced buggers, let them clean that up.'

Her mouth down at the corners, she flicked the box of shamrock on to the floor.

'They can have that too.'

'Excuse me.'

The man in charge, leaning over us, hands behind his back.

'Madam, this is a game that requires great concentration . . .'

The old fella playing Michael stuck his oar in.

'I can't hear myself think. I came here to play chess, not hear her life story.'

The whole room stopped to stare. Peering over glasses, squinting through smoke, open-mouthed, disbelieving. One bloke leaned over and moved his opponent's queen while he was staring at us.

'You're disturbing the players, I'm going to have to ask you to leave.'

★ ★ ★

Frank and Mary! Oh my God, now it was coming back to me.

It was the day last summer Dad asked me to come and visit some friends with him. We cycled for miles, beyond Ballyhack, through bare, rocky hills, dotted with sheep droppings.

'Dad, slow down.'

He'd curse under his breath, slow down for about a minute, start pulling away again. A blustery wind blew. Not far from the road were patches of ground that hadn't dried out since the winter. Eventually we came to a whitewashed cottage with a thatched roof.

'This is where Frank and Mary live. They're a great couple – real auld-timers. You'd learn a lot from them.'

As I got off my bike I heard growling, the frantic skittering of paws across earth, small stones scattering. I turned to see a vicious black dog, teeth bared, spit flying, charging straight at me.

'Aaagh!'

Dad drove his boot into the side of its head. It yelped, veered sideways, then turned in a tight circle, and went for Dad. He grabbed his pump, but didn't swing it as hard as I'd expected him to. The dog jumped up, clenched its teeth around the end. Dad lifted the dog into the air, gave it an almighty kick in the balls. It dropped to the ground, rolling over and over. The howls were terrible.

'Ha! You'll have to do better than that to best Brendan Bennett, ya mangy auld fecker.'

I felt the sickening pain between my own legs.

'Where did it come from?'

Dad was calmly fixing his pump back on to the bike.

'That's Frank's dog, Patch. Take no notice of him.'

'He should be tied up, he's dangerous.'

Dad turned, hawked, fired a white missile that struck the dog's head like a pellet from a gun.

'Go on! Feck off out of it, yacuntya!'

It flinched, began crawling away.

'It's no use tying that fecker up, he's so bleddy stupid he only goes round in circles howling, ends up strangling himself. No, the bicycle pump and a good kick in the balls is the only way to sort him out.'

I was still shaking.

'Come on. Don't be worrying about that mad auld bastard, he won't bother us any more.'

We laid our bikes against the wall. Dad knocked on the door. A tall, white-haired old man in a collarless shirt answered.

'Brendan! Be Christ, good man.'

He laughed, gripped Dad's shoulder.

'Jayzus you're looking good.'

Dad was laughing too.

'You too, Frank – you look strong as a lion.'

'Jayzus – a dandelion more like.'

They both roared. Frank looked over Dad's shoulder.

'And who's this wee man?'

'The son.'

'Ah, go on.'

His eyes shone, he waved me closer.

'Come closer.'

I stepped forward.

'Jayzus, he's the very same as yourself. Is he a good worker?'

'He is not, he's a dead loss.'

'Ah sure, he's probably one of those that's good with the brain. I'll bet he's near the top of his class in school, is that right?'

Dad looked lost. A voice called from inside.

'Frank – who's that?'

'Brendan – Brendan that lives in Wales.'

'Oho, Brendan a stór, will you come in out of that?'

Inside it was one big room. A bed at one end, fireplace, table and chairs at the other. The fireplace was big enough to walk around in. A huge, blackened kettle hung from a tripod over smoking turf. The ceiling was low, the windows small, a bare stamped-down earth floor. Mary sat in one of the straight-backed wood and straw chairs drawn up in front of the fireplace. She had short, curly grey hair, wore a thick pair of granny glasses.

'Oho, the wanderer returns. Come over here till I see you.'

They told each other how good they both looked, then she noticed me.

'Who's this?'

Frank grinned.

'Go on, guess.'

She leant forward in her chair, stared at me for a few seconds, then broke into a smile.

'Is she yours, Brendan?'

'Ah Mary, can't you see it's a lad?' said Frank.

'Go on!'

She squinted at me.

'That's never a boy.'

Dad and Frank roared. I was starting to hate her.

'Brendan *has* no daughter. It's the eldest son – Liam!'

She frowned, beckoned me closer with her scrawny hand.

'Let's have a look at you.'

Dad shoved me from behind.

'Go on.'

I stayed where I was. She got up, shuffled towards me, began looking me over again, her left eye moving in a different direction to her right. She began muttering to herself.

'Jayzus, he is and all . . . well, I'll be.'

Suddenly she gripped my hand in hers, began working it up and down like the handle of a pump.

'WELL, HELLO THERE, LIAM.'

She cackled horribly.

'He's a bit lean all the same. What do you feed him on, Brendan?'

'Pigs' trotters.'

They roared. Frank pulled up another couple of chairs, Mary made some tea, cut and buttered some soda bread. They talked about the weather, what the fishing was like off Spanish Point that summer, the terrible state of the roads. I gazed at the long wooden beam over the fireplace, the oil lamps, hats, jackets and bicycle lamps hanging down from hooks. Mary smiled, asked, 'Do you like coming to Ireland, Liam a stór?'

'I do, yeah.'

'And why wouldn't ya? Running around grand and free till nightfall, no cars to worry about.'

Dad started laughing.

'Till the telly starts anyway.'

'Would you like the television, Liam?'

'Yeah, I do.'

'I couldn't be bothered with it myself. If I sat in front of it too long I'd be getting a headache. I like the wireless though. I'd often sit and listen to the wireless of an evening.'

They didn't have a telly. Or a bathroom. There were a couple of buckets of water drawn from the well standing on a table just inside the door. Frank stirred.

'I believe *The Fugitive* is a very good programme. Do you get *The Fugitive* in Wales at all?'

'We do, yeah.'

'I'd say you'd get any amount of good programmes on the auld television in Wales.'

'Yeah, there's lots of good ones.'

They were a nice couple, I could see that, but their house was dark, gloomy and depressing and I couldn't wait to get back to the twentieth century.

Cycling back, Dad started talking about how he envied the way they lived – no clutter, no fancy-dan gadgets, no bleddy bills. He stopped by an old ruin, the remains of a cottage just like Frank and Mary's.

'What do you think of it?'

It was a dump.

'Every day, rain, hail or shine, I get on the auld bike and go looking for the ideal location – somewhere a fella could settle down for the rest of his life. But no matter how many places I see, I always end up coming back here. It's a grand spot, isn't it?'

'Mmmm.'

On the edge of a bog. Miles from anywhere.

'It wouldn't take much to make that every bit as good as Frank and Mary's place.'

I didn't like the way this was going.

'It's got no roof.'

'You'd fix that in a few days. Frank's promised to give me a hand. The walls are fine. Stick a front door in there and you'd have a grand little home. Just think, by this time next year the four of us could be tucked up inside, sitting round a turf fire, eating potato cakes and buttermilk.'

There! It would be awful.

Oh no, what had I been thinking of, telling him I was

desperate to move to Ireland? How was I ever going to get out of this?

★ ★ ★

We were in Colin's front room, his dad sat on the edge of a chair, playing his electric guitar, amp turned down low. He started singing.

'Here he comes, yeah, here he comes,
'He's coming to check up on you.
'Well here he comes, yeah, here he comes,
'The dude who loves checking on you.
'Here comes the foreman, yeah, here comes the foreman,
'Lord, I got those foreman blues.'
He played a solo, screwing up his face, teasing out the notes.
'I haven't heard that one before,' said Colin.
'I just made it up, kind of a John Lee Hooker type thing.'
He didn't even seem to be trying.
'I've got so many songs in my head. Some days I'll be walking down the street or driving the fork-lift and suddenly' – he clicked his fingers – 'just like that, a song will come to me. And I have to stop whatever I'm doing and find somewhere to go over it in my mind.'

He was so absorbed in what he was saying, he didn't notice Mrs Williams appear suddenly in the doorway. She rested her head against the wall, looking, listening. She had a funny look on her face, I couldn't figure out what it was at first. Then I realised – it was the look of love.

My husband is going to be the Next Big Thing.

My wife would look at me like that when I told her about my plans.

Mr Williams tapped his forehead.

'I get the tune taped, up here, so I don't forget it. Jot some lyrics down on a scrap of paper – I keep meaning to buy a notebook, but I never get round to it. Doesn't matter, anything'll do, some of the greatest hits ever were written down on a paper napkin in a café, or the back of a cigarette packet in a pub.'

I didn't know that. I got excited. If it was that easy, I could do it.

'That place where you found me when you brought the sandwiches, hiding in the middle of the boxes, I've got a few little hideaways like that. Every time that bloody foreman finds one, I just make another somewhere else.'

He leaned back in the chair, crossed his legs.

'Yeah, once the inspiration hits you, you just have to drop everything and get it down on paper, grab that moment.'

When we'd found him he wasn't doing anything except reading the *Daily Mirror* and listening to the radio.

'You want to watch you don't get caught,' said Mrs Williams. He reached down, picked up his mug of tea, took a sip.

'No chance.'

She closed her eyes, sighed.

'What if you got the sack? Where would we be then?'

'Maybe I won't need that job for much longer. The last concert at The Royal Oak we got three encores. Could have done more, but we'd already played everything we'd rehearsed. They bloody loved us, they did.'

'How much did you earn?'

'The manager said he'd never seen anything like it.'

'How much did you earn?'

He paused, fighting down his irritation.

'We're going places.'

'We've got a mortgage to pay and a son to feed and clothe, in case you forgot. And a few concerts in pubs at the weekend aren't going to pay for those.'

She folded her arms, pursed her lips. I couldn't understand why she was getting so cross with him; anybody else would jump at the chance of their husband becoming a pop star.

'No, but a recording contract would.'

She grabbed the end of her sleeve, laughed up it. Mr Williams's hands tensed on the arm of the chair.

'It happens.'

She shook her head.

'Not to people like us.'

'Thanks for the vote of confidence. That's really great, that is.'

'All I'm saying is . . .'

'Oh, don't worry, I understand what you're saying all right. You've made yourself very clear.'

He stubbed his fag out in the ashtray, got up, walked to the door.

'Cliff!'

He brushed past her. She rolled her eyes, followed him into the hall.

'Where you going now?'

'Out.'

'Come on, Cliff . . .'

'You never stop knocking me, do you? Never a word of encouragement. Well, let me tell you something, there are plenty of people who *are* impressed. The women practically throw themselves at me when I come off stage – and don't think I haven't been tempted.'

'Don't you *dare* talk to me like that. If you think . . .'

SLAM!

She raced out after him, opened the door, shouted down the street.

'IF YOU EVER TOUCH ANOTHER WOMAN, I'M WALKING OUT OF THIS HOUSE, AND I'M NEVER COMING BACK. AND I'LL TAKE COLIN WITH ME!'

SLAM!

Colin stared at the floor, his face turned away. I tried to think of something to say to lighten the mood but couldn't. His mam came back into the room, mouth pinched, eyes smouldering.

'Right, Colin, time you were in bed.'

'But Mam . . .'

'GET UP THOSE STAIRS NOW!'

'Um, I'd better be going.'

'Yes, Liam, I think that's a good idea.'

★ ★ ★

We had to stand in the corridor at the chess club now we'd been banned. Stuck out there in the gloomy grey cold, the thickos' waiting area, while Michael sat inside in the warmth and light. Mam opened the door a crack, stuck her head around to check on Michael.

'Ah, he's grand. Sure he doesn't need us hanging around at all. Isn't it terrific the way a little fella like him can sit so still and concentrate for hours on end?'

She fumbled through her handbag for her fags and lighter.

'He's playing that auld fella, the one that kept giving out about me. He's a right cranky auld gom, isn't he?'

She blinked her eyes furiously as the smoke from her first drag burned them, tilted her head backwards to escape it.

'Christ, the way he went on. What kind of a game is it where you daren't say a word when you're watching? Can you think of another game like that?'

'No, I can't.'

She blew a stream of smoke.

'Isn't it a shame Michael wasn't a rugby prodigy. Then you could have a bit of a sing-song and a laugh and a drink when you were watching him play. I love rugby. One day, years ago, when everything was getting on top of me I put you in the pushchair and caught the bus to Cardiff. I'd have started screaming otherwise, I swear to God.'

'You did? How old was I?'

She leant backwards, screwed up her eyes.

'You'd have been three, I think. I was carrying Michael at the time.'

'What did you do in Cardiff?'

'I walked to the rugby ground, stood outside and listened to the crowd singing. Oh, there's nothing I like more in the world than that Welsh rugby crowd singing, it'd bring tears to your eyes.'

I'd seen her transfixed in front of *Grandstand* when the rugby from Cardiff was on.

'It was fantastic – it cheered me right up, it did. You could tell they were winning from the cheers, you didn't need to see anything. A great cheer would go up, then a song, then another cheer, a song, another cheer . . . *Winning!*'

She laughed.

'Jesus, winning wasn't the word. It was a massacre. They were *slaughtering* the other lot, wiping the floor with them, rubbing their noses right in it.'

'Who were they playing?'

'Ireland.'

A thin, vengeful smile settled on her face.

'That made my day – those Irish players are all sons of doctors and lawyers. The *cream* of Irish society, if you please!'

She made a snorting noise with her nose.

'The Lords and Masters – and a meaner bunch of bleddy so-and-sos you'd never meet – they wouldn't give you the steam off their piss. Who are they to look down on me?'

She scowled, took a deep drag on her fag.

'But you only needed to take one look at the Welsh players to see they were just ordinary blokes from ordinary families, who'd worked damn hard for everything they'd got. And they were sending the bleddy Irish back home with their tails between their legs. I wanted to run on to that pitch and shake their hands.'

It didn't matter how much psychology Dad used, he'd never get her on that boat.

Unless.

Unless he came straight out and told her about Crindau being right in the front line, and everything in Ireland being so broken down and useless that no one would bother to invade it. I didn't want to die in a nuclear war, but I didn't want to live like Frank and Mary either. If Mam realised moving there was our only chance, maybe she could persuade Dad to live in a more normal house, with electric light, a television, and a bathroom.

'Would you *never* go back to live in Ireland, Mam? I mean, even if that was the only way to avoid . . . something really terrible.'

I didn't like the funny little smile on her lips.

'Something really terrible. And what would that be now, I wonder? Has your father been filling your head with all this stuff about nuclear war again?'

'No.'

'You two have got a right little double act going, haven't you?'

'What double act?'

' "Do you miss Ireland, Liam?" "Yeah." '

She gave me a piercing stare. I felt my face burn.

'Since when have you missed Ireland? Every year we go through the same thing. You don't want to go, there's nothing to do there, you've no one to play with, you'll miss all your favourite programmes on telly. Now all of a sudden you *can't wait* to go and live there. What's going on?'

She was mocking me. *Enjoying* watching me squirm. It wasn't fair.

'I . . .'

'You'd soon miss your football, and not having Colin, and Uncle Ronnie and Auntie Val just down the street, and a hundred and one other things you take for granted here in Crindau. I'd say you'd find life in the country very boring altogether. It's ten miles to the nearest town, if you could call Ballyhack a town at all. Sure it's nothing but a few shops, and a

227

dozen pubs full of fellas talking the same auld bleddy rubbish every night, and a scutty little excuse for a road spattered in horseshit running through the middle. Town me arse.'

She flicked the ash off her fag, took another drag.

'Don't get me wrong now, I love going back to Ireland. I couldn't bear not to see my family – I'm not like your father, he's fallen out with damn near every member of his. But I couldn't live there and I'd say you were too used to living in a town to be happy over there. Isn't that so?'

She was sharp as a razor. She wasn't having a nervous breakdown at all, she just hated Dad. Hated him so much it made my insides writhe.

Maybe she was right. Maybe Dad was talking rubbish. Perhaps I should switch sides? But as soon as I had the thought, I felt a sharp pain in my chest. *You can't betray him.* No, he wasn't talking rubbish – what about the documentary?

Do you see? Do you see now what I'm telling you is true?

'Jesus, that man. I should have listened to my father. The night before we got married he took me to one side and said, "Are you sure you want to go through with this? I won't hold it against you if you change your mind."'

She shook her head sadly.

'I wouldn't listen, I was too headstrong. When I said I was sure he just nodded, put on his coat and hat, left the house without a word. When he came I asked him where he'd been, he said he'd tried to make your father see sense but he was just as set on it as me. Then he went and got the bottle of poteen he had hidden in the shed and got roaring drunk.'

Both of them had told me the same story now. One of them had got the wrong end of the stick. She took a hefty drag from her cigarette.

'Oh no, I've learnt not to take any notice of his bleddy stupid plans down the years.'

She dropped the butt on to the floor, stood still, sizing me up.

'You'll be sorry if you're taken in by what he says, mark my words, Liam.'

★ ★ ★

Dad grimaced, ran his hand through his hair.

'I'm not getting anywhere with your mother. It's like talking to a brick wall.'

We were sitting out the back, me on one pile of wood, him on the other. It was Sunday morning, the bells of St Mark's ringing in the distance.

'Fecking hell, I've never met anyone so full of spite against her own kind.'

He sat hunched over, breathing heavily, the axe resting between his legs. That was how I found him. I knew straight away something was wrong. It wasn't like him to sit around when there was wood to be chopped.

There won't be a tree left standing in the whole of Wales by the time I'm finished. I'll scalp the fecking place. There'll be no chance of the bleddy Ruskies sneaking up behind Brendan.

'You only have to mention Ireland and she turns into a fecking banshee. I'm damned well tempted to tell her to feck off, get on the next boat and go to Ireland without her. Would you come with me?'

Oh my God, no.

This was all Mam's fault, she was breaking up the family, why couldn't she love, honour and obey a *bit*, at least? Would it really hurt her that much?

'We'd be happy as Larry, you and me. We'd build our own home, grow our own food, and no bleddy nagging women to bother us.'

My mind was racing, trying to think of an answer.

'But how would Mam and Michael cope without us?'

He went to reply, then shut his mouth again, sagged.

'Ah . . . I suppose you're right, we can't leave them.'

He gripped the axe tighter.

'Maybe there won't be a third world war after all, and then there'll be no need to go to Ireland anyhow.'

He went rigid.

'What kind of a fecking eejit are ya? Jayzus Christ, have you not listened to a word I've said?'

'But . . .'

I was hoping it was true. That God would take mercy on us at the last moment, destroy the communists with bolts of lightning – *ZAP!* He loved us, surely he wouldn't let them win?

'Are you soft up here?'

He tapped his forehead with his finger.

'Didn't Our Lady of Fatima warn us? Have you forgotten already? You have to be strong up here in the head as well as having a strong body if you want to survive, and there's few fellas as strong as Brendan in the head department.'

'I . . .'

'The suffering I've lived through would have finished off many a fella, but not me, no sir, not Brendan. I'm not beaten yet. Not by a long way. It's time to start working on Plan B.'

'Plan B?'

'Yes, never put all your eggs in one basket.'

'But . . .'

He dropped the axe, slapped his hands down on his legs, got up.

'I think I'll go for a walk and clear the head.'

'But Dad.'

'What?'

His mind was off somewhere else, perfecting Plan B.

'What's Plan B?'

'I made a mistake last time, did too much yakking, I should have kept me cards closer to me chest. Not that I'm accusing you of blabbing about it to your mother.'

'I didn't!'

'But she seemed to catch on very quickly to what I was up to, all the same. *It was almost as if she already knew.*'

'But Dad, I didn't.'

'I'm not saying you did.'

He hawked and spat.

'And I'm not saying you didn't. You could have let it slip without meaning to. It's easily done. "Careless talk costs lives" – that's what they used to say during the war. I've learnt from my mistakes, Plan B is going to remain top secret. You'll find out in good time.'

It wasn't fair. He'd no right blaming me.

'Dad, you can trust me.'

Something hard and dark gathered in his eyes.

'I've already explained myself, now don't provoke me.'

He pushed open the door, stepped out into the back lane.

★ ★ ★

The cigarette trade was taking off. We'd arranged to meet some new customers behind the garages near Spytty Lane. Preece's older brother and his mate, Mad Nick, hammered a football against one of the doors, bellowing between shots.

WHAM.

'BASTARD!'

WHAM.

'FUCKER!'

WHAM.

'CUNT!'

It was pointless trying to make ourselves heard above the row so we stood to one side, waiting. Eventually a bigger version of Preece with ginger hair noticed us.

'You got the fags?'

Marek held up the bag.

'In here.'

'Let's see.'

Marek opened the carrier bag, tilted it towards him. Mad Nick made a grab for it. Marek snatched it away, pointed his finger in Mad Nick's face.

'Don't you ever try that again, you hear me?'

He and Preece's brother exchanged a look. *Who the fuck does he think he is?*

'Why? What you gonna do about it?'

'Try it and find out.'

He was mad. They'd kill us. Why did he have to talk to them like that? Now the narrow passageway from the garages back to the road seemed very far away. If the people in the houses nearby hadn't heard the banging and swearing they weren't going to hear our cries for help. Mad Nick was glaring at Marek. I could already hear the siren screaming through the dark night, taste the blood pooling in my mouth.

Mad Nick laughed first, then Preece's brother joined in.

'Our kid told me you were a mad bastard.'

Preece's brother took some money from his back pocket, held it out.

'All right, Big Shot, here you are.'

Marek took it, handed over the bag. Mad Nick looked inside.

'Tidy.'

Preece's brother said, 'Where you getting this from?'

'I'm sorry, that's strictly confidential.'

They laughed again.

'You slay me, son.'

'Well, gentlemen, it was a pleasure doing business with you. We'll meet again soon, I hope.'

They were still laughing as we walked back through the passageway. We'd done it.

★ ★ ★

Marek, Colin and me had just finished some soup at the Sikorskis' house, were about to leave, when Mr Sikorski shot up out of his chair.

'You are not going out dressed like that.'

Barbara, Marek's tidy sister, had just walked past.

'Like what?'

'A degenerate.'

Her draw jopped, she spread her arms.

'*What?*'

'*Those.*'

'Tata! Everyone wears jeans.'

'I don't care what everyone else does, *you* will dress decently.'

She made a choking noise deep in her throat, stomped out of the room, back up the stairs. Marek nudged me, whispered, 'About time she was put in her place.' I wasn't so sure. She was right, everybody *did* wear jeans. There was a knock on the front door. Mr Sikorski went out and answered it, shouted up the stairs, 'Jan, your tutor, Mr Griffiths, is here.'

Upstairs, a door opened, someone trudged out on to the landing.

'Well?' asked Mr Sikorski. 'Aren't you going to introduce yourself?'

There was a painfully long pause.

'I'm Jan.'

It was the voice of a condemned man.

'Well,' said Mr Griffiths, all bright, breezy and sing-song Welshy, 'I'll come up then, shall I?'

Mr Sikorski came back into the room, shaking his head.

'That boy . . . I hired someone to help him with his accountancy exams and *this* is the thanks I get.'

Marek caught my eye, ran a finger across his throat. I couldn't understand why he hated his brother and sister so much. Or why Mr Sikorski wouldn't let Barbara go out in jeans. I'd seen the Sikorskis arguing with each other before, but I hadn't taken it seriously. It felt like a performance they put on whenever anyone visited, it never occurred to me they really *meant* it. Now I wasn't so sure. I wanted them to stop, they were beginning to remind me of *my* family.

Barbara came back down, wearing a skirt. She looked close to tears. Mr Sikorski nodded.

'That's better.'

She'd looked fine in jeans. Marek said, 'Don't let her go without searching her bag.'

'What?'

'I'll bet she has make up in there.'

'Shut up, you.'

'I've seen her uptown wearing lipstick and yucky green stuff around her eyes – she was obviously going to meet a boy.'

'You little . . .'

She lunged at Marek. Mr Sikorski stepped in between them.

'Stop this, now!'

Marek's kid sister charged through the door, shouting angrily over her shoulder.

'You're late again.'

I waited to see who would follow her into the room. No one did. She carried on talking to thin air.

'Well, don't think I'm going to sit inside waiting for you the next time. You're not the only friend I've got, you know.'

'Tata, you tell Marek not to . . .'

'Be quiet! My God, what next?'

Someone ran down the stairs at a hundred miles an hour, slammed the front door.

'What the . . .'

Mr Sikorski ran into the hall. We all followed him. Mr Griffiths was at the top of the stairs, his hands fluttering nervously around his lapels.

'I . . . I've never been spoken to like that in my life before.'

'What did he say?'

234

'He called me a murderer.'

'WHAT?'

'One minute he had his head bent over, taking notes, the next he jumped up and shouted, "Murderer! Can't you hear it? Can't you hear my soul screaming in agony at the thought of spending my life in accountancy?" Then he flung his notebook to the floor and ran out.'

★ ★ ★

Something woke me up. It came from downstairs, a door opening, closing. The cellar door. No, it couldn't be. I'd imagined it.

There it was again.

Oh sweet Jesus. It had come back to haunt me.

You should never have done that to your poor little brother.

He'd asked for it. He wouldn't stop following me.

Leee-am.

Leee-am.

Dogging my every step.

Leee-am.

Leee-am.

Taking up my space, cramping my style, breathing air meant for me. I couldn't understand it. I'd done nothing to encourage him.

Leave me alone.

Go away.

Get lost, you spaz.

Pushed him. Poked him. Twisted his arm behind his back. Still he kept coming back for more. No one could have put up with it.

Mam was out the back, hanging washing on the line.

'Michael, come here a minute.'

He came straight away, an eager look on his face. He'd forgotten how I'd made him eat dirt that morning.

'Do you want to know a secret?'

He nodded.

'Come on, I'll show you. It's down there.'

I opened the cellar door. Made him go first. Meant to give him a shove when we were a couple of steps from the bottom. A scare, that's all. Didn't mean to make him fall that far. Not all the way from the top step. Knew as soon as I saw the way his body was twisted on the floor it was bad. Head cut open. Mouth gaping. Terrified eyes.

What happened to me?

A terrible silence. I thought I was going to be sick with the fear. Mam came running when she heard the screaming.

'Oh God, what now?'

'He fell.'

She rushed past me as if I wasn't there. Almost pushed me down the steps.

I got the third degree from her at the hospital.

'Are you sure it was an accident?'

'Yes.'

'You weren't fighting again?'

'No.'

He broke his arm. Kids that age have very soft bones. They cut a patch out of his hair to put the stitches in his head.

Eventually Mam gave up asking me if we'd been fighting and turned on Dad.

'How many times have I asked you to keep that door locked?'

'Can't you keep an eye on him? What else have you got to do all day?'

'PIG!'

She snatched the key, rushed outside. Rolled up her sleeve, stuck her fag in the corner of her mouth like a man, took a run, flung it into the dark. It had been locked ever since.

There it was again.

God punishing me. Reminding me of all the terrible things

I'd ever done in my life. I'd hear the same sounds every night till I went mad. I pulled the bedclothes over my head, started humming the theme tune to *Match of the Day*.

It wasn't happening.

★ ★ ★

We kept the money from the cigarette sales in a tin hidden inside the trunk of a tree near our bunker. We counted it at the end of every week, then Marek wrote down the total in a notebook and we put it back.

'How much?'

'Seven pounds, eleven shillings and sixpence.'

Colin gave a low whistle. Marek snapped the tin shut.

'It's not enough. We need more, *much* more.'

'Why?'

Marek stopped, looked around as if he suspected someone might be listening.

'The Russians are *pouring* money into the Valleys. Once they create a hotbed of communism, they bribe them to keep them on their side. Seven pounds, eleven and six is *peanuts*.'

Colin looked deflated. I was disappointed too, thought we'd been doing brilliantly.

'So how much do we need?'

Marek gazed into the distance, rubbing his chin.

'Hundreds, no, *thousands* of pounds.'

He held up the tin.

'This is just the start. We have to start stepping up our operation.'

★ ★ ★

There was something in the air. They were gathered outside the factory gates, huddled in groups, talking, rubbing hands, stamping feet against the bitter cold. Colin and I freewheeled to the edge of the crowd on our bikes.

'Dad, why aren't you in work?'

Mr Williams barely glanced at us, went back to talking to the other blokes.

'Here's your lunch-box.'

He'd forgotten it again. One of the blokes nudged Mr Williams.

'Aye aye, here's Dai Guevara.'

A man in a blue anorak strode through the factory gates.

'You lot have really dropped me in it now.'

Mr Williams snorted.

'We've dropped *you* in it?'

'Management isn't going to negotiate with you after you've walked out. I want you all to come back to work *right now*.'

Some people looked nervous then. Mr Williams stepped forward.

'And give up the one bit of bargaining power we've got? You must be joking.'

'Believe me, this isn't going to do any good.'

'So we should just sit back and do nothing, let them lay off half the workforce, like they did in Blackwood and Pontypool. Let management and that bastard Evans decide who deserves to keep their job and who gets the push. No, thanks.'

Mr Williams pointed to a bloke to his right.

'You're asking me to keep my head down and hope it's *him*.'

He swivelled round, pointed to an old bloke lighting a fag.

'Or *him*.'

Jabbed the air in front of another man.

'Or *him*.'

Jerked his thumb at his chest.

'And not *me*. Well, no, that's not what *I'm* going to do.'

He pulled a disgusted face, as if Dai Guevara had asked him

to club a kitten to death. Put his hands on his hips, turned to the others.

'That's not what we're going to do, is it?'

'NO!'

He smiled, had them eating out of his hand. He turned back to Dai.

'We're going to stick together – you tell them we're not coming back till they promise there'll be no redundancies.'

Everyone cheered. Mr Williams unwrapped a stick of gum, popped it into his mouth, cool as you like. *This* was his stage now, and he was bringing the house down. He looked at Dai as though he was a piece of dogshit stuck on the bottom of his shoe.

'It's all right for *you* to talk, I'm damned sure *you're* not going to be made redundant.'

The sharp intake of breath around me, the look on Dai Guevara's face, told me Mr Williams had scored a direct hit.

'What are you trying to say, Williams?'

The foreman marched up to the gate, put his finger and thumb to his lips, whistled.

'You're wanted,' said Mr Williams. 'They've sent their little yapping dog out to look for you.'

They laughed, then cheered. Dai put his hands on his hips, looked us up and down.

'Go on, enjoy it while you can. Oh yeah, you're all having a great laugh now. Let's see how you feel in a few days, after you've been standing out here for hours on end in the freezing wind, management still refusing to talk to you, no money in your pocket, and no one willing to back you in this *completely unofficial action.*'

He turned away, walked back inside the gates. Mr Williams's face dropped. He caught us watching him, straightened his shoulders, grinned. Turned and flashed a V sign at Dai's back. I smiled, ignoring the sinking feeling inside.

★ ★ ★

239

There it was again. The cellar door opening. Then something heavy being dragged across the hall.

I wasn't imagining it. Not this time.

Was I?

I had to go down, find out what was going on. I'd go mad just lying here night after night. I jumped out of bed before I could have second thoughts, closed the door behind me, reached out, touched the sign with my hand.

This Is Anfield.

Straightened my back, pretended to chew gum, then walked smartly down the stairs, head held high.

Shankly! Shankly! Shankly!

I was the manager of Liverpool. I was as hard as nails. Made big men like Tommy Smith and Ron Yeats shake in their boots. Whoever was down there had better look out.

The lights were on. The cellar door open. Living room door, kitchen door, wide open. A tap running. I edged forward, peered round the kitchen door. Dad was standing in front of the sink, drinking a cup of water. He was naked apart from his underpants. He was smeared in dirt from head to toe.

'Dad?'

He turned round. Face blackened like a miner's.

'Jayzus, I've a terrible thirst on me.'

He put the cup under the running tap, filled it again. Drained it in a couple of gulps, refilled it, turned the tap off. Why was he only wearing his underpants? How did he get so filthy?

'What are you doing?'

He sipped at the water, nodded knowingly.

'I wondered when you'd come and ask how I've been getting on with Plan B. It's taken you long enough.'

He was making me nervous.

'But you told me you wanted to keep it top secret – you were afraid if I knew too much about it I might let Mam know by accident. Careless talk costs lives, you said, remember?'

He wasn't listening. He was annoyed with me.

'Jayzus, I was beginning to think you'd forgotten about me completely.'

My scalp began to tingle. I *hated* it when he was disappointed in me. Even when I'd no idea what he wanted from me, like now.

'A fella would get lonely, working away down here on his own, he'd crave a bit of company. "Ah, he'll surely come and ask me how Plan B is getting on *today*," I kept saying to myself. It just goes to show – never rely on anyone, you'd only end up disappointed in the end.'

He was setting his jaw, turning his back to me. I'd let him down. I'd hurt him. He didn't want to be my dad any more.

'But . . .'

My mind was racing, desperately trying to think of a way to make him like me again.

'But *someone* had to keep an eye on Mam. If *both* of us weren't there, she might have started wondering what was going on. But I was able to cover for you – whenever she asked where you were I said you'd gone foraging for wood, or were down the allotment.'

He lowered the cup.

'She was asking about me, was she?'

No, not once.

'Yeah, she was.'

'I'll bet she was, the nosy bitch. I'll bet she's *desperate* to know what I'm doing.'

'Yeah, you're right, she is. Don't you see? If I hadn't been there, she might have suspected something.'

He turned slightly, so that I could see his profile. His face had softened a little.

'That's true.'

'And I didn't think you wanted to be disturbed. I knew you were busy.'

He turned back round to face me. Nodded slowly, a grave expression on his face.

'I *have* been busy.'

He seemed to decide something.

'Would you like to see Plan B?'

'Yeah.'

I *was* dying to see it. He gulped down the rest of the water, dropped the cup in the sink.

'Come on.'

I followed him back out into the hallway.

'Down here.'

Down the steps to the cellar. *The cellar!*

'I bet it's different to how you remember it.'

There used to be junk piled everywhere – rusting bits of bicycle, broken pieces of furniture, stacks of yellowing Irish newspapers. All that had gone. Now there were piles of wood cut into different lengths, neatly stacked. Shovels, picks, brushes, hammers, a saw, boxes of candles and nails, filled sacks lining one wall.

'I told you I'd been busy.'

'I thought Mam had thrown away the key.'

He winked.

'Ha – so she had. I waited till she'd gone to bed, then went out with a torch and found it in the road.'

He was enjoying my surprise. Delighted to finally show someone what he'd been up to.

'There are no flies on Brendan.'

He pointed to a hole in the middle of the floor.

'There it is.'

'What?'

'Plan B.'

'A *hole?*'

He scowled, annoyed.

'It's a tunnel, you eejit.'

'Plan B is a tunnel?'

'Not just *one* tunnel, wait till you see, I've been working like the divil. Jayzus, it's no joke working in a space that small. The heat is terrific down there, that's why I have to strip off.'

I nearly jumped out of my skin.

'What's that?'

A jagged ringing from underneath us.

'That's just the alarm clock going off down in the tunnel.'

'Why do you need an alarm clock?'

'You use up the air quare quick when you're working underground. Christ, I blacked out a couple of times, I must have lost track of time. So I always bring an alarm clock down with me now and set it to go off after half an hour. I'll build some proper ventilation later on.'

He wiped his mouth with the back of his hand, the ringing slowly winding down.

'I came up a bit early this time though – I was dying of the thirst. Christ, it's a dirty job. And you'd be dog-tired after doing a day's work beforehand – most nights I only get about three hours' sleep.'

He nodded at the sacks.

'You have to get rid of all the soil, of course. Every now and then I strap a sack on to the back of my bike, ride off and dump it somewhere.'

That explained the dragging noises I'd heard. It was a relief to discover the sounds I'd heard hadn't been God punishing me for what I'd done to Michael, just Dad working. A perfectly normal explanation.

'But it'll be worth it in the end.'

'But *why* are you digging a tunnel?'

He jerked his head back in surprise.

'Why do you think?'

'I don't know.'

He was annoyed.

'The politicians, the bleddy civil servants, the Lords and fecking Ladies, the Swiss, they all have their secret bunkers already, you may be sure of that. *They* won't be caught out when the Russians attack. Do you think there'll be any room in their bunkers for Paddy? Will there fuck. We can all roast as far as they're concerned. Well, here's *one* Paddy who won't roast.'

He nodded to himself, smiling grimly.

'I'll fecking show *them*, the cunts.'

So the Lords and Ladies were already prepared for nuclear war. They'd kept very quiet about it, the sneaky so-and-sos. If *they'd* been digging secret bunkers and tunnels, it couldn't be that mad a thing to do.

'Do you want to come down and have a look?'

My insides tightened. People got trapped under the ground, died slow, horrible deaths. Screamed and screamed but no one heard.

'You'd better take your pyjamas off, mind, otherwise you'll get them filthy.'

But if I didn't do it, he'd stop wanting to be my dad. And if it was the only way to survive a nuclear war, I'd *have* to do it sooner or later.

'There's no need to be nervous, I know what I'm doing. Come on, follow me, you'll be grand.'

Not a flicker of doubt in his eyes. He knew exactly what he was doing. I trusted him. I stripped to my underpants. Dad picked up two candles, lit them, passed one to me. He lowered himself into the hole up to his chest, then ducked down, disappeared beneath the cellar floor. I followed, moving very slowly and carefully. When my feet touched the bottom, only my neck and head were left above the cellar floor. Then I got down on my hands and knees and crawled. Dad kept looking round.

'Jayzus, you could go a *bit* faster.'

No, I couldn't, I wasn't going to let that candle blow out. I looked around me at the tightly packed earth, the wooden beams supporting the top and sides. He'd done a great job.

It's a perfectly normal thing to do, the Lords and Ladies have theirs already dug for them.

I relaxed a little. I think I did.

Dad started humming, he loved it down there.

'Are you all right?'

'Yeah.'

'Of course you are. Michael wouldn't be able for it, but nothing worries you, does it?'

I grinned.

'That's right – Michael would start screaming, you'd never get him down here.'

'I've made a good job of it, haven't I?'

'You have. How far does it go?'

He stopped. It felt like we were a million miles from the nearest living soul. The deepest silence I'd ever heard. Me and Dad in the middle of it.

'I reckon this one must have reached the end of the street by now, if I keep going straight I'll reach Tredegar Avenue in another few days.'

He chewed his lip, peering into the inky darkness ahead of us.

'This is only the start. By the time I've finished there'll be a whole network of tunnels down here, it'll be like fecking Spaghetti Junction – Christ, you'll need a map to find your way around. If any Russians ever *did* get down here it wouldn't do them much good, they wouldn't have a bleddy clue which way to go.'

He paused to picture how helpless they'd be and chuckled to himself. Dad had been right all along. It wasn't such a strange thing to do. I wasn't afraid any more. Not much. I'd get used to it down there.

'What do you say? Where would you sooner be after the bomb

drops? In a bunker with Lord and Lady Muck and their yakking little poodle and bleddy miserable auld butler, or here with me?'

'Here.'

He grinned, clamped my shoulder with his hand, squeezed too hard.

'Course you would. Good man.'

★ ★ ★

Siberia is a freezing, barren place. Nothing grows there, no animals can survive. Hear the relentless howl of fierce winds scouring the land day and night, then understand why they're so desperate to get their hands on Wales.

See the communists in ankle-length coats, thick gloves, huge fur hats, cowering in the blizzard. Watching, waiting, plotting, scheming. They couldn't succeed without the help of dupes and spies, trying to weaken our country from inside. Here's one now. Standing at the top of the market steps. Long hair, duffel coat, jeans. Holding up one of his propaganda-filled newspapers.

Students And Workers – Together We Can Bring The State To Its Knees!

'Bastard!' hissed Marek. He gripped my shoulder. 'Good work, Liam.'

I was delighted. I'd finally discovered a communist menace that he didn't know about already.

'We must report this immediately. Come on!'

The copper at the desk looked up, smiled to himself, put his pen down.

'Now then, what can I do for you three?'

Marek stepped forward, slapped his hand down on the desk.

'I want to report a communist.'

The copper's jaw dropped. Had us down as kids come to report a lost puppy.

'He stands on the market steps every Saturday, calling for the government to be overthrown.'

'Get away.'

We'd probably get a reward. Cash. Or premium bonds. Our photo in the paper. *The brave trio who nipped a communist plot in the bud.*

'Yes, in broad daylight.'

The desk sergeant clicked his tongue. He was taking the news very calmly. I thought he'd be horrified.

'We can't have that.'

He shook his head.

He was making fun of us.

He took a sip from a big mug. The bastard. Marek crossed his arms.

'So what are you going to do about it?'

The copper whistled through his teeth. Then he scratched the side of his nose.

'I'll make a note of it.'

He picked up his pen.

'Calling – for – the – government – to – be – overthrown – in – broad – daylight. Hmmm.'

He took another sip of tea.

'I'll send someone to deal with it immediately.'

I didn't believe it for a second. He winked at us.

'Thanks for the tip-off.'

Out on the street, we were older, wiser, a little sadder.

'I can't believe it. He seemed to think the whole thing was a big joke,' I said.

'The police are always asking for help in solving crime,' said Colin, 'and look how they act when you give them a tip-off.'

Marek shook his head angrily.

'If that's their attitude then we'll just have to take matters into our own hands.'

★ ★ ★

Bridie was here again; she visited Mam two or three times a week now that Dad spent so much time down in the cellar, digging tunnels. I was pretending to read a library book, but secretly keeping an eye on her and Mam.

'Where does Brendan get to all this time?'

Mam paused to puff on her fag, shake some ash into the ashtray.

'Oh, God knows, he's probably down the allotment, building an early warning system, or digging a nuclear shelter or something.'

I stiffened. Bridie guffawed.

'Oh Maureen, stop. I'll wet myself.'

Mam crossed her legs.

'Ha! I wish *I* had the time to sit around worrying about nuclear war. The guttering on the roof needs repairing, we need a new back door, the carpet on the stairs needs tacking down at the bottom . . . oh no, he hasn't time to do any of that, too busy worrying about the end of the world.'

She paused for breath, had another drag. It was like someone had taken the top off a bottle, and all the bad things about Dad were flying out of it.

'And God knows how many times I have to ask him for the money to pay the bills – "More fecking money! Do you think I'm made of the stuff?" It's a wonder we haven't had the gas and electricity cut off months ago. But of course that wouldn't bother him anyhow, he's got his wood – Jesus, there's no room to move out the back any more for the stuff – and his boxes of candles in case there's a power cut and God knows what else.'

She took a swig of the whisky.

'He's always thinking up *some* fantastic scheme. Not long after Liam was born he wanted to sell the house and move to Australia. To some place in the middle of nowhere, a bleddy desert as far as I could make out. Everyone there lives in caves under the ground and spends all their time mining for some precious mineral or other – "If you found a couple of stone of that stuff you'd be set up for life." '

She laughed scornfully. I wanted her to stop.

'Can you imagine? A complete madman. Jesus, I don't care what he's up to as long as he stays out of my hair.'

'Ah, there's no bit of a laugh in him at all.'

'Will you have another, Bridie?'

'Why not?'

She unscrewed the cap on the whisky bottle, filled Bridie's glass. That was their third, they'd had two each while they were watching *The Val Doonican Show*.

'I should have married Pat, he was a grand dancer, terrible light on his feet, and he liked a sing-song and a laugh.'

'I can't imagine Brendan singing.'

'Oh, he sings all right. Gives us all a performance every night. Rushes out of the bathroom with nothing but a towel wrapped round his waist, runs through here singing "The Wild Colonial Boy" at the top of his voice.'

'Oh Jesus!'

Bridie snorted, clasped her hand over her mouth, spilt some of her whisky on her dress.

'That'd be a sight for sore eyes all right.'

'One night he ran past just as I was letting Father Gillespie in. He took one look at yer man charging up the stairs in his towel, singing, and . . .'

Mam had one hand on her chest, waved the other at Bridie.

'The poor auld craytur went red as a beetroot, started spluttering and stuttering, "I . . . I . . . I . . . I . . ." '

Bridie snorted, sprayed whisky, bent over, choking.

'Stop!'

' "I . . . I . . . I'll come back at a more convenient time, Mrs Bennett." '

249

Bridie's glass fell to the floor as she bent double. Mam slid to one side of the chair, mouth gaping like a fish, no sound coming out.

They were drunk.

It was terrible. Dad was down in the cellar, digging tunnels so we'd survive a nuclear war, and here they were, poking fun at him, nine sheets to the wind. Mam caught my eye.

'Will you look at that one? The sour face on him. You hate to see your poor auld mammy enjoying herself, don't you?'

'You're drunk.'

Her face hardened.

'You rotten little whelp. Why shouldn't I have a drink?'

Ladies weren't supposed to get drunk.

'Ah now, leave him be, Maureen.'

'What do you want from me anyway? Why do you have to always look so bloody disapproving? If you don't like what you see, why don't you go to bed?'

I threw down the book.

'I will.'

I ran out of the room. Pushed open the cellar door, closed it carefully behind me, rushed down the steps. I stripped off, lit a candle, lowered myself into the tunnel, started crawling.

Easy does it now. Not too fast, you don't want the candle to go out. There's nothing to be afraid of, Dad knows what he's doing.

I ignored the entrances to new tunnels that were springing up and headed for the faint pinprick of light straight ahead.

'Dad.'

'Hello.'

He was moving slowly, breathing heavily. He put down the shovel, wiped his brow. He looked sad and lonely.

'How are things up above?'

'Very quiet – Mam's watching the telly, Michael's in bed.'

I didn't want him to know Bridie was here, it would only upset him. The women ruled the roost up above, drinking and gossiping, the men were in control down below, doing all the work.

'It's looking good down here, Dad. You're doing a great job.'

'Thanks, son. Christ, I'm worn out.'

'I'll help you.'

He smiled gratefully, reached out and squeezed my shoulder.

'We get on grand, don't we?'

'Yeah, we do.'

He shook his head sorrowfully.

'There were eleven of us. You meet people nowadays who say large families are a great thing. Well, don't you believe them. It was fecking awful. We were always fighting, there was never enough to go round, you see. Jayzus, I wish my father had tied a fecking knot in it.'

His voice thickened.

'My father would never talk to me the way I do to you. He'd give you a belt round the side of the head as soon as look at you. Oh God, you don't know how lucky you are.'

I *was* lucky. I had a dad who talked to me, man to man, who loved me, was doing everything he could to make sure we'd survive the next world war. He was the only one with the guts to face the future.

He might as well know what kind of future he's got to look forward to. It's not going to go away just because you don't want to think about it – Jayzus, you're no better than bleddy Chamberlain.

I wasn't going to listen to a word Mam said about him from now on. He was the only one who could save us.

★ ★ ★

The police were useless. It was down to us. We stood at the bottom of the market steps, watching Mr Sikorski marching down the street towards us. He'd come straight from work, still in his overalls, face taut, determined.

251

We had no illusions about what the enemy was like. We were not gentlemen.

A war hero. A man who'd come screaming down out of a blue summer sky, heading straight for the Germans at top speed, shattering their nerves.

They thought we were madmen, that we were going to ram them. They scattered in all directions.

Who needed the police when we had him?

'That's him.'

Marek pointed out the communist. He was shouting at a couple of teenage girls coming through the market doors, clutching Criminal Records carrier bags.

'Bring the revolution to Wales!'

They giggled, turned away. Four quick strides took Mr Sikorski to the top step, toe to toe with the communist. We fanned out behind him, ready to leap into action at a moment's notice. The communist looked round, startled; he was surrounded. Mr Sikorski snatched the paper from his hands, tore it in half, flung it down the steps behind him.

'Hey!'

He pointed to the pile of papers at his feet.

'Give me those.'

'What do you think . . .'

'You are breaking the law – it is illegal to stand in a public place and call for the violent overthrow of the government.'

The girls with the Criminal Records carrier bags stood at the bottom of the steps, staring. A crowd gathered. Gawping, nudging each other, stuffing chips into their gobs. The communist squared up to Mr Sikorski.

'Piss off!'

Mr Sikorski seized his arm, twisted it behind his back, racked it up till he was standing on his toes, yelping.

'Fascist! Let me go.'

Mr Sikorski scowled, wrapped his other arm around his

throat. The girls' mouths shot open. A strangled cry came from the communist.

'I am going to escort you to the bus station. Once there I will put you on the first bus out of town, and I strongly advise you never to come back.'

The communist threw himself to the left, a desperate attempt to escape. Mr Sikorski struggled to hold him for a moment, then tightened his grip, till the communist grimaced in pain, buckled at the knees.

If I ever got into an argument with a communist I'd tear him limb from limb.

He was going to snap his neck, leave him in a crumpled heap on the steps, surrounded by his communist propaganda.

Then, at the last minute, he loosened his hold.

'Don't try that again, I'm warning you. Come on, let's go.'

He forced him down the first step. We got ready to follow them to the bus station.

'Come on, break it up, break it up.'

A couple of coppers pushed through the crowd. Mr Sikorski nodded in their direction.

'Ha! At last. I thought you'd never realise what was going on right under your nose.'

They didn't like that.

'Now listen, sunshine . . .'

'No, you listen to me – every Saturday this man, a communist, stands here, in a place where women and children are passing, spouting hateful propaganda.'

The communist started spluttering and coughing, pointing at his throat, face turning bright red. One of the coppers nodded at Mr Sikorski.

'Let him go.'

'What?'

'Let him go, I said.'

Mr Sikorski reluctantly released him. The communist

buckled, staggered backwards, a raw, desperate noise coming out of him.

'OK, he's yours. Take him down to the station and charge him with treason.'

The coppers looked at each other – what?

'OK, sunshine, I've been very patient with you, but now I'm beginning to . . .'

'He nearly strangled me.'

'SHUT UP, YOU.'

The other copper fixed Mr Sikorski with a dangerous stare.

'Look, we've got more important things to deal with. Now push off or . . .'

'More important things? What could be more important than preventing the rise of communism? I want to speak to your superior.'

'Right, that's it. You're under arrest.'

'*What?*'

The first copper tried to grab Mr Sikorski's arm. But he was too quick, and seized the copper's wrist with one hand, pushing the flat of his other hand under his chin, and forced his head backwards. The second copper drew his truncheon, was raising it over his shoulder when Marek aimed a vicious kick at his ankle.

'Shit!'

'Tata!'

Mr Sikorski had the first copper up against the wall, the second was hopping on one leg, grimacing, bringing out his whistle.

★ ★ ★

The desk sergeant was surprised to see us again, gave us a funny look, then turned away. It had taken four coppers to arrest Mr Sikorski. They led him into a room at the end of a corridor. We waited on a bench, staring at the floor. They'd arrested *him*, let the communist go with just a ticking off. It didn't make sense. *Unless they were on the same side.* No, that was crazy. Was it? There were hardly any communists in this country outside the Valleys. But then how did the communists get to be in charge of Poland when the Poles were such great Catholics?

They're very sly.

Brainwashing. Marek had seen them do it in a film, *The Manchurian Candidate.* I could see it now. What was happening in that room. Glassy eyes, robotic voices.

You – murdered – that – man – on – the – market – steps.

Mr Sikorski framed, like Ludwik, locked up for the rest of his life.

I looked up, caught the desk sergeant watching me, a curious expression on his face. I looked back down at the floor. He was in on it too, that was why he'd tried to fob us off when we came to report a communist.

We were all in great danger. I felt Marek rising from the bench, looked up to see Mr Sikorski coming out. I couldn't see any marks or bruises on him, but they had done something awful to him in there. He looked much older, worn out, the light had gone from his eyes, his shoulders sagged.

'How dare you treat my father like this. He fought for this country.'

'That so? He can tell the judge.'

'He was a fighter pilot – do you know how many German planes he shot down?'

Mr Sikorski waved his hand angrily at Marek.

'That's enough.'

We walked back outside in silence. Mr Sikorski stopped, stared at the crowds of shoppers bustling past, his eyes like an old man's looking back on a wasted life.

'Look at them – they have no idea.'

His voice was slower, quieter than normal.

'Hitler said that if his enemies had grasped how dangerous he was earlier, and taken to the streets to fight him, they could have stopped him with just a few hundred men. Just think. But they didn't take this funny little man seriously, or didn't have the stomach for a fight, and he grew stronger, till he was in a position to crush anyone who stood against him. *That* is a lesson we should never forget. Stamp out evil before it grows too strong.'

He wasn't really talking to us, but to someone only he could see, just out of reach. Maybe it was Ludwik. He turned and left without another word. I watched him disappear into the crowds, sad and stooped, a forgotten hero.

★ ★ ★

I had to try going down the tunnels on my own. I had to do it now, get some practice in before the bombs started dropping. Then it wouldn't be so hard using them when the time came. I wasn't worried about going down there on my own, not really. I brought a ball of string, unrolled it behind me as I crawled along, so I'd be able to find my way back, like Theseus. Wore a pair of old trousers so I could carry a couple of spare candles and box of matches in the pockets.

There were lots of new tunnels.

It'll be like Spaghetti Junction down here by the time I've finished.

Actually, there were *so* many tunnels it was confusing. A couple of times I'd gone down tunnels that came to a dead end after twenty or thirty feet. Surely that wasn't a good idea, starting new ones before you'd finished the others, then leaving them and going back to the ones you were digging before?

Unless.

He'd done it deliberately, to confuse the Russians in case they ever discovered where we were.

Ingenious.

It was gloomy down there, hot, claustrophobic, as silent as the grave. It wasn't going to be a picnic. But it would be worth it.

The alternative was unthinkable.

A blinding flash, brighter than the sun, the mushroom cloud, then a hurricane smashing towns to pieces. Fires that raged for months on end. The living dead, lumps of rotting flesh hanging off their bodies, staggering through the rubble.

Help me. Water. For God's sake, please help me.

Dad was the only one prepared for the worst. They laughed at him, made jokes behind his back. But hundreds of years ago they had laughed at people who said the earth was round. They laughed at people who said you could land a man on the moon. But when the bomb goes off, and we're the only ones prepared for the worst, they won't be laughing any more. Then he'll be a hero.

Don't panic. This way, there's room for everyone in the tunnels.

Uncle Ronnie and Auntie Val, Colin and his mam and dad, Marek and his family, Miss Mellon, Joe 90 and Father Gillespie.

Above ground, Dad seemed funny sometimes. Odd even. But now I realised he was the sanest man in town.

★　★　★

We poured into the streets.

Wembley, Wembley, here we come.

We'd just beaten Northampton 2–1 in the League Cup. Stevie Boy got both goals early in the second half. Northampton pulled one back with twenty minutes to go, hit the post twice, looked certain to score till their star player had to be stretchered off. Blute caught him in the head with his elbow when the ref wasn't looking.

SIX FOOT TWO, EYES OF BLUE . . .

It was fab – *FAB, Scott!* My first ever midweek game. Before it started I stared at the silver raindrops dancing under the floodlights, listening to the first notes of the *2001* theme, thinking *there's nowhere I'd rather be.*

Mr Williams and his mate Dave were passing a hip flask between them. Mr Williams took a swig, shouted up at the sky.

'We're in the last sixteen, I can't believe it.'

He tried to return the hip flask, Dave put up his hand to stop him.

'You finish it, Cliffie.'

'No, Dave, there's loads left.'

'Go on – you're on strike, man, get it down you.'

'Well . . .'

'Empty it, for Christ's sake, will you?'

People started singing.

Come on without, come on within,
You've not seen nothing like Crindau win!

We all joined in, clapping our hands as we walked. Everyone was smiling, lit up from inside. Hard-looking blokes bumped into each other in the excitement, smiled, said, 'Sorry, mate, after you.' People opened their front doors, came out and stood on their doorsteps, to stare, soak up the atmosphere, hoping some of our excitement would rub off on them. I wanted this to last as long as possible, walking through the streets in a crowd, singing, talking about the game. And I wanted to rush home, sit quietly on my own, live through it all again, again, again, sinking into the memories like a hot bath.

'Hey!'

Someone was pushing their way through the crowd.

'Watch where you're going.'

'Hey, you!'

Uproar behind us. I turned to see what was happening. Coming straight at us. Red-faced, furious, the stench of stale tobacco and fried onions coming off him.

'Oooof!'

He sent Colin and me flying, stuck his finger in Mr Williams's face.

'What the fuck?'

He was the same height as Mr Williams, but broader, much tougher-looking. He had eyes like Blute's.

'Stay away from my wife, you cunt.'

'What?'

Mr Williams was leaning backwards, trying to escape the jabbing finger.

'You've got the wrong bloke.'

'You were seen. The car park outside The Baker's Arms after one of your concerts – strutting about like the fucking poor man's Mick Jagger.'

Everyone was staring. Mr Williams looked around, held out his arms to the people squeezing past.

'This bloke is a nutter, he's got the . . .'

The man's fist was a blur. Mr Williams staggered backwards. Blood gushed from his nose.

'Dad!'

A second punch, full in the mouth, and Mr Williams dropped like a sack of spuds. The man took a step back, giving himself more room to swing his boot into Mr Williams's head. Dave jumped on to his back, wrapped his arms round his neck.

'Fuuu—'

Was swung around like a doll.

'Hey – cut it out!'

It took five or six blokes to drag the man away from Mr Williams. He lay still on the ground, his hands covering his face.

'Dad!'

Colin tried to run to him.

'No!'

I grabbed hold of his arms, held him back.

'No, Colin, no!'

That's what best friends did. Jumped in to stop their mate from doing something stupid – like rushing over to stare at your dad's horribly mangled face. Dave crouched down, put his arm on Mr Williams's shoulder.

'Cliff, are you OK, mate?'

Colin stopped struggling. Something had slipped out of him. His face was chalk-white, tears streaming down his cheeks. I released his arms. Dave started helping Mr Williams to his feet, the front of his coat caked in dirt and blood. No one singing now. Everyone staring at us.

'Stand back,' said Dave. 'Give him some room, for Christ's sake.'

'Colin, are you all . . .'

But when I turned round, he'd vanished.

★ ★ ★

I didn't know what to think about it. It was very serious, messing with other women. Against the law if you were married. Worse, Mr Williams was a Catholic so he'd broken his sacred marriage vows. Any day now, the envelope with the Vatican seal would pop through his letterbox. His heart in his mouth as he tore it open.

You are hereby excommunicated from the Roman Catholic Church for messing with another bloke's wife.

His Excellency,

The Pope.

If he'd done it. He said he hadn't, that it was a case of mistaken identity.

It happened.

Why would he do it? It didn't make sense. Mrs Williams was gorgeous. The best-looking mother in the street. A fantastic hostess.

Hi-ya, Liam, come in. There's some chips left, they always give you too much at Alonzis. Help yourself to bread and butter.

She kept the house nice and clean, always a smile and a friendly word for everyone when she walked down the street. Lots of others with her looks wouldn't give you the time of day. Why would you cheat on someone like that? It couldn't be true. Mr Williams had it all – a gorgeous wife who loved him, he could sing and play the guitar, drive a fork-lift truck, had a fantastic record collection, a great bunch of mates. Why put all that at risk?

★ ★ ★

I paused, one foot on the bottom step, the other on the cellar floor.

'What are you doing?'

Dad looked up, grinned. He was standing in his underpants, smearing himself with lard.

'Preparing for the nuclear winter.'

'What?'

'When those bastards drop the bomb they'll fuck up the weather completely. They'll start a new ice age. It'll be a divil keeping warm.'

A shiver ran through me.

'We'll have to rub lard on ourselves?'

He had a lump of it in his hands, rubbing it up and down his chest like a bar of soap.

'This is what people did in the last century, when they couldn't afford to heat their houses. When winter came, they'd cover themselves in lard, then wrap newspapers round their bodies, and leave it on right through till the spring, grand insulation. When they put their clothes on top of the lard and paper, Jayzus, they were as warm as toast. Warm as bleddy toast, man.'

261

He reached down, picked up a newspaper.

'And no bleddy bills to pay. Fecking ingenious.'

He carefully folded the middle pages of the *Argus* round his belly, held out his arms, smiling triumphantly.

'See – it sticks to you with the lard. What did I tell you?'

'Yeah.'

He took another page, started wrapping it around his arm.

'I see that hairy fecker Williams has been cheating on his wife.'

I'd hoped he hadn't heard about it; Mam was the one interested in gossip.

'It could be a case of mistaken identity.'

He snorted derisively.

'Sex mad, he is. The long-haired waster. Jayzus, she's no better, parading down the street plastered in bleddy warpaint, a skirt on her no bigger than a handkerchief.'

'But he said he didn't do anything.'

'Ha! Cop on to yourself. Sure, what else would he say? I've seen him slobbering over every woman that passes, it'd make you sick. There's no decency these days at all. The fellas at work are always boasting about how often they've done it. Jayzus, I wouldn't have any pass on it myself. It'd disgust you, so it would. If I were you, Liam, I'd stay single. You're better off doing your own washing and cleaning in the end, even though it's the last thing you'd feel like doing at the end of a hard day's work. And for companionship, get yourself a dog. For God's sake, don't make the same mistake I did. Stay single. A wife and kids would drag a fella down.'

I was going to get married when I grew up, my wife and kids wouldn't drag me down. He was sticking newspaper on to his back now.

'Your mother was always wanting a big family. Christ, the trouble I had with that one. Two is enough.'

Now was my chance, I had to find out once and for all.

'Is Michael adopted?'

He did a double take.

'Adopted me arse – he nearly killed your mother, she was over thirty fecking hours in labour with him. Jayzus, that was one fella who never wanted to come into this world, I'm telling you.'

A horrifying thought hit me.

'Am *I* adopted?'

He snorted.

'Of course you're not, you bleddy eejit. Christ, you weren't much better, you took nearly as long as Michael. Christ, I was out and bawling in a couple of hours, no trouble to me mammy at all. Ah no, I never did the poor auld craytur no harm, not me.'

Michael was my brother. The same flesh and blood. I should have felt less alone, but I didn't. I felt cheated. If he was one of us I couldn't just ignore him, wait for someone to turn up one day, claim him back and take him away. We were stuck with him for good.

'I'll bet that hairy fecker Williams gave his poor mother a terrible time – be Christ, I'll bet they had to get a pair of tongs and *pull* the lazy bastard out.'

He held out the lard.

'Do you want a go?'

'Er, no thanks.'

He turned right around, the paper stuck to him like a second skin.

'Look, no hands.'

He laughed. The headline across his back read *Mad Dog Terrorises Estate*.

* * *

They start shouting and yelling at each other over the slightest thing, couple of hours later they're slobbering all over each other again.

263

If I called round now I'd find the three of them sitting down together in the back kitchen.

Ha ha ha. Come in, Liam, we were just laughing about that mix-up after the football match the other day, weren't we, darling?

I ran down the back lane, knocked on their door. No one answered. The door was slightly ajar, I pushed it open.

'Colin?'

I stepped inside. There was a record playing at top volume, the needle stuck, the singer saying the same thing over and over.

One . . . One . . . One . . . One . . . One . . . One . . . One . . .

The table cluttered with dirty plates and mugs, empty beer bottles, an overflowing ashtray. Mr Williams shambled out of the front room. Still in his dressing gown and pyjamas at lunch time. He hadn't shaved, had a glass of beer in his hand. Swollen nose, black eye, cut lip.

'Is Colin in?'

There was a gap between my asking and him understanding the question. He shook his head, pointed at a packet of fags on the table.

One . . . One . . . One . . .

'Any left in that one?'

I picked it up, shook it.

'No.'

One . . . One . . . One . . .

I don't know how he could stand listening to it. His eyes roamed over the table, settled on another packet.

'How about that one?'

I picked it up, shook it.

'Yeah, there's one in here.'

I waited for him to understand, 1 . . . 2 . . . 3 . . .

'Let's have it.'

I handed it to him.

'Thanks.'

One . . . One . . . One . . .

He found some matches, lit up. I followed him back into the front room. He was staring at the music centre.

One . . . One . . . One . . .

He lifted the arm, switched off the turntable, picked up the single. 'Jumpin' Jack Flash' by the Rolling Stones.

'Scratched to fuck like all the rest.'

He flung it on to the pile of singles already lying on the floor. Picked up a pair of scissors from the music centre.

'This is what she used. I caught her doing it. Luckily she was still on that first box of singles. If I'd come in any later she would have knackered every bloody record I own.'

She shouldn't have done it. I could understand her being angry, but not that. It had taken him years to build up his record collection. I tried cheering him up.

'I'll bet you can get new ones at Criminal Records.'

He slumped in a chair, staring into space.

'Is Colin in?'

1 . . . 2 . . . 3 . . .

He shook his head. Looked round for an ashtray, didn't see one, flicked his ash on the carpet.

'Will he be back soon?'

1 . . . 2 . . . 3 . . .

'No idea. His mam has taken him with her.'

'Where?'

1 . . . 2 . . . 3 . . .

'She's gone to stay with her folks in Glasweg.'

Colin was gone. An awful sinking feeling in my stomach. Glasweg was right on the other side of town, miles away. Mr Williams ran his hand across his stubble.

'She won't believe me. I kept telling her, I never went near that bloke's wife. She won't . . .'

He stared into space again.

Colin was gone. I couldn't take it in. He'd always been here, right here, just down the street; he didn't belong in Glasweg.

Had he gone there for good, or would he be back in a few days? No use asking his dad. Mr Williams was letting himself go. He was in a shocking state. He badly needed to get dressed, shaved, clean the place up. Badly.

'I'm going now, Mr Williams.'

I wasn't sure whether he heard me or not.

★ ★ ★

This time the meeting place was a playground on the Gaer Estate. A cluster of tower blocks on the edge of town, wind howling round every corner. Injun country. We'd arranged to meet a friend of a friend of Preece's there. I told Marek I didn't like it.

'You aren't supposed to *like* it, it's business. How else are we going to raise funds for the resistance?

It wasn't that. The money, what it could buy, wasn't the point. Marek was in love with the danger.

'I've got a bad feeling about this.'

Everyone knew the Gaer Estate was as rough as boots. Colin wasn't going to be any use, he'd been acting like a zombie ever since that night his dad had been attacked. We'd eventually found him standing at a bus stop, blubbering like a baby, got him home in a taxi.

Marek gave me a sombre look, nodded.

'I know. Me too. Don't worry, I've taken precautions.'

We got there early, so we'd be one step ahead. Not early enough. The red glow of a cigarette guided us to the swings.

'Are you Gary?'

'Yeah. You Marek?'

'Yes.'

'Funny name.'

'Do you want to talk or do business?'

Gary stood up. He made Preece look cuddly. He nodded at the bag.

266

'That the stuff?'

'Yes.'

There was a movement behind us. I turned, saw five kids lurking in the shadows.

'We've got company.'

'What's this?' asked Marek. 'We were told it would be just you.'

'You've got your mates, I've got mine.'

'Tell them to get lost.'

'Why?'

'If they don't, there's no deal.'

'What's the matter, Mary, you nervous?'

Behind me, somebody sniggered. I was scared. I caught Colin's eye. *You ready for this, mate?* No, he was shitting himself. Brilliant. It was down to me and Marek. Gary flicked his butt to the floor.

'What's to stop us from just taking those fags off you, Mary?'

'This.'

In a flash Marek had a knife at Gary's throat.

Don't worry, I've taken precautions.

'Tell them to back off.'

My head was throbbing, my throat was parched. I hoped desperately that Marek knew what he was doing. I really didn't know if he did any more. I was pissing my pants, to be honest.

'Tell them or I'll cut you.'

A sound like something solid forcing its way down a plug-hole, Gary swallowing.

'Back off.'

His gang retreated a few steps, stealing anxious glances at each other.

'Tell them to keep going, right over to the slide.'

That was on the far side of the playground. Gary told them. Slowly, step by step, they backed away.

'Give me the money.'

Gary passed it over. Marek held it out.

'Liam.'

I took it from him.

'Is it all there?'

It was no good, I couldn't count it, my hands were shaking too much.

'Well, *is it?*'

I'd drop it all over the floor if I carried on trying to count it, so I said 'Yeah' and just hoped it was. Marek chucked the bag on to the ground in front of Gary.

'You see, even though you tried to cheat us, we stuck to our deal. We are men of honour.'

He took the knife away from Gary's neck. Gary sagged, nearly collapsed. Jerked his head back just in time as Marek flicked it under his neck again.

'My name isn't Mary. It's Marek. Understand?'

Gary made a faint movement with his head.

'It's a Polish name. Say it.'

'Marek.'

His voice had shrunk.

'Here's some advice. Don't ever try to cheat a Pole. Come on, let's go.'

We didn't look back. Walked quickly, purposefully, our heads held high. Didn't start running till we turned the corner.

* * *

I put a penny in the slot, took a candle from the box, lit it. Waited for the wax to drip down on to the little black metal saucer, then stuck it on. I put my hands together, looked up at the statue of the Virgin Mary lit up from below by the flickering flames.

Please, Holy Mother, give us strength to face the horrors ahead.

Protect the survivors in their tunnels. I know those who turn against the Church deserve everything they get, but when the war begins, please ask God to keep the casualties as low as possible – forty or fifty million. Thank you very much. Amen.

I bowed my head, blessed myself. Looked up at her again. I could see the pain and suffering in her eyes. She'd seen her only son crucified, the holy saints tortured and murdered, churches burnt to the ground by communists. She'd never once complained. Hands outstretched, head to one side, gazing down sadly. That's exactly how she must have looked to the children at Fatima. Hovering in midair right in front of them. About six feet off the ground. Any higher and you'd get a crick in your neck looking up at her, and she wouldn't want that. A shadow fell over me. I looked up, saw Miss Mellon.

'Hello, Liam. Penny for your thoughts.'

The inviting look in her eyes, her closeness, the glowing candles, the Virgin Mary looking down on us, the sweet smell of incense, soft murmuring of the organ from above. *Tell her.*

'I'm worried, Miss.'

She moved closer, lowered her voice.

'What about, Liam?'

'Nuclear war, Miss.'

The shock in her eyes; she'd thought it would be some kid's stuff she could laugh off.

There's a monster under my bed.

'Really?'

'Yes, Miss. I'm frightened, I can't stop thinking about the millions of horrible deaths.'

'Those are very morbid thoughts for someone your age.'

'Thanks.'

She'd finally realised how grown up I was – that's what morbid meant.

'Then there's the nuclear winter – the only way the survivors will be able to keep warm is to rub lard all over their bodies, then cover themselves in newspapers – it'll be awful!'

She gave me a curious look.

I nodded at the statue of the Virgin Mary.

'She warned us, didn't she? Told us what to expect at Fatima. The end of the world.'

Miss Mellon smiled a thin, sad smile. She was lovely, but there was something sad about her too. She needed someone to take care of her. Someone like me. I just needed to grow up a bit – the difference in our height might be a problem otherwise.

'It's going to happen. There's nothing we can do about it.'

'That's not true.'

She tucked a loose strand of hair behind her ear, bit her lip.

'There *is* something we can do.'

'Yes, ambush trains carrying communists into Wales.'

Her eyes widened in alarm.

'No, fighting violence with more violence is never the answer.'

It was the *only* answer, but I could see she didn't like it.

'But Miss, Hitler himself said he could have been stopped by a few hundred men if they'd acted earlier.'

She shook her head gently.

'Liam, where did you hear that?'

I shrugged, didn't want to tell her about Mr Sikorski being arrested.

'It was in the *Argus*, I think.'

She looked doubtful.

'We have to use peaceful means. Write letters to governments, sign petitions, go on marches . . .'

How would *that* change anything?

Her gaze deepened.

'Liam, is everything all right at home?'

I'm playing second fiddle to my kid brother, Mam and Dad

hate each other, Dad spends every night digging tunnels under our house. No, nothing to report.

'Yes, thanks.'

She didn't look convinced, wouldn't stop looking at me in that unnerving way, like she could tell what I was trying to hide from her.

Tell her. Go on, tell her everything.

No, don't start that again. Don't weaken now. *Careless talk costs lives.*

'I have to go now, Miss.'

★ ★ ★

I was walking down the road with Marek, had just told him about Colin's dad being attacked after the football game.

'And now he and his mam have gone to live with his nan.'

Marek nodded to himself, as if deciding something about him.

'He's on strike, isn't he?'

'Yeah.'

His expression darkened.

'Tata told me how after the war many Poles got jobs in factories.'

He started wagging his finger.

'And in some of these factories everybody walked out because they said the Poles were working too hard. And the management were forced to sack them. *Them!* The Poles who were producing three times as much as everyone else! That was their reward. They painted *Poles Go Home!* on walls. Tata doesn't agree with strikes, and neither do I.'

I didn't know about any of that, I only knew Mr Williams was a great bloke. I didn't understand what had gotten into Marek lately, the slightest thing set him off. I was glad to see something that would help me change the subject.

'Hey, Marek, isn't that your brother, Jan?'

He was walking down the other side of the road, a suitcase in each hand, his saxophone in a case slung over his shoulder. Marek peered suspiciously at him.

'What's he up to now?'

We ran after him.

'Where are you going?'

He stopped, put down the suitcases. He had angry red welts across both palms, sweat beginning to trickle down his forehead.

'I'm leaving.'

'*Leaving?*'

Jan took a deep breath. This was terrible. Now Marek's family were starting to break up, just like Colin's. Where would it end?

'I'm going to live in London. Hanka will put me up until I can find a place of my own.'

Marek took a step back, as if he might catch something.

'*Hanka?*'

'Yes, Hanka.'

We don't talk about her any more.

Jan took a long, careful look at Marek. He smiled, his eyes still sad.

'You should be pleased – now you'll have the room to yourself.'

Marek didn't smile back.

'Why are you leaving?'

'Wait till you get older, and want to do something that Tata doesn't like. Then you'll understand.'

He bent down to pick up his suitcases, paused, looked up again, smiled.

'Goodbye, little man.'

Marek clenched his fists.

'I'm *not* a little man.'

Jan walked away. Marek stood watching him.

'He'll be sorry.'

But it was Marek who looked sorry.

★ ★ ★

We'd be married in the summer, drive through Crindau in my E-type Jag afterwards, beeping the horn, tins on strings jumping and clattering behind us. I'd wear my Liverpool shirt, leather jacket, sunglasses, one hand on the steering wheel, the other round her shoulders.

'Everything all right, darling?'

'This is the happiest day of my life, Liam.'

We'd had to wait till I was eighteen.

'Do you, Liam Bennett, Crindau's star player, take Miss Mellon to be your lawful wedded wife?'

'I do.'

'I now pronounce you m . . . m . . . m . . . m . . . man and w . . . w . . . w . . . w . . . w . . .'

Come on, Gillo, you can do it.

'W . . . w . . . wife.'

Yes!

Dad tried to talk me out of it.

A wife and kids would drag a fella down, take my advice and stay single.

Mam too.

Don't do it, getting married was the biggest mistake of my bleddy life.

But I wouldn't make the same mistake they'd made. I was marrying someone I loved, not someone I hated.

★ ★ ★

It was freezing cold on the picket line, there were far fewer people than last week. There were no jokes, speeches or cheers

273

this time, everyone was cold and miserable and had disappeared inside themselves. It was the first time Colin had seen his dad since he'd been beaten up. Mr Williams was trying to act as if nothing bad had happened.

'Cold today, eh, buttie?'

'Yeah.'

Colin's voice was a whisper, his eyes avoiding his dad's. Mr Williams rubbed his hands together, stamped his feet, made an effort to make his voice bright and breezy.

'What's it like at your nan's, then?'

'OK.'

Mr Williams laughed, as if Colin had said something hilarious.

'Yeah, right – apart from the smell.'

Colin was always complaining about the smell of cats in his nan's house – she had seven.

'It's not as bad as it used to be.'

'Had them all put down, has she?'

'No.'

Mr Williams pushed Colin's shoulder.

'I was *joking*, son!'

It was embarrassing. The more Mr Williams tried to act like nothing was wrong, the more obvious he made it that something was. Colin looked as though he wanted the ground to open up and swallow him. Mr Williams lit a fag, looked round to check no one was watching, then handed Colin an envelope, *Tina* written on it. He lowered his voice.

'Give that to your mam.'

Colin looked at it suspiciously.

'Go on, it won't bite.'

Colin stuffed it in his pocket, caught my eye, nodded towards the road.

'We've got to go now, Dad.'

We were meeting Marek at the HQ. He said he'd a special mission planned for today, that we mustn't be late.

'Bye, son.' He winked at me. 'See you, Liam.'

'See you, Mr Williams. Good luck with the strike.'

★ ★ ★

Marek came into the bunker carrying a shoulder bag. He was tenser than I'd ever seen him.

'What's the plan?'

'First, let's have a drink.'

He went and got the bottles of vodka and orange, and three cups from the corner of the bunker.

'Gentlemen, a toast.'

We held our glasses up.

'To the success of today's mission.'

Marek knocked his back in one, screwed up his face, shook his head. He started making himself another straight away. Me and Colin got stuck into ours. No one said a word till we were on our third, then Marek opened his bag, brought out three balaclavas.

'We will wear these. Pull them right down over your heads. I have made eyeholes.'

We put them on. We looked at each other. We looked different; we looked frightening.

'We are going to ambush the 12.35 to Merthyr Tydfil using these . . .'

Moving very slowly, Marek took out three bottles, placed them on the floor. Each of them filled with liquid, a rag stuffed inside, one end soaked in the liquid, the other poking up through the top of the bottle.

'Gentlemen, these are Molotov cocktails.'

'Jesus, Marek.'

He met my eyes, nodded, grim-faced.

'You saw what happened to Tata, arrested for daring to touch a communist. They are getting too confident, we need to teach them a lesson, show them that we mean business.'

He checked his watch.

'It's 12.09 already, let's go.'

*　★　*

We leaned on the railway bridge, staring at the empty track in front of us.

'What's the time?'

'12.32.'

I was high on vodka, scared shitless by the thought of what I was about to do. Marek nudged me.

'Liam – do you think I'm crazy?'

I looked into his eyes, black pools that reflected nothing. I wasn't sure, just knew that I wouldn't be the one to back down first.

'You have no idea what it's like. You can visit your country every year, and see your uncles and aunts and cousins. You can go and live there when you finish school and take an Irish wife. How I envy you.'

I was pierced with embarrassment and guilt. Now I wished that going to Ireland every summer meant more to me. I felt I hadn't done anything to deserve it.

'I have no real home. The communists have stolen it. The Poles have always been victims. No one has ever cared what happened to them. Maybe that does make you a little crazy in the end.'

'Here it comes.'

Colin was pointing to the front of the train coming round the bend.

'Right!'

Marek took out a lighter, snapped on the flame. The train rattled closer. My mouth was bleached dry, my eyes felt raw, as if a layer had been peeled off.

'Ready . . .'

Twenty feet away now. Marek lit the Molotov cocktails. Colin looked like he was going to burst into tears. I looked away, didn't want to catch his fear. *Don't look at him, look down at the train.*

'Steady . . .'

The first carriage disappeared under us, the bridge shook.

'Fire!'

Colin's missed completely, fell uselessly into the grass by the side of the track. Mine bounced off the edge of the train's roof, spun into the air, struck a tree, *still* didn't break, disappeared into the undergrowth. Marek took aim, threw.

Whuumpff!

Direct hit. The flames erupted, disappeared under the bridge. We ran to the other side, saw the fire eating the roof.

'Jesus, we did it.'

Marek crossed himself.

'God guided my hand.'

There was no shouting or punching the air this time. No one spoke. The three of us stood side by side, staring at the burning carriage disappearing down the track. This was the real thing. This was war.

The flames were already covering half the roof. What if someone got hurt? *Don't think about that.*

We were wearing disguises, no one had seen us. No chance of ever being discovered. The perfect mission.

'What was that?'

A noise behind us. We turned, saw two boys, our age, goggle-eyed, crouching in the trees.

'Get them.'

They were already racing down the hill. The first one disappeared into the trees. The second tripped, got up again, but he was dazed, and we'd gained a few yards. Looked over his shoulder, saw us getting closer, panicked. Ran blindly now, scraping himself on branches, stumbling on uneven ground. Didn't notice the fallen branch. Went crashing to the ground, landed heavily, the breath exploding out of him. We were on him almost straight away, pounding his face, arms, body.

'Filthy spy.'

'Communist bastard.'

'Who sent you?'

'No one.'

'Liar!'

The terror in his eyes. The pitiful whimpering sounds escaping from him. The scratchy feel of the new balaclava on my face. The struggle to get in a telling punch as the other two threw theirs.

'How long have you been spying on us?'

'Who were you going to tell?'

'Who sent you?'

I grabbed a handful of his hair, pulled. He screamed. We hadn't signed the Geneva Convention. We'd do whatever was necessary to make him talk.

He had it coming.

'Hold him still.'

Marek took the knife from his pocket.

'Who sent you?'

Tears flooded his eyes.

'I'll ask you again – who sent you?'

He started blubbering. We shouldn't have to see that. He should take his punishment like a man. What did he expect?

Colin spat in his face.

'Which organisation do you belong to?'

Marek pressed the blade into his neck.

'I'll count to three, and if you haven't answered by then, I'll cut your throat. One . . . two . . .'

'The Boys' Brigade.'

'The Boy . . .' Marek screwed up his face in disgust. He drew back. Looked at us as though he'd smelt something rotten. 'We're dealing with amateurs.'

'Jesus!'

Colin pulled a face, pointed at a stain spreading across the front of the boy's trousers.

'He's pissed himself.'

'Ugh!'

He was blubbering like a baby now, trying to hide his face from us. Marek took a deep breath.

'Listen to me. If you want to live, you must promise never to reveal to anyone what you saw here today. And as a guarantee of your future behaviour, I will need to know your name and address, and the name and address of your friend.'

'I can't do that.'

Marek lowered his voice, brought the knife back to his throat, smiled at him.

'Oh yes, you can.'

★ ★ ★

Marek, Colin and I walked slowly down Mount Pleasant Road. The houses here had names as well as numbers – *Dingly Dell, Belvedere, Camelot.* Their own garages, a tennis court in one of the gardens. We didn't fit in. I didn't. It was pouring down. My trousers and feet soaking, rain running down my neck, wet seeping through my anorak.

Marek stopped, gripped my arm.

'That's it, number thirty-five.'

Pendragon.

'What do we do now?' asked Colin.

'This.'

Marek strode right up to the front door and knocked loudly, three times. Waved us forward to join him. A lady answered the door. She looked like she knew we'd done something, she just couldn't figure out what it was yet.

'Hello, Mrs Wilkins, is Paul there?'

She didn't drop her guard.

'What do you want?'

'We won't come in, we're in a hurry – that's my father parked just down the road.'

He pointed at a car about thirty feet away, its engine running.

'He's taking me and my friends Robert and Graham to Boys' Brigade.'

We'd interrogated the other one thoroughly, knew this was the night they went.

'I just wanted to drop something off that I borrowed from Paul yesterday.'

He was brilliant. Exactly the kind of bright, sensible, polite boy you'd want your son to have as a friend. The lady relaxed.

'I'll just get him.'

As soon as she was gone, we pulled on our balaclavas. Marek took out a gun.

'Christ! What are you doing? You said we were just going to frighten him.'

'I think this should do the trick, don't you?'

This was mad. This wasn't happening. Marek looked sharply at Colin.

'You didn't believe me, did you?'

He was holding it in both hands, its barrel pointing downwards. Old, cumbersome, heavy, his father's RAF pistol.

Paul walked into the hall, froze. Stared at the gun in Marek's hands.

'Hello, Paul, remember us?'

Paul glanced back into the room.

'Look at me!'

His head snapped back round.

'Thinking of calling your parents?'

Paul wavered. All he had to do was shout. Marek raised the gun, pointed it at him.

'Go ahead and try it. I'll blow your head clean off.'

Paul looked into Marek's eyes, decided against it. The blood drained from his face. I heard a toddler's chatter, the theme music from *Tomorrow's World*, cozy familiar sounds from just a few feet away, that belonged to another world now.

'You'd better keep your mouth shut about what you saw in Cwm Wood if you know what's good for you. Understand?'

He nodded.

'You're out of your depth, Paul. Stay away from Cwm Wood. You got that?'

Paul's face was crumbling. His shoulders were shaking, his mouth a horrible slit, tears rolled down his cheeks.

'Now go back inside and act as if nothing has happened.'

Marek took a step back, nodded to us to do the same. He called out, 'See you in school tomorrow, Paul.'

We edged our way back down to the gate, then into the road, one eye on Paul motionless in the hall, blubbering. Marek put the gun away. He'd never talk, neither of them, they were too scared. We were ruthless, desperate men now, iron in our souls. You had to fight terror with terror. I was terrified. We were out of control. I wanted someone to stop us. We walked in silence for a while, then Colin said, 'Did we *have* to do that?'

'Yes, we did. He could have ruined everything. Spies have to be dealt with very severely.'

Colin hung his head.

'I don't want to do anything like that ever again.'

'Like father, like son.'

'What's that supposed to mean?'

'You're going on strike now, yes? Just like your father.'

'You leave my father out of this.'

'Marek, you shouldn't say that. Of course you can trust Colin, and *his* dad.'

Marek laughed bitterly.

'Trust a man who cheats on his wife?'

My throat shrivelled. Colin turned on me.

'You told him!'

'I told him about your dad being attacked. I didn't accuse him of anything.'

'I asked you not to.'

'I didn't mean any harm. Marek, tell him . . .'

'There's no smoke without fire,' said Marek.

Colin's punch was wild, Marek dodged it easily. Then stood still, staring him out, daring him to try again. Colin's eyes filled to the brim.

'You're a couple of bastards.'

He ran straight into the road.

'COLIN!'

A car screeched to a halt inches from him. The driver collapsed on the wheel, blaring his horn. Colin stumbled, fell into a puddle, cursed, got up, disappeared down an alley. The driver rolled down the window, swore at us, and drove away.

'What did you say that for?'

I heard my voice cracking. Marek looked keenly into the middle distance, as if he'd just spotted something suspicious.

'We shouldn't hang around here, it's too dangerous.'

'Marek . . .'

'I'll see you tomorrow.'

He turned the corner, walked away.

★ ★ ★

Monday morning. Colin was already sitting at the desk. We'd fallen out before. The time I'd cracked him across the face with a ruler. The day he'd poured ink in my hair. We'd always made it up eventually.

'Hi-ya, Colin.'

He didn't reply. If he hadn't shifted very deliberately right to the edge of the bench, I wouldn't have known he'd heard me. I buried the hurt, the anger, carried on.

'About your dad . . .'

He turned his head in the opposite direction. Stuck his nose in the air, as if there was a bad smell coming off me.

I wasn't taking that from anyone.

'Suit yourself.'

Marek was watching, then turned away when I met his eye. It was all his fault. I wondered how long Colin would keep it up this time. He hadn't spoken to me for nearly a week when I hit him with the ruler. Thommo marched in, whistling the theme from *The Dam Busters*.

'Right! You've got *me* today, you lucky lot.'

Colin and I turned to each other.

'What's going on?'

'Where's Miss . . .'

He remembered he wasn't talking to me any more, turned away again. He could be pathetic sometimes. I shifted right to the edge of my side of the bench.

Thommo looked at the wilting flowers in the vase, turned down his mouth at the corners. Miss Mellon brought in fresh flowers every week. He snatched them from the vase, chucked them into the bin. He pulled her chair back, sat down at her desk, like it was *his* classroom.

'Right!'

Took out the register, licked his finger, opened it. Where was she? She'd never missed a day before.

★ ★ ★

283

Mam told us at dinner, she'd heard all about it at the hairdressers'.

'Miss Mellon's been sacked.'

No, it couldn't be true. Why would anyone sack her? I looked around the table, expecting everyone to be horrified. Dad shoved a spud into his gob, hadn't even heard, sat at the table with us, his eyes seeing only the tunnels. Michael stared at the wall, lost in his own world.

White knight takes black rook. Black queen moves left to protect black king.

I was the only one who cared.

It didn't make sense, she was the best teacher in school.

'God, it's a shame, if it wasn't for her we'd never have known Michael was a prodigy.'

There *was* that. Still.

'Why was she sacked?'

'She was on that big Ban the Bomb rally in Cardiff the other week.'

'She got the sack for that?'

Mam took a deep breath, put down her knife and fork.

'There's something rotten going on in that school. There was a photo of her holding a banner in the paper – she saw Mr Thompson going in to see Partridge with it folded under his arm. Partridge called her in half an hour later and wiped the floor with her. Asked her what kind of example she was setting to young children, making a spectacle of herself on the street, accused her of being a double agent for the Methodists, deliberately making Roman Catholics look bad and ruining the reputation of the school.'

We are a tiny island of Roman Catholics in a sea of Methodists.

That was a lie, she'd never try and make us look bad, she was a fantastic Catholic. She'd been framed, like poor Ludwik and Mr Sikorski.

★ ★ ★

It was halfway down page 4 of the *Argus*.

Passengers noticed smoke billowing past the window, then grew concerned when the ceiling started getting hotter. They pulled the emergency cord when the paint on the ceiling started to bubble. The train was evacuated, and passengers were forced to walk three miles along the tracks to the nearest station, Abertillery. The police have not ruled out hooliganism.

But what I remembered most was the first boy pissing himself in fear, the second crying like a baby on the doorstep. I felt sick to my stomach.

★   ★   ★

I couldn't sleep. I had too much on my mind. This was turning into the worst year of my life. A patch of moonlight shone through the window, lighting up Michael's face. The little spaz looked so relaxed, not a care in the world.

The sleeping prodigy.

His only concern how long it would take to beat his next opponent. Not a clue what was going on in the real world. Mam and Dad hating each other, Miss Mellon getting the sack, the tunnels under the house, the thousands of nuclear missiles pointed at us. No, *I* was the one saddled with all the worries, leaving him free to concentrate on being a genius.

Suddenly his eyes opened. He stared right at me, didn't look away after a couple of seconds, like I expected. Usually he wouldn't dare to hold my gaze. It was strange, I wasn't angry, I felt relieved.

I'm not alone. There are two of us. We're the same flesh and blood. The fighting has to stop, life is too short.

He wasn't adopted, he was a chip off the old block. Maybe now was the time to bury the hatchet. Our backs were against the wall. Well, mine was. We had to stick together. We needed each other. He closed his eyes again. He hadn't gone back to

285

sleep. He'd lost his nerve. Frightened I'd do something to him. But I didn't want to push him around any more. It was boring. I wanted someone I could talk to. I waited for him to open his eyes and look at me again.

'Michael.'

I made my voice as soft and light as a feather, so as not to startle him.

'Michael, are you awake?'

He didn't answer, didn't look away.

'You're my brother, my *real* brother. When I said you were adopted, I was just making it up. I checked with Dad, you're one of us. I'll never raise my hand to you again, all right?'

He shook his head.

'You're not my brother.'

'Yes, I am.'

'No, you're not, you were adopted.'

Jesus, how could a prodigy be so stupid? Still, at least he was talking to me for a change. That was a relief in itself, it was creepy, the way he hardly ever spoke.

'Listen to me,' I said. '*Neither* of us is adopted.'

'You *can't* be my brother, you're nothing like me.'

Suddenly I got it.

'Listen, you're just a kid, I know you must feel you'll never match up to me, no matter how hard you try, but in a few years you'll . . .'

'What?'

'There's no need to feel inferior . . .'

'*Inferior?*'

'Yeah, I know I must seem . . .'

'No! You don't get it, do you? You can't be my brother. I'm a prodigy, you're really thick.'

I was out of the bed and on top of him before either of us knew what was happening. My hands round his throat, squeezing tighter, tighter, tighter.

286

'I'M NOT THICK!'

A horrible sound from below me. A mangy dog arching its back, desperately trying to be sick.

'I'M NOT—'

I bore down on him with all my weight.

Go on, he asked for it. Go on. Do it! Do it!

My arms started to shake. Tears rolled down my cheek. I let go of him. I rolled off the bed, fell on to the floor, lay there.

I'd nearly killed him. Wanted to. I curled into a ball. I was shivering. Gradually my breathing slowed down. I waited till his was nearly back to normal before I spoke.

'Michael.'

The sounds coming from his bed frightened me. Desperate, heaving sobs between each agonised breath.

'Michael – are you all right?'

His breathing became more regular, broken up by little sniffles and whimpers.

'I won't touch you again, I promise. The two of us will stick together from now on.'

He lay completely still.

'Michael?'

'I'll tell Preece.'

'Fuck you.'

★   ★   ★

I pushed open the back door.

'Hi-ya, Ma— What are *you* doing here?'

Bridie looked up from laying the table.

'That's a nice greeting now.'

'Where's Mam?'

'She's out with some of the other mothers, getting people to sign a petition to try and get Miss Mellon her job back.'

'But . . . but who's going to make the tea?'

'Me.'

Mam should be here, cooking, not off somewhere messing about with petitions. She was breaking her marriage vows, she'd be excommunicated if a priest found out.

'When will she be back?'

'Ah, she won't be long. An hour or two at most. You should be proud of your mammy, she's doing everything she can to save your teacher's job.'

It *was* good that someone was standing up for Miss Mellon. No one else in this family seemed to care.

'Do you like Miss Mellon?'

'Yeah, she's great.'

'She is so, my Carmel and Eileen loved her to bits.'

Bridie checked her watch.

'Oh Jesus, yer man will be home any minute expecting his grub. Let's get moving.'

Me and Michael helped her get the plates, cups and saucers ready. She was great with Michael, even got a smile out of him, winked at me over his head to show me she realised how childish he was, how easily fooled. Prodigy my arse.

'Ah, you're a grand pair of men. I'd be lost without you.'

Dad pushed open the door. There were big black bags under his eyes, he looked like he hadn't slept for a week. He froze when he saw Bridie at the cooker.

'What the . . .'

'Brendan, how are you?'

'Where's Maureen?'

She told him.

'She should be here, making me dinner.'

'I've made it – sit down, will you, it's ready.'

'You should be at home, taking care of your own family.'

'Carmel's sixteen now, and Eileen's nearly fifteen. They're well able to look after the others for a couple of hours.'

Dad grunted, sat down, stared at his plate.

'What the feck's this?'

'Sausages, chips and peas.'

Not just any chips either – Birds Eye crinkle-cut chips. And three great big bangers each – just beginning to burst open, a bit blackened at the ends, exactly how I liked them. What a fantastic cook!

'But today's boiled bacon and cabbage.'

'We often have this at home – the kids love it.'

'I don't fecking care what you have at home, I want me boiled bacon and cabbage.'

Bridie sniffed, speared a chip.

'It's about four hours from now.'

'What?'

'The next boat train to Ireland. You'd better get on it if you want boiled bacon and cabbage, because *this* is what's for tea tonight in this house. It's all I had time to do after rushing over to help out, and *this* is the thanks I get.'

He stared at his plate. Hating what he saw, loving it, absolutely starving.

'It'll be getting cold. I'd say you'd be quare hungry after a long day at work.'

'Bleddy chips out of a packet . . .'

He speared some with his fork. Bridie picked up a slice of buttered bread, stuck some chips on it, smothered them in tomato sauce, folded the bread in half.

'You can't beat the auld chip butty, isn't that right Liam?'

Dad scowled, he *hated* chip butties. Bridie took a big mouthful. She made me want to smile the way she was carrying on, she should have been on the telly. She pulled a funny face at me, winked. I laughed. Dad shot me an angry look. She rolled her eyes to heaven.

'Mmm! Bleddy gorgeous.'

Michael looked at her, then Dad, wondering if he dare make a butty himself. Dad had his head down, shovelling the grub in.

'You're looking tired, Brendan.'

It was true. His skin was grey.

'I'm grand.'

'Well,' said Bridie, '*something's* making you awful weary-looking. God knows what you must get up to every night.'

He froze.

'I don't get up to anything.'

'There's no need to take that tone with me. I'm only making conversation.'

'I don't like conversation at the dinner table.'

'Are you dancing the night away in some nightclub? I hear you're a great man for the singing and dancing.'

'Shut your bleddy mouth, you auld hoor.'

'Or do you have yourself a fancy woman?'

Dad threw down his knife and fork.

'Feck off.'

'Have you ever thought of going to the doctor?'

'Wha . . .'

'Because I'd say you've got high blood pressure. Flying off the handle like that over someone pulling your leg.'

'Will you mind your own fecking business?' He pointed his knife at her. 'I won't tell you again!'

'See what I mean?'

She shrugged.

'Come on, eat up, boys.'

★ ★ ★

When we'd finished our tea, Dad nodded at the door.

'Thanks for your help, now feck off.'

'I'll stay till Maureen gets back.'

'Feck off, I said.'

She smiled pleasantly, as if she hadn't heard him swearing at her.

'I'll do the washing up, then go and sit with the boys for a while.'

She got up, collected the dirty plates, took them over to the sink.

'But I want to have a bath.'

She smirked, turned on the tap.

'Go ahead, I'm not stopping ya.'

'You're . . . you're *inhibiting* me, so you are. I can't relax and go about my normal routine with you here.'

'Liam, would you pass me the knives and forks, there's a good fella.'

'For feck's sake!'

Dad went into the bathroom, slammed the door behind him. Bridie started humming 'The Wild Colonial Boy'. She turned round, shouted at the bathroom door.

'I'm looking forward to the song and dance routine.'

I was getting out of there.

'I'm going to see Uncle Ronnie and Auntie Val.'

★ ★ ★

I'd only gone a few feet down the street when Mr Williams opened the front door, stepped outside. He looked different. Clean-shaven, hair washed, dressed in his best clothes. Black leather jacket, ribbed black polo-neck, white flares, cowboy boots. He looked happier than I'd seen him for weeks. He checked his pockets.

Wallet, fags, keys – all present and correct.

Ready for a big night out. Looked up, smiling at someone. Mrs Williams followed him out the door.

They'd made it up.

She looked fantastic. Long shiny red mac, white tights, knee-length black boots. She was smiling too. Colin came out next, in a brand new blue anorak with a furry hood, closing the door behind him. I pressed myself against the wall. Didn't want him to see me, think I was snooping on him.

Mr Williams ruffled Colin's hair.

'All right, mate?'

'Where are we going, Dad?'

Mr Williams smiled. The smile of a man who'd had it all, lost it, won it back again.

'The Wimpy Bar.'

'Yeah!'

The lucky pig. The times I'd stood outside the Wimpy Bar drooling over the photos in the window – burger in a bun with chips and peas; melted cheese on burger in a bun with chips and peas. Or beans if you preferred, no extra cost. A glass of Coke with an ice cream float to finish.

Other people's parents had blazing rows, things were terrible for a while, then they made it up. Mam and Dad had been having the same awful argument for years, never made it up, no kisses, hugs or trips to the Wimpy Bar to celebrate.

Jayzus are you mad? There's food at home, I'm not paying good money for greasy auld chips.

I flattened myself against the wall, watched them walking up the street in front of me. Mr and Mrs Williams hand in hand, Colin trotting alongside them, a big soppy grin plastered across his face.

I wasn't jealous.

I pushed myself away from the wall and ran down the street to Uncle Ronnie and Auntie Val's.

Auntie Val answered the door. Her face lit up when she saw me.

'Hi-ya, Liam. Come in.'

I felt tears welling up in my eyes. I wanted to hug her. No matter how awful things were, no matter how mad things got at home, Uncle Ronnie and Auntie Val were always pleased to see me. Nothing bad ever happened there.

She led me into the kitchen. Uncle Ronnie was at the table, filling in his pools coupon.

'Hi-ya, buttie.'

Pools on a Wednesday. Everything as it always was. No nasty surprises.

'Here you are, lovely,' said Auntie Val, passing me a glass of orange juice and a Wagon Wheel.

'I wanted to ask you something,' said Auntie Val. 'Have you or your mam or dad heard any strange noises late at night recently?'

'No.'

Uncle Ronnie shifted uneasily in his chair.

'Val, he doesn't want to hear about this.'

'I do.'

Strange noises in the night. It sounded exciting, scary, like a ghost story. I had to know. I unwrapped the Wagon Wheel, nibbled off a bit of the wavy chocolate coating, uncovering the crunchy biscuit underneath.

'The last couple of nights, I keep hearing an alarm clock going off every half-hour – *ring, ring, ring.* The first time I heard it, it was so quiet, it sounded so far away, I started thinking I must have imagined it. Then, just when I was dropping off, I heard it again. I know this sounds strange, but it sounded like it was coming from right under our house – are you all right, Liam?'

I was choking. A bit of Wagon Wheel had gone down the wrong way.

'Have a drink, for God's sake!'

I slurped down some orange juice but did it too quickly so it came rushing back up my nose, flushing out of both nostrils. Auntie Val got up, slapped me on the back, passed me her handkerchief.

'Thanks, I'm all right now.'

'I woke Ronnie up.'

'Half past one in the bloody morning.'

'And of course his hearing isn't as good as mine.'

'Half asleep, I was, and she's nudging me and going "Ronnie, listen, can you hear an alarm going off in the distance?" '

'Made such a row waking up he didn't hear it. Just you wait, I said, it'll go off again in another half-hour.'

'Thought she'd gone bloody gaga, I did.'

'So I made him a cup of tea.'

'With a tot of rum in it.'

'And we come down here, and sure enough, at two in the morning it goes off again – *ring, ring, ring*.'

He was going to get caught.

'We both heard it this time, *just*, so faint you'd miss it if it was in the daytime, but at that time in the morning . . .'

'With everything so quiet, like.'

'You'd *swear* it was coming from underground.'

Auntie Val tapped her foot on the floor.

'Right beneath where we're sitting now.'

'Gave me the creeps, it did.'

'Had a terrible job getting back to sleep, didn't we, Ronnie?'

'Didn't feel safe in our own house, wondering what was going on underneath us.'

I wanted to. I couldn't. Tell them it was only Dad. That they shouldn't worry.

'The next morning, I had a word with Lynette next door, told her what I've just told you. "Oh Val, thank God for that," she said. "I heard it too – I thought I was going mad, I didn't dare mention it to Martin." '

He was definitely going to get caught.

'I said to her, we should ring the council, find out if they're doing any work underground, laying pipes or something.'

'And if we don't get any answers from them, we should go to the police – for all we know there might be some maniac down there.'

'Escaped from some lunatic asylum, living underground like a bloody mole to avoid capture.'

'Oh!'

'Sorry, Auntie Val.'

I'd dropped the glass on the floor.

'I'm sorry.'

'Don't worry, love, it's not the first thing that's been spilled on that floor, and it won't be the last. Sit down and stop fussing, you're all right.'

She got the mop, cleared it up.

'What we should do is get a few blokes together, find a way down there and sort the bugger out ourselves so we can all sleep safe in our beds.'

Dad hunted down, chased through the tunnels with torches and clubs.

'A *posse*, like, that's what I'm talking about. A dozen able-bodied men.'

I leapt out of the chair.

'I've got to go.'

'You all right, buttie?'

I had to warn him.

'I'm fine – I think I left the oven on, got to run back and check.'

They looked at each other – *What's come over him?* I shot out the back door, ran down the path. I noticed something strange out of the corner of my eye.

No, it can't be.

The earth was moving in Auntie Val's herb garden. I must have imagined it. I looked again. One of Auntie Val's gnomes toppled over. A shovel poked through the soil.

Jesus!

Then, a hand.

Holy Mary, Mother of God!

Then another hand. My legs weren't there. My heart trying to punch its way out of my chest.

What's going on?

The second hand reached out blindly, grabbed a gnome. I couldn't move, couldn't look away. A head pushed its way out of the ground, shook off the soil, opened its eyes, stared at the gnome.

'What the feck?'

'Dad.'

He turned my way.

'Where am I?'

'In Uncle Ronnie and Auntie Val's garden.'

'You're joking.'

'No – look for yourself.'

He swivelled round, gazed up and down the back.

'Feck it. I thought I was halfway to Cardiff.'

Dad stared at the gnome, face screwed up in disgust.

'Bleddy stupid yoke.'

He flung it away. It crashed on to the path, its head flew off. Auntie Val carried the kettle over to the tap.

'Dad, you'd better go. Auntie Val's standing by the sink, if she looks out of the window, she'll see you.'

His head jerked back towards the window.

'Quick!'

He disappeared back under the soil. The kitchen door opened, Auntie Val gave Butch a push with the sweeping brush.

'Go on, stinker – out you go.'

She looked up, startled, when she saw me.

'Oh! Still here?'

'Ha ha, yeah.'

She gave me a funny look. Butch came running, made straight for the hole, growling. He started scrabbling at it.

'Feck off, yacuntya.'

'Dad – shhh!'

'Butch – get away from there.'

He was barking furiously, head stuck down the hole.

'Bad boy! What's got into you?'

Auntie Val scampered down the path, waving the broom in front of her.

'Stop tha – oh! Look what you've done to Harry.'

She stared at the headless gnome, her hand on her cheek.

'You've broken his head off, you rotten so-and-so.'

They were going to get a posse and hunt him down with torches and clubs. Or the police would come with nets and drag him away, lock him up and throw away the key. I pushed open the gate, ran down the lane.

★ ★ ★

The next morning *I* was there first, already sitting at the desk when Colin came in. I'd decided Colin's mam and dad getting back together was a great thing to happen. It meant he had no reason to hate me any more, that we could be friends again now.

'Hi-ya . . .'

He *still* wouldn't look at me.

'I saw you walking up the street last night. I'm glad your mam and dad have made it up.'

His head shot round like a cobra's.

'No thanks to you.'

That was below the belt. You didn't say that kind of thing to your best friend. *Your blood brother.* I held up my thumb in front of his face.

'See the mark from the knife? Doesn't that mean anything to you?'

He looked at me with contempt.

'There's nothing there.'

I looked again. He was right, there wasn't. He was staring at me like I was some kind of big thicko. Thought he'd put me in my place. Rubbed my nose in it.

My parents are back together again. They bought me a new anorak with a furry hood, and we went to the Wimpy Bar for our tea. I don't need you.

'Fuck off.'

Shock, then hurt in his eyes. It was seeing the hurt that made me do it. Soon as I saw I'd hurt him, I wanted to hurt him more. I pushed hard with both hands. He wasn't expecting it and went crashing to the floor. The bang made everyone look round. I was on my feet, standing over him.

'Come on, then.'

He got up too quickly, trying to prove he wasn't hurt. I was ready for him. Got him in a headlock. The punches he threw hit my arms and chest. They didn't hurt, not too much.

'Break it up.'

I tightened my grip. We crashed into another desk. Colin's knee smashed into the corner and he yelped in pain.

'Let him go.'

I wouldn't. I hadn't asked for this. He'd left me no choice. Down the corridor, shrill whistling, the theme from *The Dam Busters*.

'Thommo's coming.'

I let him go. He was nearly crying. I got back into my seat just in time.

'Now then, you lucky lot – sit down, Williams.'

He dropped down beside me, struggling to get his breathing under control, to prove I hadn't really hurt him. He leaned closer.

'You're dead.'

I gave him a taste of his own medicine, ignored him. He wasn't going to do anything. He knew I'd beat him. I was glad I'd done it. It was better this way.

★   ★   ★

Mam was out again tonight, at a meeting about getting Miss Mellon her job back. Nearly every parent in the school had signed the petition. Maybe Miss Mellon was right, letters, petitions and demonstrations *could* change things. Mam was doing a fantastic job, fair play to her. Bridie cooked our tea again. After we'd finished eating, Dad called me to one side in the kitchen, his face drawn and pale.

'Did you have anything to do with this?'

'What?'

'With that bleddy Bridie being here again?'

'No – of course not.'

There was a knock at the front door.

'I'll get it,' said Bridie cheerfully.

'You seem very pleased about it, all the same.'

He twisted his face up as if he'd just sucked a lemon.

'Laughing and smiling at every little thing she says, hanging on her every word, gazing up at her as if you were in bleddy love with her – Christ, I thought I was going to be sick.'

'I was only being friendly.'

I heard Uncle Ronnie and Auntie Val's voices.

'Nice to see you, Bridie love. How you been keeping?'

'But Dad, she's just helping out while Mam . . .'

His eyes hardened.

'Cop on to yourself – she's *spying* on us.'

'What?'

'I know very well what she's up to. Snooping around when I'm not here.'

Uncle Ronnie and Auntie Val were telling Bridie about hearing the alarm clock going off in the middle of the night.

'I'm warning you, don't trust that one. Listen to no one but me.'

His head jerked round.

'What are *they* doing here?'

He rushed into the living room. I stood in the doorway watching. *What now?*

'Hello there, Brendan. We were wondering if you'd heard any strange noises recently.'

299

Dad stared at Bridie.

'Did *you* put them up to this?'

Uncle Ronnie held up his hand to stop Dad right there, could see he'd got hold of the wrong end of the stick.

'You see, me and Val keep being woken up by an alarm clock going off in the middle of the night, you'd swear it was coming from under the ground.'

'Don't come round here accusing me of things.'

'No one's accusing you of . . .'

Bridie stepped between Dad and Uncle Ronnie.

'Good God, man, will you calm down?'

A nerve in Dad's cheek started jumping.

'Shut your bleddy face, you. I know what *you're* up to, ya bleddy auld hoor.'

He wagged his finger at Uncle Ronnie and Auntie Val.

'You're all in it together, aren't you?'

'Now listen here . . .'

Something dark came into Dad's eyes. He snatched the poker from the fire.

'Jesus!'

Bridie jumped back, the red-hot tip six inches from her face. He pushed the poker at her face again.

'Brendan!'

He ignored Auntie Val, his whole body tensed, ready to strike. Bridie moved back again, fought down the fear, gave him a mouthful.

'You're never bleddy right in the head. You should be locked up in St Woolos.'

Auntie Val grabbed Bridie's arm, pulled her away, before Dad could jab at her again. The veins on his neck bulged, spit flew from his mouth as he roared at her.

'Get out, now, or I'll fecking kill ya.'

★   ★   ★

I was standing on my own in the playground. Colin walked over, stood next to me. I looked away.

'Your dad is mad.'

I should have seen that coming. The whole street would know about Dad going at Bridie with the poker by now. It didn't get to me. I could see what he was doing. Could read him like a book. He couldn't beat me in a fight, so he had to try and hurt me in some other way. It was pathetic, really, when you thought about it.

'A bloody nutter. He should be locked up.'

It was like being hit very gently with soft cushions. *Can't you do better that?*

'Did you hear what I said? He should be . . .'

'At least he doesn't cheat on his wife.'

Sex mad, he is. I've seen him slobbering over every woman that passes.

His face fell. I could beat him in a fight, and I could beat him with words.

'Shut your face . . .'

'Piss off, Colin, OK.'

I walked away, left him standing there. I wanted to be alone. I walked past the bike shed, round the corner, down the steps to the boiler room. Hot, dark and musty, a heated cave. I used to hide from Preece down there. No one else knew about it.

My dad wasn't mad. He'd been working too hard, that was all.

The door opened. I looked up, saw Marek. He must have followed me. He walked over, stared at a space just past my shoulder.

'I've just told Colin he's no longer a member of the resistance.'

He met my eyes.

'What about you?'

It took me a few moments to work out what was wrong. He

301

almost looked the same. But something wasn't quite right. It was as if a double was acting the part of Marek. The old certainty was gone; he was *pretending* to be the Marek I knew.

'Do *you* still want to be a member?'

I didn't know.

'I'm planning a mission to Duffryn at the weekend.'

'Why are you going to Duffryn?'

The coppers patrolled in fours down there.

'To sell cigarettes. The struggle continues.'

I didn't see how selling fags to the scum of Crindau was going to free Poland.

'Do you want to come?'

He was mad. He'd die for Poland. He'd die in a fight after school rather than give in. He was the most fearless person I'd ever met. But he was worried now, for the first time. I should be furious with him, he'd ruined it between me and Colin. Then again, he'd stood by me when I thought I'd killed that man. While Colin was pissing himself, ready to squeal at a moment's notice. He was my blood brother.

'OK.'

'That means you still want to be a member of the resistance.'

'Yes.'

'Then I need you to sign this.'

He took out a piece of paper.

'What is it?'

'An agreement. You sign here at the bottom.'

He was already taking a pen from his pocket.

'Hang on, what does it say?'

'That you'll never go on strike.'

'*What?*'

'You saw the trouble I had with Colin. I can't afford to have members picking and choosing what they will and won't do. If you are really committed to fighting communism, then you will have no trouble signing this.'

He thrust a pen at me. I shook my head.

'You won't sign?'

'No. If you want to be my friend you must trust me.'

He couldn't keep the hurt out of his eyes. The old Marek would have. His eyelashes were flickering like crazy, his mouth was trying to escape from his control. But maybe I'd never really known the old Marek, only thought I had. Or perhaps this was the real Marek, and he'd just been putting on a show before, and none of us had noticed. I could feel my own face crumbling.

Marek said, 'You are making a big mistake.'

He took a deep breath, jerked his head back, raised his chin.

'We are no longer friends.'

He walked back up the steps, back straight, head held high. I wanted to call out. Warn him not to go to Duffryn on his own, that it was too dangerous. But it felt like an arrow had pierced my throat, just like the bugler in the tower at Cracow, and I couldn't make a sound.

★ ★ ★

Thommo did the register again after lunch. Miss Mellon just did it in the morning, but Thommo acted like he was a commandant at a prisoner of war camp, checking to see if anyone had escaped in the lunch hour.

'Davis.'

That was Joe 90.

'Yes, sir.'

Thommo looked at him.

'Are you *really* with us, Davis? I sometimes wonder if you're on the same planet as the rest of us.'

Every time he took the register he made some crack about Joe 90. Usually somebody would laugh, relieved it wasn't them. Not today. There was something in the air, we could all feel it.

303

The shock of our silence rippled across Thommo's face. He looked back down at the register, went through the rest of the names without pauses or jokes. But Joe 90 was rattled. A bubble had formed, deep down in his chest, had started floating up to his neck, his mouth. He started to panic.

Not now.

He cemented his lips together, squeezed his eyes shut.

Please.

'Right!'

Thommo closed the register.

'This afternoon we're going to . . .'

Joe 90 clamped his hands over his mouth. Too late. An enormous belch burst through his fingers, erupted into the room. Thommo went rigid.

'Disgusting boy! Go and explain your behaviour to Miss Partridge.'

Joe looked terrified. Miss Mellon would never have spoken to him like that.

'It's not fair – he can't help it. You make him nervous. You're always picking on him.'

Thommo glared at me.

'And you can go with him, Bennett.'

'But, sir . . .'

He banged the register down on the desk.

'Go on.'

I stood up. Joe 90 was frozen to his seat, tears welling up in his eyes.

'Are you deaf, boy? I said . . .'

'Leave him alone.'

Everyone turned to stare at Preece.

'You! Come here.'

Preece stayed where he was, crossed his arms. He was back. All this time he'd just been lying low, waiting for the right opportunity.

'Do you know something, Thommo – you're the biggest spaz I've ever met.'

There was a gasp. Thommo shot up. His chair crashed to the floor behind him.

'How dare you talk to me like that? Come here now or I'll . . .'

'What? You lay a finger on me and you'll be sorry.'

'Are you threatening me, boy?'

Gina Esposito started crying.

'I want Miss Mellon.'

The uncertainty in Thommo's eyes at the mention of her name gave me strength. He must have seen the mothers signing the petition outside the school, must have heard about the meeting. Must have known everyone wanted her back. I started shouting.

'I want Miss Mellon.'

Thommo's head snapped round.

'Shut up.'

I lifted my desk lid, started banging it up and down.

'I want Miss Mellon. I want Miss Mellon.'

The others joined in. First Preece, then his mates, Gina Esposito, then her friends, soon the whole class was shouting, banging their desk lids.

'I WANT MISS MELLON!'

The noise was fantastic. It was like being at Somerton Park, the crowd baying for a penalty as Stevie Boy tumbled in the box. Thommo was rushing round like a madman, shoving people back down into their seats.

'I WANT MISS MELLON!'

'Sit down and shut up.'

Every time he pushed someone back down, they'd jump to their feet again by the time he was at the next desk. The walls were shaking, the floor vibrating.

'WE WANT MISS MELLON!'

305

The door crashed open.

'WHAT IS GOING ON IN HERE?'

Miss Partridge stood in the doorway, nostrils flaring, eyes blazing.

* * *

She sent everyone home. Was going to write to our parents. I went and sat in the little square off Caradoc Road, where I'd become blood brothers with Colin and Marek. Hunched over on the bench, staring at the ground. I heard someone else arrive, stiffened.

'Hey, Bennett.'

Preece stood in front of me.

'Want a fag?'

'Sure, why not?'

He lit up a couple of fags, passed one to me, sat down. I wasn't nervous. I knew what to do. I'd seen it happen. Seen people making fools of themselves. Inhaling too deeply on their first puff, desperate to impress.

Look at me, I'm a fifty a day man.

Then double over coughing and spluttering. I took one short, shallow puff, counted to ten, took another.

'Thommo's such a spaz.'

'Yeah.'

My head began to swim. I gripped the edge of the bench with my free hand to steady myself.

'You OK?'

'Uhuh.'

Then the pain kicked in. It felt like somebody had punched me in the forehead. I gritted my teeth, held on to the hurt, invited it in. I *wanted* it to get worse, so that it would blot out everything else. I took a long drag this time. *Wham!* The fist struck again. My stomach twisted itself into a knot.

'I didn't know you had it in you, Bennett.'

'Sometimes you just can't take any more shit, know what I mean?'

'Yeah.'

Preece spat on the ground, sucked some phlegm back down his throat, took another drag. I'd left Colin and Marek behind, become a hard man. The ringleaders, that was what Partridge had called me and Preece.

'Thommo got my older brother Gary expelled.'

I waited for him to say something more, but he just held his fag upright between his thumb and forefinger and stared at it.

'Do you think *you'll* get expelled?'

'Probably. Who cares?'

I shrugged.

'Yeah, right, who cares?'

I took another small puff. Preece took a long drag, blew smoke through his nose. Then it struck me – the cigarette in my hand was one the resistance had sold to Preece. I'd crossed from one side to the other.

'Well, I got things to do – see you.'

'Yeah, see you, Preecey.'

I wasn't ready to get up yet, my legs weren't. There was cold sweat on my forehead. The pain in my head surging, pulsing. I waited another couple of minutes before moving.

* * *

I felt something was wrong after a few hundred yards. Halfway down Pugsley Street I knew for certain. Somebody was following me. I slowed down, waited till they got a little closer, whirled round.

'Do you want to come home with me?'

307

It was Joe 90. His eyes were red-rimmed, he looked like the first gust of wind would blow him away.

★   ★   ★

The house reeked of stale fried food and pine air freshener. Damp patches showed through the wallpaper. The furniture looked as though it had been nicked off a tip. He showed me into the kitchen.

'Do you want something to eat?'

'What is there?'

Not cat food.

'Toast.'

'Lovely.'

'Where's your dad?'

He beamed with pride.

'He's got a job.'

'Really? That's brilliant.'

He remembered something.

'It's only for a few weeks.'

'Still . . . what kind of job is it?'

He started pulling at his ear lobe.

'Promise not to tell any of the others?'

'This is just between you and me, Joe.'

He relaxed a bit, let go of his ear.

'He has to walk round and round this field in the rain – if it's not raining then he has to stand under a shower with all his clothes on. Then scientists examine him at the end of every day.'

It didn't make sense.

'That's not a job.'

'It is! He's getting good money.'

'Why would anyone pay him for that?'

'It's an experiment – they're trying to find out why people get colds. Then they can come up with a cure.'

'Hey!'

Smoke was pouring out from under the grill. Joe took it out, but it fell to pieces when he tried scraping off the black bits. He put some new bread under the grill. This time he kept checking it every two seconds.

'They might want to use my dad again. They're always looking for people. If he does it a few more times we'll have enough to go to Butlins this summer.'

He took the toast out, buttered it.

'We've got blackberry jam.'

'That would be great, thanks.'

He knew that I'd fallen out with Colin and Marek, and now he was trying to get in with me. He didn't know about me and Preece. He thought this was just the start, that because I'd stood up for him against Thommo I was his mate now. What would be so terrible about that? I was hardly spoilt for choice when it came to friends.

The toast was blackened, and I didn't like the margarine. But it was nice of him, all the same. I was having great fun pretending not to look down on him. This was what it must feel like being a saint.

Blessed are those who have nothing.

My face on calendars and collection boxes, feast days in my name. A plaque outside my house. *St Liam of the Hopeless Cases was born here.*

'Shall we go in the front room? It's cosier.'

'OK.'

I couldn't wait to see what was in *there*. I followed him through, sat down on the sofa. I was delighted to see how faded and covered in stains it was. Almost cheered at the sight of the stale crust and dirty handkerchief stuffed into a corner, the rips in the curtain, peeling wallpaper.

'Sorry about the mess.'

'That's all right.'

The messier the better. Being with Joe was cheering me up no end. I'd thought *I* was badly off, but imagine being him.

An unfinished game of Monopoly was scattered across the floor.

'We love Monopoly. Sometimes the games go on for days.'

There were six pieces on the board.

'Do you all play?'

'Yeah, it's great fun. If Mam lands on one of Dad's properties when he's got hotels on it he goes, "I want that money paid into my Swiss bank account," and Mam says, "Ack at Lord Muck of Crindau, you'll be lucky to get half a crown out of me." Sometimes everyone's laughing so much we can't carry on.'

'Yeah?'

'Yeah.'

He'd lost that hunted look. His face was lit up from inside.

'They're only messing, they always end up having a kiss and cuddle at the end. Then they'll say to us, "We may not be rich, but we'll always have each other, won't we?"'

'They say that?'

'Yeah, and – what's wrong?'

'Nothing.'

He'd whipped the carpet from under my feet. I was an idiot to look down on him. This was a House of Love. A place full of kisses, hugs and laughter. Joe could rush back here after being goaded, prodded and poked all day at school and know his ordeal was over.

'Liam?'

I felt sick to my stomach.

'Stop it!'

'What?'

'Stop looking like that. What's the matter?'

His big innocent eyes, roaming aimlessly behind his glasses. His pleading expression.

Please like me.

Felt the bile rising in my throat. The same urge to hurt that came over me when I looked at Michael. His weakness disgusted me. When I turned on him it was almost as if I was trying to beat and bully the weakness out of me. No, I mustn't make the same mistake with Joe 90; I mustn't hate him. It wasn't his fault. I didn't want to fall out with anyone else.

'I'm OK, really.'

I had to get out of there, before I turned on him.

'I'm going.'

He looked crushed.

'But you've only just got here.'

'SHUT UP!'

He sank back into the chair. Tears filled his eyes. I wanted to punch him for being so weak. I wanted to give him a hug, and tell him everything was all right. I vaulted out of the sofa, ran into the hall, was out of the door before he could say another word.

When I reached the end of the street I had no idea where to go. I stood there, gnawing my lip. Noticed a lady looking at me out of her window.

You're attracting attention. Move it!

I walked uptown, lost myself in the crowds. This was how it would be from now on. Bunking off school, looking in shop windows. Nicking things. Going up and down in the lift at the library in Lloyd George Square. I stopped outside Steve's Bargains, looked at the knives in the window. There was a brilliant flick knife for 7/6d. I'd need protection if I was going to be on my own. It could be dangerous uptown. I might get chased by a gang from another school; set on by drunken yobbos; followed by one of those blokes who interfered with children. I had to be prepared for anything.

'Liam, is that you?'

Dad was pushing his bike in front of him, his face grey and drawn.

'Christ, I don't know what happened to me. One minute I'm loading a pallet, the next thing I'm lying on the ground, surrounded by fellas asking me if I'm all right.'

He wiped something from his eye, stared at the knives in the window.

He was in a bad way.

'Jayzus, I must have passed out. They sent me home. Said I was in no fit state to work. *Me!* Christ, there's no better worker in the place. Feck!'

He ran his hand slowly over his forehead.

'My head is *bursting*.'

He squeezed his eyes shut, started rubbing the back of his neck, slowly swivelling his head from side to side. I was worried. He looked as though he might collapse again any minute.

'Dad, are you all right?'

He was muttering to himself.

'Feckers, they won't grind me down. Come on.'

He started walking, much slower than usual. I noticed both his tyres were flat. After a few feet he stopped again.

'Are we heading in the right direction?'

'Yeah, this is the way.'

He didn't look convinced.

'You're sure? I don't recognise any of this.'

How could he be lost after living in Crindau all this time?

'Honest, Dad, we just carry on straight down here, follow Clytha Road till we reach the traffic lights, then turn right down Lime Street.'

He looked at me gratefully.

'Jayzus, it's a good job I bumped into you. I've lost me bearings completely.'

He brought his hand up to his eyes, rubbed them tenderly.

'Christ, I don't feel too good, to be honest with you, son.'

He looked around at the crowds, a horrified expression on his face.

312

'Christ almighty, where do they all come from at all? You'd *never* see this many people on the streets at home in Ireland. This is a terrible country for crowds, it must be *bursting* at the seams with people. It'd unnerve you, so it would.'

He was frightening me.

'How in God's name did I ever end up *here*?'

He seemed to shrink, desperately clutching on to the bike for support.

'Come on, let's go home.'

He grabbed my shoulder.

'Stick close to me. If you got lost here, God knows how long it'd take me to find you.'

* * *

As soon as he opened the front door I sensed something was wrong. Then I saw it.

'Dad – look.'

'What?'

I pointed to the cellar door, wide open.

'Feck.'

He pushed past me, shouted down the steps.

'Who's there? Show yourself.'

His mouth dropped open. I rushed over. Mam was at the bottom of the stairs.

'What are you doing down there?'

'No, Brendan, the question is – what are *you* doing down here?'

He started bellowing.

'You've no business poking your nose into my things. How the feck did you get down there?'

She didn't bat an eyelid.

'You left the key in the lock.'

Her voice was completely calm. The mask was off now, she

was ready to take command. She started walking up the steps, never taking her eyes off Dad, no sign of nerves.

'Going behind my back when I'm at work, you sneaky bitch.'

She ignored him, looked at me for the first time.

'Liam, go upstairs and pack your case, you're coming with me to Bridie's.'

'But . . .'

'Go on.'

I looked at Dad. He was struggling to catch up with what was happening. Mam squeezed past him, pushed me gently towards the stairs.

'Hurry up, there's a good lad.'

I heard them from upstairs while I was throwing some things into my case.

'You bleddy madman, what the hell were you thinking of? I hope to God you haven't gone and weakened the foundations with your bleddy holes.'

'Don't be fecking ridiculous, I know what I'm doing.'

She laughed in his face. The sound of it set my teeth on edge. I walked on to the landing. Mam was putting on her coat, her back turned to Dad.

'It's the only chance we've got to survive the next world war, don't you see?'

'I see all right, I see that you're stark, staring mad. What in God's name did you think you were doing, threatening Bridie with a red-hot poker?'

She looked up, saw me.

'Come on, Liam. Let's be going.'

She was in command now. Had the bit between her teeth. I realised she'd been the stronger one all along. She hadn't been having a nervous breakdown, she just hated Dad so much she'd let things get on top of her for a while. He was silent as I walked down the stairs. Mam opened the door, stepped outside.

'Now then, Liam.'

Dad's arms dangled limply at his side. He had the same expression on his face he'd had uptown, staring at the crowded pavements.

How in God's name did I ever end up here?

His voice was a whisper as I walked past.

'Don't go.'

The expression on his face was terrible. Bursting with pain and humiliation.

'Liam!'

Mam was stretching out a hand towards me.

'Come on.'

She had Bridie. She had Michael.

'I'm staying here with Dad.'

Mam's mouth fell open. Dad had no one. He needed me. I couldn't do it.

'You are *not* staying with him. Come here this minute.'

Dad leapt in front of me, slammed the door in her face. He flipped open the letterbox, started yelling.

'You heard him – he wants to stay with me. Now feck off to Bridie's and leave us alone!'

She started banging on the door.

'Let me in.'

'Feck off.'

'Let me in or I'll get the police.'

Dad pulled the bolt across. She started pounding on the door with her fists.

'I'm going to walk away from this door now, so you can shut your bleddy hole, because no one will hear you.'

The letterbox opened from the other side.

'Liam!'

'I'm all right, Mam. Don't worry.'

'Of course he's all right. Why shouldn't he be? Leave us alone.'

'I'll be back – and I'll bring the bleddy police with me, you madman.'

'You can bring the fecking marines for all I care, ya bleddy hoor.'

The letterbox shut. Opened again.

'Liam – you stay away from that cellar, you hear me?'

'Yes, Mam.'

Dad grabbed my arm, pulled me away from the door. The clicking of Mam's shoes on the pavement growing fainter, the silence in the hall growing deeper. Dad let go of me, wiped one eye, then the other with his finger.

'Good man, Liam. You made the right choice. Christ, the last place you'd want to be stuck is in that bleddy auld Bridie's house, listening to those two prattling away. Fecking hell, that'd be a fate worse than death.'

He laughed. Too loud. Too long. Like someone stabbing the same piano key over and over.

'Right!'

He turned round. His eyes were wet. When he spoke his voice was a hoarse whisper.

'It's just you and me now, Liam. It was always going to be just you and me in the end.'

★   ★   ★

We carried the filled sacks up from the basement, stacked them behind the front door.

'They'll have a hard time getting in now.'

'But Dad, how will we get out?'

'Come on.'

He rushed back down to the cellar, was already stripping to his underpants by the time I reached the bottom step.

'Right, let's get going, we've wasted enough time already.'

I started taking off my clothes. Dad lit a couple of candles, lowered himself into the tunnel entrance. I took a candle, followed him. The network of tunnels was getting bigger all the time, we passed more new turnings that I'd never entered. After a few minutes, we reached the spot where he'd finished working last night. He rubbed his hands together, laughed.

'Ha! The Paddies are the fellas for work.'

I filled a sack with soil while he dug. All the time I was waiting. I wasn't sure what for. I didn't have a plan exactly. Just knew that this was where I needed to be, and that I'd think of *something*. Dad wasn't well right now, had collapsed once already today, needed someone to keep an eye on him. I was the man for the job.

His movements were getting slower, clumsier, his breathing more laboured. He was talking to himself.

' "I'll bring the bleddy police with me, you madman." Jesus, have you ever heard the like? What kind of a way is that to talk to your husband?'

'Dad.'

'She's got a nasty streak in her, that one.'

'Dad!'

His head jerked in my direction. Squinting in the candlelight, sweat rolling down his face.

'What?'

'Shall we have a break?'

'Christ, we've only just started.'

'You're tired – you're slowing down. You've collapsed once already today.'

He wavered, then dropped the shovel, wiped his forehead.

'It's no joke digging every night, then going to work the next day. It'd be too much for most fellas.'

'You're right, it would.'

A plan began to form in my mind.

'They'd have collapsed after a few days. There aren't many like me.'

I needed to keep him talking.

'No, there aren't.'

Him and Mam never got anywhere when they tried to talk to each other. But he'd listen to me.

'You need a proper rest, Dad. You'd feel much better if you went and lay down on the bed for a bit.'

There was a vacant look in his eyes, I wasn't even sure if he'd heard me, but I had to keep trying.

'You relax, have forty winks. I'll keep watch downstairs. I'll wake you up if I see anyone coming.'

I'd let Mam in. Call a doctor. He'd give him an injection while he slept. Then a tonic to build him up again – *take three times a day, after meals*. He'd be right as rain in a few days.

'Well?'

He sighed, slowly rubbed his temples.

'You're a good son to me, I don't know what I'd do without you. Christ, you're the only one I can trust. Everyone else is against me – your mother, Bridie, Ronnie and Val . . .'

'They're just worried about the noises at night. Just wait till they find out what you're doing down here.'

'What are you talking about?'

There was an edge in his voice now.

'Once we explain that it's not an escaped lunatic they've been hearing, that it's you.'

'*Tell them?*'

'Yes, tell them you're only digging tunnels so we can survive the next world war. Explain that there'll be plenty of room for them too.'

He looked horrified.

'Have you gone fecking mad?'

'But . . .'

'How in fuck's name do you think a couple of pensioners would cope down here? Ronnie can hardly walk, let alone crawl on his hands and knees.'

'I could help him.'

'Christ, cop on to yourself, willya. These tunnels are for us, there'll be no room for anyone else.'

'You can't leave them!'

'You fecking watch me. Oh yes, Ronnie thought he was very clever, he thought I didn't notice him laughing at me. He probably thought he was dealing with some bleddy thick Paddy. Well, he'll be laughing on the other side of his face when the bombs start falling, and he's no place to hide. Let's see how bleddy funny he finds that.'

'No!'

'Him, and Val, that hairy fecker Williams and his bleddy dolly bird wife with her tiny skirt, they'll all be running around bawling and screaming, no idea what's hit them.'

'Dad, you don't mean it.'

'Yes, I fecking do. Once the war starts it's going to be all about the survival of the fittest.'

My God, he really *did* mean it, he'd leave them all to burn.

'I hate you!'

I snatched my candle, started backing away.

'Come back here.'

I kept going.

'Liam!'

He'd looked exhausted a minute ago, but now he was steaming towards me like a train. I turned into another tunnel to my right that I'd never been in before. Put my hand in a pile of something soft. I froze. I looked down. Saw my fingers plunged deep inside something coiled and brown. No, please, not that. I held up my hand. It was.

'Aaaaaagh!'

The stench. The feel of it. Shit. Human shit.

'God, God, God!'

I was going to throw up. *Christ, no!* I'd dropped the candle. I was in total darkness now, under the ground, my hand covered in my dad's shit.

'Help me!'

Dad's candle was coming closer.

'Quickly!'

His face in the ghostly glow, horrified, as if it was my fault.

' Jayzus, you're a right fecking mess.'

'Get it off me.'

He found my candle, lit it with his, stuck it in the earth in front of me. I was holding the shit-covered hand as far away as I could.

It's not part of me.

'Where are you going?'

He'd left me, carried on crawling up the tunnel, the light from his candle growing dimmer.

'Don't leave me here.'

He was coming back, clutching a toilet roll. He started wiping my hand clean. I closed my eyes.

'Christ almighty, you're covered in it.'

'GET IT OFF ME!'

I clenched my teeth, screwed my eyes shut. His hands tugging at mine, grunting as he wiped, tugged, chucked.

'Hold still, for Christ's sake.'

He stopped.

'There.'

I opened my eyes. My hand was clean. It didn't matter. I could still feel his shit on me. I'd never be clean again.

'Why didn't you use the toilet?'

'You fecking eejit, we're on red alert. Do you think I have time to crawl the length of the tunnel and run up to the bathroom? Where did you *think* we were going to go when the war started?'

I hadn't thought. Hadn't wanted to.

'What the hell did you think you were playing at, running away from your own father like that?'

'I don't want to stay down here in the dark with you.'

His face was raw, wounded. But I didn't care if I was hurting him any more. I had to get away from him. He frightened me.

'Come on now, son, don't talk like that. Stop pretending, you know you're just like me.'

Michael takes after his mother, but you're like me.

It wasn't true.

You're never bleddy right in the head. You should be locked up in St Woolos.

'I'm not! Don't say that.'

I started edging away.

'Come back.'

'You're mad!'

We both froze. The words hung in the air between us. His face tightened.

'Mad, am I?'

He made a wild lunge.

'Feck!'

Cracked his head on one of the beams, collapsed on the ground, moaning. I had to get out of there. Now. He was blocking the way, I'd have to go back, crawl away from the cellar, then turn around, find another way out. There was a turning to the left ahead. Something told me not to take it. I kept going. Heard him getting up, scrabbling after me, cracking his head on another beam.

'UGH!'

There was another left turn coming up.

Take this one.

The wrong decision, it petered out after a few yards. *Jesus!* What had he been doing down here all this time? I scrambled back out, saw him heading for me, breathing hard. It sounded painful, like every breath was scalding his chest.

'Liam!'

I carried straight on till I saw another turning to my right. I prayed it didn't end after a few yards like the last one. I had to get out of the tunnel I was in, it was taking me away from the cellar, to God knows where.

Keep calm.

This one didn't go in a straight line like the others, it began curving round, seemed to be going in a circle. Why? Then I noticed a turning to my right. Should I take it? No. Keep going. Wrong decision, it ended a minute later. A tunnel to nowhere, just like the other one. What had he been doing down there? The terror gripped me, squeezed.

There's no way out.

I was in the labyrinth.

Please, God, get me out of here. Please, sweet Jesus, please.

I crawled back, heading straight for him now. The flame of his candle ten feet away. His damaged face, his haunted eyes. Then, at the last minute, I took the turning I'd just passed, praying it wasn't another dead end.

'Come here!'

He was right behind. Nothing would slow him down. I should have listened to Mam.

Liam – you stay away from that cellar, you hear me?

She'd been right all along. She'd tried to warn me, but I wouldn't listen.

You'll be sorry if you're taken in by what he says, mark my words, Liam.

Bridie, Uncle Ronnie, Auntie Val, Mr Williams, they were all right. Dad was mad. How could I not have realised? Suddenly I was shouting.

'HELP!'

Pointless. No one would hear me. Even if they did, what could they do? The door was locked and barricaded. I'd helped him do it. Then came down here with him of my own free will.

I started crying. I was the biggest eejit of all time. I'd never understand anything. Got the wrong end of the stick every time. Michael was right, I was a big thicko. Hot tears streamed down my cheeks, salt trickled into my mouth. Something dark and bitter slid down the back of my throat.

I was going to die down there.

'Jesus!'

The alarm went off. Where was it? If I could find my way back to the alarm, I'd be OK, I'd know where I was.

The alarm.

It was a warning. The air was running out. No air, you die.

'Oh God.'

I had to stop crying, it was using up too much oxygen. I had to calm down, stop panicking, move slowly, make the air last.

'Liam!'

If I moved slowly, Dad would catch up with me.

Please, please, Mary, Mother of God, guide me to safety. Get me out of this labyrinth. I'll devote the rest of my life to God, become a missionary, work with hopeless cases.

Just ahead the tunnel joined another. I looked to my right – a shovel and sack, the alarm, the place where we'd been working.

Yes!

I'd be out of there in a few minutes.

'Liam!'

It'd take a hell of a blow to put me down.

I was nearly there.

'Come here.'

He was just a couple of feet behind me now. I saw light streaming down. The entrance to the cellar. I'd run straight up the steps, run to the bathroom. Lock the door behind me. Climb out of the window.

I'd made it. I started hauling myself up. Felt a trembling behind me. A low rumbling, the sound of splintering wood. Dad yelling.

'FECK!'

I hope to God you haven't gone and weakened the foundations with your bleddy holes.

323

The tunnel was collapsing behind me.

I pushed myself through the hole, fell face-first on to cold concrete. Desperate, heaving breaths punching their way out of my chest. I wanted to stay there till I fell asleep. Wake up and find out I'd dreamed it.

Behind, the soft, slow, whispering sound of earth rising higher, filling up the tunnel. Then silence.

He was still down there. I wasn't going to look back. I couldn't bear to, I was too frightened of what I might see. He was still down there. My own father. Praying that someone would come and help him. No, there was nothing I could do. It would be madness going back, I was lucky to escape with my own life. Buried alive. Imagine that. How could I ever live with myself if I didn't try to help? I looked back. The entrance wasn't there any more.

I'd nearly killed the man on the train. I'd nearly killed Michael. Now I'd killed my own father.

My stomach was a raw wound. I was soaked in cold sweat. I'd pissed myself. I had to get up. I couldn't leave him behind.

You're a good son to me, I don't know what I'd do without you.

No matter what he'd done, he was still my dad.

My teeth were chattering. My underpants and legs were warm and wet. I forced my shaking legs to work. I got up. I fetched a shovel from the wall, started digging. Please, God, let him be alive. He couldn't be very far down, he was only just behind me when the tunnel collapsed. It was down to me now.

It's just you and me now, Liam. It was always going to be just you and me in the end.

'DAD!'

I had to stop, wipe away the tears. I couldn't stop shaking. I couldn't stop.

Come on, don't be soft. Be a man.

I gritted my teeth. I dug, I cried. I cursed and swore.

'Come on, you bastard. You fucking weakling. Is that the best you can do? Fucking come on!'

Tears, snot, cold sweat pouring out of me.

'You useless cunt. Harder, faster, you fucker, you bloody stupid . . . *Jesus!*'

The shovel struck something soft. I flung it aside, sank to my knees, started clawing at the dirt with my hands. Brushed it away from his hair, his head. There was a bloody gash where I'd cut him with the shovel.

'Dad! Are you all right?'

No answer, instead, someone hammering at the front door. Shouting through the letterbox.

'Is there anyone there?'

A man's voice.

'Open up, it's the police.'

I was clawing the dirt like a dog, uncovering more of his face. He looked terrible. A death mask. A mummy with the bandages peeled off. I touched him. His skin was frightening, cold and clammy, lifeless. I grabbed his face with both hands, squeezed.

'*Please!*'

'Liam, it's Mam. Are you in there?'

She'd come back. She'd brought help. I just needed to let her know I was here. I opened my mouth, tried to speak, an animal noise came out. I couldn't talk any more. I'd stopped being human.

'Liam!'

I didn't know if he was alive or not. Didn't know how you could tell. His head fell forward. I picked it up, forced his eyes open.

'Wake up!'

'Stand back.'

Something crashed into the front door, once, twice. It split, cracked, slammed to the ground.

'Is there anyone there?'

Blood was trickling out of his mouth now, dribbling down his chin. I forced his mouth open. It was a bloody mess. He'd bitten his tongue off. No, my fingers found it, bloated and slick with blood. He was breathing. I think he was. I lifted my head towards the cellar door. I opened my mouth. I cried out. This time the words came.

'Mam – help me!'

Two policemen came running down the steps.

'Get the boy out of there – and call an ambulance.'

One of them grabbed me, carried me upstairs in his arms. The light nearly blinded me when we reached the top. Mam and Bridie were waiting there.

'Oh Jesus, Mary and Joseph.'

Uncle Ronnie and Auntie Val were standing in the gap where the front door had been. Auntie Val had her hand over her mouth, Uncle Ronnie's eyes were wet.

'You all right, buttie?'

The copper carried me into the living room, put me down on the sofa. Mam dropped to her knees, pulled me to her, squeezed me so tight I thought my bones would snap. There was a fierce strength in her.

'Mam – don't let go.'

'I won't.'

And she didn't.

Acknowledgements

For their helpfulness and support, my heartfelt thanks to the following people: Clare Alexander and Kate Shaw at Gillon Aitken; everyone at the Centerprise Literature Project, especially Eva Lewin; Laurence Roberts; Jane Rogers; Stuart Williams at Secker & Warburg. And, of course, Joanna and Anna.

I am indebted to the following wonderful books:
Forgotten Few: The Polish Air Force In The Second World War, by Adam Zamoyski (John Murray, 1995), which helped inspire Mr Sikorski's wartime memories. *Bloody Valentine: A Killing in Cardiff*, by John Williams (HarperCollins, 1995), from which I adapted the vivid description of Tiger Bay in the 1930s for Crindau Docks.